His Captive Lady

"With tenderness, compassion, and a deep understanding of the era, Gracie touches readers on many levels with her remarkable characters and intense exploration of their deepest human needs. Gracie is a great storyteller."
—*RT Book Reviews* (4½ stars, Top Pick)

"Once again, author Anne Gracie has proven what an exceptionally gifted author is all about . . . Absolutely one of the best romances I've read this year!"
—*CK²S Kwips and Kritiques*

The Stolen Princess

"Anne Gracie's talent is as consistent as it is huge. I highly recommend *The Stolen Princess* and look forward to the rest of the series."
—*Romance Reviews Today*

"Anne Gracie always delivers a charming, feel-good story with enchanting characters. I love all of Ms. Gracie's stories and *The Stolen Princess* is no exception. It stole my heart, as it will yours."
—*Fresh Fiction*

continued . . .

THE
Spring Bride

ANNE GRACIE

B
BERKLEY SENSATION, NEW YORK

BERKLEY SENSATION

An imprint of Penguin Random House LLC
375 Hudson Street, New York, New York 10014

THE SPRING BRIDE

A Berkley Sensation Book / published by arrangement with the author

BERKLEY SENSATION® and the "B" design are registered trademarks
of Penguin Random House LLC.
For more information, visit penguin.com.

ISBN: 978-0-425-25927-6

PUBLISHING HISTORY
Berkley Sensation mass-market edition / June 2015

PRINTED IN THE UNITED STATES OF AMERICA

10 9 8 7 6 5 4 3 2 1

Cover art by Aleta Rafton (Lott Reps).
Cover design by George Long.

Penguin
Random
House

In memory of
Winnie Salisbury
(née Winnie Williams)
who many years ago showed me
the beautiful North Wales of her childhood and youth.

And with thanks, as always,
to my writing friends in whom I'm so blessed.

Prologue

London, 1805

"Tell us about the night you were a princess, Mama."

"She *felt* like a princess, she wasn't really one," Jane's big sister, Abby, corrected her.

Jane didn't care. A princess was a princess. "Mama? Tell us."

Mama smiled. "Don't you ever get sick of it, darling?"

Jane shook her head fervently.

"Well, I was just eighteen, and it was the grandest ball of the season. Everybody was there, dukes, earls, even a royal prince."

"And what were you wearing, Mama?"

"You know very well what I was wearing, you've heard it a hundred times."

"Mama!"

"Very well, I was wearing a beeeyoutiful ball gown, rose-colored silk that swished like water when I walked."

"And a gauze overdress—go on," Jane prompted.

"A gauze overdress with hundreds of tiny crystals sewn on it that caught the light—"

"And glittered like a shower of diamonds," Jane finished for her.

"See, you know it better than I do."

"Go on. And on your head . . ."

"On my head I wore a most elegant little headdress of pink pearls and diamonds—of course, they were paste, but—"

"And you came down the staircase, and everybody turned to look at you . . ." Jane didn't want to hear about paste, which wasn't as good as diamonds—not that she'd ever seen any kind of jewelry, except for Mama's gold wedding ring—but everybody knew a princess wore diamonds.

"Yes, little tyrant, and everybody turned to look at me in my beeyoutiful glittery pink dress." Mama laughed, but the laughter turned into a coughing fit that ended with her lying back on the bed, handkerchief pressed to her mouth, exhausted.

Abby fetched Mama some water and a clean handkerchief, slipping it into Mama's hands so that Papa wouldn't notice the blood on the old one. Abby was always secretly washing blood out of Mama's handkerchiefs.

After a while, Jane asked, "Mama, why aren't you a princess now?"

"Oh, I'm still a princess, my darling." Mama opened her eyes, and looked over Jane's head at Papa, who was standing behind her, silent and grim. "That night I met and fell in love with your papa. He's my prince, and always will be." And she smiled up at Papa.

And Jane could see for herself that Mama really had been a princess because the smile made her beautiful again, so beautiful, as if someone had lit a candle inside her.

"You'll always be my princess," Papa said in a choked voice, smoothing Mama's hair back and kissing her on the forehead.

Jane loved Papa dearly, but she knew he wasn't a prince. A prince lived in a castle, not one poky little room in a smelly old building.

Mama was supposed to have married someone else—a rich man who did live in a castle. Papa too was supposed to marry another lady, but then they met each other and fell in love. And because they fell in love, they had to run away and get married, because their parents wanted them to marry the other people. The rich other people.

That was why Jane and Abby had never met their grandparents, even though Abby was almost twelve and Jane was nearly six. Because they were still angry. Papa and Mama had been cast out, cut off without a penny. That's why they had no money. Papa did his best, but there was never enough . . .

If Mama were a princess now, she wouldn't be a thin shadow of herself, faded, sad and sick. And Papa wouldn't be so tight and angry and sad. Jane and Abby would be princesses too, and they'd all be living in a castle, not a cold, dark little room, where rats scrabbled behind the walls. And none of them would ever be cold, or hungry or frightened.

"I'm going to be a princess too, when I grow up," Jane declared. "And I'll have a pink glittery dress and wear diamonds and—"

"Janey darling, it's just make-believe," Abby began.

"No, I will!"

"Ah, sweetheart, no matter what you wear, you'll always be Papa's little princess," Papa said, picking Jane up and twirling her around and around. And everybody laughed.

But Jane had no doubt of it. Twirling high in Papa's arms, she looked down at the dingy little room spinning around her, Mama lying weak and thin in her bed, and Abby crouched beside her with a clean cloth. It wasn't always going to be like this. Everybody said Jane was the image of her mother, and that meant she could be a princess too. She just had to find a prince with a castle.

Chapter One

But there certainly are not so many men of large fortune
in the world as there are pretty women to deserve them.

—JANE AUSTEN, MANSFIELD PARK

Mayfair, London, March 1817

"That was a lovely treat, thank you, Abby." Jane squeezed her sister's arm affectionately as they walked through Berkeley Square. "I can't believe I had to wait eighteen years to taste ice cream."

Abby laughed. "You've made up for it in the last few months—is there any flavor at Gunter's you haven't tasted?"

"No," Jane admitted, "but I still haven't decided which is my favorite."

Abby laughed again. "And it's not even summer yet." It was barely even spring. The plane trees that lined the square were only just beginning to bud and a few scattered clumps of snowdrops were in bloom.

Jane squeezed her older sister's arm again. "Ice cream or not, it's lovely to have the catch-up, just the two of us. I love Damaris and Daisy—you know I do, but sometimes . . ."

Abby nodded. "Sometimes you just need to be with your big sister, I know. It's the same for me." She paused, then glanced at Jane. "Are you nervous about your season? Your first ball, it's what, ten days away?"

"A fortnight," Jane corrected her. "And no, I'm not nervous. Not really." She shook her head. "Well, nervous in a good way. If you want to know the truth, I can't wait. All those years in the Pillbury Home wearing gray and brown serge and never dreaming—well, *only* dreaming about going to balls and parties and routs, wearing pretty dresses, dancing until dawn and going to plays and concerts and picnics, as Mama did. But I never truly believed it would happen, that one day . . ." She hugged her sister, then gave a happy little twirl. "It's so exciting, Abby. I feel so very lucky."

"We are lucky," Abby said, sobering a little. "All of us. If it weren't for Lady Beatrice . . ."

"I know. But she insists we rescued her, which is true too, in a way. And truly Abby, she's enjoying this as much as any of us. She couldn't be more delighted if we were her real nieces."

Abby laughed. "Good thing I married her nephew then, which makes it almost true."

"'*Nonsense! Your marriage to Max has nothing to do with it. If I want nieces, I'll dashed well have 'em!*'" Jane declared in an excellent imitation of Lady Beatrice, and they both laughed.

Abby linked arms with Jane again and they resumed walking. "Oh, Jane, I'm so happy. Happier than I ever dreamed possible. You have no idea. Marriage is . . ." She gave a blissful sigh and then blushed. "But you'll find out soon enough. You'll meet a handsome young man—maybe even next week at the ball—and you'll fall madly in—"

"Do you think Damaris and Freddy will have arrived in town yet?"

Abby gave her a sharp glance, but accepted the change of subject. "Damaris's last letter said they expected to arrive in London today or tomorrow, so they might have, yes."

"Oh, good. I can't wait to see her. Her letters from Venice contained some beautiful sketches—it seems like a magical place. I wonder if I'll ever get to see it."

"Jane—"

But Jane didn't want to talk about falling in love, which was all Abby talked about these days. "Watch out," she said, pulling Abby back as a curricle whizzed past them. "You're not in the country now, Abby—we have traffic in London, remember."

They crossed the street and mounted the front steps of Lady Beatrice's house, where Jane and Daisy still lived.

Max, on his marriage to Abby, had rented a town house around the corner. He'd offered to house Daisy and Jane there as well, but Lady Beatrice had objected strongly. "Stealing my gels? Losing Abby and Damaris to you and Freddy is bad enough. What's wrong with newlyweds today—don't you *want* privacy?" Delivered with a gimlet stare magnified by her favorite lorgnette.

Abby and Max hadn't argued. And Freddy, taking the hint, had also arranged the hire of a town house for the season, within easy walking distance of Berkeley Square.

The front door opened silently before Jane could even reach for the bell. Featherby, their butler, placed a white-gloved finger over his lips in mysterious fashion and stood back to let them in.

Daisy was sitting on the stairs, halfway up. "Daisy?" Jane began.

"*Sssh!*" Daisy made extravagant shushing gestures. Jane and Abby exchanged glances. What on earth was going on?

Featherby, tapping his finger against his lips to reinforce the need for silence, pointed to the door to the drawing room, which was ajar. Voices wafted out. Lady Beatrice and a male visitor. Nothing unusual there. So why were Daisy and Featherby behaving so mysteriously?

"What—" Jane began.

"*Shhh!*" Daisy made fierce, emphatic gestures, beckoning to Jane to come up and to be quiet.

Mystified, Jane obeyed. Featherby stepped in front of the sitting room door, blocking them from the sight of the unknown visitor while Jane and Abby slipped past and hurried silently up the stairs.

"What's going on?" Jane whispered.

"Sit down and listen!" Daisy tugged her down beside her on the stairs. "It's about you."

Jane sat. So did Abby. The three girls leaned against the rails, listening intently to the voices coming from the drawing room.

The man, whoever he was, was talking about himself. "Of course, you know my family and my circumstances, Lady Beatrice, and naturally my eligibility is not in doubt—"

Eligibility? "What's he talking about?" Jane whispered.

"He's making an offer for you," Daisy whispered back.

"For *me*?" Jane squeaked. She turned and stared at Daisy. "Who is he?"

"Lord Cambury."

Jane gave her a blank stare. "*Who?*"

"Lord Cambury. He came to the literary society a couple of times."

Jane shook her head, none the wiser.

"Little fat bloke. Thirty-three or so. Natty dresser. Balding." Daisy mimed a comb being dragged across a scalp and Jane suddenly remembered. Lord Cambury.

Lord Cambury? There must be some mistake. He couldn't possibly be offering for her. She'd barely exchanged a dozen words with the man. She leaned closer to hear the conversation coming from the drawing room.

But Featherby, who had been hovering casually near the drawing room door, suddenly turned and gestured urgently. Lord Cambury's voice grew louder, saying, "Tomorrow then, Lady Beatrice. I look forward to it."

He was leaving. The girls rose and hurried up the stairs out of sight.

At the landing, Jane turned and peered down cautiously between the rails. She caught a glimpse of a pink and shiny pate, over which thin strands of fair hair had been carefully combed, and then Featherby was handing Lord Cambury his hat, coat and cane.

The front door closed behind him and Jane let out the breath she hadn't even realized she'd been holding.

Featherby glanced up and said in a voice that carried up the stairs, "Yes, m'lady, Miss Jane and Lady Davenham are here with Miss Daisy. I'll call them down, shall I?" The girls hurried downstairs.

"Tea, m'lady?" Featherby asked as they entered the drawing room.

Lady Beatrice nodded. "And something stronger for me." Featherby bowed and withdrew. Lady Beatrice pulled out her lorgnette and regarded Jane through it. "Well now, you're full of surprises, miss."

Jane's jaw dropped. "*I* am?"

Lady Beatrice frowned. "You didn't expect this?"

"I'm not entirely sure what 'this' is." She glanced at Daisy. "Daisy said Lord Cambury was making an offer. Of marriage. For me."

Lady Beatrice nodded. "Nothing wrong with the gel's ears. Not that any of you should be listening at doors."

Daisy gave her an unrepentant grin. "Best way to keep up with all the news."

"Minx." The old lady shook her head, sending her vivid red curls bobbing. "But you're quite right." She turned to Jane. "Lord Cambury has made a formal offer for your hand."

So it was true. Jane stared at her, stunned. "But . . . he hardly knows me." She tried to remember the times she'd spoken to Lord Cambury, and could recall only the most commonplace exchanges—a comment about the weather on one occasion, and her partiality for cream cakes on another.

"And from the sounds of things, you don't know him either," Abby pointed out.

"Nevertheless, it's an excellent offer," Lady Beatrice said. "He's rich, as rich as Golden Ball they say, only without the vulgarity. Lord Cambury prides himself on his exquisite good taste."

William, their footman, brought in the tea tray with a large pot of tea and a plate of cakes and other delicacies. Featherby followed, bearing the brandy decanter. Under Lady Beatrice's supervision, he poured her tea—more brandy than tea.

Abby poured for the rest of them, just tea with a little milk. For a few moments the silence was broken only by the clattering of teacups and spoons.

"What did you tell him?" Jane blurted out as soon as William and Featherby had left.

"That it was your decision, of course."

"It's ridiculous," Abby declared. "As if Jane would even consider such an insulting offer. So he's rich and a lord. Does he think he is so rich and important that he doesn't even have to bother courting her?" She looked at Jane expectantly.

Jane said nothing.

"Ridiculous, perhaps," Lady Beatrice said after a moment, "but it's quite a coup for your sister. The caps that have been set at Cambury these past ten years—you have no idea, my dears—and he's offered for Jane before the season has even begun!"

She drained her cup and signaled for Abby to refill it with tea this time. "Whether or not you accept him, your success is assured, my dear. What a season this is going to be! Two of you brilliantly married already and now, a magnificent offer for Jane—and from Cambury, of all men."

"What do you know about him?" Jane asked.

There was a sudden silence.

Abby put the teapot down with a thump and turned to her sister. "You can't be seriously considering him, Jane. You don't even know him—you said as much yourself."

"That's why I asked Lady Beatrice what she knows about him," Jane responded tranquilly. "I'm curious." She glanced at Abby. "I have a right to know, after all."

Abby bit her lip. "Of course."

The old lady picked up her teacup and regarded Jane for a thoughtful moment. "Good family, of course—been here since the conquest. I'm fairly sure I attended the boy's christening." She took a sip of tea, grimaced and signaled for Abby to add some brandy to it.

"As for Cambury himself," she continued, "I've heard nothing to his detriment. His aunt, Dora, Lady Embury, comes occasionally to my literary society." Nobody said anything and the old lady added, "You gels must know her. Large lady, lives on the other side of the square. Often dresses in purple—not the shade I'd advise for a woman of her high color—and could talk the leg off an iron pot. Owns a herd of little yappy dogs."

"Oh, yes, I know who you mean," Jane said. She'd seen and even patted the dogs in the park.

Lady Beatrice continued, "According to Dora, her beloved Edwin—Cambury—is a perfect paragon—a dutiful nephew—his parents died some years ago—visits Dora often enough to keep her happy but doesn't appear to be tied to her apron strings. Even walks those dratted little dogs for her on occasion." She shook her head. "As for what he does with himself, from what he said, his passion in life seems to be collecting beautiful things. He told me he considers himself 'a connoisseur of beauty.' "

She snorted. "In fact, it's more or less how he referred to you, Jane—said he wishes to acquire a beautiful wife to complete his house full of beautiful objects. Houses," she corrected herself. "He has three that I know of. One in London, another his country seat—Cambury Castle—"

"A castle?" Jane echoed.

"Yes, quite a magnificent estate—and a place in Brighton—he's a member of the Prince Regent's set."

"Coxcomb! I don't care whose set he's part of or how many houses he owns, or how much his aunt dotes on him," Abby said hotly. "Jane deserves better than a man who doesn't even bother to get to know her before offering for her hand, a man who wants to *add her to his collection of beautiful things*—I've never heard of anything so outrageous—and I hope you told him so, Lady Beatrice."

The old lady made a vague gesture. "It's not for me to say who Jane will or won't marry. She must decide for herself. Cambury's coming back tomorrow at three to speak to her."

"Good. Jane can tell him herself, then." Abby turned to Jane. "And I hope you send him away with a flea in his ear. The arrogance of the man!"

Jane didn't respond. She couldn't think straight. She'd expected—well, hoped—for an offer of marriage from some eligible gentleman, but not before the season had even started. And certainly not from someone she'd barely exchanged a word with. Or anyone so . . . rich. With a *castle*.

"Jane?" Abby said, frowning. "You will send him away, won't you?"

Still Jane said nothing. She had no idea what she would do. She could feel everyone's eyes on her.

"It's what you've always said you wanted, isn't it, my dear?" Lady Beatrice asked after a moment. "To make a good marriage to a wealthy man?"

"Oh, but that was before," Abby said. "Back then, when we were destitute and quite horridly desperate. I'd say any one of us would have agreed to marry a virtual stranger then, just to get a roof over our heads and to know where our next meal was coming from."

"And to be safe," Jane added.

"Exactly. But now we're in a completely different situation. We're not in need of anything. And Damaris and I are married and so very, very happy—more so than either of us dared to dream of." There was a catch in her voice as she said it.

Jane was in no doubt of her sisters' happiness. Abby fairly glowed with love and joy and so had Damaris as she'd left with Freddy after Christmas on their honeymoon trip to Venice.

Abby continued, "So there's no need for anyone to make a marriage of convenience now. Everything's set for Jane to make her come-out, and over the next few months she'll meet dozens of eligible and handsome young men, and I just know she's going to fall in love with one of them, and be happier than she'd ever dreamed of."

Jane smiled. She knew what her sister wanted for her. Abby wanted Jane to have what Abby had—everything her heart desired. But Jane was different from Abby.

"Is he a kind man, do you think?" Jane asked Lady Beatrice. It sounded like he was, seeing he walked his aunt's dogs for her. His liking dogs was promising.

"Jane, you can't possibly be taking this offer seriously," Abby burst out.

"Why not? It was made seriously, wasn't it?"

"But—" Abby began.

"Now, Abby," Lady Beatrice said warningly.

"But she's thinking of accepting him—can't you see?" Abby turned back to her sister. "What about love, Jane? You can't marry without love. You simply can't. You can't imagine how wonderful it is, Jane, to be in love and to know that you're loved in return."

Jane swallowed and glanced away.

Abby gave her a narrow glance, then her tone changed. "Look, you don't need to decide now; there's plenty of time to meet the right man, to fall in love. You'll have dozens of eligible offers, just wait and see. Isn't that right, Lady Beatrice? Once the season gets started, she'll be knee-deep in suitors, all clamoring for her attention."

Jane didn't say anything. She didn't want to be knee-deep in suitors. The very idea made her uncomfortable. Men always seemed to want something from her—she'd never quite understood what. They seemed to imagine she was someone different, some-one who matched her face.

She didn't want dozens of men clamoring for her attention; she just wanted to be . . . safe. And comfortable.

She'd been so looking forward to her season, wearing pretty dresses and going to balls and parties and concerts—after twelve years in the Pillbury Home, wearing cast-offs and hand-me-downs from the older girls, what girl wouldn't? She'd looked forward to dancing with a succession of handsome young men too. She hadn't thought much beyond that.

Oh, she knew marriage was the aim of it all, and she wanted to be married, of course she did; you had to be married to have children, and Jane wanted children more than anything.

But it had all been a bit vague in her mind. She'd vaguely imagined she'd meet a nice eligible gentleman and he would propose, and she would accept and then, at the end of the season, she'd get married.

And then her life—her real life—would start. She'd have a husband and a home and soon, she hoped, she'd be blessed with her own little baby. It was all she'd ever wanted—a home of her own and children. And of course, a husband made all that possible.

But dozens of suitors . . . staring . . . and clamoring . . .

"Jane—" Abby began again, but Lady Beatrice held up a magisterial hand.

"Hush, Abby! I know you want what's best for your sister— we all do—but it's Jane's decision and she needs time now, to think it over. In peace."

Abby gave a rueful smile. "Of course. I'm sorry, love." She rose and gave Jane a hug. "I didn't mean to be telling you what to do. It's a bad big sister habit—I forget sometimes that you're eighteen and all grown up now. You'll do the right thing, I know you will."

Jane hugged her back, grateful not to have to explain herself while her thoughts were still in turmoil.

"I'd better go," Abby said. "I said I'd meet Max at four, and I'm already late." She kissed Jane. "Don't do anything rash, little sister."

"I won't."

Daisy stood as well. "I got work to do, so I'm goin' too. See you upstairs, Jane?"

Jane nodded. "In a few minutes." She wanted to talk to Lady Beatrice alone.

Abby took her leave in a round of hugs, and Daisy hurried away upstairs. Jane sat down again, facing Lady Beatrice. There was a short silence while she organized her chaotic thoughts. Lady Beatrice sipped her "tea" and nibbled on an almond cat's tongue.

"I've never had a marriage proposal before," Jane said

eventually. "It's a little daunting. So I have until tomorrow to make up my mind?"

"Not at all. He might press you for an answer, but if he does and it makes you uncomfortable, refer him to me. I have no intention of letting anyone rush you into a decision. Marriage is a serious matter, my dear, and this decision will affect your entire life. So take as much time as you need."

"But if he's coming back tomorrow . . ."

"You can tell him you need more time to think it over. It does men good to be kept waiting—how often do I have to tell you gels that? Men want what they can't have. They're hunters by nature, and the harder the thing is to catch, the more they value it. Keeping them waiting and guessing is part of the game."

Jane gave her a troubled look. "It's not a game to me."

Lady Beatrice reached across and patted Jane's hand. "I know it isn't, my dear. It's all very serious, isn't it—and you're quite right to take your time and think it through very carefully. And even if you decide to refuse Cambury, it won't hurt your reputation at all when it gets out that you'd been asked."

"Oh, but I'd never tell anyone—"

"Pish-tush, who is talking about *telling*?" The old lady gave an airy shrug. "But such things often happen to get out—I can't imagine how—but I assure you, it won't hurt your chances for it to be known that Cambury made an offer for you before the season has even started." Lady Beatrice grinned. "Every eligible miss—and her mother—will be ready to scratch your eyes out. I've lost track of the number of dazzling beauties that have set their caps at Cambury—and failed. So whether you accept him or not—either way, it's a triumph!"

She chuckled gleefully, then saw Jane's worried look and assumed a solemn expression. "But there, I don't wish to put any pressure on you, my dear. It's entirely up to you. If you don't want him, tell him so, and if you're not sure, simply tell him you need more time."

"But if I make him wait, he might change his mind."

The old lady eyed her shrewdly. "He might. Would that distress you?"

Jane bit her lip. That was the trouble; she didn't know.

Chapter Two

I lay it down as a general rule, Harriet, that if a woman doubts as to whether she should accept a man or not, she certainly ought to refuse him.

—JANE AUSTEN, *EMMA*

"Gawd, I'm fair knackered." Daisy stretched and groaned. She and Jane were getting ready for bed.

"'*Vulgarity, Daisy, m'gel, vulgarity,*'" Jane said in Lady Bea accents. "Turn around and I'll get you undone."

Daisy laughed and turned her back for Jane to unlace her. "I'm never gunna sound like a lady, am I? I'll have to get someone else to run me posh shop. If I ever get it, that is."

"You'll get it," Jane told her confidently. "We got a lot done today. Two more outfits finished."

Daisy shook her head. "Yeah, but there's piles and piles of work still to do." She plonked herself down on the bed with a sigh. "I dunno how I'm gunna manage it all, to tell the truth, Jane."

"Even with Polly and Ginny helping?" Lady Beatrice had given two of the maids permission to help Daisy every afternoon.

Daisy nodded. "Even then. I reckon I might have over-reached meself, Jane."

"Nonsense." Jane gave her a hug. "You're just tired."

Daisy's dream was to become a fashionable dressmaker—fashions to the *ton*—and the plan was for her to make a splash this season, having designed and made all Jane's clothes for her come-out, most of Abby's and some of Damaris's—only some because Freddy had taken Damaris to Paris on their honeymoon. Damaris had written apologetically that Freddy had insisted on buying her the most beautiful dresses and two gorgeous pelisses, that she didn't have the heart to say no to him and she hoped Daisy wouldn't be offended.

Daisy had admitted to Jane that far from being offended, she was a bit relieved—it was a bigger job than she'd imagined, making clothes for all three of them for a whole season. Of course, Jane and Polly did all the seams and hems and Ginny, who was skilled at fine needlework, did some of the fancywork while Daisy designed, cut, fitted and did the rest of the fancywork. And Abby lent a hand when she could.

Still, it was a stretch.

They'd all underestimated the amount of work it would be. And the space it would take.

That's why the two girls were sharing a bedroom—Daisy's bedchamber was so taken over with garments in various stages of manufacture, a dummy with a half-made dress pinned in place, rolls of fabric, patterns, pins, reams of braid, beads, lace, fringes and whatnot. "Me cave of gorgeousness," Daisy called it, but her bed had become so buried under dressmaking materials that finally she'd moved the bed and her personal belongings into Jane's room.

It was cosier this way, Jane thought. For most of her life she'd shared a dormitory with other girls, and though she'd enjoyed the luxury of having her own room when they first came to live with Lady Beatrice, she had to admit she enjoyed sharing with Daisy, and talking over the day's events as they drifted off to sleep. Not to mention the convenience of having someone to help you dress and undress without having to summon a maid.

"But enough about me," Daisy said. "Have you worked out what you're going to do about Lord Comb-it-up?"

Jane pulled her dress over her head. "No, I haven't decided."

Daisy frowned. "You ain't gunna marry him, surely? You don't even know him."

Jane sighed. "Probably not." She wasn't dismissing him out of hand, though. A rich man of good family, with nothing known to his detriment, a dutiful nephew who was kind to animals. There was nothing alarming about that.

And he owned a castle. Oh, she'd grown out of that silly child-hood fantasy, but still . . . if she said yes to him tomorrow . . .

Daisy reached for Jane's stay laces. "I saw your face when Abby said that about you fallin' in love." As she spoke, she glanced at Jane's reflection in the mirror. "Yeah, that's the look. So, how come you ain't so excited about meetin' some handsome young gent and fallin' in love?"

"It would be nice to fall in love," Jane said uncertainly. "But . . ."

"Cor, these strings is knotted tight! So what's the problem? It's not the broffel, is it? I mean you weren't touched or nuffin'." It was how they'd met—Jane and Damaris had been kidnapped and sold into a brothel, and Daisy, who'd been a maid there, had, with Abby's assistance, helped them escape.

"No, it's not that. It's just . . . It's not so simple. I can't fall in love with just anyone. I have to make sure he's the right kind of man."

There was a short pause, then Daisy said bluntly, "You mean rich, don't you?"

Jane sighed. "I know, it sounds awful, but you must under-stand, Daisy, a girl like me, without a bean to my name except the allowance dear Lady Beatrice makes us out of the goodness of her heart, well . . . I need to marry a rich man if I'm to have . . ." She trailed off.

"What? Pretty dresses? Jewels? Lots of parties—what?"

"Children."

"*Children?*" Daisy stared at Jane in the looking glass. "Gawd, Jane, you don't need a rich bloke to get kids."

"*I* do." She knew very well the consequences of being too poor to support children. She'd lived them and she would rather die than submit her own children to such a fate. "I think it's more sensible to choose a man for what he can offer, instead of trusting to luck to fall in love with the right kind of man."

And a rich man who was good to his aunt and who liked dogs didn't sound like the wrong kind of man.

She continued, "Trusting to love is like a leaf trusting the wind to blow it to safety. You never know where you might end up. So I don't plan to fall in love at all. I will choose a husband carefully and then I'll fall in love with him."

"It don't work like that." Daisy shook her head knowingly. "Not for you. When the time comes, you won't be able to 'elp yourself. You'll fall in love, just like Abby and Damaris; they never expected it neither. There y'are, it's done now."

Jane pulled off her stays and stepped out of her petticoat. "Nonsense. People *choose* whether they fall in love or not."

Daisy snorted.

"They do, they just don't realize it," Jane insisted. She shrugged off her chemise and slipped her nightgown on. "I've observed it in others. There's a period of time at the beginning when a person thinks, 'Him? Or not him?' And they either find reasons not to like him, or else they spin rose-colored stories about how wonderful he is."

She climbed into her bed. "People *choose* to fall in love." And plenty of people who made convenient marriages fell in love, she knew; it happened after the marriage, that was all. Because they chose to make the best of things.

Daisy climbed into her bed. "Some folks might think like that, mebbe. But not you."

"Why not me? You think I'm being a coldhearted, designing female? Maybe I am, but there's nothing wrong with being ambitious. You are, for your business."

"Yeah, but bein' ambitious and fallin' in love is poles apart. Anyway, I'm tough, me. I was brung up in the gutter, I know what I got to do to succeed and I'll fight to make it 'appen. And sure, plenty of ladies are ambitious to marry the richest bloke they can find. But not you—you got a heart as soft as butter."

"I haven't!" Jane said indignantly.

Daisy laughed. "So who was it who brought Damaris out of the broffel with 'er, endangering 'er own escape—but would you take no for an answer?"

Jane frowned. "That was different. Damaris saved me from that horrid auction. I couldn't leave her there."

"And then there was that cat and 'er kittens you brought in—fleas an' all. Without knowing how Lady Beatrice would react. You coulda got us all kicked out."

"The building was going to be demolished, they would have been killed. And we got rid of the fl—"

"And we both know what you do wiv pennies—"

"That's diff—"

"Face it, you're as softhearted as they come, Janey girl. And knowin' you, you'll find the most impossible, unsuitable bloke in the *ton* and fall for 'im like a ton o' bricks."

"I won't. I absolutely will not do anything so foolish!" She felt oddly panicky at the thought.

"Pooh, you won't have no choice in it, just like Abby and Damaris didn't. And if anyone's made for love, you are. You can say what you like, Janey, love'll find you anyway. Now go to sleep. We got a lot of work to get through in the morning. Your turn to blow out the candle."

Jane slipped out of bed and blew it out. She climbed back into bed. *You'll find the most impossible, unsuitable bloke in the* ton *and fall for 'im like a ton o' bricks.*

She wouldn't. She absolutely wouldn't.

"Jane! Jane, wake up!" A hand was shaking her shoulder, hard.

"Wha—" Jane sat up abruptly, staring around her wildly. Her heart was pounding.

"You was dreamin' again." Daisy was sitting on Jane's bed. "'Nother nightmare."

Jane blinked, and her dazed thoughts slowly came into focus. She glanced at the window. The curtains stirred slightly, letting in a few slivers of gray predawn light.

"You all right now?" Daisy asked.

Jane nodded. "Thanks, Daisy." It was the same dream as always.

Daisy didn't move. "You been dreamin' a lot lately. Cryin' and callin' out."

"Sorry. I don't mean to wake you." She hesitated, then, "What do I say?"

"Can't make out the words, just a lot of muttering, thrashing around and yelling—but that ain't the point. I keep tellin' you, it's the night air. Everybody knows night air is bad for you, but you will insist on sleepin' with the window open."

"I don't like it shut," Jane said.

Daisy slipped off the bed and stumped over to the window. "Yeah, well, too bad, because I'm shuttin' it now. It's bloody freezin' outside and we got at least another hour before it gets light enough to start sewing, so I'm gunna get some sleep." She pulled back the curtains and sniffed appreciatively. "Mmm, must be an east wind. Smell that? You can always smell the bread from the bakery when there's an east wind. Best smell in the world, that is."

Jane repressed a shudder.

"Mmm, lovely it is. Makes me hungry." Daisy took another deep sniff, then closed the window and pulled the curtains closed. "Funny that," she said as she climbed back into her bed.

"What is?"

"You often seem to have bad dreams when there's an east wind. Night." She laughed. "Or whatever you say when you're goin' back to sleep in the mornin'."

"Night. And thanks, Daisy." Jane snuggled back down in the warm bedclothes. She wouldn't get any more sleep, she knew. She never did after she'd had the dream.

Daisy never asked what Jane's nightmares were about. She took it for granted that everyone had terrible memories from before. "It's normal, innit?" she'd said once. "But we're the survivors, and bad dreams is what we pay for bein' survivors." It was a comforting philosophy. Dreams were frightening while you were having them, but they couldn't hurt you, after all.

And Jane was a survivor.

London, 1804

A fist thumped on the door. Hard. Three loud thumps. With every bang the door rattled. "Come on, little girl, open the door!"

Silence. Jane didn't move. Besides, she wasn't a little girl anymore. She was six.

"I know you're in there, little girl."

She scarcely dared to breathe.

"I've got a bag of sweeties for you. Just open the door and you can have them."

Sweeties? She loved sweets, had only tasted them a few times in her life, but she still didn't move. Mr. Morrison, the landlord, frightened her, sweets or no.

Besides, she was not to open the door to anyone, Abby had said. Not to anyone. Only Abby.

Outside in the hallway, Mr. Morrison's voice lowered. There was someone with him. Jane crept closer to the door and pressed her ear against it.

"She's in there, I know she is. And alone—her sister works at the bakery and won't be back for hours."

"Then get that bloody door open. I 'aven't got all day."

Jane froze. She knew that voice, low as it was. It was The Man. *The Man.* She started to shake. The Man had tried to take her before. Oh, where was Abby? She bit on her knuckle and stared at the door.

The first time he'd just grabbed at her in the street, but Abby was there and she'd pulled Jane back and The Man had gone away.

The second time she'd been playing in the street with the other children, and a boy had come eating an orange, not a boy she'd seen before, but he'd come right up to Jane and given her a piece, and oh, it was delicious, so sweet and juicy and the boy had said a man was giving out oranges to children for nothing, just go around the corner.

Only when Jane had gone around the corner, it was The Man—and he was waiting for her. He'd thrown a bag over her head and would have stolen her away, only she'd screamed and the other children—Mama called them street urchins, but they were Jane's friends—had rushed up in a group and attacked The Man, and he'd dropped Jane and she'd escaped and run home to Mama, and safety.

But Mama was dead now, and Jane was alone.

The knock on the door came again, softer this time, and Mr. Morrison said, trying to sound friendly but she could tell he was cross, "Now don't be foolish, girl. You know me. Nobody's going to hurt you."

A key scraped in the lock and the handle turned. Shivering, Jane watched it like a snake. Last month Mama had made Abby put a bolt on the door. Mr. Morrison didn't know about the bolt. But was it strong enough to keep out him and The Man?

The door rattled, but stayed shut. Mr. Morrison swore.

The Man had come here once when Mama was alive. Mama had been expecting Mr. Morrison, come about the rent, and had told her to hide in the wardrobe like a little mouse and to keep the door closed and not to move or come out—no matter what she heard—until Mama called her.

It was Mr. Morrison, but he'd brought The Man with him. Jane had seen him through a crack in the wardrobe door. She'd listened as he told Mama he could give Jane a good job and a good home and plenty of food and he'd pay Mama ten pounds for her—ten pounds! But Mama got angry and started coughing and telling The Man to get out and that he wasn't to lay a finger on either of her daughters, but The Man had said he didn't want the other one, only Jane.

He told Mama she wasn't long for this world anyway, and that sooner or later he'd get Jane. And if not him, that someone else would get her, that Jane was worth good money in the right hands, and if Mama sold her to him now, she could buy medicine for herself and food for her other daughter.

Mama had called him a filthy procu-something, and told him to get out! Get out! And to stay away from her daughters! The more angry and upset Mama got, the more she coughed, and the man had laughed because in the end she could hardly talk for coughing.

He'd stopped laughing when Mama had coughed blood on him. He'd sworn and backed away.

People got frightened when Mama coughed blood. Jane and Abby were used to it. After the man had gone, Jane fetched the cloth and the bowl of water and gave Mama some drops from the little blue bottle and soon Mama was quiet again.

That was when Jane had asked Mama why The Man wanted Jane and not Abby. Abby was stronger and quicker and much cleverer than Jane. Abby was twelve and could read and write and do everything. She even had a job already, at the bakery. Jane was only six and not very good at anything much.

"So why, Mama?" she'd asked. "Why did he want me, and not Abby?"

Mama had cupped Jane's cheek with her thin, white hand and said in such a sad voice, "Because you're beautiful, my darling. Because you're beautiful."

She'd told Jane then that The Man was a very bad man, a wicked man. And that she must watch out for him and stay away from him, that when Mama was gone, Jane must stay with Abby at all times and not wander off.

Mama had died last week but Jane wasn't allowed to go to work with her sister. Abby's boss said he wouldn't allow a child of Jane's age in the bakery, that she would be a nuisance and get underfoot—no matter that Abby promised him Jane would not. So while Abby was at work, Jane had to stay here, alone, in the small room that was their home. Abby said it was safer here than playing in the streets.

Jane didn't feel safe at all. At least in the street there were the other children.

The door rattled again. "Open this door at once!" Mr. Morrison yelled.

"Oh, fer Gawd's sake, just break it down," she heard The Man say. "I'll pay for the damage."

Jane looked frantically around the room. There wasn't any place to hide. They'd be sure to look in the wardrobe. There was no way out except the door. Even the window was boarded over from when it had been broken so long ago.

The window! In the summer, Abby had loosened some of the nails so they could get some fresh air into the room. *Crash*! The door trembled. A crack appeared down the middle.

Jane flew to the window. With fingers that were shaking and clumsy, she worked the loose nail out. One of the boards swung down, leaving a narrow gap. She could see outside, to daylight.

Crash! It was the sound of splitting timber but Jane didn't wait to see. In a flash she was wriggling through the gap between the boards. It was a very tight squeeze.

Behind her she heard the door splinter. She heard a shout and footsteps.

She squirmed frantically, heard something rip, felt someone grab her foot, but she kicked back and fell to the pavement in a heap, one shoe missing.

"Come back 'ere, ya little bitch!" Mr. Morrison shouted, but Jane didn't wait.

She picked herself up and ran and ran and ran, not stopping for breath, not caring that she had only one shoe, not caring that there was a stitch in her side, not stopping until she reached the bakery and ran around the back and there was Abby in an apron too big for her and covered in flour. She hurled herself at her big sister. "Oh, Abby, Abby, Abby!"

And Abby's arms came around her. "What's happened, Janey? What are you doing here? And where's your shoe?"

Shaking, and gasping for breath, she managed, "He came,

Abby—The Man—with Mr. Morrison and I didn't open the door to them just like you said, but he banged so loudly and, and then The Man said to break the door down and, and—" She broke off, sobbing.

"Hush, love, you're all right," Abby soothed. "You're here with me now, you're safe."

"I got out of the window." She looked down at her one remaining shoe and shivered. "Someone grabbed my foot as I was climbing out. He got my shoe, Abby. The Man got my shoe."

"Yes, but he didn't get you," Abby said firmly. "And that's all that matters."

"We can't go back there, Abby. He paid Mr. Morrison to let him in."

"What's that child doing here?" a deep voice boomed. "I told you, no children!" It was the baker, fat and red-faced with a big beard.

"Wait here." Abby sat Jane down on an upturned bucket and hurried away to speak to the baker. Jane couldn't hear what they said, but several times the baker turned to look at her. He was frowning.

The minute Abby came back, Jane said, "I won't go back, Abby. He'll—"

"Hush. I'll go when I've finished work, but only to collect our things."

"What about me?" Jane sent a nervous glance at the baker.

"He said you can stay in the yard during the day," Abby said.

"You told me there were rats in the yard." Jane was scared of rats. She'd been bitten by a rat when she was little. She still had the scar.

"There are two cats and a little dog to keep the rats away," Abby told her. "You'll like that, won't you?"

Jane nodded. She loved animals, except for rats.

"Are you hungry?"

Jane nodded. She was always hungry.

"I'll bring you a nice warm bun to eat." Abby fetched the bun and gave it to Jane. It was the best thing about working in a bakery; there was always stale bread for Abby to bring home. Most days it was all they ate.

"Abby, where will we live now?"

There was a short silence. Abby glanced at the baker, who was pulling trays of bread from a fiery oven.

"He said we can sleep in the shed for a night or two, on the flour sacks, just until we find somewhere else. Don't worry, we'll work something out. I'll write some letters. We can't go on like this," Abby said.

"Letters like Mama used to write?" Mama wrote letters but she never got any answers.

Abby sighed. "I know. But what else can we do?"

J ane lay curled up in bed, thinking about the past.
Don't do anything rash, Abby had said.

But Abby's idea of rash wasn't Jane's. Abby thought it would be rash for Jane to accept a man of good reputation, good family and good fortune, just because she didn't know him very well. Didn't love him.

But Abby had been twelve when Mama and Papa had died. Abby had memories of when they'd been happy. Abby trusted in love. And she'd been lucky.

Jane had only a few memories of those days. She mainly remembered hunger, and being cold and uncomfortable. And frightened. For most of her life she'd been alone, without family.

Trust in love? Hope to be lucky in love?

Mama and Papa had—and look where that had ended; Papa in his desperation shot as a highwayman, Mama coughing her lungs out with consumption and their children left destitute and alone, aged twelve and six.

It was only by the purest luck that she and Abby weren't living in poverty still.

Luck, and Daisy . . . And Lady Beatrice . . . And a chain of random lucky events . . . But you couldn't rely on luck forever.

The pinkish light of dawn edged through the gap in the curtains. Jane huddled the warm bedclothes around her. No, she wouldn't do anything rash.

Chapter Three

*Oh, Lizzy! do anything rather than marry
without affection.*

—JANE AUSTEN, *PRIDE AND PREJUDICE*

L ord Cambury arrived at exactly three o'clock.
   Punctuality was good, Jane thought. It showed that
politeness was important to him, and that, in small ways at
least, he kept his word. While he was greeting her and Lady
Beatrice, and being seated in the drawing room, Jane examined
him carefully.

He was rather tubby around the waist, only a few inches taller
than she, and physically unthreatening. He was neatly and styl-
ishly dressed in immaculate fawn breeches and gleaming black
boots, his neckcloth was elegantly arranged, but not overly elabo-
rate, and the cut of his coat showed the hand of a master tailor.
His hair was carefully styled to disguise his bald pate, and
pomaded into place. *Lord Comb-it-up.* Jane tried not to think
about Daisy's comment. His encroaching baldness wasn't his
fault, poor man.

After a short exchange of polite commonplaces, and his
refusal of any refreshment, Lady Beatrice left Jane alone with
him. She sat, smoothing her skirt over her knees, trying to
appear calmer than she felt.

"Y'look lovely today," Lord Cambury told her with an
approving smile. "All my years in society, don't think I've ever

seen a more beautiful young lady—and believe me, I've looked."
He held up his hands, making a frame of her face with his fingers,
then altering it. "Perfect proportions, no matter what angle you
take."

Jane blushed and thanked him. She never felt comfortable
when people talked about her beauty. "I believe you walk your
aunt's dogs on occasion."

"Yes, fond of dogs."

"So am I. And are you fond of cats too?"

"Don't mind 'em, though I don't keep 'em. Make me
sneeze."

"Ah."

There was a short pause, then Lord Cambury said, "Went
to your literary society last week. Heard you read."

"Yes, I remember."

"Don't generally read much. Boring."

"Oh."

"Pretty voice, though. Don't mind listening."

"Thank you." There was a short silence. She couldn't think
of a thing to say. It was hard to pretend this was an ordinary
morning call, when she knew the real purpose of his visit. She
was absurdly nervous.

"Your guardian inform you as to the purpose of my visit?"

So there was to be no beating about the bush, no attempt at
flirtation, no pretense that this was to be anything but a straightforward arrangement. Jane relaxed a little. "Yes, she did." Lady
Beatrice wasn't her guardian, not in any formal sense, but that
didn't matter.

And then he launched into the speech she'd overheard most
of the day before on the stairs. She listened politely as he outlined
his desire for a beautiful wife to add to all the other beautiful
things he had collected in his lifetime, adding delicately that he
hoped she would give him beautiful children, eventually—he
needed an heir, of course.

He explained his eligibility, though not in the detail he had
to Lady Beatrice the day before. He did describe all three of his
houses and their contents in great detail, as if she were marrying
his houses as well.

There was some truth in the notion, she decided. She was,
after all, marrying him to get a home.

It was all a little strange, but Jane didn't feel at all uncomfortable with him. He did stare at her, but not in *that* way, the way so many men did that usually made her uncomfortable. It was almost as if she were a painting or a statue, rather than a person.

He finished his speech, hesitated, then carefully lowered himself onto one knee and said, "Miss Chance, will you do me the honor of becoming my wife?"

Jane took a deep breath. This was the moment. With a simple "yes," she could secure her future. And that of any children she might have. But she respected that he hadn't tried to flummery her with false declarations of love, and she owed him the same honesty.

It seemed she was going to do something rash after all.

"Please sit down, Lord Cambury," she found herself saying. "There are one or two things I need to clarify before I answer your very flattering question."

He frowned, rose with only a slight degree of difficulty, brushed off his breeches and sat down again.

"Thank you for your offer," she told him. "I am deeply honored by it."

"But?"

"But you need to know something about me before you ask me again." His frown deepened, but she continued, her voice shaking a little. "You asked Miss Chance to be your wife. I am . . . I am not Miss Chance. *Chance* is a name we made up—my sisters and I—when we were in trouble and fleeing from an evil man who intended us harm. My real name is Jane Chantry."

His expression didn't change. "Of the Hertfordshire Chantrys."

She couldn't tell if it was a question or not, but she decided to treat it as one. "I believe so, though my sister Abby and I have never had any contact with my father's family." The Hertfordshire Chantrys had never acknowledged Jane and Abby's existence, not when they were born and Papa wrote to his parents, not when Papa was killed and Mama wrote to them, nor when Mama died and twelve-year-old Abby wrote to tell them she and her little sister were now orphaned, destitute and alone. The Hertfordshire Chantrys had offered no help, shown no interest.

"We've never had any contact with our mother's family, the Dalrymples, either. Our parents died when I was six, and Abby and I went into an orphan asylum."

"Orphan asylum?"

Jane raised her chin. "Yes, the Pillbury Home for the Daughters of Distressed Gentlewomen. I lived there for twelve years."

His sandy brows rose. "And what about the *Marchese di Chancelotto*?"

She swallowed. "I'm afraid he is a figment of Lady Beatrice's imagination that somehow caught the *ton*'s attention and became accepted as fact. We cannot publicly deny it without embarrassing Lady Beatrice, so we don't. We owe her everything, and would not for the world cause her any distress." Though it was doubtful whether anything could embarrass Lady Beatrice.

The old lady had made up the outrageous story one night at a dinner party, out of a mischievous desire to annoy her nephew, Max. None of them had dreamed anyone would take it seriously, but the story had spread and become established as truth, much to the old lady's delight.

He frowned. "And Lady Beatrice is . . ."

"A dear and beloved friend. But no blood relation."

"Yet your sister married her nephew. He know about this?"

"Yes."

Lord Cambury sat back in his chair, looking thoughtful. "I see. Your other sisters?"

"Equally dear and beloved, but no relation to Abby and me. Nevertheless, we are committed to each other as sisters of the heart, and nothing would ever prevail on me to deny them," Jane said firmly.

"I see."

No, he didn't. There was worse to come. She took a deep breath and smoothed her hands over the fabric of her skirt again. They trembled a little. This was going to be the hard part. "I need to tell you how we met, but first, I want your word as a gentleman that you will repeat this to no one, for the secrets I must reveal are not mine alone."

He gave her a narrow look, pursed his lips, then nodded briskly and gave his word.

In a quiet voice, and not looking at him as she spoke, she explained how on the very day she'd left the Pill, she'd been drugged and kidnapped, how she'd woken up in a brothel, and how Damaris, who'd also been newly kidnapped, had helped save her from the virgin auction by brewing a potion of herbs that had made Jane too ill to be sold.

She told him how Daisy, who'd worked in the brothel as a maidservant, had smuggled them out with Abby's help, and how they'd inadvertently caused Abby to lose her position as a governess. She told him how the four girls had vowed to band together as sisters and to take care of each other, and she finished by telling him how they'd come—at Lady Beatrice's invitation—to live with her as her nieces.

She finished, and Lord Cambury said nothing for a long time. Jane waited anxiously, having no clue what he was thinking—his face was quite hard to read—and when he finally spoke, it was to ask for a cognac.

Jane rang for Featherby, and after he'd brought his lordship a cognac, she said, "Would you rather I left you alone for a while, Lord Cambury? I know I've given you quite a lot to take in."

He drained the glass, set it down carefully and fixed her with a stare. "Still a virgin?"

She was a little taken aback by the bluntness of the question, but said calmly, "Yes. Neither Damaris nor I were touched in the brothel." Her face heated and she forced herself to add, "And though I was displayed almost naked, I don't believe they were looking at my face."

"Hmm." He poured himself another cognac, a smaller one this time, and sipped, looking at her, pondering the tale she'd told him. "Even blushing, you're beautiful."

Jane blinked. Was that all he had to say? "So I presume you will wish to withdraw your offer."

"Hmm, what's that? No, admire your honesty, as a matter of fact. Didn't expect you to confess."

"Confess?"

"Knew most of it already—the Italian *marchese*, for a start." He saw her surprise and explained, "Had you investigated. Knew it for a lie. Knew too you were no relation to Lady Beatrice and your so-called sisters. Knew about the Chantrys and the Dalrymples too." He frowned. "Didn't know about the brothel, though. Comes as a nasty shock, to be frank."

"It was a nasty shock to me too," she said thinly.

There was a long silence while he thought it over. "Still a virgin, no harm done. And beautiful. And you come of good stock—wouldn't have offered for you, otherwise—the Chantrys and the Dalrymples are well-respected families."

Not by her, Jane thought. Anyone who could abandon two small orphaned girls to their fate, just because their parents had eloped, was not deserving of her respect, or even to be called a family. But she didn't argue.

"Are you saying your offer still stands?" she asked cautiously.

"Reason I decided on you is your good bloodlines and perfect face. That hasn't altered. Have to confess your frankness pleases me too—never expected honesty from a beautiful woman. Pleasant surprise." He finished his cognac and set the glass down with a snap. "So yes, the offer still stands."

From his pocket he produced a small box containing a ring. It was a diamond, large and more ornate than Jane would have chosen. He slipped it on her finger and she thanked him prettily. It felt very heavy on her hand.

Because she wasn't yet used to it, she told herself.

Jane broke the news to Lady Beatrice after Lord Cambury had left. The old lady frowned. "You've accepted him already? Curses! I meant to tell you to send for me before he left. I wanted to talk to him about settlements. Drat the man!"

"I did mention settlements," Jane said. Settlements were vital to her future security; they concerned the financial and other arrangements made for her and her children if she were left widowed. Without settlements, they could be left with nothing.

Lady Beatrice brightened. "You did?" Then her face fell. "And I suppose he told you not to worry your pretty head about such things. Men will persist in thinking we females are brainless ninnies."

Jane smiled. She'd expected him to say something of the sort, but she'd thought it all out beforehand. "I told him my agreement was conditional on him working out a satisfactory settlement with Max—I hope that's all right. Max is my brother-in-law, after all."

"And an absolute shark in business." Lady Beatrice beamed at her. "Clever girl. You handled it brilliantly. Max will be delighted to take it in hand, and he'll ensure you're well provided for, you can be sure of that. I must confess, I am surprised to find you so . . ."

"Mercenary?"

"Not at all," the old lady said indignantly. "*Practical* was the word I was looking for. It's not mercenary to want to secure your future and that of any children. A great many gels only think of love, and never consider their future."

"I know. My mother and father did exactly that."

There was a short silence, then Lady Beatrice patted her hand. "So they did, my love, so they did. I understand now." She brightened. "So when do we announce it?"

"I agreed to let Lord Cambury announce it as soon as the settlements have been signed. He wishes us to marry at the end of the season."

"A spring bride?" Lady Beatrice's delicately plucked eyebrows shot up. "Good heavens. The man must be besotted."

"No, I don't think he is," Jane said. The whole affair had been remarkably calm and straightforward. Businesslike. Somehow that had reassured her more than anything.

She showed Lady Beatrice the ring.

Lady Beatrice examined it, then nodded. "Well, well, well, you appear to have it all under control. I must say, my dear, I never suspected that behind that lovely face of yours there was such a wonderfully sensible brain." She pulled Jane into a hug. "I'm so proud of you, Jane. Cambury, and before the season has even started! Oh, the cats will be out in force when they hear that, mark my words!" She chuckled in anticipation.

J ane told Daisy straightaway, and informed the rest of her family that evening at dinner. Damaris and Freddy had arrived to a joyous reunion, and the whole family—including Mr. Patrick Flynn, who was a close family friend—were gathered around the dinner table.

As she'd expected, there was an outcry, particularly from Abby, but Jane was prepared for it. She stood firm and refused to explain herself—she knew her reasons would upset Abby more than anything—Abby would blame herself, and she didn't want that.

And Lady Beatrice and, quite unexpectedly, Flynn, Max and Daisy supported her, reminding Abby it was Jane's life and her decision. Damaris didn't argue one way or the other; she simply hugged Jane tightly and wished her happiness. Freddy congratulated her, told her Cambury was a dashed dull dog, but would probably make her a decent enough husband. And eventually, Abby decided arguing further would only alienate her sister, and gave up and embraced her and, with tears in her eyes, wished her all the happiness in the world.

That night, Jane slipped into bed, and pulled the bedclothes around her. She'd done it. She was as good as promised in marriage to a wealthy man of good character and good family.

She'd be safe now, from the risk of falling in love.

Chapter Four

*May I ask whether these pleasing attentions
proceed from the impulse of the moment, or are
the result of previous study?*

—JANE AUSTEN, *PRIDE AND PREJUDICE*

"Sir?" A clerk poked his head into the Honorable Gilbert Radcliffe's discreet Whitehall office. From the outer office, Zachary Black watched, faintly amused by the clerk's excessive caution. Surely he didn't look that dangerous?

"Yes, Evans, what is it?" Radcliffe sounded preoccupied, busy.

"There's a man here asking to see you." The clerk lowered his voice. "*Demanding* to see you."

"And?"

"The thing is, sir, he's a *gypsy*."

"A gypsy?"

"Yes, sir. Dirty and disreputable-looking. I would have shown him the door, only the fellow asked for you by name, sir, insisted you'd want to see him, and wouldn't take no for an answer." He added doubtfully, "I could try to have him removed, if you insist, sir, only he's quite large and I fear it would be . . . difficult."

"An ugly customer, eh? Well then, send the fellow in. I'll deal with him."

The clerk turned to Zach and stepped back to let him pass. "Watch yourself, gypsy. Mr. Radcliffe might be a gentleman but he won't put up with any nonsense."

Zach winked at him, and sauntered into the office, saying in a roughly accented voice, "Gen'leman give me a message for some toff called Mr. Gilbert Radcliffe—that you, is it? Said I was to give it only to 'im. Said Mr. Radcliffe would give me a gold guinea for it."

The Honorable Gilbert Radcliffe leaned back in his chair, regarding his visitor through narrowed eyes. His gaze took in the darkly bristled jaw, the worn, faintly foreign clothing, the muddy boots, the shabby sheepskin coat with the faded but outlandish embroidery—and most damning of all, the small gold earring. "Gold, is it? For a scoundrel such as yourself?"

"Gold, 'e promised me." Zach edged closer. "And gold is what I'll 'ave."

Gilbert Radcliffe wrinkled his nose. "Faugh, that smell . . . Have you been sleeping in a barn?"

Zach's mouth twitched, but he whined in an aggrieved voice, "I come a long way wiv this message, I 'ave."

"Shall I call someone and have the wretch removed, sir?" said Evans from the doorway.

"No, no." Radcliffe waved him away. "Bring a pot of tea and two cups."

The clerk gave him an incredulous look. "*Tea*, sir?"

"And some biscuits?" Zach added hopefully. "Ginger ones?"

The clerk gave him a dirty look and glanced at Radcliffe, who nodded. "Yes, and biscuits—ginger if you have them. And shut the door behind you." When the clerk had gone, Radcliffe looked at Zach and shook his head. "He probably expects you to steal the spoons."

Zach gave him an indignant look. "I'll have you know, Gil, I haven't stolen any spoons for, oh, weeks."

Gil laughed. He rose and threw open a window. "You do realize you smell rather like a sheep."

Zach grinned. "I know. It's the coat." He proudly gestured to the ragged sheepskin coat, covered in faded, once lurid embroidery, now grimy with age and hard wear. Fringed with lank curls of greasy wool, it still bore the faint odor of sheep. "Blame the rain. When it's wet, the *eau-de-sheep* intensifies. The smell is practically undetectable once it dries out."

"Right now, however, it's appalling."

"Appalling? How can you say such a thing? Why, this coat cost me two whole shillings, I'll have you know. *Two!*"

Gil shuddered. "And the cat-skin waistcoat? There's no possible excuse for that."

Zach stroked it lovingly. "Dreadful, isn't it?"

Gil shook his head. "You used to be quite an elegant fellow at school. I almost didn't recognize you." He held out his hand. "But it's dammed good to see you, Ad—"

Zach cut him off. "I don't answer to that name." There was a short silence, then he added quietly, "I've been Zachary Black for the last twelve years and I see no reason to change. How are you, Gil?" The two men shook hands.

"So I'm glad you got my message, and even gladder that you came, but why a gypsy, may I ask?"

"Easiest way to cross a border I know of," Zach told him. "Nobody notices gypsies, especially if they're traveling in a group, which I was." He saw Radcliffe's expression and added, "Legacy of the many misspent hours I spent playing with the gypsies as a boy. I'm an honorary member of the tribe now. Been very useful over the years."

"Did you manage to get the evidence?"

For answer, Zach pulled a tattered-looking oilskin packet from an inside pocket and tossed it onto Gil's desk. The room fell silent as Gil opened the parcel and pored over the documents within.

Zach had received Gil's note nine days before—a grimy screw of paper passed from hand to hand. In it Gil had told him to bring the evidence himself, that his presence in England was imperative. On the strength of that note, he'd left the Hungarians to their own political devices and headed straight for London, making excellent time.

Such notes—always written in Gil's hand and in a code only Zach could read—had ruled his life for the last eight years, carrying instructions from this shabby office at the Horse Guards in Whitehall to whichever part of the Continent Zach was currently working. On behalf of king and country.

This was the first time he'd been back in twelve years. It felt rather strange.

The clerk came with the tea and biscuits, depositing the tray in silence. He glanced at Gil, and then at Zach, a little puzzled, but Gil was absorbed by the contents of the documents in front of him and said nothing. Zach just winked and reached for a biscuit, and Evans left, his curiosity rampant but unsatisfied.

Zach poured his tea, added two lumps of sugar and sipped it slowly, savoring it. English tea. How long had it been? He was on his second cup and his fourth ginger biscuit before Gil finally looked up. "Excellent. It is just as we suspected. And now we have the proof. I won't ask you how you obtained these—"

"Good, because I won't tell you. Now, tell me, Gil, why the devil did you insist I bring them myself? I could easily have sent those papers the usual way. My people are as reliable as ever they were. There was no need for me to return to England."

Gil reached for the pot and poured himself a cup. "Actually, there is."

"Because my father is dead? I knew that months ago, and it makes no diff—"

"It does, if you want to live in England ever again."

Zach frowned. "What do you mean?" He wasn't sure he did want to live in England.

Gil added milk and stirred sugar into his tea. "I've heard a whisper."

"You always do, they're your stock-in-trade."

"The thing is, I don't know the full details—and no, you know me better than to expect me to furnish you with unsubstantiated rumors—but you'd better get along to Smith, Entwhistle and Crombie—"

Zach frowned. "My family lawyers?"

Gil nodded. "I have no doubt they'll be able to explain. And you might need these." He pulled a large faded envelope from a drawer and passed it to Zach. "And Ad—Zach, I wouldn't waste any time, if I were you."

Frowning, Zach picked up the envelope. He'd left it with Gil twelve years before, against . . . he wasn't sure what. He turned it over. The seal was still intact. "Like that, is it?"

Gil nodded. "Do you have somewhere to stay?"

"Do you think the Pulteney will take me dressed like this?" He laughed at Gil's expression. The Pulteney Hotel was the most fashionable hotel in London. "It's all I have with me. I didn't plan on staying in England longer than a day or two."

Gil sighed. "I suppose you'd better stay with me, then. Here's the address of my lodgings." He scribbled something on a card and handed it to Zach. "Show this to my man. He'll lend you my shaving gear and find you something respectable to wear." He narrowed his eyes at his old friend. "That appalling coat and especially that"—he glanced at the cat-skin waistcoat and shuddered—"abomination are not to be seen in my vicinity, understand?"

Zach shook his head sorrowfully. "Gilbert, Gilbert, and I thought you liked cats."

"I do. That's the problem."

Zach laughed.

The head clerk of Smith, Entwhistle and Crombie, attorneys-at-law, was as unimpressed with Zach's appearance as Evans had been. A proper client would have handed the clerk a calling card, but for the last six years Zach hadn't carried any kind of identification, let alone a gentleman's card. Gypsies didn't. Nor did spies. And until he knew what this was about, he had no intention of explaining and certainly not to a pompous little clerk.

"Smith is in, I presume."

The clerk's glance flickered briefly to one of the doors that gave off his room. "Not to the likes of you, he isn't."

"In there, is he? Right." Before the clerk could react, Zach had stepped around him and entered the far right-hand office. He shut the door behind himself and snibbed it firmly.

A slender man of about thirty, with hair already going gray, rose from behind his desk, frowning. "What is the meaning of this intrusion?"

"Sorry, Mr. Smith," the clerk called from the other side of the door. "I couldn't stop him."

"You're Smith?" Zach had been expecting an older man.

"Yes, but as I said—"

"Ah, you must be the son. I was expecting your father, but I suppose he's retired now." Zach sat down, choosing the most comfortable-looking chair.

"Now look here—" Smith began.

The clerk rattled at the door handle, shouting, "Shall I fetch a constable, Mr. Smith?"

"I wouldn't," Zach told the lawyer mildly. "It would be rather embarrassing. Particularly for you." He sat back and crossed his legs, apparently indifferent to, if not totally oblivious of, the clerk hammering on the door and shouting through the heavy oak panels.

Smith visibly hesitated.

"Mr. Smith?" the clerk shouted again. "Shall I fetch help?"

"No, it's all right, Griggs," Smith called.

There was a short silence from the other side of the door, then, "Are you sure, sir?"

"Quite sure."

It was so obviously a lie, Zach couldn't help but smile.

Smith frowned, as if he'd had a sudden thought. He leaned forward intently. "Have we met before?"

"Once, a long time ago. My name is Zachary Black."

Smith shook his head. "I have a very good memory for names. I don't know any Zachary Black."

"Your hair was black when last we met."

Smith's hand crept briefly to his hair. He frowned.

"It was but a brief meeting. You came with your father to Wainfleet, summoned there, I assume, by my late father."

"*Wainfleet?*" Smith stared at him in disbelief. "Your late— You can't mean—good God! No, you cannot be—" He stared at Zach in shock. "But you're *dead*!"

"Am I? Are you sure?" he said dryly.

"Well, of course I didn't—I mean—good God! I should have recognized you by those eyes alone!" Smith sat in his chair with a *plop*. "Cutting it a bit fine, aren't you? The hearing is in two weeks."

"The hearing?"

"To declare you legally dead." He frowned at Zach's expression. "You didn't know? Your cousin Gerald has—since your father's death he's—"

"Ah, Gerald. He always did want what was mine." So that was it.

"Yes, but—oh, dear—you don't understand. Apart from your cousin, there are other . . . complications." Smith pulled out a handkerchief and mopped his brow, though the room was far from warm. He took a deep breath, which seemed to calm him somewhat. "I am sorry, you've taken me rather by surprise. Now, first things first. Can you prove this?"

"Prove what? That I'm alive?"

"That you are Adam—"

"I don't call myself that anymore. Haven't used the name for the last twelve years, not since I left Wainfleet. Zachary Black, that's who I've been."

Smith leaned forward over his desk. "But can you prove you are your father's son?"

"As much as any son can prove his father." Zach pulled out the envelope Gil had given him and tossed it onto Smith's desk. "It's all in there."

Smith opened the envelope and examined the papers within. He took his time, scrutinizing each document carefully. Zach sat back. So he was to be declared dead, was he? It would almost be amusing, except that Cousin Gerald would get everything, and he didn't like Cousin Gerald. Never had.

He watched the lawyer check and double-check the papers, searching for a flaw in the evidence. Finally he looked up. "Can anyone verify these?"

"You mean is there anyone who will vouch that I am who those documents say I am? Yes, of course." Zach listed half a dozen names, mostly former schoolfellows, adding, "And Gil Radcliffe, at the Horse Guards, can vouch for my activities during the late war."

Smith, busily noting down the names, brightened. "During the late war? You were a soldier, then?"

"Not quite."

"Oh. Some kind of spy, I gather." The disapproval in his voice told Zach a good deal. Smith belonged to the majority of Englishmen who regarded spying as an ungentlemanly occupation. Gentlemen fought in the open, man-to-man, face-to-face. Spies lurked in the dark, trading in lies and secrets.

Zach rather enjoyed the life. And ungentlemanly or not, spies risked their lives for information that saved hundreds, sometimes thousands, of others. He gave a faint smile, neither confirming nor denying the charge.

"Your father might vouch for me too, assuming his memory is still intact. I was just a lad the last time we met, and no doubt I've changed a good deal, but we met several times."

Smith nodded. "I don't doubt it; now I know who you are. You aren't much like your father, but your resemblance to your late grandfather is unmistakable, especially around the eyes. Ill health forced Father to retire, but his brain is as sharp as ever. He'll gladly identify you."

Zach added with a glimmer of dark amusement, "No doubt Cousin Gerald will also identify me, though not, I fear, gladly."

Smith pursed his lips. "I did advise him to wait until all legal ends had been tied up, but . . ." He made a faint gesture of frustration.

"Always was a greedy little tick. So is that all? Can you have the hearing stopped, or must I appear and prove my identity?"

"I will try, but I think—I am sure, in fact, that your cousin will insist on the hearing. It has been, as you know, twelve years since you've been seen in England, and well, he—"

"Having considered himself owner of all that is mine, he will be bound to dispute my claim," Zach finished for him. "He can carry on all he likes—and knowing Gerald, he will—but there's no denying I'm alive and well. So is that all, then? I can leave it in your hands?" He rose.

"Ah, no." Smith looked, if possible, even more worried now than when Zach had arrived. "There is"—he swallowed—"a complication."

Zach seated himself again. "Complication?"

"Something rather more serious."

"Indeed?" Zach waited.

"I foresee no difficulty in establishing your identity, sir. But that in itself is the problem."

"I don't follow you."

"The difficulty is—" Smith took a deep breath. "The moment you have proved your identity, you will be arrested."

There was a short silence. "On what charge?"

"Murder."

Chapter Five

*Surprises are foolish things. The pleasure is not
enhanced, and the inconvenience is often considerable.*

—JANE AUSTEN, *MANSFIELD PARK*

"Murder?" Zach repeated mildly. He'd personally killed five men in his life, each one an enemy of his country and killed in the line of duty. And in time of war. And though he'd been indirectly responsible for the deaths of several others—again, overseas and in the service of his country—not one of those acts could be called murder.

"Yes, *murder.*" Smith seemed to feel the need to stress the word, to underline the gravity of the situation.

"And who, pray tell, am I meant to have murdered?"

Smith seemed astonished that he would have to ask. "Your mother, of course."

"My *mother*?" Zach eyed Smith narrowly. "This is a joke, I apprehend."

"A joke?" Smith said, shocked. "I would *never* joke about murder."

"Then to accuse me of murdering my mother is simply ridiculous."

"You didn't kill your mother, sir?" Smith looked relieved.

"I suppose in a manner of speaking I was responsible for her death," Zach admitted with a careless shrug. He was hungry and wanted to get this nonsense over with.

Smith's jaw tightened.

"But I can't honestly be blamed for it," he continued. "Don't tell me they're charging babies with murder these days?"

Smith said in a scandalized tone, "Sixteen is hardly a baby."

"Sixteen?" Zach shook his head. "I was three weeks old when my mother died of childbed fever. I was, some might say, responsible, but it was hardly my fault."

"Ah. No." Smith flicked through the documents that remained in front of him, and gave a *tsk!* of annoyance. "My apologies, my—sir, I inadvertently misrepresented the situation. I am referring to your father's second wife, your *step*mother. It's her murder you're accused of."

Zach sat forward. "Cecily is dead? When did this happen?"

"Twelve years ago, sir. The night you left Wainfleet."

Zach sat back. "Nonsense. I saw her several weeks after I left Wainfleet—we left there together—and she was in the pink of health. And she's written to me on and off over the years. I think the last letter was at Christmas." He frowned. "Or was it the year before? Oh well, she's not dead, that's the important thing."

Smith leaned forward and gave him a searching look. "Do you have those letters?"

Zach shook his head. "Of course not. Why would I keep them?"

Smith sighed. "They might have helped prove she was alive. You'll have to prove she is, you know. Can you?" The man still seemed to have doubts.

Zach shrugged. "I expect so. It'll be a damned nuisance, though."

"A *nuisance*?" Smith echoed him, incredulously. "You are facing *a murder charge*."

"Yes, and it's a blasted inconvenience. But tell me, I'm curious—setting aside the fact that I had no reason to want poor Cecily dead, how am I supposed to have killed her? And why, for heaven's sake?"

"The 'why' is a matter of speculation. As to how"—Smith consulted his notes—"you—er, *someone* hit her over the head and threw her body in the lake at Wainfleet."

Zach snorted. "Rather crude of me, I would have thought. Oh, don't look at me like that, man, it's a mistake."

Smith looked troubled. "Your stepmother's body was most positively identified."

He raised a brow. "By whom?"

"By your father."

"My *father*?" Now that was a surprise.

"And at least three servants." Smith glanced at the file before him and added, "The body had been stripped of jewelry: her rings, in particular, were missing. And . . ."

Zach's stomach rumbled. Outside he could hear carts rattling over the cobbles and a pie man calling his wares. He hadn't yet broken his fast, apart from the ginger nuts. "And?" he prompted after a moment.

Smith cleared his throat uncomfortably. "A young man answering your description sold some jewelry in London some weeks later, jewelry which your father identified as belonging to his late wife—your mother, I mean. And some belonging to your stepmother. The jeweler swore an affidavit and your father identified the jewels." Smith scanned Zach's face. "Do you have any explanation for that, sir?"

Zach wrinkled his nose. "It's true I sold my mother's rubies," he admitted. "But they were hers by right, and not entailed, and were therefore mine to sell. I sold some jewels for Cecily too— jewels that my father had given her and not part of the estate—and I gave her the money. What else was she to live on? My father never made her an allowance."

"And the rings?"

Zach made an impatient gesture. "I know nothing of any rings. I never touched the dead woman, whoever she was. As far as I know, Cecily is still wearing her rings. Or if she isn't, she will still have them. Probably," he added. Cecily had no reason to keep the rings, not for any sentimental reasons.

"So you didn't do it, sir? Kill her, I mean."

"Of course I didn't do it. I don't hurt women," Zach said irritably. He'd helped Cecily to escape his father for her own protection, dammit. "But it'll be a blasted nuisance having to prove it."

"More than a nuisance, I fear," Smith said. "Forgive my blunt speaking, sir, but in my view—and Father's too—the evidence against you is quite strong. It's been twelve years since the murder, and for almost all of that time you have been absent from this country. It's going to be very difficult to disprove." Judging by the expression on his face, the lawyer thought it more like impossible.

Zach wasn't the slightest bit worried. He knew Cecily was alive and well and living in Wales. It was almost amusing. Or it would be, if it wasn't so blasted inconvenient. He'd planned to leave England almost immediately. After seeing Gil, he realized that he'd be delayed by having to prove his identity and deal with the various matters arising from his father's death. But this . . . a murder charge could hold up things for a ridiculously long time.

"So the instant I prove my identity, I'll get clapped in irons and hauled off to prison?"

"Not in *irons*." Smith sounded horrified by the suggestion. "You are *a gentleman*, after all. But prison certainly."

"You relieve my mind," Zach said dryly. He gave a short laugh. "So my choice is to claim my inheritance and risk hanging for murder—unless I produce, alive and well, the stepmother I have not seen for twelve years—or to remain Zachary Black and live by my wits, as I have the past twelve years."

Smith nodded. "In a nutshell. And until we locate your stepmother, it would be better if you continued under your current name. If you give me her last known address, I will have her traced and obtain a certified witness statement."

Zach nodded. He'd given Cecily his word not to divulge her whereabouts to his father, but his father was dead, and Cecily now had nothing to fear. He gave it.

"In *Wales*?" Smith exclaimed in surprise. From the way he said it, it might have been Outer Mongolia.

"Yes, with an old school friend who'd been widowed. And her letters came from the same village, so you should be able to locate her easily enough."

"I hope so, sir. If we're not able to find her—"

"I'll go to Wales myself, find her and fetch her back here." She probably would welcome a visit to London after all this time. Cecily did like to shop.

The lawyer shook his head. "Not a good idea, sir. Better if you left it in the hands of, er, impartial witnesses. Don't want any accusations of, er, tampering with the evidence, do we?"

"Rubbish. How could producing the woman I'm supposed to have murdered possibly be construed as tampering with the evidence?"

The lawyer grimaced. "There was a case last year that caused quite a scandal. A noble gentleman's long-lost heir who'd been missing for twenty years appeared to claim his inheritance. He was very convincing, but eventually was proved to be a fraud. Someone had noticed his resemblance to the heir and coached him thoroughly to impersonate the heir."

He added with an apologetic expression, "People get suspicious now when heirs or witnesses conveniently turn up out of the blue. We wouldn't want to be accused of finding a woman who looks like your stepmother and coaching her, now would we? Best leave it to us, sir."

Zach considered it. It seemed ridiculous to him, but he gave an acquiescent shrug. He preferred to do things himself rather than to leave them in the hands of unknown people. But having crossed Europe quickly by the fastest—and most uncomfortable—route possible, he could not deny that being spared a journey into North Wales had a definite appeal. Come to think of it, he was due a few sybaritic luxuries himself.

"In the meantime, I would advise you to, er, lie low."

"Lie low?"

Smith nodded apologetically. "It would not do if someone recognized you before we located your stepmother. So where can I contact you?" His pencil was poised to note it down. "Your address?"

Zach gave him Gil's address. "That's temporary. I'll let you know if and when I find something more permanent." He picked up his hat. "Is that all?"

Smith nodded. Zach stood and walked to the door. He glanced back at the lawyer and grinned. "Rather a piquant situation, don't you think?"

"*Piquant?*" Smith stared. "I'd call it *damnable.*"

"You think so?" He opened the door. "But then, I've always quite enjoyed a challenge." He winked at the glowering clerk and headed for the exit.

It looked like he'd be staying in England for some time, blast it. He hadn't planned to stay more than a few days, but now he'd found there was a plot afoot to deny him his home and birthright—by Cousin Gerald, the little weasel—he was damned if he'd tamely hand it over.

In the meantime, he just had to stay invisible. No difficulty with that. Staying invisible was what he did best.

Zach walked along, munching on a pie—a good, solid English meat pie—and turning the lawyer's revelations over and over in his mind. It didn't make sense.

Who was the dead woman?

Twelve years ago, he'd escorted Cecily to her widowed friend in Wales, traveled back to London, sold the jewels and then returned to Wales to give Cecily her share of the money.

It couldn't possibly be Cecily.

Not unless she'd returned to Wainfleet after he'd left her that second time, and he would have sworn that wild horses wouldn't have dragged her back there.

His father would have if he'd found her, but how could he? Zach hadn't told a soul and Cecily had just wanted to disappear forever—somewhere his father would never find her.

Besides, Smith had said the woman must have died the night he and Cecily had fled Wainfleet, which was nonsense. And in any case, there were his letters from Cecily.

So why had his father identified the dead woman as Cecily? His father *and* three servants. Damn. He should have asked Smith which servants.

His father had been a brute and a bully, but he'd also had a great deal of family pride and it wasn't like him to lie—not this kind of cold-blooded lie, the kind that would make his only son a wanted man. Blackening the family name.

Unless he'd been in a rage . . . In a rage, especially a drunken one, there was nothing his father would not do, up to and including the beating of his fragile young wife and his only son senseless.

Had his father identified the dead woman as Cecily to hide the humiliating fact that she'd left him, fled his house with her sixteen-year-old stepson? Had he imagined, in some blind, drunken, idiotic rage, that they'd eloped? And blamed his son for the murder?

It was possible.

Or had he beaten up some other woman in a rage and identified her as Cecily to cover up his crime? That too was possible.

But it didn't explain the servants who'd also identified the dead woman as Cecily. Zach kicked a pebble along the pavement. It just didn't make sense.

It wasn't as if he could just walk up to Bow Street and seek answers to his questions. If Smith was right, the only response Zach would get was arrest and imprisonment, followed by a long wait in jail until the case came to trial and his innocence was proved—and that would be damned inconvenient.

No, dammit, he'd just have to lie low until they could prove Cecily was alive and well. It was annoying, but that was all.

In the meantime, he was here, in England. He finished his pie and brushed the last of the few crumbs of pastry from his fingers. An England in which his father was dead. He wasn't sure how he felt about that.

He crossed the road, pausing to let a wagon rumble by. He was coming to a more fashionable part of town, where elegant little shops displayed the kind of wares most people couldn't dream of owning. Quite why he'd wandered in this direction he wasn't sure; perhaps it was merely a desire to reacquaint himself with an area he remembered from his youth.

Not that anyone who'd known him then would look twice at him at the moment. There were still enough shabbily dressed people, even in this area, for him not to stand out.

With a faint jolt of surprise, he realized he was enjoying himself. He'd missed London, missed the sound of English, in all its variations, all around him; the call of hawkers, the shouts of street urchins, the genteel murmur of a pair of well-dressed ladies as they passed him in the street, the distant bellow of a frustrated carter, shouting at people to get out of the road—all in different accents, but all English.

He was home. It was a strange feeling.

Ahead, a small knot of fashionably dressed people emerged from one of the shops, just as an elegant town carriage pulled up. Some ragged children loitered nearby but the fashionable people swept past them.

It was the girl that caught Zach's eye—a slender creature dressed in blue and gold, like something out of a fairy tale. She was the last out of the shop, and after she emerged, she waited a few steps behind her companions searching for something in her reticule.

Zach's attention was drawn to the comedy of errors playing

itself out ahead of her; a large footman in livery, a maid, and a companion by the look of her, all laden with parcels, fussing around a frail-looking, aristocratic old lady who was struggling to climb into the landau, crossly batting away any helping hands, and knocking several parcels to the ground.

He glanced back at the golden girl. The street urchins had gone, but now her attention was not on the fuss around the old lady, but on something else happening down a narrow side alley. Even as he watched, she stiffened and ran into the alley. Had the children stolen something? Was she in pursuit of them? Foolish if she was.

Her companions didn't seem to notice; the old lady continued to struggle to mount the carriage without assistance, the footman, juggling parcels, began to load them carefully into the boot of the carriage, the other two females fussed around the old lady while the coachman fended off abuse from the traffic he was holding up.

Curious as to what would cause such a gently nurtured flower of the aristocracy to venture alone into a dirty London side street, Zach closed the distance in a few long strides and looked down the alley.

And with a muttered curse started running.

A group of youths were gathered in a circle, kicking at something—Zach couldn't see what, but clearly the girl had. She burst into the knot of ruffians at full pelt, giving the biggest one a hard shove that caught him off balance and made him stagger.

The tallest youth quickly recovered from his surprise, grabbed the girl and shoved her hard against the wall of the alley. Zach put on speed, but before he could reach them, the girl's knee came up in a most unladylike move. She connected too. The leader bent double, swearing horribly. His friends closed in.

She faced them white-faced and tense, holding her reticule up like a weapon. She opened her mouth—to scream, he supposed—but then she saw Zach coming. She instantly swiped at one of the thug's heads with her reticule. The youth ducked, and she missed his head, but as a distraction it was sufficient.

Zach grabbed the two nearest thugs by their collars and slammed them hard against the wall of the alley. They subsided there, groaning. The remaining three youths swung round to face him warily. They eyed his rough clothing. "She's ours, gypsy. Bugger off."

Zach's reply was to place himself between the girl and the youths.

"You ain't from 'round 'ere," one of them said, drawing a knife. "You dunno who you're dealing wiv."

In a swift movement, Zach kicked the knife from the youth's hand. It clattered against the cobbles. "Consider ourselves introduced."

"Best not interfere if you plan on livin' long," his friend said, sounding suddenly less assured.

Zach gave the youth a cold smile. "Try me."

"Behind you," the girl warned him. Zach jabbed an elbow in the throat of a lad who'd recovered from being flung at the wall and was creeping up on him from behind. He reeled back, choking and coughing.

"Next one who makes a move toward myself or the young lady, I'll break his neck," Zach said calmly.

The three young men exchanged glances and edged away. One of them held up his hands. "We don't want no trouble, mister."

"Then get out of here—and take that rubbish with you." Zach jerked his head at the youth stirring groggily on the filthy cobblestones and the one still clutching his throat.

Hastily the three gathered up their mates and hurried away down the alley.

Zach waited until they'd gone, then turned to the young woman. "Are you all r—" The words dried on his tongue. The sounds of the city faded away. He stood, neither knowing nor caring where he was, drowning in a pair of wide blue eyes, blue as the sky on a Greek summer's day . . .

She stared back, not moving or saying a word.

The moment stretched. Then her eyelashes fluttered. Breaking his gaze, she glanced away, and took in a long, shivery-sounding breath.

The city sounds and smells rushed back. Zach blinked. What the devil was he doing? He *never* lost concentration. He glanced back down the alley, but the youths were well and truly gone. His gaze returned to the young woman. She was staring at him again, and again he was caught by that blue, blue gaze.

Mastering himself, he dragged in a ragged breath and said, "Are you all right?" His voice sounded hoarse.

She was trembling—and no wonder—but even as his hands

went out to steady her, she seemed to gather herself and edged away from him.

Damn, he'd forgotten how he was dressed. "Miss?" he said, remembering his role at last.

In danger of drowning again in that blue gaze and losing his ability to think, he lowered his eyes, and found himself focusing on her mouth instead.

Bad idea. Satiny, full, eminently kissable mouth. Wild roses and strawberries.

"Y-yes." It was hesitant, and she bit uncertainly on the lower lip with small, even teeth. He felt his body stir.

He dragged his eyes off her mouth, and dropped his gaze.

A slow blush spread upward from the neck of her dress, and Zach suddenly realized where he was looking. Damn.

He hauled his gaze off her chest, noted in passing that the blush had turned her cheeks to wild roses blooming. It made him want to stare at her lips again, so in sheer self-defense he focused on her hat, a ridiculous little blue and gold confection perched rakishly on top of a head of soft, guinea-gold curls.

"Are you sure?" he said, his voice annoyingly husky.

Under cover of straightening her hat, she took another few deep, shaky breaths before answering in a voice that trembled only a little, "Sorry. Yes, I'm perfectly all right, thank you. And very grateful for your assistance." And then she smiled up at him, a dazzling sunburst of a smile that made him catch his breath.

He should have been relieved at her quick recovery, but something about that smile, so bright and . . . and composed— and for all its brilliance, it was false, because she was still shaking. It fanned a small spark of anger within him. She had nothing to smile about, dammit.

She must have seen something in his expression, for she took a step backward and stumbled. He caught her by the arms, and could feel her pulse fast and fluttering. She wasn't all right. Not at all. She went to pull away. It fanned his temper further.

"What the hell did you think you were doing?"

The smile slipped. She opened her mouth to respond, but he continued, "Did you think you could just barrel into a bunch of street toughs and interfere with whatever it was they were up to? Did you imagine that they would listen—"

Chapter Six

I did not then know what it was to love.

—JANE AUSTEN, *SENSE AND SENSIBILITY*

His words washed over her. Jane tried to gather her scattered wits. She'd never seen such eyes, gray but with the faintest hint of green, like a sage leaf buried in pewter or polished steel. And if she wasn't looking up at him, seeing for herself the tanned, darkly stubbled skin, the overlong tangle of thick, dark hair, the bold blade of a nose and the faded, gaudily embroidered sheepskin coat, she would have thought he was . . . someone else. A different kind of man.

But he was a gypsy and a stranger, and although she was grateful for his help—very grateful—she stiffened as his words finally filtered through to her.

"Why on earth would you think they'd listen to you? Because you're a rich young lady and they're just street scum?"

He had no right to speak to her in this fashion. Speak? He was yelling at her. She frowned. The man—the handsome, brave and noble gypsy—the man who'd saved her from a nasty encounter with those horrid boys—like a hero in a novel—and then stolen her breath and her composure for goodness knows how long—was *yelling* at her.

Oh, not loudly, for his voice was low and vehement. But those steely gray eyes were blazing and his hands gripped her fore-arms tightly, as if he'd like to shake her.

The fact that what he was saying was embarrassingly true—oh, not that she thought those boys would show any respect to a lady—far from it, she simply hadn't thought before she'd acted—only made things worse.

He glanced at the reticule dangling from her wrist. "And how could you imagine that frivolous bit of fluff would be any kind of a weapon?"

She finally found her voice. "I usually carry a stack of pennies in my coin purse but I gave—I don't have them today." She tried to pull free of his grip, but he wasn't finished.

The deep, low-voiced tirade continued, "You cannot possibly be so naive. Even the most sheltered young lady ought to kn—"

"The weight of the pennies acts like a cosh."

"A cosh?" The steely eyes narrowed. "So you're not that sheltered, are you? That move you put on that thug . . ."

Jane felt her cheeks warm again. Of all the things he had to notice . . . She lifted her chin. "I don't know what you're talking about."

"When you kneed him in the—"

"I did no such thing," she interrupted hastily. No gentleman would refer to such a thing, but of course, a gypsy would have no such delicate scruples. She turned aside, knowing she was blushing. Again. Though for a different reason. "You're mistaken."

"I'm not." His grip relaxed and the anger faded from his face. He sounded almost amused, which annoyed her.

"Yes, you are. I didn't—a lady would never—" She caught herself up and said haughtily, "I cannot even imagine what you are suggesting." She hadn't even thought about it, had just reacted in a move she'd learned a lifetime ago, in another life.

His lips twitched and she could see he was prepared to argue the point, but before he could say anything, Jane heard a whimper, and seized on it gratefully. She turned. "Did you hear that? He's still here, poor little fellow."

"Who is?"

"The dog. Why do you think I came down here?" She scanned the shadowed corners of the alley as she spoke. "Those beasts were torturing him. I could hear him yelping in pain."

"A dog? You risked your life for *a dog*?" He sounded incredulous.

"They were *torturing* it." Jane searched through the rubbish in the alley, trying not to notice the dirt and the smells.

"And that justifies risking your life, does it?"

"I didn't think," she admitted. "I just heard a dog yelping in pain and those horrid beasts laughing so evilly, and . . . I . . . I just had to stop them." She shuddered, recalling the way the leader of the toughs had thrust her hard against the wall. And how this tall, unshaven stranger had plucked the youth off her and flung him yards across the alley, with such easy, practiced violence.

"All on your own?"

She swallowed. "All right, it was foolish of me, I admit. But I didn't think they'd turn so nasty. Besides, I thought William was behind me. He usually is."

"Who is—"

"Oh, there he is." She started toward a pile of rubbish in a corner from which a quivering black nose poked.

"Be careful," the gypsy ordered, following her. "If the animal's hurt, he'll bite."

People said gypsies were dangerous, that they would steal you away. This one was protective. And bossy. And annoying.

Though those eyes of his . . . they could steal a girl's soul.

If she wasn't careful.

"He won't bite me." She'd never had an animal bite her yet, except for that rat, when she was little. "You won't hurt me, will you, sweetheart?" she crooned softly as she pulled away the dirty sacking that the dog had sought refuge in, poor frightened creature. It growled, but it was a halfhearted effort. A warning as much as anything. "Oh, just look at the state of you, poor baby."

Half starved, with his ribs sticking out, and bleeding from a dozen injuries, the dog crouched on the damp cobbles, shivering, eyeing her warily. But not in a fierce or dangerous way, she knew. She was much more confident with animals than men.

Behind her, the tall man looked at the dog and made a small exclamation under his breath. "I should have given each of those young thugs a good thrashing."

Jane agreed, but all her attention was on the dog. She tugged off her gloves and tucked them in her reticule. She hadn't touched the dog yet, was just letting him get used to her scent. And to the sound of her voice. "There, there, sweetheart, everything will be all right now," she murmured. "I'm here now. Nobody shall harm you again. Now, don't be frightened, I just need to see how badly those horrid beasts have . . ." Judging the moment right, she reached out to touch the dog.

Again, the gypsy grabbed her, this time by the wrist.

Jane jumped. The dog flinched and growled again.

She froze a moment, staring down at the big hand holding her wrist so firmly. Warm, brown, masculine fingers wrapped around her bare skin. She would have imagined a gypsy's hands would feel rough but his didn't. She tried to remember how those hands had smashed into those young thugs. His grip was strong, but he wasn't hurting her.

With dignity, she turned her head to glare at him. An unhand-me-sir sort of glare. A society-lady-to-gypsy sort of glare.

It ought to have put him in his place.

It didn't.

Their gazes locked for an endless moment. Gray-green eyes bored unapologetically into hers, warm, hard fingers gripped her firmly. The noise of the city, the dismal reek of the alleyway, even the dog faded again from her awareness. Such bright, hard, unsettling eyes. Soul-stealing eyes. She swallowed and fought to maintain her composure.

He was a stranger, a gypsy—and an angry one, judging by the glitter in his eyes—and this was the second or third time he'd touched her, yet she felt no sense of threat. Well, not physically.

It was a different kind of danger.

He was so close she could feel the warmth of his big body, could see each dark bristle in his skin, the rough darkness of his jaw, the mobile fascination of his mouth.

Fascination? What was she thinking?

A chance-met gypsy in a small side alley. Rough. Tough. Intimidating. He'd handled those boys with a casual violence that ought to have horrified her.

Instead, it had thrilled her.

She ought to be repelled by him.

She wasn't. Far from it. Something about him drew her in some strange way. The thought sparked a warning deep within her.

"What do you think you're doing?" She wrenched her gaze off his face and glanced pointedly at his hand. A surprisingly clean hand, tanned, but with clean, well-trimmed fingernails. He didn't smell dirty either. There was a scent of woodsmoke and damp wool and old leaves and underneath it all a scent of . . . she didn't know what, but it was dark and masculine, and somehow . . . enticing.

He moved, and another sliver of stark awareness rippled through her.

"Don't touch him, he's frightened and hurt; he could be savage." His voice was soft, but his hard, silvery gaze stripped her of her defenses.

"He's not savage and he won't bite me." She carefully detached her arm from his grasp. "Thank you, but I know what I'm doing." She bent over the dog, but all the time she could feel the man's eyes on her, his gaze sliding over her.

She was used to men staring at her. All her life it had happened, even when she was a child. Usually she hated it, hated the way they stared, their eyes running over her, hot and heavy, weighted with expectations that made her feel . . . anxious. Uncomfortable. And sometimes frightened.

But this . . . She didn't know quite what she felt.

The intensity of that hard, silver-edged gaze made her . . . not uncomfortable, exactly, so much as aware. Alive. Breathless. On edge.

Nonsense. It was merely a reaction from the scuffle with those horrid boys, she told herself. She was no longer used to witnessing violence. Only occasionally, in her dreams.

Beside her he shifted, and again, she absorbed that faint exotic, manly, outdoorsy smell. The forbidden. Dark, exciting. Dangerous. She shivered.

The sooner she got herself away from him, the better.

Footsteps sounded behind them, and he released her and whirled, fists at the ready.

"Oh, there you are, William," Jane said quickly, not certain whether she felt relieved or disappointed. "I knew you'd get here eventually. I told this gentleman you were close by." There she went again, calling the gypsy a gentleman.

The expression on William's face showed how ludicrous he thought the appellation too. "This feller bothering you, Miss Jane?"

"Not at all. In fact, he saved me from the unwanted attentions of some extremely nasty young men." She turned back to the dog.

William peered over her shoulder and grunted. "A dawg. I might o' known it."

"The poor little fellow has been cruelly injured." She reached for the dog again.

"Don't! If it's hurt, it'll—"

"Miss Jane knows what she's doing," William told the gypsy, adding in a pointed fashion to Jane, "Though what she's doing down a dirty alley with a dirty gypsy and a dirty stray dawg, when she *ought* to be sittin' in the carriage along with the other ladies, is something I'd like to know the reason for."

"Hush." She let the dog sniff her fingers, then stroked him softly. When he relaxed a little, she ran her hands gently over the animal's body. He quivered under her touch, stiffened a few times and whimpered once, but otherwise suffered her attentions with a patient air. And when she'd finished her examination, he tried to lick her hand.

She turned her head and said to the gypsy. "See, I told you, he's not savage. He's got some nasty cuts and abrasions—even some burns, the beasts—but I don't think anything is broken. Maybe a cracked rib or two—I can't tell yet—but he's going to be all right, I'm sure of it."

She rose to her feet. The gypsy and William reached out a hand to assist her at the same time. The gypsy won. It was the fourth time he'd touched her. His grip was sure and strong on the bare skin of her hand. Her pulse leapt at the contact.

William bristled, but before he could take offense at the familiarity, the man had released her.

"Want me to get rid of this fellow, Miss Jane?" William asked.

"Not at all." To cover her flustered reaction to the gypsy's touch, Jane brushed off her skirt, frowning as she noticed a muddy stain. "As I said before, he's been very helpful."

William snorted, unimpressed.

"Yes, William," the gypsy said, "I was *very* helpful. Just as well, seeing you were too busy with *parcels* to notice that your mistress was in trouble."

William stiffened. His glare intensified.

With a smile that was pure, studied insolence, the gypsy adjusted his nonexistent cuffs.

Honestly, men—they might as well have been two dogs, circling stiff-legged around each other, hackles up, looking for a fight. Jane decided to defuse the moment. "Give the man a shilling for his trouble, please, William."

The gypsy's smug smile vanished. "A *shilling*?" Black brows snapped together and he stared at Jane first in surprise and then . . . was that amusement? The gray eyes gleamed, the hint of green more in evidence now.

Wasn't a shilling enough? Or perhaps she'd offered him too much? She didn't have much experience in tipping. It was a male concern. She glanced at William, but he didn't seem surprised, just unhappy at having to pay the man anything, even though he knew she'd repay him when they got home. He frowned at her with a mulish expression, conveying a silent message that she understood perfectly well.

But William didn't understand that the gypsy had saved her from a truly terrible situation. And Jane didn't want to explain to her footman—to anyone, really—just how foolish and reckless she'd been.

"William?" she prompted.

With every evidence of reluctance, the big footman produced a shilling and begrudgingly handed it to the gypsy, who flipped the coin in the air, and pocketed it with a grin.

William jerked a thumb. "Now, hop it, you."

The gypsy leaned against the wall. "I'm quite happy here, thanks."

With a visible effort, William turned away, saying, "We should go now, miss."

Jane ignored him. She was carefully removing the blue satin ribbon that was threaded through the waist of her pelisse.

Bemused, Zach watched her. The ribbon was threaded under her breasts, gathering the fabric of the coat in to emphasize her slender figure. The ribbon drawstring gave the garment its shape. The more she tugged, the more it lost its shape.

"You're unraveling that thing," he pointed out.

"Yes, I don't have a leash."

"Leash?" Zach looked from her to the dog. It was a beaten-up, barrel-bodied, squint-eyed brindle creature with a blunt nose and a face like a fistful of wrinkles, quite the ugliest-looking brute he'd ever seen. "You mean you're going to *keep* it?"

In his experience, ladies of quality kept overbred bundles of dainty fluff, not—he looked at the dog again—whatever this was. There was a Staffordshire or bulldog somewhere in its ancestry, he'd wager. Along with a dozen other breeds. And possibly a warthog. Whatever, it was not a dog for a lady.

"You're going to make a pet of *that*?"

"Why not?"

"Because it's the ugliest little brute I've ever seen."

She turned an indignant look on him. "You don't imagine I'm going to leave him here to be abused and mistreated again, do you? Just because he's not *pretty*? His looks aren't his fault. And the patience with which he endured my examination tells you more about him than his looks. In any case, he's half starved—look at those ribs—and hurt. I wouldn't leave any animal in such a condition. It's obvious nobody cares for the poor little fellow. So you'll come home with me, won't you, darling?" She finished tying the blue satin ribbon around the neck of the dog, and straightened.

The dog shook itself, wagged its ragged excuse for a tail—which involved wagging its whole body—and sat on her foot with an air of ownership. She laughed and patted its head. "Brave little fellow."

Zach watched, amused. Talk about beauty and the beast.

"Miss Jane, you can't." The words burst from the big footman. "Not this . . . creature. I've never seen such a—" Miss Jane's silky brows rose and the big man broke off, saying in a pleading manner. "Please, miss. Lady Bea will never stand for it."

"We're keeping him, William," Miss Jane said firmly. "Lady Beatrice needs a guard dog."

William looked at the dog and made a choking noise.

Zach grinned.

"The cats won't like it," William persisted weakly.

"They will get used to each other," she said. The dog scratched itself vigorously.

"It's got fleas," William said, in the manner of a man who has faced defeat before.

"We'll bathe him. You'll see, he's going to make a wonderful addition to the household."

"What are you going to call him?" Zach asked. "Brutus?"

"Haven't you gone yet?" the footman growled.

"Apparently not," Zach told him.

"Brutus? No," she said seriously. "A name like that would cause people to expect the worst of him. But he has a lovely nature, I'm convinced. People place far too much emphasis on looks." It was an interesting statement from a pampered society beauty, Zach thought.

"Like William," she added.

"William?" Zach glanced at the big, ugly bruiser, incongruous in his stylish footman's livery. A former prizefighter, he'd wager, with a cauliflower ear and a nose that had been broken more than once. "I can see the resemblance."

The footman gave him a warning growl.

Miss Jane continued, oblivious, "People are sometimes nervous of William, because of his looks, you understand, but—"

"Time to go, Miss Jane," the footman interrupted. He'd gone a little pink about the ears.

"But really, he's the gentlest, kindest, sweetest-natured soul—"

"Aw, give over, Miss Jane," the footman muttered, turning a delicate shade of puce.

"I don't know what my sisters and I would have done without William," she finished warmly.

"What about naming him RosePetal?" Zach suggested into the silence that followed. "The dog, I mean, not William. To signify his beautiful nature. The dog's, not William's."

The footman glowered and flexed his big meaty fists in a warning manner.

"RosePetal?" She wrinkled her nose and gave him a severe look. "Heavens, no. He's not an *effeminate* sort of dog. A name like RosePetal would embarrass him."

Zach looked at the snaggle-toothed, bandy-legged canine cannonball and agreed solemnly that no, he wasn't an effeminate sort of dog.

"But I doubt he's easily embarrassed," he added. In fact, given the enthusiasm with which the animal was snuffling at its own genitalia, he doubted embarrassment was even in its vocabulary.

The large footman cleared his throat. "Miss Jane, if you think Lady Bea is going to let that animal—with all its dirt and fleas and blood and who knows what else—into her nice new landau . . ."

Miss Jane frowned. "I see what you mean. William, I don't suppose you'd walk him home for me?"

"No, miss, I would not," William said firmly, with the air of a man who has snatched victory from the jaws of defeat. "The animal no doubt will—"

"I'll walk him home for you," Zach offered.

"Oh, no, you won't," William began.

"The very thing," Miss Jane exclaimed with a dazzling smile for Zach. "Thank you."

Now that, Zach thought dazedly, was a genuine smile. He took the end of the blue satin ribbon from her. "What's the address?"

"Berkeley Square, number—"

"Miss Jane, you can't give out your address to any riffraff you meet in the street!"

"Ah, but William, I'm not your run-of-the-mill riffraff," Zach said, enjoying himself hugely. "I'm the riffraff that saved Miss Jane from a group of thugs, when her *footman* was worrying about *parcels*."

William glowered.

"That's true," she said. "And I'm sure he'll take very good care of the dog."

"Very good care," Zach assured her.

She gave him her address. "Give the man another sixpence, William. It's quite a long walk to Berkeley Square. William, or Featherby, our butler, will give you another shilling when you deliver the dog," she assured Zach.

"But—" William began.

Zach promptly held out his hand. It was quite fun, being tipped by a footman. He'd always experienced tipping the other way around. Besides, he could do with the change. Most of the coins he had were foreign.

William sourly produced a sixpence and handed it over, along with a look that suggested that if Zach valued his skin, neither he nor the dog should come within half a mile of the house on Berkeley Square. "Now come along, Miss Jane, Lady Beatrice is waiting."

But Miss Jane wasn't finished. "Thank you, Mr.—"

"Black, Zachary Black, at your service," Zach said, bowing slightly, and although he knew it was the height of bad manners to ask a lady her name, he was currently being riffraff so he added, "And you are—"

"The likes of you don't need to know 'er name," the footman growled before she could say anything.

She gave Zach one of those bright impersonal smiles she seemed to think would put him in his place. Again. He grinned knowingly.

The smile faltered. She looked away, a slight pucker between her brows. "Take good care of my dog, won't you, Mr. Black?"

"I will indeed," Zach assured her, holding the blue satin ribbon that was attached to the ugliest dog in London.

He watched her walk down the lane toward the waiting landau, then, assisted by the big footman, climb lightly in. Zach and the dog made slower progress, reaching the main street just as the carriage pulled away from the curb. She was facing the other way, but she turned her head and looked at him. He couldn't read her expression.

The carriage turned a corner, and he stood a moment, gazing at nothing, just the busy street, and found himself thinking of small purple flowers hiding among heart-shaped dark green leaves. *Violets?* Why on earth was he thinking of woodlands and violets? In a busy London street?

And then it came to him. Her perfume. The scent of violets.

Then a smell wafted up that smelled nothing like a violet. He glanced down at the dog. "Faugh! And I'm guessing flatulence isn't the worst of your habits either, is it? The girl is clearly a little unhinged to want to bring such an unrefined creature into her home, but who am I to complain, since it provides me with an excuse to see her again? Come along then, RosePetal, let's get you to Berkeley Square."

Chapter Seven

How quick come the reasons for approving what we like.

—JANE AUSTEN, *PERSUASION*

"Where on earth did you get to, gel?" Lady Beatrice demanded as Jane climbed into the carriage. She was huddled in fur up to her ears. "It's demmed freezing sitting here, and the racket is atrocious." The street was filled, in fact, with traffic blocked by her ladyship's waiting carriage, and the racket was the loudly voiced complaints coming from the other drivers. Lady Beatrice's driver sat awaiting her ladyship's instructions, sublimely unaware of the insults hurled his way.

"Well, gel, did you forget something?"

"Um . . ." Jane began, trying to think of how best to break the news of her new pet. She gave William, taking his place at the back of the landau, a warning glance, in case he planned to take it upon himself to explain for her. On the way back to the carriage, he'd made no bones about his disapproval of her behavior. Or the company she kept.

"Oi! What's happened to your pelisse?" Daisy demanded. "It's got a dirty mark there. And you've gone and lost that blue satin ribbon, and it took me ages to find the right shade of blue—and it was the end of the roll."

"Sorry, Daisy." Jane hadn't thought twice about using the

ribbon as a leash, but now she felt a twinge of guilt. It hadn't occurred to Jane that the ribbon would be hard to replace.

"Well, get along, man, don't dillydally." Lady Beatrice leaned forward and poked the driver with her cane. "You're holding up the traffic."

Jane hadn't intended to look back, but as the carriage moved off, she turned her head, just as the tall gypsy emerged from the alley with the dog. He stood watching, still and silent. Those eyes, like polished steel, followed her.

Daisy, sharp-eyed as usual, followed her gaze. "Now there's a good-looking feller," she said with approval in her voice. "Pity about his clothes."

"Did we get everything we needed?" Jane asked, trying to change the subject. "I'm so looking forward to the dance lesson this afternoon. We never did learn the waltz at the Pill." At least she wasn't the only one who found the tall man . . . noticeable.

Lady Beatrice twisted in her seat and peered at the gypsy through her lorgnette. "Hmm." She nodded. "Give him a shave and a bath and put him in a decent coat and breeches and he'd make quite a sight."

"Leave him in nuffin' at all, fresh from the bath, and I'm bettin' he'd look even better," Daisy said, and Lady Beatrice gave an earthy chuckle.

Jane tried to think of dogs, ice cream, satin ribbons—anything except the tall gypsy dressed in nothing at all.

It was a miserable failure. She could feel her face heating. And not just her face.

The carriage pulled slowly—agonizingly slowly; she could feel his gaze on her still—into the street, while Daisy and Lady Beatrice continued their bawdy observations about the appeal of tall, dark men in general and the gypsy in particular. Jane looked straight ahead and tried not to hear them, tried not to think of the way those long, tanned fingers had gripped her wrist, the way that deep voice had shivered through her awareness.

There was something about that voice . . . She frowned, trying to place an elusive impression. When he'd spoken to those boys, he sounded like . . . like some kind of rough . . . And yet the way he'd spoken to her when she was bent over the dog, if she hadn't seen him, she might have thought she was talking to . . . Except . . .

The carriage lurched and she lost her train of thought.

"Good, strong-looking shoulders," Lady Beatrice was saying. "I like a man to be a man, not like some of the wispy little fashion plates you see cavorting at Almack's these days."

Jane wished they would stop. It wasn't seemly to talk in such a way about a chance-met vagabond. Especially one with such strange, compelling eyes. Not that they could see the color of his eyes. And she knew very well, from personal experience, close personal experience, how strong he was. A shiver passed through her, which was strange, because she wasn't a bit cold. On the contrary.

"A gypsy, I reckon from the look of—" Daisy broke off and squinted hard at the man and the dog. Especially the dog. "Oi! That's my ribbon he's holding, the one you just lost."

Ah. Jane swallowed, and thrust the gypsy from her mind. The ribbon.

Daisy turned to Jane with a narrow look. "Jane? 'Ow did that gypsy get hold of my blue satin ribbon? He's tied it to a flea-bitten mongrel."

A heavily laden wagon pulled out behind them, and the gypsy and dog disappeared from sight. The carriage turned the corner and the old lady and Daisy sat back in their seats. Daisy turned to Jane with an expectant look.

Which to explain first, the dog or the ribbon? Jane moistened her lips and wondered how best to present her case. "You know how we've been talking about needing more protection."

Lady Beatrice and Daisy looked at her. "No."

"We have William for protection," Lady Beatrice pointed out. "Has something happened to frighten you?"

"No, no, not at all," Jane said hastily. "I didn't mean protection, so much as company."

"Company? We got plenty of company," Daisy said impatiently. "The house is never empty, what with morning callers that come in the afternoon, and the literary society folk and—and everyone else. But what *I* want to know is how that gypsy feller got hold of my ribbon, because you won't convince me it fell out of its own accord; my clothes don't fall to bits. So did he pinch it from you? They can, you know—gypsies—pinch things from you wiv-without you even noticing."

Jane would have liked to blame the gypsy, but people could

be imprisoned and transported to the other side of the world for stealing a handkerchief or a loaf of bread, and for all she knew, a ribbon, so she couldn't. Besides, the dog would be delivered soon, with the ribbon around its neck.

"I gave it to him," Jane admitted. "The dog needed a leash."

"So you gave him my blue satin ribbon?" Daisy said incredulously. "From your new pelisse? Which wivout that ribbon now looks like a bloomin' sack."

"I'm so sorry, Daisy, I didn't realize that shade would be hard to replace, but after all, a dog is more important than a pelisse."

Daisy and Lady Beatrice both stared at her in utter disbelief. "That—that's heresy!" Daisy sputtered.

"Quite right," Lady Beatrice said crisply. "Dogs are all very well in their place, but *nothing* is more important than the fit of a pelisse."

"But I had to give it to him. He was injured, and might have run away."

"Who? The gypsy?" Lady Beatrice asked.

"No, the dog." She took a deep breath. "Don't you think it would be nice to get a dog?"

Lady Beatrice stared. "A dog? Why on earth would I want a dog?" She said "dog" the way some people would say "elephant," as if the whole idea were too outrageous for words.

Jane cast around for a reason that might appeal. "I believe it's tremendously fashionable at the moment."

Daisy, who was assiduous in keeping up with all the latest fashions and fads, shot Jane a narrow glance, but said nothing.

Lady Beatrice pursed her lips, put up her lorgnette and thoughtfully regarded Jane through it. "What kind of a dog were you thinking of? A poodle? A pug? An elegant little Italian greyhound, perhaps?"

"N-no, I was thinking of something . . . sturdier. A dog with, with personality, rather than any particular appearance."

"*Personality?*" Lady Beatrice uttered the word distastefully and shook her head. "No, no, my dear, that cannot be right. If dogs are in fashion this season, they must be an accessory and thus chosen with as much care as a hat or a pair of shoes."

"An *accessory*?" Jane was disgusted. "A dog is not an accessory. It's a creature with feelings and—"

"Bloody hell, you're talking about that 'orrible-looking mutt, aren't you?" Daisy said. "The one the gypsy was holding."

"Yes," Jane confessed. "And I'm not really asking you, Lady Beatrice. I—I've adopted him."

"Who, the gypsy?" Lady Beatrice winked at Daisy and chuckled, then broke off, eyeing Jane sharply. "You adopted a *dog*?"

Jane nodded, and the old lady rolled her eyes. "Foisting yet another wretched animal on us, gel?"

"Foisting? But you *love* the cats," Jane pointed out indignantly, smarting a little under the accusation, all the more discomforting because it was true.

"Cats," Lady Beatrice said majestically, "are different."

There was no arguing with that.

Daisy joined in, "If you wanted a dog, why choose a bandy-legged, ugly brute like that one?"

"How would you know what he looks like?" Jane retorted. "You weren't even looking at the dog—you were staring at the gypsy." And making unseemly remarks about him in the bath. Or out of it.

Daisy snorted. "I was lookin' at my blue satin ribbon first, and I could see perfectly plain that it was tied around the neck of the ugliest mutt in London." She turned to Lady Beatrice. "Truly, it's an 'orrible-looking animal."

"He—he's not the handsomest of dogs, it's true," Jane admitted, "but he has a noble soul and will make a wonderful companion, I'm sure."

"Noble soul?" Daisy made a rude sound.

"Oh, pish-tush, enough squabbling, gels." The old lady waved her hand. "I'll take a look at the animal and decide for myself. I presume it's being delivered?"

Jane nodded, but didn't explain by whom. Daisy slanted her a knowing look and gave a snort of laughter. Jane tried not to look self-conscious, but her cheeks felt uncomfortably warm.

"I'll inspect the creature when it arrives," Lady Beatrice said as the landau pulled up in front of their house. "Now, hurry up and change out of your street clothes, gels. Damaris and Abby will be joining us for luncheon. They should be here shortly."

"Just Damaris and Abby?" Jane asked. "Not the men?"

"Max doesn't take luncheon—says it's a meal for ladies, and

I daresay Freddy is the same." She added waspishly, "Having an ale and bread and cheese at noon, or a meat pie bought in the street, isn't luncheon, apparently. Because men have no need of luncheon." She snorted.

As Jane and Daisy changed out of their street clothes, Jane explained what had happened in the alleyway. "I don't know what would have happened if he hadn't been there, Daisy . . ."

"I knew it," Daisy said. "That handsome gypsy feller got you all of a flutter, din't he?"

Jane blinked. That wasn't the impression she'd tried to give. In fact, she'd absolutely minimized the gypsy's involvement in the telling of the story. "He did not. And I was *not* all of a flutter."

"Mmh-hmm," Daisy said in a don't-believe-a-word-of-it way.

"Was he handsome?" Jane added airily, if belatedly. "I didn't notice."

Daisy made a rude sound.

"As I recall," Jane turned indignantly, "it was *you* waxing lyrical about his appearance—*naked from his bath*, you said— you and Lady Beatrice, quite shameless, you were. *I* wasn't the slightest bit interested."

Daisy said nothing. She didn't need to; her look said it all.

"And *if* I were in a flutter—which I *wasn't*—it was no doubt because of those horrid, wicked boys—from whom he rescued me—"

"Handsome *and* heroic—he gets better and better. Sounds like you 'ad a lucky escape. Bit silly to take on those blokes on your own, though. Good thing 'e came by when 'e did."

"I know." Jane sighed. "I'm always the damsel, never the knight."

Daisy twisted around to stare at her. "Never the night? It wasn't dark."

"No, knight with a *k*." Then remembering that it was less than a year since Daisy had learned to read, she said, "A knight in shining armor, with a sword."

"Why would you want—oh, you mean other people come to your rescue. Good thing too. Right mess you'd be in if they didn't." Daisy took Jane's pelisse and laid it on the bed. "I'll

find you a new ribbon for this. Unless you've made arrangements to meet your feller again to get it back."

Jane turned away. "He's not 'my fellow.' And you're making
far too much of it. It was nothing, really nothing."

"Right. That's why you were staring back from the carriage—
starin' at *nothin'*, like he was a big bowl of strawberries and cream
and you all starvin' hungry."

"I was looking at the dog," Jane said with dignity.

"Oh, *the dog* got you all flushed and bothered, *I* see." Daisy's eyes were dancing.

"I wasn't flushed. Or if I was, it was the relief—yes, the relief
of saving that poor animal from those dreadful ruffians."

"Has he got a name, this gallant knight of yours?" Daisy
asked casually, putting her own pelisse away.

"Zachary Bla—oh, stop it! There is no need to look so knowing, it was only polite to ask; he'd just offered to bring—" She
broke off. "I was being polite, that's all."

"Polite." Daisy nodded. "And of course, you usually go around
introducin' yourself to gypsies you meet in the street. Lady Bea
know about this interesting little habit of yours, does she?"

"He's not a gypsy—at least I'm not sure." She frowned,
considering his accent.

She caught Daisy's speculative look and felt her cheeks warming. "Oh, don't be silly, Daisy, you know I couldn't possibly be
interested in someone like him."

"Because you're betrothed to Lord Comb-it-up?"

"Don't call him that. And yes, I am betrothed. And I
wouldn't dream of looking at any other man."

Daisy shrugged. "No harm in looking, I reckon, and your
bloke is a right tasty eyeful."

Jane glared at her. "He's not *'my bloke'*—it's quite ridiculous
to talk like that." And she didn't like Daisy referring to him as a
"tasty eyeful" either, even though in all honesty—no, she wasn't
even going to think it.

Daisy ignored her. "Speaking for meself, I quite like a feller
who's a bit rough 'round the edges—as long as he ain't rough
with me. I don't fancy them all smooth and polished and, and,
natty, like Lord C—" She caught Jane's eye. "Like some o' those
fellers that come to the literary society." She wrinkled her nose.
"Nothin' of interest there. Nothin' to set a girl's pulse racin'."

Jane tried not to think of how the gypsy's touch, the look in those hard, green-gray eyes—even his smell—had set her pulse racing. "Marriage is not about that kind of thing," she said, tidying her hair in the looking glass.

Daisy gave her an incredulous look.

"It's not," Jane insisted. "It's for security and for having children." *And having a home in which to raise them. And protect them.*

"If you say so. Me, I don't never plan to get married so what would I know?" Daisy added with a grin, "But I wasn't suggesting you *marry* the gypsy, lovie—just that you fancy him to bits."

"I do not! I don't fancy anyone."

Daisy gave her a thoughtful look. "You never talk about love or fancies, or anythin' like that, do you, Jane? Why not, I wonder? Even Lady Bea does it sometimes, and Abby and Damaris never stop."

"That's different," Jane said. "Besides, Abby and Damaris are married now."

"Yeah, but you don't have to be married, or in love, to fancy a good-lookin' bloke. It's only natural, and it ain't nothing to be ashamed of." Downstairs the front doorbell jangled and Daisy's face lit up. "Ooh, that'll be Abby and Damaris now. I can't wait to see 'em—it's been that long since we had a proper talk, just us girls, without the men. Besides, I'm starvin', so 'urry up, Miss I-Never-Noticed-He-Was-Handsome." She hurried toward the stairs, whistling a jaunty tune.

Jane, following, pressed her lips together as she recognized the tune; *Away with the raggle-taggle gypsy-o.*

She was not, absolutely *not*, about to have her head turned by a handsome gypsy. The very idea was ridiculous. Ludicrous. Impossible.

She was a betrothed woman.

Zachary Black was merely delivering a dog for her.

It took forever to get to Berkeley Square, partly because of RosePetal's determination to investigate interesting smells and christen lampposts, and partly because Zach had spotted a market, where he'd bought some healing herbs and a pot of ointment from a gypsy woman, and a red leather collar and a lead—a chain, because he didn't trust the dog not to chomp through a leather one.

"A fine laughingstock you made of me in your blue satin ribbon," he'd told the dog severely as he buckled on the collar. "The ugliest dog in London in the prettiest ribbon. Apart from which, I don't trust you an inch. If you spotted a cat or some other mortal enemy, would you respect the restraining powers of a blue satin ribbon?"

The dog looked up, panting gently through that atrocious but endearing snaggle-toothed grin.

"I didn't think so. No honor at all. And this collar is too smart for you by far, I know, but you're coming up in the world, RosePetal. Just think of it, she's offered me two shillings—two! Aren't you impressed? I wouldn't have given tuppence for you." He clipped on the chain. "Don't get any ideas about it changing your status in life, though—she's probably forgotten you by now. Or changed her mind about keeping you. Girls like that are impulsive. They don't think things through. Look at the way she charged into that pack of bullies."

It still stunned him, the way she hadn't hesitated. Foolhardy, and impulsive, yes, foolish too. But undeniably brave. And all to rescue a street mongrel—and an ugly one at that. In Zach's experience, ladies usually cooed and fussed over pretty little creatures, balls of fluff, or puppies—appealing-looking animals.

"Not you," he told the dog. "Not an appealing bone in your body, is there?"

The dog glanced up at him, wagged his entire behind at Zach and grinned that tongue-lolling, lopsided, hideous grin. Zach laughed. "Your appeal, while not immediately obvious, is an acquired taste. But she didn't know that when she risked her skin for you, did she? Those louts could have hurt her quite badly."

She was an intriguing mix. She was clearly a sheltered young lady of the *ton*. There was no hint of vulgarity in her voice or demeanor, and her clothes were of the finest materials and what he took to be the latest mode, though he was more *au courant* with ladies' fashion on the Continent.

And there was a definite innocence about her. Those blushes couldn't be faked.

Yet she knew what a cosh was, and how to use it. And then there was the instinctive way she'd used her knee to disable their leader. Where had she learned that little trick? It wasn't the kind of thing young ladies of the *ton* were taught. A brother, perhaps? It was intriguing.

No, she was intriguing.

Not to mention enticing. That mouth of hers, so soft and lush, like silken-skinned cherries. Would it taste as sweet? He grinned to himself. She'd probably rather die than kiss a gypsy.

Though she'd shown no sign of the scorn that respectable people—particularly respectable ladies—showed gypsies. The big footman now, he'd shown Zach the kind of reception most gypsies received.

Not Miss Jane; she'd treated Zach almost as politely as if he'd been a gentleman. Even called him one once. Why? Because he'd saved her pretty hide from a mauling by those thugs? Or because his act had slipped? He had forgotten himself for a moment—and that did disturb him. He *never* forgot who or where he was—his life depended on it.

Why would he lose concentration today? Because he was back in England after all these years? Because he was, despite what he'd told Gil, growing weary of the life he'd been living? Whatever the reason, it was a warning.

Zach rolled up the blue satin ribbon and tucked it in his pocket. She wouldn't want it back, not after it had been around the dog's dirty neck. He'd return it if she asked for it. Of course.

He continued on his way, ruminating on the enigma of Miss Jane. She was full of contradictions. A lady with a footman, who airily told the footman to pay the gypsy and yet didn't talk down to him, or try to freeze him out, as most ladies would. She'd also talked to the footman as if he were someone she both liked and respected. William wasn't simply a servant to her; he was a person, with feelings.

Perhaps she didn't know any better. She was young—only eighteen or nineteen. Perhaps that was it. She probably treated everyone politely. Well brought up. Or perhaps she'd been raised by nonconformists or radicals.

But would nonconformists or radicals keep servants dressed in livery? And who was this Lady Beatrice with the new carriage who wouldn't want a dog in it? A relative? Her grandmother?

He pondered William's reaction to the dog. Clearly it was not the first time Miss Jane had brought home a stray.

"She might want you," he told the dog as they turned the corner into Berkeley Square. "But will that old lady feel the same? I doubt it. You are not most ladies' vision of an ideal pet. And who could blame them?" he added as the dog stopped to scratch vigorously behind one ear. "Such attractive habits you have."

Two fashionable-looking ladies were looking at him askance. He raised his shabby hat to them and gave a flourishing half bow, which caused them to turn hastily away. Grinning to himself—he did enjoy playing the disreputable vagabond—he led the dog across the park toward the address she had given him, and rang the front doorbell.

A very dignified butler answered, took one look at Zach and the dog and said, "You will find the tradesmen's entrance around the side," indicating the direction with a regal sweep of his white-gloved hand. Clearly he had been expecting them.

He went to close the door, but Zach stuck his foot in it and said pleasantly, "Not a tradesman; doing a favor for Miss Jane."

The butler narrowed his eyes and subjected Zach to a swift, though thorough scrutiny. "Nevertheless, the animal must be delivered through the tradesmen's entrance."

Zach didn't move. The butler looked at Zach's foot. "I would hate to have to call William. Miss Jane would be so embarrassed by a scuffle on her aunt's front doorstep."

Zach frowned. The butler added smoothly, "Such an incident would hardly add to the young lady's case for keeping the animal."

The fellow had him there. With a grin, Zach withdrew his foot. "Rolled me up, by George, foot and guns, without even an exchange of fire. Smart fellow. Come along then, RosePetal, we've been put firmly in our place." To the butler he said, "Tell Miss Jane the dog and I will be waiting for her in the square."

The butler frowned. "But the side entrance—"

Zach smiled. "Did you forget? Neither the dog nor I are tradesmen."

Chapter Eight

I have not the pleasure of understanding you.

—JANE AUSTEN, *PRIDE AND PREJUDICE*

Luncheon was a light, informal affair: cucumber sandwiches, a little cold chicken and some lemon curd cakes, washed down with cups of tea. And since they hadn't been all girls together since Christmas, there was no shortage of conversation. Not that there ever was when all four girls were together.

It was wonderful to have her sisters back, and under normal circumstances Jane would have loved nothing better than to spend the rest of the day talking with them and hearing all their news.

But the matter of a tall, dark gypsy kept intruding into her thoughts.

Because of the dog, she told herself firmly. She had to get him cleaned up and presentable-looking before Lady Beatrice saw him. As he currently was—muddy, bloody, beaten-up and flea-ridden—she wouldn't have a hope of being allowed to keep him.

It would be different when she had a home of her own. She wouldn't have to ask anyone's permission to adopt a dog then. Except Lord Cambury. And he liked dogs.

She kept glancing at the clock on the mantel. How long would it take him to get to Berkeley Square?

"Jane, gel, what the deuce is the matter with you?" Lady

Beatrice asked, interrupting a story Damaris was telling. "You keep looking at the clock. Are your sisters boring you, or are you expecting someone to call?" Clearly the dog had not even crossed her mind. And a good thing too.

"Of course I'm not bored," Jane, embarrassed, assured them. "Truly, I'm not. Go on with your story, Damaris. It all sounds utterly delightful."

To her surprise, they all laughed.

"Delightful indeed," Damaris said with a chuckle. "I was in the middle of relating my travel-sickness woes—not something I had intended to bore you all with, but Abby did ask. And despite the misery getting there—though Freddy was so sweet, you wouldn't believe—I do not regret going to Venice. Freddy was right—it's a magical place."

Jane blushed. "I'm so sorry, Damaris, I was woolgathering."

"That," Lady Beatrice said crisply, "was apparent. I would have expected you'd show some interest in the land of your birth."

Jane's jaw dropped. The land of her birth? As if Lady Beatrice hadn't made up the entire story of them being born in Venice, when she knew perfectly well they'd all been born in England.

Damaris and Abby giggled. Daisy rolled her eyes. Of them all, Daisy was the one most disapproving of Lady Beatrice's flights of fancy. Lies, Daisy often said, never did nobody no good.

"Is there something wrong, Jane?" Abby asked.

"She's waitin' for an 'andsome gypsy to bring her an ugly mutt wearing a blue satin ribbon," Daisy said.

Abby laughed. "Have you taken up fortune-telling, Daisy?"

"No, it's true. I'm getting a dog, but he's not really that ugly," Jane said. "He's like we were, before Lady Beatrice rescued us—homeless and without a family or anyone to care—"

"Very affecting, I'm sure," Lady Beatrice interrupted. "However, we have yet to decide whether the dog stays or not. You may show it to me, and then we'll see." She bent and picked up Snowflake. "There are the cats to consider."

Jane prayed that her dog was the cat-friendly type. And that the cats were dog friendly.

"What's this about a gypsy?" Abby asked.

"Some horrid boys were torturing him," Jane said.

"Who, the gypsy?"

"No, the dog. The gypsy helped me get rid of the boys. He's

bringing the dog here. I asked him to because he was too dirty to ride in the carriage."

"Who, the gypsy?" Lady Beatrice asked.

"No, the dog. He was all muddy. The gypsy is actually quite clean."

Lady Beatrice snorted. "Believe that when I see it."

Jane rose. "The front doorbell rang a moment ago. It's probably him."

Lady Beatrice held up a magisterial hand. "Stay where you are, gel. Well-bred young ladies don't answer the door, especially not to gypsies. Besides, gypsies know better than to approach the front door of a gentleman's residence."

"But—"

"In any case, there is no need for you to speak to the fellow yourself. What is the point of having servants if they can't deal with such trivial matters? Featherby or William will give him a coin for his trouble and that will be the end of the matter. Finish your luncheon and listen to your sisters' news. Now, tell me, Damaris, did you meet the doge in Venice?"

Jane, frustrated, sat back in her chair as Damaris responded that no, they hadn't met the doge, but they'd met a number of other Venetian noblemen and ladies. She described some of the occasions.

Jane did her best to concentrate. Of course she wanted to hear her sister's news, she was interested, she truly was, but Venice was a long way away, and she'd never heard of any of these people, and her dog and Zachary Black would be here at any minute—if not here already.

It was only polite to thank him herself, surely? She felt Daisy's shrewd gaze on her and plastered an interested expression on her face.

She tried not to fidget, tried not to think of a pair of silver-green eyes gleaming in a tanned face. And the way her pulse had leapt when he touched her.

Finally luncheon came to an end. Lady Beatrice allowed Abby to assist her upstairs, where she would lie down for a short "composer" before supervising their dancing lesson later on. Damaris and Daisy hurried away to get in a fitting for a dress Daisy had almost finished, and Jane was free to go and find her dog.

Zachary Black would have left by now, which was disappointing—though only because she would have liked to thank him personally, she told herself. Being polite. Really, she was eager to see her dog.

Jane looked into the front hall, but there was no sign of anyone. No doubt they'd taken the dog to the kitchen. He'd be hungry. She headed through the green baize door and entered the servants' area.

"There's something not right about that gypsy," Featherby was saying to William. Jane drew back and listened.

"Well, of course he's not right—he's a gypsy," William responded.

"Is he, that's the question."

"Course he is, Hewitt," William said. "You saw that coat of his."

Featherby nodded. "I did see his coat." His nose wrinkled. "I *smelled* his coat, and yet . . ."

"And yet, what? If he looks like a gypsy, smells like a gypsy and acts like a gypsy, what else would he be?"

"I'm not sure." Featherby rubbed his chin in a thoughtful manner. "The way he acted at first, I thought he might try to push his way in, but as soon as I mentioned that it might embarrass Miss Jane—" He shook his head. "He took it almost like . . . like a gentleman. *And* he refused to use the tradesmen's entrance as if such a thing were beneath him."

William snorted. "Didn't sound like a gentleman to me. His accent is as rough as guts."

Jane frowned. The more she thought about it, the more she was sure Zachary Black hadn't any accent when he'd talked to her. But when he'd addressed those young thugs and William . . . he'd sounded different.

Then again, both she and Abby could speak with different accents: the accent they'd grown up hearing in the streets—very like Daisy's, in fact—and Mama and Papa's accents, which sounded more like Lady Beatrice's. Mama and Papa always corrected Abby or Jane whenever they heard them speaking like street children.

Abby was better than Jane at the street accent; Jane could hardly remember those early days. She'd entered the Pill aged six, and everyone there had to speak like a lady or suffer the consequences.

But sometimes, when she was with Daisy, she found herself echoing Daisy's Cockney accent. Maybe the gypsy was like that, taking on the accent of whoever he was with. A kind of protective coloring. Like a chameleon.

"It's just a feeling," Featherby said. "Still, you'd better make sure you go with Miss Jane when she goes to the square."

"You think he'll still be waiting?"

Jane's heart leapt. He was still here? Waiting for her? She felt suddenly breathless.

"I'd bet my last guinea on it. He struck me as a man who doesn't give up easily."

William snorted. "You should have let me hit him, Hewitt. I'd'a made him give the dawg up."

"A vulgar brawl in a lady's residence, William? *Not* while I'm in charge."

"As if I don't know better than that," William said, aggrieved. "I would'a done it outside, a'course. Around the corner."

"You're not to hit anyone." Jane stepped forward. "Now, where is my dog, please?"

"The gypsy wouldn't give it up without you being there to hand it over to, miss. Says he has instructions for you." William snorted. "Instructions! The cheek of him. I'll give him instruct—"

Featherby interrupted smoothly. "The fellow is waiting across the road, in the square, with the animal, Miss Jane."

"Very well, I'll go. The dog will need a bath before we bring him inside, so could you have somebody take the tin bathtub and some hot water and towels into the back garden, please?"

"You're planning to wash the animal yourself?" Featherby sounded shocked.

"Of course," Jane said. "He's going to be my dog, and besides, he has injuries that I'll need to tend to."

Featherby managed not to express his disapproval, but she could tell from the utter smoothness of his expression that it was an effort. "Before you go out, Polly will fetch you another pelisse, there being something amiss with the one you wore this morning." He rang a bell. A maid appeared and he added, "Miss Jane's pelisse, Polly, if you please. The warm one—the wind has freshened quite nastily. You will attend Miss Jane in the park. William, you will go as well, only no fisticuffs—do you understand? And, Miss Jane, when you go, leave by the front door, if you please, not the servants' entrance."

Zach had filled in the time waiting by buying a couple more meat pies from a wandering pie seller. He gave one to the dog, who gobbled it up in two noisy bites. "No manners at all," Zach observed. "You're going to have to do better than that if you're to take up residence with a lady, you know. They tend to frown on things like gobbling."

"Mr. Black." The soft female voice was so close, Zach was startled into dropping the remnants of his pie. How had he missed her approach?

A loud slurping sound at his feet indicated the pie had not been neglected.

She looked radiant in a red wool pelisse and a blue velvet hat that exactly matched the color of her eyes.

"Thank you so much for waiting, Mr. Black. I was sorry to think you might have left without me thanking you." She glanced up at him with a shy little smile, and Zach's brain simply stopped working.

"Jane," he managed to mumble. Quite the orator.

Luckily, she was accompanied by a maid and the large footman. "Oi, gypsy, not so familiar—" the big footman growled, and Zach found his brain again. He dragged his gaze off her face.

"William," he said with every appearance of delight. "How I've missed you." The big footman glowered.

"William, would you wait over there with Polly, please?" she said, pointing to a bench that was close, but took them nicely out of earshot. The big footman reluctantly moved away and she turned back to Zach, her cheeks a little flushed. "I have not given you permission to use my name, sir." Her skin looked as soft as a baby's. Her lips were moist.

"You haven't given me your name at all," he pointed out. "So I have no choice but to call you Jane."

She hesitated, then, "It is Miss Chance."

"Mischance?" Zach smiled. "I wouldn't say that. Quite a fortuitous meeting, if you ask me."

"Not mischance—Miss. Chance," she said seriously. "My surname is Chance."

"Oh, I see. A fine name, Chance. Like Miss Fortune, or Luck, or Miss Fate. If I'd had my wits about me, I'd have introduced myself as Zachary Fortune and then we could have been cousins."

"Nonsense." She looked uneasy. No wonder. He sounded like a lunatic.

"You're right," he said. "It would not at all suit me to be your cousin, not at all."

Her flush deepened and she glanced away. "You are impudent, sir." She turned her attention to the dog and, for the first time, noticed the collar. "Oh, you bought him a collar. And lead. Thank you. I must pay—"

"No," Zach said firmly. "It is a gift."

"But I can't accept—"

"A gift for the dog."

"Oh." She looked down at the dog and tried not to smile. "Then thank you. He's very grateful, I'm sure. It's a very handsome collar. Red suits him."

"Red suits you," he said quietly.

She didn't respond. She gently scratched the dog behind the ears. "Look at you, so dirty. I'm going to give you a bath when we get home, will you like that?"

"Which reminds me, I got you these." Zach took from his pocket the bundle of dried herbs wrapped in newspaper and the small stoppered pot he'd bought at the market.

She made no move to accept them. "What are they?"

"The packet contains some herbs that are good for healing. Steep them in hot water and use the water to rinse the dog after you bathe him. Then apply the ointment to his injuries. It will hasten the healing process."

Still she hesitated.

"They're old gypsy remedies. Very reliable."

She took the newspaper packet and sniffed it cautiously. "Is that lavender I can smell?"

"Yes, lavender is cleansing. And calendula and comfrey and various other herbs. Nothing harmful, I assure you."

"My sister Damaris knows about herbs too." She removed the stopper from the little pot and sniffed the ointment within. "A little pungent, but rather nice. There's lavender in this too, I think."

"Yes, a bit extra in the ointment. I thought you'd appreciate a sweeter smell"—he glanced down at the dog—"to counteract the rather powerful *eau-de-dog*."

She laughed then, and the sound was like sunlight on diamonds. Her eyes sparkled and Zach felt his breath catch. He stood there, staring down at her, unable to think of a thing. She gazed back at him. The silence stretched.

"Miss Jane?" It was the footman.

She started, blushed and turned around. "Yes, William?"

"It's time for you to be getting back." He sent Zach a gimlet glare.

"Oh, that's right, my lesson, I almost forgot." Still blushing, she turned to Zach. "We're practicing the waltz," she confided. "I'd better go. Thank you so much for bringing my dog, Mr. Black."

"My absolute pleasure," Zach murmured. She gave him a warm look, her blush deepened and Zach's brain seized up again.

"Here y'are, gypsy." William stepped between them, thrusting a coin at Zach. "I trust that'll be the last we see of you."

Zach had forgotten her promise of payment when he delivered the dog. He accepted the shilling with a grin. "You never know, William, fate is such an unpredictable mistress, is she not?" William scowled.

He turned to Jane and gave her a raffish bow. "I shan't say good-bye, Miss Chance, but *adieu*. Perhaps, if you happen to walk your dog in the mornings, say around ten, we might happen to meet."

She hesitated, then shook her head. "I'm sorry. Good-bye, Mr. Black, and thank you again for your assistance." She turned away, leading the dog, the footman and maid bringing up the rear.

Zach watched her crossing the square, and smiled to himself. A lady of virtue indeed. She'd given him his marching orders, no doubt about it.

Trouble was, he'd never much liked orders.

Chapter Nine

*Where there is a wish to please, one ought to overlook,
and one does overlook a great deal.*

—JANE AUSTEN, EMMA

"Well," Lady Beatrice said after dinner. "Let's see this dog, then." They were all gathered together—Abby and Max, Damaris and Freddy, Daisy and Jane—in the smaller, cozier drawing room. Lady Beatrice had even invited Flynn for the first family "at home" dinner since Freddy and Damaris had returned from Italy, which said a lot for her affection for him, but Flynn had already commenced his hunt for "the finest young lady in London" and was engaged for the evening.

"Now? But the dog hasn't had time to settle in yet," Jane said. It was too soon. She'd bathed him and anointed his injuries, but he still looked very much the worse for wear. Besides, she hadn't yet discovered the extent of his house training—if any—and more to the point, his attitude toward cats.

All three of the half-grown cats were present: Snowflake lay, as usual, curled in Lady Beatrice's lap, Marmaduke was stretched out along the back of the sofa, while Max-the-cat dangled bonelessly over the knees of his namesake, Max-the-man.

"Is the animal clean?" the old lady asked.

"Yes." She'd bathed him three times, using lavender soap—lavender having healing properties as well as smelling lovely—and in the last rinse she'd used a decoction Damaris had made of the herbs Mr. Black had given her. The dog was as clean as she could possibly make him, and smelled pleasantly herbal, though still a bit doggy underneath. Which was only to be expected.

"Well, bring it up, then. No time like the present, especially since all the family is here. We'll see how this creature from the streets conducts itself in polite company." She stroked Snowflake in a meaningful manner.

Praying silently that the dog would rise to the occasion, Jane went to fetch him.

He was currently confined to the lower regions of the house, partly because Daisy refused to allow him in the bedroom she shared with Jane, and partly because the status of his house-trained-ness—or otherwise—was as yet not established.

She found him asleep on a pile of old rags in the scullery. To Jane's delight, he greeted her ecstatically, writhing in joy, grinning his endearing, ugly grin and making happy doggy sounds. He really was a darling.

She clipped on his lead, sending a silent thanks to Zachary Black for thinking of it. The dog—she had a name for him already, but didn't want to tempt fate by using it before she'd been given permission to keep him—looked so much more civilized in the smart red collar and lead. She prayed Lady Bea would let him stay.

One day she'd have a home of her own and be able to keep whatever animals she wanted to. But that day was yet to come.

She took him upstairs, pausing outside the drawing room to give him a last pat and to whisper, "On your best behavior, please."

She led him into the middle of the drawing room. There was a moment's silence, then, *Mrrrow! Hisss! Spit!*

Three half-grown cats shot into action. Snowflake shot off Lady Bea's lap and leapt onto the dresser behind, skidding across the polished surface and sending a china ornament flying to its doom. Marmaduke leapt vertically in the air and came back down on the top of the sofa. Hissing, he backed away along the length of it, poised to flee, his fur all on end.

Max—the man—gasped as his feline namesake dug claws into his thighs, arched his back and hissed at the canine intruder. Max, swearing under his breath, pushed the cat off. He landed on the floor, and stood facing the dog, stiff-legged, ears flattened, alternately growling and hissing.

"Good God," Max said, rubbing his thigh and staring at the dog. "Could you have found a sorrier-looking mutt?" Jane didn't answer. She and everybody else were watching to see what the dog would do.

She tightened her grip on the leash, but he made no move to attack the cats. His ragged tail waved gently. That was a good sign, she thought. Unless he thought the cats were dinner.

Max-the-cat approached warily, just a few steps, stiff-legged, claws out, ready to attack . . . or flee.

The dog watched the cat, but didn't move. His tail continued to wag.

Jane prayed.

Max-the-cat arched his back, *mrrowled* malevolently and hissed.

The dog sat down. His tail went *thump thump thump* on the floor. Then he scratched behind his ear. Vigorously.

"I hope that's not a flea," Lady Beatrice said.

"It's not," Jane assured her.

Slowly the cat's fur unstiffened. His ears rose a little, setting more to curious and wary, rather than attack. He crouched down, watching the dog with baleful yellow eyes, *mrrowling* occasionally under his breath, but without the same vicious tone—more of a warning sound. Jane started to breathe.

"Undo the chain." Max's voice made her jump.

"But—"

"They've met each other now. Might as well see how they behave while we're here to prevent any carnage."

"No," Jane said. "Not yet. He's not ready."

Max raised a brow.

"It's my dog," she told him.

"That's yet to be decided," Lady Beatrice said.

"Oh, but—"

"Look," Damaris said softly.

While they'd been talking, Max-the-cat had edged closer and closer. As they watched, he leaned forward tentatively and gave the dog a cautious sniff, then drew back, ready to pounce or flee. The dog, panting gently, gave an amiable grin—at least Jane thought it was amiable. To everybody else, she was sure it looked horrific. His tail went *thump thump thump*.

Again the cat drew cautiously near, one paw raised in

warning. He smacked the dog, once, twice. Everyone held their collective breath.

The dog eyed the cat, yawned hugely, then flopped over on his side and . . . went to sleep.

"Well, I think that answers the question," Freddy's voice said into the silence. "He's quite clearly a Menace to Cats." Everybody laughed.

"So may I keep him?" Jane asked breathlessly. "Please?"

Lady Beatrice eyed the dog with a pained expression. "It's a demmed ugly creature. Are you sure you don't want something . . . prettier?"

"No, I want this dog. He needs me." Jane knelt and stroked the dog's head. He opened one eye, licked her hand and went back to sleep.

Lady Beatrice made a helpless gesture with her hand. "Very well, if you must."

Jane jumped up and hugged her. "Oh, thank you, Lady Beatrice. You'll see, he'll be the best-behaved dog, I'll make sure of it."

Lady Beatrice waved her away. "Take the animal back downstairs, gel. It looks as fatigued by all this as I am."

"Do you have a name picked out for him yet?" Abby asked as Jane led the dog toward the door.

"Yes, of course," Jane told her. "Almost from the first moment I met him."

"Well, don't keep us in suspense," Freddy said.

"It's Caesar," Jane told him. "Because I'm certain he has a truly noble nature. And he's just proved it."

As she closed the door behind her, the room exploded into laughter.

"Never mind," she told Caesar. "They will come to love you eventually."

"Now you look like a down-on-his-luck clerk," Gil said in disgust. Deeming Zach's appearance too appalling to take him to dine at his club, Gil had sent his manservant out to fetch steak and kidney pudding from the inn around the corner. "Dashed shabby. It's almost as bad as that gypsy outfit."

"Flatterer." Zach examined his reflection in the looking glass. He was delighted with the new clothes. The gypsy look had outlived its usefulness. It had helped him cross countless borders virtually unnoticed, but now that he was in London— and frequenting fashionable areas—it would draw the wrong kind of attention.

Besides, the cat-skin waistcoat would not, he was sure, be approved by a young lady who was fond of animals.

When he'd left the lawyer's office, he'd had every intention of heading for Wales to fetch Cecily. Why kick his heels waiting around in London when he could do the job perfectly well himself? The lawyer was being ridiculously overcautious, prosing of substitutes and coaching them. Cecily was herself not a substitute.

But then he'd met Miss Jane . . . And he was . . . intrigued.

On the way back from Berkeley Square, he'd found a second-hand clothes market and selected a plain dark blue coat, a gray waistcoat, a couple of white shirts and a plain black hat. Nothing too fashionable—he rather thought he'd like to continue in his anonymity, see what happened.

Gil's valet had taken one discreetly horrified look and whisked the clothing away to be cleaned and thoroughly pressed with a hot iron, as much, he said with dark disapproval, to remove any lurking livestock as for the appearance of the garments. For they were, he'd murmured to his master, distressingly lower class.

Zach had smiled. You could tell a lot about people from the way they treated those who were beneath them on the social scale.

"It's the perfect degree of shabbiness," Zach explained to Gil. "I don't want to be mistaken for a gentleman, but neither do I want to be denied entrance at your lodgings." He'd kept his own buff breeches and his boots, which were comfortable and well worn. Gil's valet had cleaned and polished them to a brilliant shine, but Zach had dusted them up a little, saying such a shine was above his touch.

Gil rolled his eyes. "Believe me, no gentleman would be seen dead in that outfit. But for a clerk who's down on his luck, or a seedy debt collector, it's perfect."

Zach frowned. "Seedy?"

"The bristles. A respectable clerk would shave."

"Ah." He ran a hand over his bristly chin. The bristles might need to go in that case. He was sure Miss Jane Chance wouldn't want to be seen with a seedy-looking character. "I thought it more . . . piratical?"

"Oh, of course, piratical. Definitely. What was I thinking?" Gil said dryly. "Tell me, do you intend to keep the earring?"

Zach fingered his earring. "I did wonder if it might be fashionable. Saw a chap with an earring on the stairs earlier."

"Big, dark-haired fellow? Dressed as a gentleman, apart from an eye-blinding waistcoat?"

"That's the one."

"Flynn, an Irishman. Took over Freddy Monkton-Coombes's rooms and his valet when Monkton-Coombes got married a couple of months ago. You know Monkton-Coombes, don't you? A Cambridge man."

"Never went to university, remember?" By the time Gil and his other school friends had gone to university, Zach had been living by his wits, more or less, on the Continent for several years.

"Of course. Forgot for a minute. Well, Flynn's the only chap I know who wears an earring. Apart from sailors—you sure you don't wish to dance a hornpipe?"

"Mockery does not become you, Gilbert." Zach removed his earring.

Over dinner, Zach explained what he'd learned from the lawyer.

When he'd finished, Gil signaled for his manservant to clear the table, then he poured them both a brandy. "So, a murder charge. That complicates things."

"Nonsense, it's just a misunderstanding. Cecily is alive and living in Wales, as you well know, having forwarded her letters over the years."

Gil nodded. "Still, since your cousin has moved to have you declared dead, it could stir the murder thing up. So it's wise to do as the lawyer says and lie low."

Zach rolled his eyes. "The fellow's ridiculously overcautious. I could easily fetch Cecily myself from Wales, but he insists on sending his own man. Had some crazy notion that I'd be accused of coaching a woman to impersonate her."

"Ah, he'd be thinking of the Breckenridge affair."

"The what?"

"Case last year. Duke of Breckenridge's long-lost heir turned up after being missing for twenty years. Old man in tears of joy, fatted calf killed—you can imagine the fuss." He gave Zach a shrewd look. "Turned out to be a fraud. Left a nasty taste in everyone's mouth. As well to err on the cautious side."

"It's ludicrous. Cecily is alive, she isn't a fraud, so there's no case. I was intending to go and fetch her anyway—damn sight more efficient to do it myself rather than hang around here kicking my heels and *lying low*." Zach snorted. "Skulking around, hiding, more like."

"How shocking," Gil said. "How anyone could expect you to skulk, or hide, or lie low? *Tsk tsk tsk!*"

His words forced a reluctant grin from Zach. "That was different. It was my job. There was a worthwhile purpose to it."

"And keeping your neck from getting stretched is not a worthwhile purpose?"

"There's no question of my neck getting stretched," Zach said irritably. "Cecily's alive."

They subsided into companionable silence.

After a while Gil said, "So you'll stay for the hearing?"

"To assert my status as the living heir? Of course."

"Good." Gil pulled out a card and wrote on the back of it. "Then take this to my tailor tomorrow—his address is on the back—tell him I sent you, and order yourself some decent clothes. You'll need to look like a gentleman." He passed Zach the card, and sat back. "And after that?"

Zach sipped the brandy thoughtfully. "Not sure, to be honest."

"Wainfleet?"

"Can't leave it to rot." Much as he felt like it.

Wainfleet had always been very much his father's domain. Now it was his. He wasn't sure how that made him feel.

"If I could sell it, I would, sight unseen, but the damned place is entailed, so I'll have to put in a manager, I suppose."

"And then you'll do what? Return to the same work? After eight years of it?"

Zach shrugged. "Why not?" But truth to tell, he didn't know what he wanted. Yesterday his plans had been simple, his future crystal clear: Get the Hungarian papers to Gil, then return to the Continent and take up where he'd left off. Now . . . now the past was rising up to haunt him. There was a court case, possibly two. And obligations.

And a girl with wide, fathomless blue eyes . . .

"Aren't you tired of that life? It's not the same now, since we've defeated Boney."

"There's still a need for intelligence and information."

"Of course, but . . ."

"But what?"

"Nothing," Gil said. "If you enjoy it, I suppose . . . I just thought now, since you have alternatives . . ."

And there was the rub, Zach thought. Gil's words had struck closer than Gil knew. Zach had been getting weary of traveling, of dwelling in the shadows, living a life of adventure and uncertainty. It had been exciting at first, but after eight years—and a war—the zest of danger had palled.

He'd served his country well but now, being here in England after twelve years abroad, had . . . unsettled him. Against all his expectations, it felt almost like—no, that was ridiculous. He'd never felt at home in England. Or anywhere else. Certainly not at Wainfleet.

What to do with the rest of his life? He had no idea.

He drained his glass. "I hate making plans. They inevitably fail." It was easier to go where chance took him.

"Not inevitably," Gil reproved him. Gil prided himself on his ability to plan. "Still, if you're planning to stay and thwart your cousin's claim—not to mention sorting out that murder charge—there'll be plenty of time for you to make up your mind. You're welcome to stay here as long as you need. The guest quarters are a little poky, but—"

Zach laughed. "I've slept in coal cellars and haystacks. Your spare room is palatial by comparison."

Silence fell. They sipped their brandy. The fire hissed and crackled gently. Outside, the patter of rain against the windows and the incessant rumble of the city that never slept.

"Tell me, Gil, what do you know of the Chance family?"

Gil frowned. "Chance family?"

"In particular a Miss Jane Chance, lives with a Lady Beatrice someone on Berkeley Square."

Gil nodded. "Freddy Monkton-Coombes, who I just mentioned—fellow who used to live downst—"

"Chance, I said, not Monkton—"

"I'm getting there. Freddy married Miss Damaris Chance—Miss Jane's sister. Lady Beatrice—well, strictly speaking, she's the Dowager Lady Davenham, but she's a law unto herself, the old girl, and prefers to be called Lady Beatrice—daughter of an earl, you know. She's said to be the girls' aunt."

"Said to be?" Zach frowned.

Gil made a vague gesture with his wineglass. "All a bit havey-cavey, if you ask me."

"Everything is havey-cavey to you," Zach pointed out. "You're probably suspicious of your own mother."

"Not my mother," Gil retorted, unperturbed. "Above rubies, my mother. M'father, now . . ."

Zach gave a snort of amusement. "So tell me about these sisters and their havey-cavey aunt."

"Oh, there's nothing havey-cavey about Lady Bea, apart from being a little eccentric. Ancient noble family, counts half the *ton* as her friends and the other half she's related to. But the sisters appeared out of nowhere six months ago—supposedly from Venice. The story is they're the daughters of Lady Bea's half sister Grizelda and a Venetian *marchese*." He paused and eyed Zach over his wineglass. "The *Marchese di Chancelotto*." His lips twitched.

"The *Marchese di Chancelotto*?" Zach choked on his brandy. The name was outlandish. Nothing like any Italian or Venetian name he'd ever heard.

Gil nodded. "Precisely so."

"So the girls are adventuresses?"

Gil shrugged. "Not clear. They're very popular. Lady Bea conducts what she calls a literary society. Everyone who's anyone attends, and the girls read the books aloud, so even though the season hasn't yet commenced, they're very well known, especially with the older set, who positively dote on them."

"And nobody's ever called them on their story?"

"Well, it's not called 'polite society' for nothing. In any case, the eldest girl married Lady Beatrice's nephew, Max, Lord Davenham, who must know the truth, and another married Freddy Monkton-Coombes, Davenham's best friend."

"Which suggests that there's nothing havey-cavey about the girls."

"That or they're such charmers their husbands don't care," Gil said. He took a sip of brandy. "But you asked about the younger sister, Jane, did you not? She's not out yet—none of them are—but she's reputed to be a beauty, a diamond of the first water."

"She is."

Gil glanced up sharply. "How the devil do you know that?"

Zach shrugged. "Ran into her in a dark alley."

Gil gave him a skeptical look. "Planning to run into her again?"

Zach didn't respond.

"Even though you said the lawyer advised you to lie low?"

"I also told you, the whole thing is a mistake."

Gil drained his glass. "You never did like following orders, did you?"

Zach gave him a lazy grin. "I followed yours, didn't I?"

"No, you got the results I asked for," Gil corrected him. "There's a significant difference."

Zach tossed and turned in his bed. It was ridiculous that he couldn't get to sleep. He could sleep anywhere—he prided himself on it—a moving coach, a haystack, a cold cellar, even with enemies close by who planned to kill him. Anywhere. Anytime. It was a skill he'd honed over the years. Sleep when the opportunity presented itself.

And yet here, in Gil Radcliffe's very comfortable spare bed, with its feather mattress, fine linen sheets, warm blankets—and in perfect safety—he couldn't sleep. He turned over again, punching his pillow into a better shape, and contemplated his sleepless state. He was tense, restless.

It had been a long time since he'd had a woman. Perhaps that was the problem. No doubt Gil could direct him to some establishment where he could have his needs met . . .

He considered it. The idea didn't appeal. Zach was choosy about the women he took to bed.

Too choosy.

Curse it. He punched the pillow again. He knew what the problem was and there was no possible solution to it. The last woman he should be thinking about was Miss Jane Chance. She was an innocent; a sweet, young, sheltered miss, the last person a jaded fellow like him should be thinking lustful thoughts of.

A gypsy—if not in truth, in lifestyle.

But Gil was right, he wasn't good at doing what he was supposed to.

He shouldn't be thinking about Jane Chance, but he was. He shouldn't be thinking about returning to Berkeley Square in the morning either, but he was.

He'd spent years relying on his instincts, and now they were at war, and all over this one girl.

Admittedly she was ravishingly beautiful.

But he'd known many beautiful women in his life, and though he admired beauty in a woman, it didn't necessarily call to him, didn't compel him to possess a woman, or even to want to know her better. It certainly didn't usually keep him awake at night.

But those wide blue eyes, blue as the Mediterranean on a summer's day, and just as easy to drown in . . . and that complexion, silken English peaches and cream. And the softest-looking, most kissable, cherry-dark mouth he'd seen in a long time . . .

He groaned and turned over. He was leaving England as soon as practicable. He shouldn't be thinking about any female except some temporary woman who wanted nothing more than a night or two of bed sports.

But he couldn't get Miss Jane Chance out of his mind.

How long had it been since he'd felt that . . . instant connection with a woman? Had he ever? Not lust—well, not just lust, but something . . . else.

Whatever it was, it had shaken him. When had he *ever* lost concentration like that? Not since he was a boy.

He'd lived with danger and deception so long that it was like a second skin to him now. He never forgot who he was supposed to be and that danger was ever present.

But today . . . his accent had slipped—several times—and he'd forgotten for a moment—actually forgotten—about those young thugs.

And all because of a pair of wide blue eyes, open and trusting.

And that mouth, tender and ripe and moist . . .

All right, so she appealed to his baser desires; she also intrigued him. On the surface she was the loveliest specimen of womanhood he'd seen in a long time. And yet she'd attacked a

bunch of thugs over an ugly stray mongrel—and was going to keep said mongrel in her elegant Mayfair mansion, what's more.

And according to Gil—and who would know better?—she had secrets, and not the kind of tame little secrets any gently raised girl would have. A fabricated background with a faux Venetian *marchese* for a father, no less. And that scuffle with the street toughs had revealed a streetwise awareness that no sheltered miss ought to have.

The skill with which she played the innocent young girl, how much of that was real? He thought again of the way that slow, enticing blush had risen from the neck of her dress, and he stirred restlessly.

He'd known a lot of women skilled in the arts of arousal and deception—it was inevitable in his line of work—but he'd never met a woman who could blush on command. Could she be as innocent as she seemed?

Were those blushes and that rosy, delectable mouth signs of a promise as yet unawakened?

Probably, he told himself grimly. And that was the very reason he shouldn't be going within a mile of Miss Jane Chance. She was young—eighteen or nineteen—and if not totally sheltered, she was, he was sure, untouched. And if he'd learned one thing in his lifetime with women, it was that you don't dally with young innocents.

Women tended to view bed sports differently, and some—especially the young ones—tended to confuse sex, even harmless flirtation, with . . . emotions. They had a tendency to deceive themselves about the meaning and significance of such acts.

He'd seen that in his father's young second wife, Cecily, met her as a dewy young bride, dazzled and infatuated by her handsome older husband.

His father was certainly pleased with his pretty young bride.

Zach at sixteen might have developed a bit of a crush on her himself. She was pretty and gentle and helpless in a way that might have appealed to a young lad, except that he had just discovered the joys of bed sports with a comely local widow five years his senior, and he only had eyes for her.

Zach was just relieved that his father was too busy with his new bride to bother making Zach's life a misery. It gave him a new sense of freedom. He could stay away from the house as

long as he wanted; his father never cared. So Zach kept out of the newlyweds' way.

When he finally noticed his father's young bride, it was because she was moving with a stiffness he recognized. And when he looked at her, really looked, he'd seen that the happy glow of young bridehood had disappeared and that she'd gone quiet and was no longer so pretty, but was somehow pinched-looking.

She'd sat silently at the dinner table that night as his father broached his second bottle of wine for the evening, pleating and repleating her table napkin with nervous fingers, watching her husband with quick, furtive glances and an expression that Zach recognized with a sick inner certainty. Dread.

And he realized why his father had eased up on him lately. He'd found a fresh victim.

Cecily's plight, her helplessness in the face of his father's bullying ways, had awakened Zach's protective instincts. And look where that had got him.

He had no plans to stay in England. He had no plans at all, and girls—respectable, young, unmarried girls—particularly young, unmarried girls with exotic invented backgrounds— would be all about plans.

So it would be pointless—pointless and foolish—trying to see her again. Much more sensible to go to Wales and fetch Cecily.

He closed his eyes and tried to sleep.

And pictured that rose-silken mouth, lips slightly parted . . .

His body stirred with awareness. He turned over and jammed his eyes shut.

And found himself drowning once more in a pair of wide blue eyes.

His mouth curved with cynical self-knowledge: She was not for the likes of him. Dammit. He punched the pillow again.

Chapter Ten

*An engaged woman is always more agreeable than a
disengaged. She is satisfied with herself. Her cares are
over, and she feels that she may exert all her powers of
pleasing without suspicion. All is safe with a lady
engaged: no harm can be done.*

—JANE AUSTEN, MANSFIELD PARK

The gypsy was the first thing Jane thought of when she
woke. The curtains were stirring with the breeze from the
open window, but she could hear no rain. Good. She could take
Caesar to the park.

*Perhaps, if you happen to walk your dog in the mornings,
say around ten, we might happen to meet.*

A slow smile curved her lips. Of course she wouldn't meet
him—that was out of the question—she was a betrothed
woman.

Still, it was exciting to have a man suggest an assignation.
And not just a man—a stranger. A dark, unshaven gypsy
stranger who gazed at her with the most beautiful eyes. As if
he'd like to eat her up.

Like the big bad wolf.

A little thrill of excitement rippled through her. She lay
snuggled in the blankets, the cool air from the window fanning
her warm cheeks.

It wasn't as if anything could come of it, after all. She
wouldn't be meeting him alone and unchaperoned. Young,
unmarried ladies of the *ton* didn't go anywhere alone. Besides,
ever since that kidnap attempt last year—right in Berkeley

Square!—Lady Beatrice was stricter than ever and William or Polly or one of her sisters always accompanied Jane when she went out.

What if he did come to the park again? What would she do?

She'd never so much as flirted with a man before. Growing up, she'd had so many problems with men trying to touch her—in the street, and even in church, twice!—and expecting things from her, and imagining she felt about them the way they felt about her. She'd learned not to give men the slightest bit of encouragement.

Though discouragement didn't always work. Some men enjoyed the challenge. Even when she was a young girl and had no interest in boys or men or anything like that, it had been a problem.

At school, the drawing master had kept her back one day, and with no warning he'd grabbed her and tried to kiss her. Luckily Mrs. Bodkin had come in and stopped it. But the drawing master had blamed Jane, saying she'd tempted and encouraged him—and it was so untrue! He was old and hairy and had gray hair sprouting even from his nostrils and ears. She hadn't even thought of him as a man, just the drawing master.

But even though he'd been dismissed, Mrs. Bodkin had subjected Jane to a severe lecture on forwardness, temptation and brazen behavior, and she'd been punished every night for a week afterward by having to copy out tracts from the Bible about the sins of women.

She'd learned not to tell anyone if a man was bothering her. Nobody except her sister ever believed she wasn't to blame, and Abby had left the Pill by the time Jane was twelve. So she'd learned to recognize the signs and do her best to avoid them.

Now, for the first time ever, she was tempted to follow Daisy's suggestion and flirt with a man. Not just any man, with Mr. Zachary Black, of the darkly handsome face, the gleaming silvery eyes and the dashing smile that caused her insides to curl up deliciously. She hugged the thought to herself.

The idea of an assignation with a dark and dangerous stranger thrilled her. But she couldn't bring herself to do it. An assignation was a little too . . . calculated.

But if she took the dog out later, and they happened to meet. Nobody could say she'd made an assignation then, could they?

And if he didn't wait for her? Well, that would be that.

In the meantime, how had Caesar fared in his first night in a lady's residence? Jane quickly threw off her bedclothes and dressed hurriedly, hoping her dog had not disgraced himself.

To her great relief and pride, he had not. It seemed he'd also made a friend below stairs: Cook had seen him dispatch a rat in the yard that very morning. "Snapped its spine with one bite, miss—a joy to watch 'im, it was." She gave Jane a choice bone for the dog, adding, "I never thought much of dogs, to be honest, but 'e's better than them spoiled, useless moggies of 'er ladyship's, any day."

It was a good sign, Jane thought. Cook was very influential with the other servants, and if she approved of Caesar, he would be well treated in Jane's absence.

After breakfast, teeming with repressed impatience, she sat upstairs with Daisy, sewing the seams of the dresses she would wear during the season—Daisy wouldn't trust her with anything visible. They sewed until the clock chimed half-past ten, then Jane set her sewing aside, went downstairs and clipped Caesar's leash on.

She was determined not to hurry. She didn't have an assignation. She'd made it very clear she wouldn't meet him at ten. So.

In the square, she casually glanced around. There were nursemaids talking in small clumps while around them children played, bowling hoops and playing hopscotch. She saw one or two people walking dogs and taking the air, but of a tall, dark gypsy there was no sign.

She tried not to feel disappointed. Of course he hadn't come. She'd made it quite clear she had no intention of meeting him. So.

She felt William glance sideways at her, and immediately started walking briskly along one of the paths, leading Caesar, affecting an airy unconcern as if it hadn't even occurred to her to look for anyone.

If Mr. Black didn't care enough to wait, he wasn't worth looking for.

Caesar suddenly jerked at the chain, pulling hard away from

the path. A rat? A squirrel? "Caesar!" she reprimanded him. But the dog took no notice. He strained eagerly at the leash.

She looked up and saw what the dog had noticed already: Zachary Black, on the far side of the square, rising from a bench. Her pulse leapt. She tried to look unaffected. It wouldn't do to look too interested.

Caesar had no such compunction. Panting, wagging his tail and uttering small yips of delight, he towed Jane firmly in the tall man's direction, practically choking himself in the process. For all his skinniness, he was a strong little dog.

She was breathless and laughing by the time she reached him.

No wonder she hadn't spotted him at first. He'd discarded his gypsy coat and earring. In a plain dark coat, well-worn buckskin breeches and boots, he ought to have looked quite ordinary, but he was so tall and broad-shouldered and strode toward her with a careless arrogance, as if he owned the square—which he quite obviously didn't.

With his overlong hair and dark, unshaven jaw, he didn't look the least bit gentlemanlike, and even looked slightly menacing, so why should she feel a delicious shiver of awareness the moment he fixed her with that silvery gaze and strode toward her, she didn't understand.

"Miss Chance, fancy meeting you here on this fine crisp morning." His eyes gleamed as he gave her a small, casual bow. "William, delightful to see you too." He glanced at Polly and gave her a nod and a wink. "There's something on that bench over there, William, fetch it, would you? It's a gift for—"

"She don't accept gifts from gypsies," William growled. "And you don't order me around."

"It was a request, not an order. And I wouldn't dream of offending Miss Chance by offering her a gift," the gypsy said with a virtuous air that deceived no one. "This is for RosePetal— the dog," he added when William gave him a blank look. "I hope you don't mean to tell me that after one night in a lady's establishment, the dog is now too high in the instep to accept a small token of my friendship."

William hesitated.

"It's over there on that bench, William. But if you're unable to carry it, I'd be delighted to bring it home for Miss Chance." Without even looking to see if William had obeyed him, he squatted down and energetically scruffed at the loose folds around the dog's neck. Dog bliss if Caesar's expression was anything to go by.

Jane glanced at William, and with a scowl, he tromped toward the bench.

"Oh, you like that, don't you, RosePetal?" Zachary Black said. "You have landed on your feet, haven't you? Spoiled rotten already, I'll wager."

His hands were bare, big and elegantly shaped with long, strong fingers. His knuckles were grazed. Wounded in her service.

"He's called Caesar now," Jane told him. Her words came out a little throaty.

Zachary Black laughed as he straightened, but not in an unkind way. "He'll always be RosePetal to me. Though perhaps I should start calling him Lavender now. He smells a good deal better, and that ointment looks to be working already."

"It is. We bathed him with the herbs you gave me too. Thank you so much for them."

William returned carrying a large, shallow, woven willow basket.

"Oh," Jane exclaimed. "A bed for Caesar—thank you—it's exactly what I needed."

"I thought so, when I saw it in the market."

He was spending quite a bit of money on her—her dog—Jane thought. "Can I pay you for—"

He put up a hand. "Not at all. It's my pleasure. As I said, it's a gift. For *the dog*." He smiled at her, a swift slash of white in the tanned face. She felt her cheeks warm. When he smiled at her like that . . .

"Shall we walk? That dog needs exercise," he said, and Jane nodded.

"So tell me," he asked as they strolled along the path, "how has he settled in? I hope he didn't disgrace himself on his first night."

"Not at all," Jane told him, matching her steps to his. Walking made things easier; if she didn't have to look at him, her brain wouldn't get so scrambled. "In fact, he has done amazingly well, much better than I expected for a dog raised in the streets."

Dark brows rose. "Housebroken?"

Jane laughed and crossed her fingers. "It's early days yet, but so far so good. He also impressed Cook by killing a rat."

"Oho, that's the sort of ingratiating creature you are, is it, RosePetal?" Zachary Black said. "Very clever, making friends with the cook. And I see someone has bathed you—I bet that was a shock."

Jane laughed. "Yes indeed, but he was quite the gentleman about it—in the end, that is. He struggled at first—I was quite drenched—"

"You bathed him yourself?" he said, surprised.

"Of course. He's my dog, after all, and it's important he knows that. And as I said, he put up quite a fuss at first—he was fearful of drowning, poor lamb, but eventually he accepted his fate and simply endured." She smiled and added, "You should have seen the profound expression of martyrdom on his face. It is a shame dogs cannot be actors, because I'm sure he played the martyr better than any actor I've seen on the stage."

He chuckled.

"Of course, the cuts and abrasions must have hurt, but he never once snapped or growled or threatened me in any way. He really is a very gentle creature."

"That might be why those lads were kicking him. They'd probably hoped to make him a pit dog, and he didn't have the temperament for it."

She shuddered. "It's wicked the way men set innocent creatures to fight against each other, simply for their own entertainment."

They walked on a little, then he said, "Didn't you say you also had cats? How did that go?"

"To tell you the truth, I was terrified he'd attack them—we have three, you see, all half grown, all from the same litter, and—"

"Don't tell me, you rescued them too."

She stared at him. "Well, yes, I did. How could you know that?"

He gave her a lazy smile. "Just a feeling."

The smile seemed to curl around her insides and it was a moment before Jane could gather her wits and continue the story. "They were in a place we—er, an old building, scheduled for demolition, and they would have been killed. We brought the mother cat with us, but she abandoned them—and us—soon afterward."

"And so you kept all three kittens, of course you did, why would I even ask? So how did these lucky cats react to RosePetal's arrival?"

She laughed. "They were horrified—they spat and growled and climbed up the furniture."

"And RosePetal?"

She described how, as everyone watched, Max-the-cat approached the dog, "with menace in every claw and whisker. He's the bravest and most dauntless of the kittens. Well, of course I had no idea what Caesar would do, and I was so worried, because Lady Beatrice was by no means convinced we needed a dog and she's very fond of the cats—and then . . ." She glanced down at the dog and smiled.

"Then?"

"Caesar rolled over and just . . . went to sleep. You should have seen the cat's expression. And everyone else's."

He laughed then, a rich, deep laugh that warmed her insides. A sudden flush of heat rippled through her, and though she glanced away as if perfectly composed and indifferent, she could not help but be aware of his stance, the close proximity of his tall, hard body, the angle of his head as he looked at her. And the intensity of his gaze, which she affected not to notice.

Her neck ached with the effort not to turn her head and look, gaze, stare her fill of him.

The trouble was, he was beautiful. The faint tan of his skin, unfashionable as it was, only made the contrast of his white teeth and brilliant silvery eyes stronger, and the dark slash of his brows, the high, angled cheekbones, and the dark, bristle-roughened jaw . . . She felt her hand closing in a fist. She longed to stroke that jaw, feel the roughness under her palms, feel the hard line of his jaw beneath.

As for his mouth, framed by that dark roughness, the way he smiled was a pure invitation to sin . . . He could have been created by Michelangelo or Machiavelli or some other brilliant and scandalous Italian. And she needed to remember that.

He was dangerous. Associating with him was like playing with fire.

Such a relief that he was quite, quite impossible. And that she was safely betrothed.

His gleaming, brilliant gaze dropped to her mouth and it

was as tangible as a touch. Her lips tingled. She felt her face warming.

William cleared his throat in a meaningful manner, and Jane glanced at him and realized they'd done two complete circuits of the square. "I'd better go now," she told Zachary Black. "I have a lesson to attend."

A dark brow rose. "More lessons?"

She nodded. "You have no idea how many things there are to learn for my season. Thank you so much for Caesar's basket. I'm sure he's very grateful—or will be tonight when he sleeps in it."

He bent and patted the dog. "I'm not sure gratitude is even in his vocabulary, though it ought to be. But joy certainly is, isn't it, you rascal?" he added as Caesar grinned his crooked, sloppy grin and wagged his entire body in delight.

They said their good-byes. He made no further suggestion about any future meeting, and Jane, of course, was not so far gone to impropriety as to suggest one.

Besides, she hadn't flirted with him at all. Apart from a few unruly and quite inappropriate thoughts, she'd only talked to him, as if she'd known him forever.

Chapter Eleven

The mere habit of learning to love is the thing;
and a teachableness of disposition in a young
lady is a great blessing.

—JANE AUSTEN, *NORTHANGER ABBEY*

"No, no, no!" Lady Beatrice rapped her ebony stick on the floor. "Don't bob up and down like a dratted maid-servant! You're not concentrating. Slow and graceful, Jane, how often must I remind you?"

Jane, Damaris and Abby were assembled in the front drawing room of Lady Beatrice's house, practicing their curtsies. Daisy sat on the sidelines ostentatiously sewing.

Now that Abby and Damaris were back in London, almost every morning had been devoted to lessons in deportment, lessons in how to behave in every conceivable situation—and after that, dancing lessons. Though Jane, Abby and Damaris had been gently born, and spoke and behaved as ladies should, none of them had grown up in a gentleman's residence, or had what Lady Beatrice considered an acceptable upbringing.

And none of them were up-to-date with the dancing, though Abby and Jane knew some of the country dances.

As for Daisy, for reasons of her own, Lady Beatrice insisted she attend the lessons too, even though Daisy declared loudly and often that it was a waste of her precious time, she wasn't makin' a blasted come-out, and she had sewin' to do.

Having longed for daughters all her life, Lady Beatrice was

determined that nobody—not the highest stickler in the land—
would have any excuse even to glance sideways at her beloved
nieces. They would, each one of them, shine. Even Daisy.

So she drilled them all like soldiers.

"Watch your sisters. Abby! Damaris!" She rapped her stick
on the floor and first Abby, then Damaris walked to the middle
of the floor and sank into a slow, graceful curtsy.

The old lady snorted. "See, Jane? Perfect. Daisy, you next."

Daisy looked mutinous. "Why should I? I ain't going to make
any grand come-out so why should I make a fool of meself
pretending?"

It was her bad leg making her self-conscious, of course, but
in this, Lady Beatrice was adamant. "Your intentions are neither
here nor there—no niece of mine will leave my house less than
perfectly trained—for whatever she might encounter."

Daisy opened her mouth to argue, but the old lady flapped her
hand in irritation. "Yes, yes, yes, I know you intend to become
the most fashionable dressmaker in the *ton*, and I approve, even
if it is *in trade*." She wrinkled her nose briefly. "*But* I have yet
to hear why that exempts you from knowing what any lady should—
and if you try and tell me one more time that you *ain't no lady*"—
she imitated Daisy's accent so well that it set the others
giggling—"I'll—I'll smack you, Daisy! Now, I asked you to
curtsy, miss, so get on with it."

With a very bad grace, Daisy put her sewing aside, stomped
into the middle of the room and sank into a slow curtsy. The
old lady watched her with a critical eye and nodded. "Excellent.
See that, Jane? And Daisy has a bad leg to match her bad mood.
Now, your turn again."

Jane sank once more toward the floor.

"Slowly, child, slowly! And don't bounce up!"

Jane skipped across the room to bestow a hug on the old lady.
"I promise you I'll be perfect on the day, dearest Lady Beatrice.
I'm just so excited. It's my dream, you see—doing what Mama
did—making my come-out, dancing and going to parties, just as
Mama did."

Abby smiled. "She used to make me tell her Mama's stories
over and over again."

Jane nodded vigorously. "And even after Abby left the Pill,

I used to dream of making my come-out, just like Mama. Being Cinderella."

"Cinder*ella*?" Frowning, Lady Beatrice raised her lorgnette. "You mean that gel who went around with no shoes, dirtying her feet in the cinders of the fire? You used to dream of being *her*?" She sounded appalled.

"Yes," Jane said sunnily. "And you're my fairy godmother."

"I am *not*!" Lady Beatrice declared, revolted. "I would *never* drive around in a pumpkin pulled by rats or whatever horrid creatures they were. It's a vile notion, quite disgusting. As for the woman's choice of footwear—ridiculous! What use, pray, is a *glass* slipper? Cold, inconvenient and dashed uncomfortable, I'll be bound. No flexibility in glass, you see, so the gel—even if she was used to wearing shoes at all, which she wasn't—would be clumping all over the dance floor like a clumsy dratted elephant."

She pondered the stupidity of glass slippers, and snorted. "Ridiculous! Only use for a glass slipper would be for a gentleman to drink champagne from." She sighed reminiscently. "Did I ever tell you about the time the Duke of—" She broke off, recalling her company, and cleared her throat. "What are you all standing about grinning for? Jane, again, if you please."

"You're quite right." Jane, laughing, bent to kiss the old lady again on her powdered cheek. "You, my darling Lady Beatrice, are better than any fairy godmother could *ever* be."

Lady Beatrice, deeply pleased but determined not to show it, gave a sniff and said gruffly, "Well, this Cinderella won't be going to the ball unless she learns to curtsy better than that. And stop twirling like that, you're making me quite dizzy."

Jane laughed, and gave a last happy twirl. "I know, I'm just enjoying myself."

"Get away with you, gel. It's not my lessons that have you in alt—it's that dratted animal you saw fit to bring home. You're in a hurry to get back to it, I know—why, I don't know, for it's the ugliest creature I've seen in all my life."

"I know, but he has a beautiful nature. And you're right, I am a little worried about leaving him shut in downstairs." She gave the old lady a guilty look. "I'm not sure if he's housetrai—er, used to living in a house yet."

Lady Beatrice shuddered, and flapped her hand in a long-suffering manner. "Go on then, I can see I'm not going to get a bit of sense out of you. Ring that bell on your way out, and tell Featherby to bring tea for your sisters and me. And mind you don't get muddy paw prints or dog hairs on that dress. It was once my favorite, even if has been made over." She shot a dark look at Daisy.

"As you wish, my lady," Jane said and gave her a deep, slow, utterly perfect curtsy, then bounced up and danced across the room to tug on the bellpull.

"Hah! See, you *can* do it, you wretched gel! Only don't! Bounce! Afterward!" With each word, Lady Beatrice banged the floor with her ebony stick.

As Jane reached the door, the old lady called, "And don't be late for your dancing lesson. Half an hour until that little Frenchman comes!"

"Wouldn't miss him for the world." Jane blew her a kiss and hurried away.

Sinking back in her seat, Lady Beatrice sighed. "I'm too old for this." She rolled her eyes in a long-suffering way that deceived nobody. She was enjoying herself hugely.

"Where are you going, missy?" she demanded, spotting Daisy hurrying toward the door.

"I ain't got time to sit around drinkin' tea. I got sewing to do."

"You work too hard," Lady Beatrice told her. "You're looking quite worn, my dear."

Daisy shot her an incredulous look. "Dun't matter what I look like, does it? Them clothes won't sew themselves. 'Specially when I got to waste time making curtsies."

"*Those* clothes," Lady Beatrice, Abby and Damaris said together.

"That's right. And this is me chance in a lifetime to make somefing of meself, and I don't aim to waste it." She opened the door, where Featherby, the butler, was about to enter. He stood back to let Daisy pass through the door first.

"You'll be back here for the dancing lesson, Daisy," Lady Beatrice reminded her in a firm voice.

Daisy turned around. "Why do I have to learn to dance?"

she said, exasperated. "I ain't going to any of those toff balls—I don't want to go to them—and I got work to do!"

"You still need to learn," Lady Beatrice insisted. "Every lady should be able to dance."

"Yeah, but I ain't no—" Daisy stopped, remembering the old lady's earlier threat. "Wiv a gammy leg like mine, there's no point in me even trying to dance."

"There is a point, even if you don't see it," the old lady said austerely. "You will oblige me in this, Daisy. Thirty minutes. And if you 'forget,' Featherby will send William to fetch you." She glanced at Featherby, who bowed slightly in acknowledgment of what they all recognized as an order.

"All right, but it's a waste of my precious bloomin' time," Daisy grumbled and stumped off. She hurried to the bedchamber she shared with Jane, and found her struggling out of her dress.

"'Ere, let me." She started undoing the hooks at the back. "The old girl still wants me to go to them dratted dancing lessons. Talk her out of it, can't you, Jane? What do I want with dancing? She knows I don't want to be no fancy society lady—I just want to make dresses for them."

Jane stepped out of the dress, and shook it out. It really was very pretty. "Abby already tried yesterday after you argued last time, and if Abby can't change her mind . . . She won't be budged on it, I'm afraid."

Daisy muttered something rude under her breath. She tossed the dress over Jane's head and nimbly did it up. She tugged it straight, glanced at Jane in the looking glass and said slyly, "That big handsome gypsy fellow—you met him this morning, din't you?"

"Who?" Feeling Daisy's shrewd gaze on her, she added airily, "Oh, him. As it happens, I did bump into him in the park. Purest coincidence."

Daisy laughed. "Coincidence, my foot. That's why you was all flushed and excited—nothing to do with being Cinderella."

Jane felt herself redden. "It was. And I wasn't. It was . . . nothing." She tried to look as disinterested as possible.

Daisy quirked a skeptical brow. "So you never talked to him. Just saw him at a distance, eh?"

"He brought m—brought Caesar a basket to sleep in. It was only polite to thank him."

"Politeness again, is it?"

"Well, it w—"

Daisy snickered. "Admit it, lovey—you fancy him."

"Oh, very well, yes, maybe I do. A little. Did. But you're the one who said it was only natural to admire a well-made man. And that's all it is. Was." It was all it could be—and a very good thing. A man like Zachary Black could never fit into her plans.

Daisy held her hands up. "Don't mind me. I don't blame you, he's a good-looking feller all right. But you don't know nothing about him, Jane, so you need to be a bit careful. Are you goin' to meet him again?"

"No of course not. I doubt I'll ever see him again." Which was, Jane admitted privately, a very good thing. Probably. "Now, I really must check on Caesar."

"So what did you do today?" Gil asked, but a moment later his manservant brought in dinner—roast beef, mashed potatoes and gravy from the inn around the corner again—and conversation lapsed for a while.

Gil had decided that shabby clothing aside, it would be unwise for Zach to dine at his club. There were men there who might recognize him, men they'd been at school with. And if his cousin got word of Zach's arrival, he'd no doubt stir up trouble.

"And it would be wise," Gil added, knowing Zach of old, "not to antagonize Gerald until the murder charge has been dealt with."

Zach laughed at his friend's minatory expression. "Don't worry," he assured him. "I have no desire to see Gerald or any of the fellows we went to school with. This beef is very good. It's been a long time since I've enjoyed good, plain English fare." Zach addressed himself to his dinner again.

"So did you visit my tailor today?" Gil asked after a while.

"No, I'll go tomorrow. Might order a few things."

"A few?" Gil shot him a surprised glance. "But I thought . . ."

Zach sipped his wine. "Been a while since I had anything new. Nice drop, this burgundy. Very soft."

There was a long pause. He could feel Gil's gaze narrowed on him. "It's that girl, isn't it? The Chance chit."

Zach gave him an innocent look and gestured to his shabby clothing. "Don't you agree I need better clothes? Your manservant certainly does."

Gil didn't rise to the bait. "You went back to Berkeley Square, didn't you?"

"Briefly. Just wanted to check that she was going to be able to keep the dog." At Gil's expression, he added, "I felt responsible. You know I've always been fond of animals."

"And is she?"

"Is she what?"

"Keeping it."

"Yes."

"Good, then you'll have no further reason to go back into an area where, of all of London outside my club, you're most likely to be recognized."

"More of this excellent mashed potato?" Zach passed Gil the dish.

Silence fell as they finished the meal. Gil's manservant removed the dishes and Gil brought out a bottle of port. "So you've changed your mind about going to Wales?"

"Mmm. Decided to leave it to the lawyer," Zach said.

"Decided on a little female dalliance, more like," Gil said dryly. "Though dressed like that—it's a strange way to court a girl. Girls of the *ton* expect a man to be dressed to the nines."

"I'm not courting anyone," Zach said. "Besides, she thinks I'm a gypsy."

Gil's brows rose. "And yet she talks to you?"

"She's not your average young society miss. Besides"—Zach grinned—"I think she likes me." Though she persisted in giving him no encouragement. No overt encouragement at any rate. The way her eyes had lit up today when she saw him was enough encouragement for him.

"What if someone recognizes you?"

Zach shrugged. "Why would they? It's twelve years since I was last in England, and according to my cousin, everyone thinks I'm dead. And even if they didn't, I don't look the same. I was a mere scrubby schoolboy when I left, and was not known to the *ton* at all. Stop fussing—nobody will recognize me."

There was a short pause, then Gil shook his head. "You're incorrigible. The number of times in the past you were ordered to stay away from something, that it was too dangerous, and yet you—"

"What's life without a little risk?"

"There's a difference between calculated risks and courting death."

Zach forced a laugh. "Really, Gil, perhaps it's time you did some courting of your own. First you assume—despite my appearance—that I'm courting a young lady of the *ton*, and now you have me courting death. Which is patently ridiculous. A walk with a pretty girl, that's all it was—nothing serious."

The following morning Zach found himself propping up a plane tree in Berkeley Square, waiting for the sight of Miss Jane Chance and her atrocious dog. He wasn't quite sure how he'd arrived there: One moment he was strolling along, heading toward Gil's tailor in Old Bond Street, and the next thing he realized he was here, in Berkeley Square.

He hadn't intended to come. Last night, in the dead of the night, he'd resolved to stay away from Miss Jane Chance of the fathomless blue eyes.

He'd thought about Gil's concerns and decided he was right. It was an impossible fit—she was a being of sunshine and laughter, while Zach was a creature of the shadows.

Perhaps, if he hadn't fled his home with Cecily when he was sixteen, if he hadn't wandered the world since then, and if he hadn't found a vocation as a spy . . .

A dirty business, spying. Nothing clean or honorable about it, though the cause was just enough. Or had been while England was at war . . .

Still, he had all day to visit the tailor. It wasn't as if he had anything else to do, and it was, after all, just another walk in the park.

Physically she delighted him, the smooth silk of her complexion, her quick, bright smile—not the practiced one she used to hide behind, the genuine, spontaneous, unexpected one that was full of warmth and . . . an invitation to delight.

It reeled him in, the lure of that smile.

The morning was cool with a brisk breeze, but the sky was clear and weak sunshine warmed the cold earth, as well as Zach. Green clusters of bulbs not yet in bloom sought its pallid warmth. An English spring.

He looked up and grinned. Here she came, being towed along at the end of a chain by a loudly panting, straining, four-legged cannonball. She was laughing and reprimanding the dog in the one breath, and when the creature finally stopped at his feet and she looked up and saw who it was, the look in her eyes . . .

Warmth. And welcome.

It caused an unfamiliar tightness in his chest.

"Good morning, Miss Chance, I see you were dragged helter-skelter across the square by this disreputable fellow." He bent to give the dog a vigorous rub. "Is that any way to treat a lady, sir—is it?" RosePetal grinned and writhed happily, agreeing it was indeed.

Zach straightened. "Shall we stroll around the square for a bit? It's a little chilly standing still in this breeze."

And without thinking, he offered his arm.

She hesitated, and he withdrew the offending limb at once. Fool! He'd forgotten for a moment who he was supposed to be. She was a respectable young lady. It wasn't proper for her to take his arm.

But she surprised him by stepping onto the path with a look that indicated she might not take his arm, but she would walk with him. Zach was impressed. Not many ladies of his acquaintance—in fact, none he could think of—would walk in public with a disreputable-looking fellow such as himself. Especially not in such a fashionable district, with half the *ton* to witness it. She had unexpected character, this girl.

They strolled along the path, Zach matching his longer stride to her smaller one, her footman and maid following. Today she wore a pair of tiny blue earrings that bobbed and swung as she moved, blue as her eyes, blue as a Greek summer sky. They were half hidden by curly wisps of hair. He longed to smooth back those gossamer curls, to trace the delicate whorls of her small, elegant ears.

Ye gods, fascinated by a woman's ears?

Yet he was, undeniably, though her ears were the least of it.

Why did she fascinate him so, to draw him back here, day after day, to walk chastely under the eye of her maid and footman in the sight of half of fashionable London? He ought to be on his way to Wales to fetch Cecily, so he could sort out the murder nonsense and head back to Europe.

He could feel the footman's glare boring into his back. A good fellow, William. Protective.

She needed protecting, associating so easily with a shady fellow such as himself.

"So are you really a gypsy, Mr. Black?" she asked after they'd walked for a minute or two. There was no hint in her voice of the contempt respectable people usually reserved for gypsies, just warmth and sincere interest. And a hint of doubt. He'd let his act slip more than once with this girl.

Zach shrugged. "I'm a member of the tribe. I travel with them from time to time." It wasn't a lie.

She glanced at his ear. "I see you've taken out your earring. I know another man who wears an earring. His friends say he's a pirate. He isn't, of course, they're just joking. He used to be a seaman."

"I was a pirate once," Zach said without thinking. She gave him a doubtful look and he hastened to assure her, "Only we were called privateers. It was during the war and we captured an enemy ship and rescued some English hostages."

She still looked at him dubiously so he added, "I gave up the sea after that." He glanced around cautiously, leaned closer and said in a low voice, as if imparting a deadly secret, "I get seasick."

She laughed. "So did Admiral Nelson, I believe. It didn't stop him."

"Admiral Nelson was a pirate? I'm shocked! Appalled! And all this time I've thought him one of England's heroes."

She laughed again. "He *was* a hero. And of course I didn't mean he was a pirate, I meant seasickness didn't stop him living a seagoing life."

"Well, it's not for me. *Terra firma* for me, every time." That laugh of hers, so warm and spontaneous. He vowed silently to make her laugh as often as he could, saving up the sound to take back with him when he left England again and returned to the shadows.

She cocked her head curiously. "Were you truly a pirate?"

"Privateer. Which means it's legal. And patriotic."

They strolled on under the still bare trees. Spring was coming late to England. "Where do you come from, Mr. Black?"

"Here and there. Nowhere in particular. I'm on the move most of the time."

She gave him a quick sideways glance. "So where were you, say, a month ago?"

"A month? Hungary."

Her brows went up. "Hungary? Really. How exciting. What's it like in Hungary?"

So he told her a few stories about Hungary, and she wanted more—she seemed eager for details, and it didn't seem mere politeness, so he found himself telling her about some other places he'd lived in the last twelve years—Vienna, Paris, Rome, Saint Petersburg, Copenhagen.

"It all sounds so exotic and fascinating," she said. "I've never been anywhere interesting."

"Nowhere?" he queried, thinking about her supposed Venetian background.

"Only Cheltenham and London. And I almost went to Hereford once."

Zach was intrigued. "Almost? What happened?"

She shook her head, as if banishing an unpleasant memory. "It doesn't matter," she said in a false, bright tone. "Tell me about Saint Petersburg. I've heard a little about it—they call it the Venice of the North, don't they?"

"Yes, though when I was there first, it was winter and the city was a frozen wonderland."

"It sounds beautiful. What's Russia like?"

He groped for words to explain. "It is . . . complex. I have only been to Saint Petersburg, and that is gloriously beautiful, and primitive, and sophisticated. And cruel. Tens of thousands of peasants died in the building of the city. They were conscripted—had no choice. They were owned, body and soul."

"You found it disturbing." Her eyes were wide and somber.

He nodded. "Though all that was last century." Lord, this was no way to entertain a young lady. He brightened his tone. "So to answer your question, Miss Chance, Saint Petersburg is like a cluster of exquisite, metallic, golden orchids growing on an ancient oak whose roots are buried deep in primeval mud." And fed on blood.

"You've been there more than once, then?"

He nodded.

"Why did you go there?"

He glanced at her, so wide-eyed and earnest, and decided to tell her the truth, though in a manner he knew she wouldn't believe. He glanced around with exaggerated caution, and whispered, "I was a spy."

As predicted, she laughed, taking it as a joke. Her laugh was like the burbling of a mountain stream, clear and joyous.

"The second time I went to Russia, I fell in with a bunch of Cossacks—have you heard of Cossacks?"

She shook her head, so he proceeded to entertain her with a tale of wild Cossacks at the Russian court.

At the end, she said, "So you travel all the time?"

"I have for the last twelve years." Suddenly it seemed a long time.

"And you don't have a home?"

"No." That wasn't quite true anymore, he thought. He owned his father's house now. Though it had never been any kind of home for him. Or for Cecily.

"That's sad."

"Why?"

"Everyone needs a home."

"Home is wherever I lay my head," he said lightly.

She gave him a thoughtful look. They walked on. "I couldn't live like that," she said eventually. "Having a home is very important to me. One day I'm going to have a home of my very own."

He glanced across at the tall white house on the other side of the square. "Isn't that your home?"

"N—well, yes, of course it is. In a way."

He gave her a quizzical look, and she added, "We live there by the kindness and generosity of Lady Beatrice."

He didn't like the sound of that. "And in return, she requires certain things of you?"

"Oh, no, not at all—well, in a way, but only—oh, it's hard to explain, but truly, there is no need to look so concerned. She is the kindest, most generous soul, and I love her dearly." Seeming to think he needed more convincing—which he did—she added, "She's sponsoring my entrance into society. She was prepared to do it for my sisters too, only—"

"You have sisters?"

"Yes, but two of them are married now, and the third, well, Daisy has other plans."

"Any brothers?" he asked, thinking of that knee-to-the-groin trick she'd demonstrated in the alley.

"No brothers, just my two brothers-in-law."

"Miss Jane, it's time to go," the large footman growled from behind. And Miss Jane obediently gave Zach a sunny good-bye and hurried away across the square, her dog pulling against the lead and glancing back in a martyred fashion at Zach. He wanted to stay with Zach.

Foolish animal not to appreciate a home with a warm, affectionate woman; there'd be no future with a man like Zach.

Chapter Twelve

She was of course only too good for him; but as nobody minds having what is too good for them, he was very steadily earnest in the pursuit of the blessing...

—JANE AUSTEN, *MANSFIELD PARK*

Over the next week, Jane bumped into Zachary Black in the park almost every day. It wasn't in any way planned— not on her part, at least. She took Caesar for a walk every morning, but never at quite the same time—there were other things to be fitted into her days; life was getting busier as the start of the season drew closer.

The Duchess of Rothermere's ball was said to be the event that would launch it this year. Jane could hardly wait. Her very first ball, and the dress Daisy had made for it was a secret—Daisy even made Jane wear a blindfold for her fittings. It was all quite thrilling—and of course, she trusted Daisy implicitly.

But almost every day, no matter what time Jane took Caesar out, Zachary Black somehow managed to turn up. Sometimes he had a small gift for her. No, not for her, for the dog, he would point out each time with a virtuous air—for William's sake—and a faint, wicked smile for her. It had become a small private joke between them.

One day it was a small metal disk with a hole drilled in it. "In case this rascal wanders off, so people will know he's a dog of distinction, and not a mere mongrel stray," he said when he gave it to her.

Caesar was elegantly engraved on one side, surrounded by an engraved wreath of olive leaves. That made Jane laugh. Her address appeared in plainer script on the other side.

It was quite delightful, meeting up with him so often—it was fast becoming the highlight of her day—but it also worried Jane a little. Oh, not that anything could come of it—they came from such different worlds, it was not possible.

Society was organized into strata for a reason; she'd been taught that all her life, in the schoolroom at the Pill and by experience. Mama and Papa had been cut off because they'd eloped—not just disowned by their parents, but cut off from the rest of their society as well. And without money, Papa could not live as a gentleman.

She knew from Abby that Papa had tried and tried and tried to find work. He even bought special clothes so he would look the part. But the minute he opened his mouth, everyone knew he was a gentleman and treated him accordingly; he either didn't get the job or was sacked or for one reason or another found to be unsuitable.

Most people simply didn't feel comfortable ordering around someone they felt instinctively was their social superior. And those who did enjoy it were bullies who tried to make poor gentle Papa pay for every slight they'd ever received. Hence Papa's final act of desperation.

And because they were so poor and friendless and didn't belong anywhere, Abby and she had been in dire straits when their parents had died. If it hadn't been for the Pill . . .

They'd learned their lesson there too. The Pill was full of girls whose mothers were gently born but who had come down in the world for one reason or another.

Jane and Abby had been given a miraculous chance to return to the society that their parents had entered by birthright—and lost. Yes, Jane was very aware of the importance of behaving according to one's station in life.

She knew she should not be walking out daily with a gypsy—even if he was more respectably dressed these days, and that she was always accompanied by her maid and William—at Featherby's insistence.

Featherby, who was the kind of butler who seemed to know everything, didn't approve. Jane was certain that if Lady Beatrice knew, she would speedily put a stop to it.

Even Daisy didn't approve.

Nobody else knew about her daily meetings with Zachary Black, not even Abby, and if she did, she wouldn't approve either, Jane knew.

So why did she continue to meet him?

And more to the point, why did he keep coming back? He knew as well as she did that there could be no future in it for either of them. Did he have nothing else to do with his time?

"Not at the moment," he said when she asked him one day. "I'm at something of a loose end."

"But don't you have work to do?" she'd asked him on another occasion.

"Not at present," he said, apparently quite, unconcerned, though his eyes gleamed as if he were amused at her anxiety on his behalf. But then he'd changed the subject and, as they strolled along, in the fascination of walking and talking with Zachary Black, Jane quite forgot to wonder or to worry.

Afterward, particularly at night, when she was lying wakeful and unable to sleep, she did quite a lot of wondering about Zachary Black. And not a little worrying.

Who was he? So many things didn't add up. He was full of entertaining tales, and she could listen to that deep voice forever, but several times when they'd just been walking in silence—and not awkward silences as she sometimes felt with Lord Cambury—she'd glanced at Zachary Black and seen an expression in his eyes as he'd gazed off into nothingness . . .

It was an expression that caught at her heartstrings. He seemed so alone, so lonely.

And then, just when she'd felt she had to reach out and touch him, to reassure him that he wasn't alone, he'd turn his head, and that shuttered, desolate look would disappear and he'd say something amusing, or tell some lively and entertaining story and she'd be left wondering if she'd imagined the bleakness in him.

It spoke to her, that bleakness. In the night when she lay sleepless, trying to put all thoughts of a tall gypsy out of her mind, she couldn't shake the thought that despite his so-called gypsy tribe, he was a man who walked very much alone.

Alone—and disturbingly beautiful. She'd never before thought of a man as beautiful. Handsome, yes, rugged, certainly—even pretty. She'd met several pretty young men before, but they'd never struck her as particularly masculine.

Zachary Black's was a beauty that was purely, utterly masculine. And it kept her awake and restless and shivering long into the night. And not from the cold.

L ord Cambury too called on Jane every day, and the more Jane saw of him, the more she thought she could be comfortable with him.

He made morning calls every afternoon, making polite conversation on a variety of unexceptional topics, and staying the correct twenty minutes before taking his leave.

His visits caused some exchange of glances between their other lady visitors, but nothing was said aloud, and until the negotiations over the settlements were concluded, no announcement would be made.

Several times he escorted Jane on a slow promenade in Hyde Park at the fashionable hour, bowing to various acquaintances and stopping to chat every few minutes. His acquaintances were all rather older than him, and quite a bit older than Jane, but they were all very kind and flattering. And being with Lord Cambury, she noticed, discouraged the starers and the oglers, which she appreciated.

He attended the literary society both times during that first week and only fell asleep once, but not when it was Jane's turn to read. When she read, he sat up straight, smiled benevolently at her and listened with feigned fascination. She knew it was feigned, as his conversation afterward revealed that he hadn't taken in a thing about the story.

His fascination, it turned out, was from the picture she made, with the afternoon light slanting across her just so. After they were married, he told her, he would have her portrait painted in just that pose.

He was at all times kind, courteous and considerate of her comfort. And while his company wasn't particularly exciting, he did make her feel safe and comfortable, which was very pleasant. And if she found his conversation a trifle dull at times, well, that was quite her own fault—she needed to learn more about the things he was interested in, that was all.

Besides, it would be different when they were married. She would be busy with the household and . . . and things. And he would stop referring to her looks so frequently. That was the thing she found least comfortable. But it would pass, she was sure, once he was more used to her.

"Cor, 'e does go on, don't 'e?" Daisy commented once after Lord Cambury had joined them for part of their promenade and treated them to a lecture about various artworks he owned, and how Jane resembled and complemented them.

"He means well," Jane said. Daisy didn't get out very often these days, and she valued her walks in the park and resented anyone disrupting them. And Lord Cambury tended to behave as if Daisy didn't exist.

"It was all that talk of you bein' 'is beautiful ornament that got me," Daisy said. "You want to watch out, Jane—after you're married, 'e'll probably stick you on a shelf or in a glass case or something."

Jane laughed. "Well, if he does, Daisy darling, I'll rely on you to pop in regularly to keep me dusted."

"Me?" Daisy snorted with mock indignation. "I got enough to do. Dust yourself, you lazy cow!"

They both laughed, but then Jane said, "You do like him, don't you, Daisy?"

Daisy shrugged. "I wouldn't say 'like,' but I don't mind 'im. He seems an easygoin'-enough gent. He just talks a lot about stuff I couldn't care less about, that's all. But I'll not fault you for snappin' 'im up." She grinned. "Once you're a fine, rich lady, I'll be able to make you lots of lovely expensive clothes, won't I?"

Jane laughed. "And if I were poor?"

"Oh, I'd still make you lots of lovely clothes, but me profits would be terrible!"

It was just after noon on a crisp, clear, perfect spring day, and despite her lateness, Zachary Black was waiting for her in the square, standing tall and still beside one of the budding plane trees. Jane's heart jumped a little when she saw him and a little fizz of anticipation ran down her spine.

Caesar jumped a lot and, as usual, insisted on dragging her toward him, eagerly huffing and puffing, practically choking himself against the restraint of the red collar and chain.

"Mr. Black," she said, trying not to show how truly pleased she was to see him. The previous day when she'd walked Caesar around the square, she'd looked and looked for a tall, raffish figure, and the disappointment she'd felt when she realized he wasn't there had quite shocked her.

"I had business to attend to yesterday," he said, as if she'd asked him to explain his absence—and indeed she had wondered, but only in her mind. Jane wasn't sure how to respond. She ought not to encourage him, she knew, but . . .

"And how is this rascal?" he asked, squatting down to give the dog a hearty rub.

"He killed another rat in the back lane, so Cook is now devoted to him." She added, "He keeps trying to chase off the butcher's boy, though, which isn't quite such a popular move."

He laughed. "And the cats?"

"Still wary, but they seem to have come to terms with him. He actually seems to like them—not just tolerate, but like. It's not very dogly behavior, but I'm very grateful for it."

"Shall we walk?" he said.

They strolled, several feet apart. A pastry seller, pushing a brightly painted cart and ringing a bell, passed them on the road beside the park. "Those gypsy wagons you mentioned the other day," she said. "They look very pretty and colorful, but they must be very small—for a family, I mean." And for a man of his height. "Do your people really live in them, winter and all?"

"Winter and all," he told her.

She frowned. "But isn't it terribly cold?"

He gave her a slow smile. "We snuggle up."

"Oh." She felt her face heating. "Yes, I suppose so."

"What about your house?" he asked. "Not that one"—he gestured toward Lady Beatrice's house—"your dream house, the one you plan to live in one day. What would that be like?"

"I want a home, not just a house."

He slanted her a surprised glance. "What's the difference?"

"A house is a building, a home is where a family lives, a place that's warm, comfortable and—" She stopped, feeling that what she'd been about to say would sound foolish. And embarrassing.

"And?" he prompted.

"Where children can play and grow up."

"That's not what you were going to say."

"No." They walked on and turned the corner, then slowed to watch a little boy rolling a hoop to his smaller sister. She kept dropping it and knocking it over, but the small boy never once lost patience. He showed her how to do it, over and over.

"All children should be like that," she said quietly.

"Patient?"

"No, happy. Carefree." She felt him looking at her. "And safe. The difference between a house and a home," she added softly, her eyes on the two little children, "is love."

They moved on. Zach found himself unexpectedly touched, by her words and by the way she'd watched the little boy and his sister. There was a depth of yearning there that surprised him. He'd imagined she was the type who'd grown up having everything she wanted provided for her, with no effort.

Then again, he'd grown up with all the material things any child could want, but by her definition he'd never actually lived in a home. Not even when he was the size of that small boy. He'd never felt safe, never felt loved—not when his father was at home.

Or had he? Certainly his father had been a brute, and unpredictable at the best of times.

Zach had been sent away to school when he was seven, but before that, there must have been people who'd cared for him. Servants, at least, and surely one or two of them had cared for him more than just because they'd been paid to? Had he blocked them from his memory, the way he'd tried to block all thoughts of his childhood home?

He was responsible for those people now. The thought pricked his conscience. He didn't want to be responsible for anyone.

The nurse collected the children and Zach and Jane resumed their walk. He thought about her expression as she watched the children. And he wondered.

"Tell me something," he said, standing back so she could step around to avoid a puddle. "When we first met, you were using your reticle as a cosh."

She tensed, and darted him a cautious sideways glance. Zach pretended not to notice. "Was I?" she said in a careless voice. "I don't remember." And a moment later she added, "What's a cosh anyway?"

Zach hid a smile. For a girl with invented Venetian antecedents, she was a terrible liar. He didn't bother explaining. She knew very well what a cosh was. But her affectation of ignorance increased his curiosity. "You said you usually carried a stack of pennies in a coin purse. Why pennies?"

"Oh, I probably just meant change, loose change. Oh, look, is that a squirrel?"

No, a red herring, Zach thought. "You were quite specific at the time; you said pennies."

She shrugged and looked away.

"Only you said you'd given them all away."

"I did not. I said no such thing."

That touched a nerve, he thought. "No, you're right. You stopped halfway through the sentence, as if it were a guilty secret."

"What nonsense."

They strolled on a little way. "Whom do you give pennies to?" he asked quietly. He thought he knew, but he didn't understand why she would hide such a thing. And why specifically pennies?

She stopped and turned toward him. "I don't know what you're talking about. Besides, it's not your business how I spend my money." She took a deep breath and said firmly, "Caesar is healing well, don't you think? That ointment you gave me seems very efficacious."

"Why pennies, I wonder. Why not halfpennies, or farthings, or threepences or sixpences or even shillings? You said pennies."

She made an impatient gesture. "I told you I don't remember. And a gentleman would not persist with a topic of conversation a lady has indicated quite clearly she has no interest in."

Her expression made him smile. "Ah, but then I'm not a gentleman—I'm a gypsy, remember? And the first time I saw you, you were surrounded by street children."

"Oh?" she said in an attempt at vagueness that didn't deceive him in the least.

"Yes, and after a few moments they'd melted away. You gave them pennies, didn't you? That's why your purse was almost empty when you tried to use it later as a cosh. I'm not at all critical of the act, but I'm curious as to why you collect and give pennies, instead of sixpences or some other coin that would make more of a difference to their lives."

She hesitated, and then said a little crossly, "Well if you must know, it's because if I gave them sixpences or anything bigger than a penny, it would be taken from them by some bigger person, that's why. A copper coin is not worth fighting over, but with a penny you can buy a loaf of bread, or a half loaf and some cheese, or"—she made a vague gesture—"that kind of thing. With a penny they won't go hungry. It's not much, but it's something. And that is all I wish to say on the matter."

"Very well, I won't press you further," he said, intrigued and not a little impressed by her reasoning. Young ladies of the *ton* didn't generally have any idea of the realities of life in the street. Most simply thought of street children as nuisances to be avoided. But Miss Jane Chance had clearly given their situation a lot of thought. And responded in a surprisingly practical way.

They moved on, and as they walked back in the direction of her aunt's house, a large, well-upholstered woman in a buttoned-up purple pelisse came toward them. In front of her, attached to white leather leads, scampered two white balls of fluff.

Seeing them, the woman halted in mid-path. She looked at Jane in seeming outrage. The balls of fluff yapped and growled hysterically, apparently just as outraged to see RosePetal in their park as the woman was to see Jane in hers.

"Lady Embury." Jane smiled warmly at the woman. "How lovely to see you. Don't mind Caesar, he won't hurt a fly."

Caesar barked a couple of times at the yapping balls of fluff, fooling nobody, as his tail hadn't stopped wagging. He was, Zach had to admit, a fearsome sight, however—even in welcome.

The woman completely ignored Jane's greeting. Her gaze swept Zach from head to toe, eyeing him with magnificent disdain. He instantly swept off his hat and gave her a raffish bow.

She stiffened, glared at Jane and then passed them with her head turned pointedly away. She marched away, dragging the fluff balls with her.

Jane looked after her in surprise. And perturbation.

"Who was that old tartar?" Zach asked.

"A neighbor. A friend of my aunt's. She's the aunt of—" She broke off.

"Whose aunt?"

Jane just shook her head. She'd gone pale. The incident had obviously upset her. "She attends my aunt's literary society sometimes. I—I cannot think why she would give me the cut direct. I—I have to go home now." She hurried across the square toward her aunt's house.

Zach followed. "It was me, wasn't it? The blasted harridan cut you because of me." Damn. He knew it wouldn't be precisely approved of for Jane to be seen walking with an unprepossessing fellow such as himself, but that a friend of her aunt's would give her the cut direct, in a public square . . . The sight of Jane's ill-concealed distress infuriated him.

"You're not going to let that woman upset you, are you?"

She didn't respond.

"You were hardly behaving improperly. Granted I'm not the most ideal companion for a walk, but we were in the full public eye, for heaven's sake, hardly the illicit meeting her attitude implied. *And* you were accompanied by your maid and footman." He gestured to William and Polly walking stolidly behind them.

Jane took no notice. "I'm sorry, Mr. Black. I must go now." She was about to cross the road when she stopped suddenly, turned and faced him. Her face was pale, the set of her jaw resolute. "And I'm very sorry, but I must ask you not to return. I cannot meet you again. Too much is at stake." Her eyes were apologetic, but her words were clear. "Good-bye, Mr. Black."

Chapter Thirteen

Angry people are not always wise.

—JANE AUSTEN, *PRIDE AND PREJUDICE*

Jane hurried home, feeling slightly sick. Lady Embury wasn't a close friend of Lady Beatrice's, but she came quite regularly to the literary society and had always been pleasant enough. And since the betrothal, she'd become quite warm toward Jane.

But now Lady Embury had given her the cut direct. In public.

It could only be because she'd been seen with Zachary Black.

But what was wrong with that? It was a public square, she'd only ever walked and talked with him and she'd been accompanied by her maid and footman.

It wasn't as if she'd encouraged him.

Well, perhaps she had. A little. But what was wrong with walking and talking? And being friendly?

Zachary Black was a fascinating man, and he seemed interested in what she had to say too. And if she thought of him rather too often for her own peace of mind, well, one couldn't be blamed for that, surely? One couldn't help one's thoughts.

Her thoughts were private, secret, her own little . . . fantasy.

One's actions were what counted, she reminded herself, and

she had done nothing underhanded or illicit. Certainly she'd done nothing to jeopardize her betrothal.

She had a cup of tea, which did a little to settle the hollow feeling in the pit of her stomach, then went upstairs to join Daisy. Sewing seams was always quite soothing. There was nothing to worry about. She'd overreacted. Lady Embury probably hadn't meant any such thing; she was just distracted.

Two hours later, Featherby came to the door. "Lord Cambury is downstairs, Miss Jane, asking to speak with you."

The sick, hollow feeling returned to her stomach. She tidied her hair, striving for composure. She had done nothing wrong.

Lord Cambury came straight to the point. "Aunt tells me you've been associating with some low fellow in the square opposite. Won't do, y'know. Can't have my betrothed associating in public with shabby fellows. Bad *ton*."

Seeing Lord Cambury's grim expression now, as he waited for her explanation, she wondered whether he might be jealous. He'd never indicated a hint of any warm feelings toward her, but it was possible, she supposed.

The trouble was, she didn't know him very well. Hardly at all, to be truthful.

"I have talked to a man in the park several times, but I assure you, Lord Cambury, there has been no impropriety."

He snorted. "My aunt saw you with her own eyes, talking and laughing with the fellow. So what have you got to say to that, eh, missie?"

Jane stiffened. She'd intended to apologize, but the thought that his aunt was spying on her and telling tales was infuriating. "I don't see what business it is of Lady Embury's who I walk with in a public square opposite my home. Especially since I am accompanied at all times by my maid and footman."

He frowned. "My aunt is my family. And what my betrothed gets up to while I'm not there is my business."

"*Gets up to?*" Jane flashed. "I don't '*get up to*' anything!"

"Seen walking out with a dashed shabby fellow. More'n once too—practically every morning this week."

Jane forced herself to sound calm and reasonable. "I'm not 'walking out,' as you put it, with anyone. It's true that I've met him on several occasions but none of them were by prearrangement.

His behavior each time has been perfectly polite, and mine above reproach." She was shaking; she wasn't sure quite why. Was it nerves? Or indignation? Or guilt?

He poked his head forward. "You saying he's not shabby?"

"I just told you that he has behaved like a gentleman every time."

"Gentleman?" He made a contemptuous sound. "What's his name?"

"We haven't been introduced." It wasn't a lie.

"Aunt said she saw him offer you his arm."

"He did, but—"

He broke in, appalled. "You *touched* him? You might have caught fleas. Or worse!"

"Don't be ridiculous," she snapped, seriously annoyed now. "As I was about to say, I did not take his arm—which I'm sure your aunt saw—but only because we hadn't been introduced. He is as clean as you or I."

Lord Cambury snorted again. "I doubt that. Shabby, my aunt said. Outmoded old coat, unshaven. Needs a haircut."

Jane frowned. "Yes, his clothing is rather well worn, though what's that got to—"

"See? Shabby." Satisfied that he'd made his point, he sat back in his chair.

"I don't see what an outmoded coat has to do with anything."

He sat up, clearly shocked. "It's everything, dash it. Consider my reputation."

"*Your* reputation?"

He gave her an incredulous look. "Good God, gel, the Prince Regent himself consults me on matters of taste and beauty. No point in becoming betrothed to the most beautiful gel in the *ton* if she's seen in public with some shabby good-for-nothing, now is there? The company you keep reflects on *me*."

Jane could hardly believe her ears. He wasn't objecting so much to her meeting another man—it was Zachary Black's *clothing* that was the offense, and its effect on his own reputation. Presumably an exquisitely dressed villain would be preferable.

"I forbid you to see any more of this rogue."

"I will try, but I cannot promise—"

"Cannot? Cannot? Will not, more like!" His eyes bulged

with outrage. "Obstinate chit. I was about to send the notice of our betrothal to the *Morning Post*, but I can always change my mind, you know. Nothing has been made public yet."

"Ch-change your mind?" Jane faltered, shocked by her own recklessness in challenging him. She hadn't had the dream once since she'd accepted Lord Cambury's proposal. She couldn't lose it all now, not for the sake of a few hours of pleasant conversation with a man who might fascinate her to a frightening degree, but who could never offer her anything more. "No—please, you do not understand. I have never encouraged this man to meet me, never made any arrangement. For myself, I am happy to promise, but whether he will take any notice . . ."

Lord Cambury leaned forward. "Hah! The fellow bothering you? I'll have the rogue dealt with if he is."

"Dealt with? What do you mean?"

"Could give him a good thrashing, teach him a lesson."

"You?" She couldn't imagine it. Short and tubby Lord Cambury would never get the better of a powerfully built man like Zachary Black.

"Of course not me! I would not so demean myself. Send men to do it, of course."

"I beg you will not," she said, horrified.

"*Beg?*" He frowned. "What is this fellow to you that you would *beg?*"

"Nothing," she lied. "But he once performed a, a signal service for me, and in common decency you cannot have him beaten."

"What kind of signal service?"

"He rescued my dog from a gang of thugs who were torturing him and all set to kill him."

He sniffed. "That ugly creature? Better to have let it die."

Jane's jaw dropped. "I thought you liked dogs."

"I do—properly bred 'uns, not ugly, ill-bred mongrels. Was meaning to speak to you about it, matter of fact. Planned to get you a proper dog once we're married. *If* we marry." He gave her a long, brooding look which indicated he was by no means certain that they were going to be married.

The sick, hollow feeling grew in Jane's stomach. She forced herself to concentrate on the matter in hand. "He—the gentleman in the park—also rescued me from the unwelcome attentions of those same street thugs."

"Did he? Hmph."

"Yes, they were very rough and nasty and I, I feared for my life. But he drove them off and saved me. Which is why I am polite to him when we happen to meet in the park." She scanned his face, but had no idea what he was thinking. "So yes, I do beg you not to send men to beat him up. It would not be honorable, or just." She added desperately, "And I know you to be an honorable gentleman."

He gave her a long, brooding look. "I protect what's mine, missie."

Jane nodded. "Yes, of course, and . . . and I appreciate it." She was shaking.

He rose and picked up his gloves, ready to take his leave.

She rose. "Lord Cambury?"

"Yes?"

"The betrothal . . ."

He gave her a long look, then gave a gruff nod. "I'll send the notice today."

Relief swamped Jane, so much so that she had to sit down again.

He pulled on his gloves. "Expect beautiful women to be difficult. Part of their charm, I'm told. But you're skating on thin ice, missie, very thin ice. I have a title and a reputation and I will do whatever it takes to protect them—understand?"

She nodded.

"Will you attend the Duchess of Rothermere's ball for the launch of the season?"

She stared at him in surprise at the abrupt change of topic. "Yes, of course, but—"

"See you there, then. Reserve me two dances, yes? Supper dance and a waltz." His gaze sharpened and he tapped her arm with two fingers. "*Tsk, tsk.* No frowning, now. Don't want wrinkles."

He departed, leaving Jane sitting limply, shaken but relieved. She'd almost thrown away her chance of a future—a home, and a handsome settlement for herself and her children. All because of her fancy—her stupid, irresponsible fancy!—for a handsome gypsy.

* * *

"What the devil is the matter with you?" Gil demanded later that evening. "You've been glowering into your glass all evening."

"Nothing." Zach merely wanted to strangle something or someone. Preferably a puce-faced old bitch with two yapping puff balls. That blasted harpy had upset Jane for no good reason.

No good reason that he could see.

I cannot meet you again. Too much is at stake.

What the devil did that mean? What was *at stake*?

"Not bad news from the lawyer, is it?" Gil persisted.

"No. Tell me, Gil, what's wrong with a fellow taking a walk in a public park with a girl?"

Gil frowned. "What girl? You mean the Chance girl?"

"Doesn't matter who. Is it scandalous in London these days for a girl to walk with a man—not touching—two feet apart—in a public park, with a maid and footman in tow?"

"No, of course it's not."

"Hah!" Zach punched his fist into his hand. "I knew it! So why would that harridan give her the cut direct?"

"What harridan?"

"Lady . . . Lady somebody." He snorted. "Harpy, more like. Lady Elbury, Endbury—no, Embury, that was it—Lady Embury."

"Lady Embury? Oh, then that is interesting."

Zach sat up. "You know something. What?"

"Well, it's just a whisper . . ."

"Dammit, Gil, this is no time for blasted discretion."

"Well, I've heard a whisper that Lord Cambury has been—"

"Not Cambury—*Em*bury," Zach said impatiently.

"Lady Embury is Lord Cambury's aunt," Gil said calmly. "Now do you want to hear what I have to say or not?"

Zach scowled and flung himself back in his chair. "Go on."

Gil regarded him a moment and then grinned. "This girl has really got you wound up, hasn't she? I don't think I've ever seen you this way over a woman."

Zach said tightly, "She was given the cut direct by Lady whatsit, simply for walking in the park with me. It's a matter of righting a wrong."

"Oh, the white knight again, is it?" Gil grinned, and when

Zach muttered something rude, he laughed. "Well, the whisper is that after years of searching the *ton* for an incomparable, Lord Cambury has finally found his ideal."

Zach gave him a blank look. "So?"

"Lord Cambury is a collector of beautiful things. I'm told he requires exceptional beauty in a wife as well."

"What does that have to do—oh, my God—you don't mean—"

Gil nodded. "Word is, he's made an offer for the Chance girl and been accepted."

There was a short, stunned silence. Zach looked down at his hands, and carefully unclenched his fists. "Betrothed?" he said in what he hoped was an even tone. "I don't believe it."

Gil raised his brows. "It's hardly surprising—she's young, a diamond of the first water and her invented family background suggests she's angling for a rich husband. She's quite clearly on the marriage mart."

Zach was unable to think of a suitable response. His fists had clenched again. It seemed so, so damned *reasonable* the way Gil put it, but he refused to believe it could be so. "No. If she were betrothed, she would have told me."

Gil's brows climbed a little higher. "Confide in you? Concerning a betrothal that is not yet official? To one of the richest barons in the kingdom?" His eyes danced, but he continued in an amazed tone, "Well, I'm shocked. I cannot imagine why she would not immediately inform you—and any other chance-met gypsy strangers she met down a dark alley or in a park. Most extraordinarily secretive behavior on her part."

There was another short silence. Zach glowered at his friend. "You're enjoying this, aren't you?"

"Immensely."

"Swine."

"Another cognac?" Gil refilled both their glasses.

Zach picked up the glass and swirled the cognac moodily, staring into its golden depths as it caught the firelight. "What's he like then, this Cambury fellow?"

"One of the Regent's set, with all that you'd expect—wealth, property, the best of good *ton*—"

"Yes, yes, but what's he *like*?"

"Really?"

"Yes. Charming? Good-looking?"

"Short, balding and running to fat."

"Ah." Zach liked the sound of that. "What else? Does he keep a string of mistresses? Does he beat them? Drink like a fish? Gamble to excess? Come on, Gil, you know what I'm asking— what are the fellow's dirty little secrets? What does your famous nose tell you?"

Gil screwed up the famous nose and rubbed his chin thoughtfully. Then he shrugged. "He's dull."

"Dull?"

"As ditch water. Worse than ditch water, which at least produces the odd tadpole and frog. He's boring, tedious, stupefyingly, yawn-makingly dull."

"Dirty linen?" Zach asked hopefully.

Gil shook his head. "No mistresses that I've ever heard of— none of the other either. Member of all the usual clubs, dutiful nephew, regular churchgoer, drinks, but in moderation— everything in moderation actually, apart from the huge sums he spends on his artworks. He's a collector of art and things of beauty—has a passion for it, and goes on and on and on about it, *ad infinitum, ad nauseam*—"

"All right, enough of the Latin. So he overspends?"

Gil shook his head. "So wealthy it can't signify. Sorry, my friend, but the fellow is perfectly inoffensive."

"Inoffensive?" Somehow Cambury's very inoffensiveness was offensive.

Gil nodded. "All things considered, an excellent match for your girl."

"She can't possibly marry him!"

"Why not?"

The question hung in the air for a full minute.

"Because—" Zach glared at his glass and groped for a reason. "Because she can't, that's why."

"Oh, well, in that case . . ." With a faint smile, Gil settled back comfortably in his armchair.

Zach glared at him. "A warmhearted, lively girl like that, you can't yoke her to a fellow who's criminally boring!"

"Better than one who's criminally wanted for murder."

"I keep telling you, that's just a stupid mix-up!" Zach grabbed the poker and stirred the coals in the fire savagely. Sparks flew everywhere.

"Any news from the lawyer's man?" Gil said.

Zach shook his head. "Too soon. Won't be back from Wales yet." He stared into the fire, brooding. "Dammit, Gil, what the devil am I going to do?"

"About Cecily?"

"Not Cecily—that's all quite straightforward. The moment we produce Cecily, the problem's gone. What am I going to do about Miss Chance?"

Gil was silent for a moment. "Tell her who you are. If you say she's in the market for a rich husband . . ."

"I can't ask her to throw over a sure thing like Cambury while my own affairs are in a mess. Not while I'm—technically, at least—a wanted man." Besides, he didn't want to be just another potential rich husband to her.

Gil grimaced. "I see your point." He gave Zach a thoughtful look, and said, "Do you think Cambury knows the girl's background is a fabrication?"

"I doubt it."

"It'd be one way to scotch the betrothal . . ."

Zach considered the suggestion. It was tempting, very tempting. Cambury sounded exactly like the kind of stuffy fellow who would recoil from any whiff of a shady background in his future bride.

But he couldn't do it. If Cambury was who she really wanted, Zach wouldn't ruin things for her. Much as he'd like to. He couldn't betray her like that. Not even for her own good.

He tossed back the cognac and poured himself another glass. And a thought occurred to him.

"What if Cambury isn't her choice at all?" he said to Gil.

"What do you mean?"

"What if that woman she lives with—Lady Whosit—"

"Lady Beatrice."

"Yes, her so-called guardian. What if the old lady—or the sister—is forcing her to accept the fellow because of his wealth? That makes more sense to me."

It was obvious, now he came to look at it. She was the youngest of the sisters. Their aim in coming to London was to hook themselves rich husbands. Two of the sisters had already done so—Davenham and Monkton-Coombes must have been easily gulled. And now the older sisters were forcing Jane to marry a frightful bore for the sake of his money, damn their eyes.

Gil considered it, then shook his head. "Don't see it myself. Doesn't sound like the old lady at all."

Zach didn't argue. It all made sense to him now. She was being pressured into it.

"If you ask me, your best hope is that Cambury bores her into calling it off," Gil said.

"Good thing I won't ask you, then," Zach said dryly.

"Well, what else can you do?" Gil drained his glass and set it aside.

It was the question that occupied Zach's thoughts for the rest of a very sleepless night.

Chapter Fourteen

Oh, what care I for my house and my land?

What care I for my money-oh?

What care I for my new wedded lord?

I'm off with the raggle-taggle gypsy-oh.

—TRADITIONAL FOLK SONG

Jane woke before dawn, sweating and shivering, despite the chill draft coming from the window that was open, just a crack.

The dream again. She hadn't had it for days, not since she'd accepted Lord Cambury's offer. But this time the dream had suddenly changed, and she found herself struggling to escape a tall, dark gypsy, who seized her and carried her off into the night.

Only she wasn't so much struggling, as clinging to him . . . *You're skating on thin ice, missy.*

She was, she knew it. She didn't understand Lord Cambury at all. What kind of man got more upset by her being seen talking to a man in a shabby, worn-out coat than he had been about her being kidnapped and taken to a brothel?

Whatever, she would learn from her mistake. Obviously appearance mattered to him a great deal—in all things. She must not jeopardize her future for the sake of a few hours' conversation with Zachary Black.

No matter that her heart beat faster at the sight of his tall, lean figure striding lazily toward her. No matter that the minutes she spent talking to him flew by like seconds, and that at night, in her bed, she relived those moments over and over, like a squirrel counting her nuts before winter.

Zachary Black was not any kind of man she could marry. He had no money, no home, no job, and worse—it didn't seem to bother him in the least. And even though she was sure Max would give him a job if she asked, she wasn't at all sure Zachary Black would take it. It was clear from the tales he told that he liked his wandering life.

He was, as Daisy had said, just a passing fancy and she would be a fool to think anything else.

Her future was elsewhere, with Lord Cambury. And she had other things to think about, like the ball tonight, her first ever ball.

Jane took Caesar to the park later that morning. William followed like a large, silent shadow three paces behind her. She had no expectation of seeing Mr. Black. It was Caesar snuffling and dragging at the lead that alerted her.

She stopped dead.

How dare Zachary Black put her in this position again? She had told him in no uncertain terms that she could not—would not—see him again. That it was too much of a risk. Yet there he was, his tall, lithe figure strolling across the park with that self-assured gait that seemed so much a part of him.

She ought to turn around, march back across the street and disappear into Lady Beatrice's house.

But her traitorous feet—not to mention the dog—refused to budge. One more time, a small voice inside her said. One more time.

A cacophony of yipping to her left drew Jane's attention. A large woman in a fur-edged puce pelisse stood glaring across at Jane. Lady Embury. Perfect.

Her wildly excited dogs got all tangled in their leads, but Lady Embury took no notice. Her eyes narrowed, and her large bosom puffed with outrage.

Jane's spine stiffened. She would not be accused—silently or otherwise—by that woman. She would not live her life under Lady Embury's thumb—now or in the future.

She forced herself to bow politely.

She could almost hear the woman's sniff of outrage in response. What was she supposed to do? Apologize for being in a public square? For being approached by a man she had not asked to approach her? She would not.

A firm crunch of gravel behind her told her Mr. Black had arrived. She turned to greet him with cool composure. "Mr. Black, I did not expect to see you again."

He ignored the dog snuffing happily at his boots. "You're betrothed!" It sounded like an accusation.

Her spine stiffened further. She hadn't intended to discuss it, but she supposed if he knew why she'd told him she couldn't see him any longer, it would help. "Yes, but how did you know? It hasn't been formally announced yet."

He dismissed her question with a curt gesture. "They're forcing you, aren't they?"

Her brows drew together. "Who are you talking about? Forcing me to do what?"

"Lady Thingummy—your guardian or aunt or whatever you call her. Owns the house you live in." He indicated it with a jerk of his head. "She's forcing you to marry this fellow, isn't she?"

"No. Lady Beatrice loves me. She would never force me to do anyth—"

"Pressuring you, then—for your own good."

"No, I told you—"

"Your sister then—the one who's married to her nephew."

"No, of course not. Nobody is forcing me—or putting any pressure on me—to marry Lord Cambury. Quite the contrary, in fact."

"Quite the contrary?" He frowned. "You mean they *don't* want you to marry the fellow?"

Belatedly she realized it was quite inappropriate to be standing in the park discussing her betrothal with him. "I don't wish to discuss it."

"You mean you're marrying the fellow of your own free will?"

She didn't answer.

"Why, for God's sake?"

She stepped around him and continued walking, dragging a reluctant Caesar after her.

"Why on earth would you choose to marry such a man?"

He sounded so appalled by the idea that it gave her pause. She stopped and turned toward him. "Is there some reason you know of why I shouldn't?"

There was a short, tense silence, then the words burst from him. "He's all wrong for you."

"I asked for a reason, not an unsolicited opinion. Do you have one?" She waited for him to explain further.

"Nothing that I know of," he said sullenly, "but—"

She marched off, her temper growing. She was fed up with people telling her what she could and couldn't do. What business of his was it whom she chose to marry? How dare he question her choices? It wasn't as if he was planning to offer her any alternative, was he? It wasn't as if he could. And now, to confront her in this, this accusatory manner!

Zachary Black caught up with her in a handful of steps. "You can't marry him."

She was walking as fast as she could without running; he seemed to stroll, damn him. "Why not? He's a respectable gentleman of the *ton*, with a good reputation, a dutiful family man who—"

"My father was a gentleman of the *ton* with a reputation as a dutiful family man, but he was an animal when he drank, and he beat me and his wife—possibly both wives, only my mother died before I knew her—savagely." Zach broke off, shocked. He'd never told anyone that before.

She swung around and stared at him wide-eyed. "Your father beat you? That's dreadful."

Zach said nothing. He hadn't meant to say that.

Then her brow creased in puzzlement. "A gentleman of the *ton*? I thought your father was a gypsy."

"My real father." It wasn't a lie, but he knew how she'd interpret it—that his father had begotten him on a gypsy woman.

"Oh, I see."

"You cannot trust Cambury—trust any so-called gentleman—on reputation alone."

Her brow pleated with worry. "Do you know something ill of him? Have you heard rumors or, or anything?" He didn't answer, so she added, "Mr. Black, are you trying to tell me that Lord Cambury beats women too—is that what you're saying?"

Zach was tempted to lie, and say yes, but with those wide blue eyes gazing anxiously into his, he couldn't lie to her. He sighed. "No, I've heard nothing to his discredit."

Her lips pressed together. Her eyes sparkled with some emotion he couldn't read.

"But he's all wrong for you. He'll bore you to death in a week. You can't marry him, just because he's rich—there are more important things than wealth, you know."

She made no reply; she simply marched away, her head held high. Her cheeks were a little flushed.

Zach followed. "Listen—I have . . . feelings for you, and I suspect you have feelings for me. But I won't pursue an unwilling girl. If you tell me now, and to my face, that you harbor no tender feelings for me, that I am mistaken, I'll leave you alone."

She hesitated, as if she were about to say something, but in the end she kept walking, saying nothing.

The words burst from him unrehearsed and unplanned. "Be clear on this; it's marriage I'm talking about." He hadn't meant to say that either, but once the words were out they felt right.

She stopped dead, and for a moment he thought she was going to ignore him. But she straightened her shoulders and turned toward him. "I'm flattered by your interest, but I cannot encourage you. I am already betrothed. Before I became betrothed, I considered marriage very carefully and rationally; it was not a light or frivolous decision I made to accept Lord Cambury's offer." Her face was set, but her eyes were troubled.

"Carefully and rationally, eh?" He sent her a burning glance. "So love doesn't come into it at all?"

She looked uncomfortable. "For something as serious and binding as marriage, a girl in my position needs to consider a range of factors."

"What sort of factors? You mean money, property, a title—that sort of thing?" His temper was growing. He wanted to grab her, to toss her over his saddle and ride off into the sunset with her.

She didn't deny it. Her flush spoke for her.

He felt his lip curl. "So your sole intent is to snag a rich husband."

"N—y—oh, you make it sound so cold-blooded, and I'm not."

He laughed, a short, hard sound. "Yes you are. Still, you deserve better than a fellow like Cambury." She kept walking and Zach said, following, "You can't let yourself be sold off like this—"

"Oh, grow up!" she snapped.

His jaw dropped. "What?"

"I said, grow up!" she repeated. "Oh, it's all so easy from where you stand, isn't it, Mr. Black? You look at me and see the fine clothes, and you see I'm living in a big house in the best part of town and you imagine it's all so perfect, don't you?"

"I—"

"You can't possibly imagine—can you, Mr. Black?—that I might know what it is to be hungry, what it is to be cold, what it is to have nowhere safe to sleep at night—" She broke off and took a deep, steadying breath.

"I didn't—"

"I have *nothing*, not a penny of my own but the allowance Lady Beatrice gives me—and she has no reason to give it—I am no kin to her. It is nothing but kindness—charity, if you will." Her eyes glittered with unshed tears. Angry unshed tears.

"I have little education, no skills, nothing but my face to recommend me. Lady Beatrice has given me the opportunity to make the kind of marriage that will secure my future—mine and any children I might have—and neither you, nor anyone else, is going to stop me from having it, no matter how much I might—" She broke off, shaking her head. "Oh, please, just go. And don't come back. I do not wish to see you ever again."

"Jane—"

"You don't have permission to use my name!"

He caught her wrist. "You're wrong, you know—quite wrong."

"Let go of me!" She tugged angrily at her arm and he released her.

"You have a great deal more to offer a man than your lovely face and figure," he said urgently.

She stared at him a moment, then shook her head. "Please, just leave me alone. I cannot—"

"Don't sell yourself short."

She stiffened. "*Sell* myself?" She swallowed and said bitterly, "And what if I do? It's none of your business, is it?"

Belatedly he realized how she'd interpreted his words. "I didn't mean it like that—" But it was too late. She'd turned and was marching angrily away.

His hands clenched into two hard fists.

William stepped on the path facing Zach, his posture indicating that if Zach wanted to make an issue of it, he'd be delighted to oblige.

Zach didn't. It would be a relief to throw a punch or two, but *grow up*, she'd said.

Jane returned to Lady Beatrice's house feeling shaken by her outburst but also, strangely, feeling better for it. Served him right, she thought as she took Caesar out the back and refilled his water bowl.

She watched the dog lap up the water. Stupid, insufferable, arrogant man, telling her how she should live her life.

She picked up a brush and started grooming Caesar. "You'd think a gypsy would understand the hard realities of life, wouldn't you?" she told the dog angrily. "But no! Apparently not."

"You and I know better, don't we, Caesar?" She stopped brushing for a moment, staring at nothing, thinking about his words. *You have a great deal more to offer a man than your lovely face and figure.*

Such a nice thing to say, but then he'd followed it with that slap in the face.

"Sell myself?" she said to Caesar. He pricked up his ears.

It was true.

"No, it's not true," she told the dog. "It's a . . . an exchange, a bargain. Lord Cambury and I will each get what we want out of this. It's what marriage involves."

More or less.

"Stupid, stupid man." She wasn't talking about Lord Cambury.

She sighed. "I know—it's just as equally stupid, stupid me. Why do I feel this way? I don't want to, and yet . . ." He tempted her—too much—but they both knew he was an impossible choice.

She'd known falling in love was a reckless and dangerous thing. Jane had been certain she could prevent it happening, certain she could make herself fall in love with whomever she married. Or at least learn to love him. People did it all the time—made sensible marriages with nothing more between them than respect and goodwill. And then, after marriage, they came to love each other. Learned to love each other.

It was a much more sensible and prudent way to build a secure and contented life. And Jane had planned to be just exactly that kind of sensible.

Instead, she was letting herself think—and dream—far too much about someone who was nothing like the kind of man she should marry. Simply because the mere sight of him walking toward her made her whole body tingle, as if champagne were fizzing gently under her skin.

She'd been playing with fire, and if she'd been burned, well . . . it served her right. All he had to do was look at her, and she became ever so slightly breathless. How could it happen, that simply walking and talking with someone in a park could make her feel so . . . alive? When she was with him, listening to his stories, laughing at his mischief, walking beside him as he matched his pace to hers, happiness just seemed to bubble up inside her, like a mountain spring of clear, cool water, endlessly bubbling.

Foolishly bubbling, when all she wanted to do was laugh and twirl and dance and be happy. Because that was how being with him made her feel.

But it was impossible. Utterly, hopelessly impossible.

She *knew* it was an illusion, that life wasn't like that. Fairy-tale happy endings didn't happen to everyone—certainly not Jane. She needed to be sensible . . . And to grow up.

Daisy had been right. *You'll find the most impossible, unsuitable bloke in the* ton *and fall for 'im like a ton o' bricks.*

Only he wasn't even a member of the *ton.* "Hopeless," she muttered.

"Be clear on this; it's marriage I'm talking about."

Caesar gave her a reproachful look. "Don't look at me like that," she told him. "I know you think he's wonderful, but you're just as dizzy-brained and undiscriminating as I am. But don't worry, I will not let us suffer for my lack of judgment."

The dog nudged her hand and she resumed brushing, telling him severely, "I will *not* live in a gypsy wagon, cooking over an open fire, raising my children in the mud and endlessly traipsing around the world."

And yet . . . the way he looked at her, the way he bent his head toward her and listened—really listened, as if what she had to say was worth hearing. As if he cared what she thought and felt . . .

And she could not deny the appeal of his big, lean body; his deep voice; his strong, brown, long-fingered hands, so capable of delivering swift, brutal justice, and yet so gentle with her. And with Caesar.

And when he smiled that slow smile . . .

But he was stupid and arrogant and blind and interfering, she reminded herself crossly. And impossible!

My father beat me savagely . . .

Was that why he wandered, homeless, rootless, alone?

Stop it. There was no point wondering, she told herself crossly. She'd told him she never wanted to see him again.

Be careful what you wish for.

She wanted him to go—she did. She didn't need the . . . the torment.

Torment? What nonsense. He was simply not possible and that was that.

But would he stay away?

"Doubtful," she told Caesar, giving him a last sweep of the brush. "He never has before. Though now he knows I'm betrothed . . ." She put the brush away. "Perhaps I'll get William to walk you for the next few days, just to be on the safe side."

She had a future to think of, one that didn't contain any tall, dark man with piercing silver-green eyes. She had to put him right out of her mind. "And I will," she told the dog. "He was just a passing fancy. He means nothing to me. Or to you, do you hear me?" Feeling better for the decision, she refilled Caesar's water bowl, gave him a last pat and hurried upstairs to the sewing room.

She found Daisy sitting cross-legged in the window seat, sewing on beads and singing softly under her breath:

"Oh, what care I for my house and my land?
What care I for my money-oh?
What care I for my new wedded lord?
I'm off with the raggle-taggle gypsy-oh."

"Stop it, Daisy!"

Daisy looked up in surprise. "Stop what?"

"That song."

"What s—oh." Daisy grinned as she recalled what she'd

been singing. "Bit close to the bone, is it?" And then she saw Jane's expression and sobered instantly. "Oh, no. Like that, is it, lovie?"

"N-no," Jane said, but her voice wobbled.

Daisy put her sewing aside, slipped off the seat and fetched Jane a handkerchief. "Oh, lovie, I knew this would happen. You always were too softhearted and apt to take in strays."

"He's not a s-s-stray."

Daisy sighed. "I know. But he might as well be; you can't pin a gypsy down. And when he's tall and dark and too good-lookin' for his own good . . . the big 'andsome rat. What's he done?"

"I . . . I told him I never wanted to see him again."

Daisy slid an arm around Jane's waist. "It's prob'ly for the best then, i'n' it?"

"I know." The tears she'd been fighting spilled down her cheeks and she scrubbed them vigorously away with the handkerchief. "I won't cry over him, I won't."

"That's the spirit, lovie. No fella's worth cryin' over."

"He's arrogant and irritating and interfering."

"That he is," Daisy agreed, who'd never even spoken to him.

"I hope I never see him again."

"Good," Daisy said briskly. "Now go and wash your face—and your 'ands and under your nails if you've been petting that bloomin' dog—and then come back. We got a few hours yet before you need to get ready for the ball. You can hem or do a seam."

Jane stared at her a moment, then gave a tremulous laugh and hugged her. "Oh, Daisy, you are wonderful. Always so down-to-earth and practical."

Daisy grinned. "Got to be. If I don't look after me, nobody else will."

It was a timely reminder, Jane thought as she went to wash her hands and face.

The lady in that song, oh, no doubt she'd be happy with her gypsy the first few weeks or even months, but when the first baby came along . . . what then? She'd regret the loss of her fine feather bed and her house then. Babies needed to be warm and dry. And safe.

*   *   *

Zach trudged through the streets, oblivious of all that surrounded him, his thoughts in turmoil. She was marrying a dreary little fat bore for money. For money!

And fool that he was, he'd said she was selling herself. And though he hadn't meant it that way, it was true.

She was cold-bloodedly selling herself—albeit in marriage—for money. And he couldn't blame her.

She'd known cold, known *hunger*, for God's sake—a child of the *ton*—and had known *what it is to have nowhere safe to sleep at night.*

When? How? Why?

What the hell had happened that had made a sweet-natured, warm, generous, well-connected beauty think she had nothing but her face to recommend her? Think she had to marry for money?

When she was clearly yearning for . . . something more.

He thought of the way she'd gazed at those children, the way her eyes softened.

Grow up, she'd said. And she'd made the most grown-up decision of all. He supposed he couldn't fault her for knowing what she wanted. *The opportunity to make the kind of marriage that will secure my future—mine and any children I might have.*

Aye, that was it—safety, security and children. And a home.

He couldn't blame her. That's what women did—nest. Turn houses into homes. Raise children. Keep them safe.

Zach paced along, unseeing. Jane Chance knew exactly what she wanted out of life. It was more than he knew.

What did he want? He could only think of one thing: Jane Chance.

And if he was to have any chance of getting her, he had to *grow up*!

What a thrice-damned fool he'd been! What had he offered her so far to tempt her away from her well-heeled, fat, little, titled bore? A few hours' dalliance—conversation in a public park—with a scruffy, down-at-heels gypsy. What a temptation that was!

She wanted to make something of her life, something worthwhile—to build a life better than . . . whatever she'd experienced in her past.

And what had he been doing? Drifting. Playing games, as he

had for the last eight years. He'd always enjoyed it, the pitting of his wits against others, slipping from one identity into another, and the risks—the risks had been a big part of the fun of it.

Oh, they were serious games, on His Majesty's business and under Gil's sober direction, but still, what had he achieved? More important, what did the future hold? The gathering of intelligence was important, but was it of such importance now that the war was over? Wasn't it rather a . . . shabby occupation now that the lines were not so clearly drawn?

The Hungarian affair had left a sour taste in his mouth, to be sure. He'd done what was asked, and done it well, with his usual flair. But people's lives would be ruined by the contents of the documents he'd brought to England, people he knew . . . and some he even liked.

He wasn't convinced that his government had any business interfering with the political affairs of another country. It would go on regardless, he knew, but did he have to be part of it?

Twelve years out of England, eight of them working for his government in secret . . . Did he really want to continue living this way, living in the shadows, changing his name, his identity, his appearance whenever the situation warranted it, and moving on, always moving on? Connecting with no one?

He thought of the women he'd lain with. A series of temporary liaisons. He'd always kept women at a distance; emotional connections were dangerous in his business, and he'd made a point of avoiding the kind of women who wanted anything other than his body for a short time. He'd always kept it light—a practical exchange, a convenient coupling, a passing fancy. Nothing serious.

He thought of a pair of wide blue eyes, as clear as a Greek summer sky, and a smile that was like morning sunshine dancing on water.

He was twenty-eight. The dirty little secrets of foreign governments would always be there for the ferreting out, would always provide work for such as he. He could go on for years like that if he had to.

But he didn't have to anymore. He couldn't wipe away the dark years of the past, couldn't remove the stains of the things he'd done—you can't turn the clock back—but a fresh start? Maybe.

He might not have a home to offer her, but he had a house.

It was a beginning. The question was, what shape was that house in? And could he build a future out of it? A future that might tempt a girl bent on marrying for money?

A t breakfast the next morning, Gil pointed to a paragraph in the *Morning Post*. "It's official."

Zach glanced at it and gave a curt nod. The announcement of the betrothal of Miss Jane Chance to Lord Cambury. "I know."

"Word is, they plan to marry before the end of the season," Gil said. "Spring wedding and all that."

Zach grunted. He didn't want to think of it. "I'm going out of town for a few days," he told Gil.

Gil frowned slightly. "To Wales?"

"No. Waste of time. Cecily will be on her way to London by now. I'd probably pass them on the road and not even know it. I'm going down to take a look at Wainfleet. See what needs to be done. What?" he added, catching Gil's surprised expression. "I have responsibilities, you know."

"I know. Just didn't expect you'd be embracing them so quickly."

"Well, I am. It's time I grew up."

There was a short pause, then Gil said, "And if you're recognized?"

"It won't be an official visit; I just plan to sniff around quietly, get a sense of how things are going."

He rose from the table. "I'll be back in a couple of days. If Cecily arrives in London before I return, will you look after her?"

Gil agreed, and Zach took himself off to pack. He sent a note to the lawyer, instructing him to deal with Gil in Zach's absence, and headed out of London.

It would take him less than a day to reach Wainfleet. It was raining, so he hired a yellow bounder for most of the way, intending to stay at the local inn and hire a horse for the last few miles. And to explore.

Sitting for long hours in the chaise gave him plenty of time for reflection.

He'd thought her pampered and spoiled, sheltered from the harshness of life, and her revelations had shocked him. That she'd known hunger, and cold . . . And had had nowhere safe to sleep? *Safe to sleep?* His imagination turned over possibilities, each one more disturbing than the last.

She'd seemed so . . . innocent.

Yet he had no doubt every word was true, and not just because of the passionate conviction in her voice. The inconsistencies he'd noticed about her, they all made sense now.

She'd known poverty. Serious, frightening poverty.

No wonder she wanted a rich husband. And a home of her own. He couldn't blame her.

Once or twice he found himself smiling, thinking of the way she'd ripped into him. Little vixen. He'd deserved it too. It had been the kick in the pants he'd needed.

As twilight fell, and the coach stopped to light the lanterns, he reflected that she'd be preparing for her very first ball. He recalled the way her whole face lit up with excitement as she'd told him about the lessons she'd been having, the dress she was to wear, which she hadn't even been allowed to see properly yet . . .

Small, innocent pleasures. She took nothing for granted.

If he hadn't been such a fool, hadn't enjoyed playing the gypsy, hadn't listened to the lawyer's idiotic advice about lying low, he might have been there tonight to lead her into her first waltz.

There would be other balls, he told himself.

It didn't help.

Chapter Fifteen

*To be fond of dancing was a certain
step towards falling in love.*

—JANE AUSTEN, *PRIDE AND PREJUDICE*

Jane held her breath. "Ta-da." Daisy whipped off the cover she'd draped over the long cheval looking glass and Jane saw for the first time what her dress looked like on.

"Oh, Daisy . . . Oh, Daisy . . ." Jane twirled around slowly, gazing at her reflection in the looking glass. The fabric swirled gracefully around her body as she moved, flowing like water, like mist. The gauzy white silk had a subtle and delicate cross-weave that threw up the palest pink shadows in the folds of the skirt. A specially imported fabric, compliments of Max and Flynn. The bodice was decorated with hundreds of tiny pink crystals, which winked in the gaslight.

"It's the most beautiful dress I have ever, ever seen," Jane breathed. "Oh, thank you, Daisy. It's . . . oh, I cannot think of the words to describe how I feel."

"You look like a princess in a fairy tale," Abby said, blinking back tears. "Oh, Jane, you're the very image of Mama. I wish she and Papa could see you now. Oh, dear, oh, dear, I think I'm going to cry."

"Oi! Stop that now," Daisy interrupted. "We don't want nobody drippin' tears all over my good silk, now do we? If I'd wanted watered silk, I'd'a used it."

Laughing and crying at the same time, Abby stepped back. She turned to her husband and said helplessly, "I'm not sad, truly. It's just that she's the image of our mother. And it was always Jane's dream to make her come-out, as Mama did. But we never thought it would h-h-happen."

"I know, love," Max said gently, and passed his wife a pristine white handkerchief. Then he handed Jane an oblong box covered in white brocade. "A small token from your sister and me, in memory of your first ball."

With shaking hands, Jane opened it. It contained a necklace of pearls and crystals, and a pair of pearl drop earrings. She gasped and looked at Abby.

Abby nodded. "It was as close as we could get to the necklace Mama described. But we thought you'd prefer pink."

"Oh, I do. Thank you so much, I love it. I've never seen pink pearls before," Jane murmured, taking the necklace out of the box and holding it up against herself. "Can you do it up for me, Abby?"

"South Sea Island pearls," Max told her.

Abby fastened the necklace, then when Jane had donned the earrings, she hugged her. "Enjoy your first ball, little sister."

"And you enjoy yours, big sister," Jane responded happily. It wasn't right that all the attention was on her—it was the first ball for all three of them—Abby and Damaris too. She wished Daisy would come too, but she'd refused.

"Don't crush the dresses," Daisy warned. Abby was dressed in vibrant green silk, the hem of which was embellished with delicate swags of gold net, held up by tiny gold embroidered tassels. Around her neck she wore a magnificent necklace of emeralds.

"Quite right," Lady Beatrice said, appearing at the door. "The gel looks lovely—well, both of them do, but Jane especially. You've done a superb job, Daisy, m'dear. The choice of that fabric is a triumph."

"Yes, Daisy," Abby agreed. "And the one you made for Damaris is stunning. So original, and so very modish. You're going to have people lining up with orders after this."

"Are you quite sure you won't come, Daisy?" Lady Beatrice asked her. "I did arrange it with the duchess—she said I was welcome to bring you—and you ought to be there to witness the sensation your dresses will cause. It's your first ball too, you know—*your* dresses."

Daisy shook her head. "No time. I got work to do. Them—*those* dresses is launchin' me business tonight. I don't need to be there."

"No, not if you're as stubborn as a mule," Lady Beatrice muttered.

Everyone was quiet in the carriage on the way to the ball, Abby no doubt thinking of Mama and Papa—as was Jane, in a way.

This was always Jane's dream, Abby had said.

Jane thought of Mama's story, and a small part of her wished that the man waiting for her on the other side of the ballroom would be tall and dark with gleaming silvery-green eyes.

No, that was nothing but a foolish fantasy, she told herself firmly. An impossible dream. She had a very nice, very suitable man waiting for her and he would give her everything she'd ever wanted.

She looked across at Abby and Max, sitting opposite, and caught them in a burning exchange of glances. Abby, whose arm was linked through Max's, sighed happily and snuggled closer to her husband's big body, not caring in the least whether she crushed her gown. Max covered her hand with his, and looked down at his wife with an expression so intimate, so intensely private and loving, that Jane had to look away.

She swallowed. Everything she'd ever wanted.

Almost.

The Duchess of Rothermere's majordomo stood at the head of the stairs leading down into the ballroom and announced each person as they arrived. Lady Beatrice came first, wrinkling her nose at being called the Dowager Lady Davenham, then Max and Abby—Lord and Lady Davenham, and finally Jane, a mere Miss Chance.

Lord Cambury was waiting and came forward as they were greeting the duke and duchess. In formal ball dress, he looked quite distinguished, though it had to be said that black satin knee breeches and white silk stockings were not the best design for a man of his figure.

Jane smiled warmly at him. He scanned her appearance critically, then gave her a little nod of approval. He stepped forward and presented his arm to Jane, who accepted it at Lady Beatrice's gracious permission.

The others went inside, but Lord Cambury stood chatting a moment longer, accepting the duke and duchess's felicitations on their betrothal and talking of this and that, apparently oblivious of the delay he was causing to the line of others waiting to enter.

It was deliberate, Jane realized; he wanted to make an entrance. Their first appearance as a couple since their betrothal had been in the papers. Finally he left the duke and duchess and led Jane to the other side of the ballroom, where Lady Beatrice, Abby and Max had already joined Damaris and Freddy.

As they crossed the dance floor, a hush fell. Jane, who already had butterflies in her stomach, felt them intensify. Had she made some mistake? Was her gown caught up at the back? What were they all looking at? Why was nobody talking anymore? She kept walking, head high. Lady Beatrice had trained her for this. The old lady's voice rang in her head: *If anything goes wrong, ignore it. Pretend it's perfect. Attitude is everything.*

She was halfway across what now seemed an immense expanse of dance floor when suddenly there was a loud gasp on her left. Jane paused, glanced over.

A plump, elderly lady stood stock-still, staring at Jane as if in deep shock. She held out her hand to Jane, took two tottering steps toward her and fainted.

Jane, horrified, moved to help the lady, but Lord Cambury tugged her back. "Come along. Not our business. Plenty of others here to help." And it was true; the lady was immediately surrounded by people producing smelling salts and calling for burned feathers.

Jane hesitated. "I think she wanted to speak to me."

"Possibly, but no state to speak to anyone now," her betrothed pointed out. "Now come along. All in hand, see?"

Jane glanced at Lady Beatrice, who beckoned her forward.

"What do you think happened?" Jane asked when she reached the others.

Lady Beatrice shrugged. "Probably had herself laced in too tight. It happens, even in these benighted times when women barely know what a corset is."

"She seemed to want to tell me something."

"Probably just gasping for air," Lady Beatrice said. "Don't worry yourself, my dear, the duchess herself is attending to her." The opening bars of a piece sounded from the orchestra. "Ah, excellent, the music is starting and here is Lord Cambury all eager to lead you out for the first dance of the evening. Off you go and enjoy yourself, there's a good gel."

Jane did as she said, but though she danced every dance, and lacked no choice of partners, she became increasingly aware that something was not right. Abby and Lady Beatrice seemed to be deep in conversation with Max, and not dancing at all. Damaris and Freddy too were close by, also not dancing.

But each time she returned to them, between dances, they were full of smiles and denied anything was the matter and sent her off to dance and enjoy herself. But she was sure something was wrong. They were treating her like a child.

It became clear to Jane that a little subterfuge was required. When the next dance was about to begin, she excused herself apologetically to her partner and disappeared into the ladies' withdrawing room. A few moments later she threaded her way back to where her family was gathered.

Hidden behind a large potted palm, her arrival went unnoticed. Abby was saying distressfully, "No, I won't have Jane upset at her first ever ball."

Max's deep voice rumbled, "It's your first ball too, my love."

"Yes, but I never dreamed of balls and pretty dresses the way Jane did. I won't let that woman ruin it for her."

Jane stepped forward. "What woman, Abby? The one who fainted? But I've never seen her before. Who is she?"

There was an awkward silence, then Abby said, "It's nothing, love—go and dance."

Jane didn't move. "I'm eighteen, Abby. I'm not a child anymore, to be protected from the truth."

"She's right," Max said.

"Can't we tell her about it later?" Abby pleaded.

"If you don't tell me, someone else will," Jane said. She turned to Damaris and Freddy. "Do you know?" Damaris gave Jane an apologetic look. Freddy just shrugged.

"Then, Abby . . ." Jane turned to her sister and waited.

Abby, clearly upset, shook her head. Max put his arm around her. To Jane, he said, "The woman who fainted is Lady Dalrymple."

"*Lady Dalrymple?*" Jane stared at Abby, wide-eyed.

Abby nodded. "Our grandmother." Her lips tightened. "The one who left us to starve in the gutter."

Chapter Sixteen

This was a letter to be run through eagerly, to be read
deliberately, to supply matter for much reflection, and
to leave everything in greater suspense than ever.

—JANE AUSTEN, MANSFIELD PARK

A long with the flowers, gifts and flattering notes from
gentlemen admirers that were delivered to Jane at Lady
Beatrice's house first thing the next morning, and invitations
to even more parties and balls, there was one note that threw
Jane's emotions into even further turmoil.

She knew whom the note was from, even before she opened
it, for it was sealed with a wafer that said simply *Dalrymple*.
She broke it open and read the short message in a kind of daze.
In sloping copperplate handwriting, it said:

My dear Miss Chantry,

I hope you do not mind me addressing you thus, and
forgive me if I am mistaken—but I believe you to be my
granddaughter, the child of my beautiful, beloved daugh-
ter, Sarah, who was tragically lost to me five-and-twenty
years ago. You are so very like her, my dear girl, that last
night, when I saw you cross the floor at the Duchess of
Rothermere's ball, time might have stood still.

I do not pretend to understand how you have come to
be making your come-out under the auspices of the

dowager, Lady Davenham, I suppose because your older sister is married to her nephew. When I saw her with you, I knew at once she must be the older sister I knew you had—she is unmistakably a Chantry, whereas you, my dear, take after your mother's side of the family.

I would very much like to meet you, my dearest granddaughter. I have written to your sister too. I do not know by what miracle I have found you girls at last, but it seems that God has finally consented to answer my prayers.

Your loving grandmother,
Louisa Dalrymple.

Ten minutes later Abby arrived, waving a similar note. "Did she write to you? I assumed as much. How dare she?" Abby was shaking. "How *dare* she?"

Jane held her note out to Abby, who read it furiously. Jane read Abby's. It was almost the same.

Abby flung down the note, sat down, then jumped up and paced around the room. "*Her 'beloved daughter'*? *'Tragically lost' to her*?" Angry tears ran down her cheeks. She dashed them away. "How *dare* she say such a thing when she left Mama to die in slow agony in that filthy, squalid, horrid little place!"

She picked up the note, scanned it again, then flung it back down. It fluttered to the floor. "Do you see? She *knew* about us—*'I knew at once she must be the older sister I knew you had'*! And now she wants to see us. Now! The hypocrisy of it sickens me! We could have died for all she did for us."

Jane bent to pick the note up.

Abby paced back and forth. "I don't know how many letters we sent, telling her of our desperate situation, and asking for her help. I know Papa wrote to her—several times—when Mama first became ill—and had she received the proper treatment in time, she might still be alive today." She dashed hot tears aside.

"And after he was killed, Mama wrote to her parents, and to Papa's parents as well, asking for help, since she was so ill and could not provide for you and me." She wiped her cheeks with shaking hands. "She asked them to take the children—us!—if they still did not wish to have anything to do with her, because they—we!—at least were innocent. Not that I would have left her, but you were so little and sweet and helpless." Hot tears poured down Abby's cheeks.

Jane was shocked. She hadn't known. Some of it, yes, but not that Mama had offered to give them up. To protect them. Leaving herself to die alone. Tears prickled at the back of her eyes. Poor, desperate Mama.

"And you know I wrote to them after Mama died." Abby added bitterly, "I suppose we must be grateful that the Chantrys are dead, that they at least will not come out of nowhere to fawn so sickeningly on us."

"Are they dead?" Jane looked up. "I didn't know."

Abby made a dismissive gesture. "It was ten years ago. Influenza, I think. Max told me some time ago."

"Why didn't you tell me?"

Abby looked at her in surprise. "Sorry, I didn't think. What would have been the point?"

"I would have liked to know," Jane said. "They were my grandparents too."

Abby hugged her. "I'm sorry, love. I didn't think of it. Max told me on our honeymoon, and then it was Christmas and . . ."

"Damaris's grandparents came to Christmas," Jane said quietly. She'd only just discovered them too. And they her.

Abby looked at her, dismayed. "It never occurred to me to tell you. I didn't think you'd care. We haven't exactly been blessed with our grandparents, have we?"

Jane looked at the note still in her hand and bit her lip. "What are we going to do about this?"

"Burn it," Abby said. "If that woman thinks she can crawl into our lives now—she's widowed, you know, and no doubt wants granddaughters to tend her in her old age."

"She's widowed?"

Abby nodded. "Max found out all about her last night, after we left the ball. She must have been finding out about us at the same time, for how else did she discover our address? Max told me her husband—"

"Our grandfather."

"Yes, apparently he died just over a year ago. And Lady Dalrymple has remained at her country estate—the dower house—for the last year, but she's out of mourning now and has returned to society."

Jane considered that. "So we're bound to see her at other events."

Abby gave an indifferent shrug. "We might. So what? I don't intend to recognize her."

Jane chewed her lip.

Abby frowned. "Jane? You're not thinking of seeing her!"

Jane sighed. "I don't know. I'm confused."

"What's confusing?" Abby exclaimed incredulously. "She left Mama to die, and us to starve. And now, when it is convenient for *her*, she wants to claim us!" She stared at Jane, shocked. "You can't want to see her, surely?"

Jane's emotions were in turmoil. She didn't know what she felt or thought. It was all too much to take in. She loved Abby dearly and owed her everything for her care when Jane was a child, but Jane was a child no longer, and she would decide for herself what to do.

She rose and hugged Abby. "Hush, love, I don't know what I'll do yet—I need to think."

"You can do what you like," Abby said, "but I want nothing to do with her."

Zach drew his horse to a halt and gazed down at his childhood home. It looked achingly familiar, and yet somehow not what he'd expected. He'd remembered the building as big and cold and stark, but now, looking down at it, and having experienced European architecture at its finest, he was surprised to find it elegant, even graceful in its simplicity. Almost modern, and yet it had been built in the seventeenth century.

The absence of the firm hand of his father was in evidence: The drive needed raking, the lawn was in need of a trim, and the flower beds looked forlorn and rather weedy, but it was spring, after all, and the mullioned windows gleamed in the pale spring sunshine. He could see no people, though, which surprised him.

Jane Chance claimed a house was not the same as a home. He remembered Wainfleet as a house, despite the people—or maybe because of them. His father had insisted on rigid formality, so few of the servants had any time for a small boy. Zach had sought his entertainments elsewhere.

He looked at the lake where he was supposed to have drowned Cecily and remembered house parties in the summer with boating on the lake, ladies in wide-brimmed hats and light summer gowns being rowed by gentlemen. And picnics set up by the lakeside. He was never allowed to participate—such events were for adults, not small boys. He'd watched from his room.

Today the surface of the lake gleamed like polished pewter. It could do with a good clear-out too; those reeds were starting to take over.

His horse shifted restlessly, tossing its head, and Zach moved on, moving away from the house. He had no plans to get any closer. He doubted many people would remember him, let alone recognize the man he'd become, but if anyone did, there was bound to be a fuss and he didn't want to be bothered with all that just yet.

Besides, it was the estate he was interested in, not . . . *feelings*. He had no interest in wandering down the unpleasant byways of his childhood memories.

He rode around the estate, coming across familiar landmarks with unexpected pleasure, noticing changes. But the more he saw, the more disturbed he became. He'd come here just to remind himself what he'd left, to see what was to be done—but mostly just to get away to think.

He'd never seriously thought about marriage before, had, in fact, assumed it wasn't for him. But Miss Jane Chance had him thinking all sorts of things he'd never before considered.

The more he saw of Wainfleet, the more he noticed things that needed doing: fields lying fallow that should have been plowed and ready for spring planting—if not already planted—swampy areas that should have been drained, coppices and orchards that needed attention now, before the spring growth, fences that were sagging and ought to be repaired; all small things on their own, but adding up to a pattern of neglect that concerned him.

His father had, he thought, been a good steward of the land—old-fashioned, and hardheaded in his opinions, but responsible. He'd drummed into Zach the duty the younger generation owed to those who came before.

His father had been dead a year. And since then, it looked as though nothing had been done.

Zach's fault. He'd assumed the estate manager, whoever it was, would simply continue on as before.

There was work for him here. Not just repairs and the restoration of order, but new possibilities, new methods of farming that could bring prosperity to tenants and landlord alike. A chance to build something fresh and new and good out of something old.

Grow up, she'd told him.

His mind spun with possibilities.

He rode on, circling around the estate, and came to the edge of the forest at the rear of the house. He'd spent many hours of the day in this forest. A faint, overgrown path wove through the trees. Just past there was a stream where he'd fished sometimes, and a clearing where the gypsies used to camp each year. He'd haunted their camp as a boy, absorbing their lore without realizing it. It had helped shape his life, and on occasions to save it.

He dismounted, tied his horse to a tree and followed the little path.

And heard a crash and a sharp, sudden cry. He raced toward the sound and found, beneath a large spreading oak, a small boy of about seven or eight, lying on the ground, still and unmoving in a tangle of small branches.

He bent over the boy. To his relief, the child's eyes were wide and aware. One arm was bent at a slight angle. Broken, Zach thought. The boy stared up at Zach with a panicked look on his face, his mouth moving like a beached fish, unable to breathe.

"It's all right," Zach told him in what he hoped was a calming voice. He hadn't had a lot to do with children. "You've had the wind knocked out of you. It'll come back in a min—ah, there you are," he finished as the boy sucked in a desperate lungful of air.

The boy said nothing, gasping in air until the panicked look faded. He tried to sit up, but fell back with a cry of pain. His face turned a greenish white; his skin looked clammy.

He cradled the injured arm up against his chest and looked at Zach. His lips were clamped together in a desperate attempt not to cry. He looked sick with pain and utterly miserable.

"I think you've broken your arm," Zach told him. "Hurts like the very devil, doesn't it? Now, just lie there a moment and we'll see if you've done any other damage." The boy lay back, gritting his teeth, his face pinched with pain, dead white and clammy.

"I'm Zach," he told the boy as he tested the child's other limbs. "Fell out of the tree, did you? I've done that before."

The child said nothing; clinging to his dignity—and the contents of his stomach—Zach thought. He flinched and gasped when Zach felt his ankle, but he never uttered a sound. Brave little chap. Stoic. A farm boy by his clothing.

"Can you wiggle your toes on this foot?" He touched the lad's knee.

The boy tried it, winced and nodded.

"Good, then it's not broken, though I'm sure it hurts like fury as well. So a broken arm and a sprained ankle, eh? And a good few bruises and scratches. But don't worry, we'll get you fixed up," Zach said in as soothing a voice as he could manage. The boy looked sick as a dog already. No use adding worry to the mix. "So what's your name, lad?"

"Robin," the boy whispered. "Robin Wilks."

It was a familiar surname. There had always been Wilkses at Wainfleet. In Zach's boyhood the cook was a Mrs. Wilks, a stout and motherly woman who had a fondness for growing boys and an understanding of how they were always hungry; she'd sneaked him treats time out of memory. But that Mrs. Wilks was old even then, too old to be the mother of this child. She'd be retired by now.

He might yet escape recognition.

"You can't walk on that ankle, lad, so I'm going to carry you home. Where do you live?"

The boy hesitated then, realizing he had no choice, said, "In the big house."

"Wainfleet?" Zach asked with a sinking feeling. The irony of it didn't escape him.

The child nodded.

"Well, Robin Wilks, I'm going to lift you up now and I'll tell you straight, it's going to hurt like the devil, so I won't hold it against you if you have to yell. You're a brave lad, I know."

He scooped the boy up as gently as he could, being careful

not to bump the broken arm, which was tucked against the boy's narrow chest, but the little fellow gasped again, and fainted. Just as well, Zach thought as he made his way down through the forest, spare the child any further pain.

Taking the shortcut he'd taken so often as a child, he cut between the stables and the kitchen gardens, crossed the court-yard and headed for the kitchen. Under normal circumstances he would have expected to come across any number of people—gardeners and under-gardeners, grooms, stable boys, whatever, but he met nobody at all. It was very strange.

But just as he reached the kitchen door, it was flung open and a stout, familiar figure stood there, aged considerably, but instantly recognizable: Mrs. Wilks. She took the situation in at a glance. "Oh, Robbie, Robbie, what have you done to yourself now?" She hadn't even looked at Zach.

The boy had regained consciousness, and managed to say, "Don't fuss, Gran, I'm all ri—" but then he fainted again.

"Oh, dearie, dearie me! Come ye in, come ye in—oh, thank you, sir—yes, put him down on the chair there. Wilks, Wilks!" she called, and returned to her grandson. "That arm—"

"Is broken," Zach told her, "but the ankle is, I think, only sprained. He fell out of a big oak." She'd barely glanced at him; all her attention was on the boy.

"That'd be right. Never out of trouble that one." She hurried back to the door, calling, "Wilks!" again—presumably the boy's father, but when finally a man came running, he was white-haired and stooped and even older than she was. He was a groom, Zach recalled. The old man didn't look at Zach either.

She told him, "The boy's gone and broken his arm. Fetch Ernie."

"Ernie?" Zach had been about to slide quietly out the door and make himself scarce, but the name stopped him.

She didn't answer for a moment, but clucked over the boy, who was looking ominously green, and set a bucket down beside him. "In there, Robbie, if you're going to toss up your breakfast." He did, and she handed him a cloth to wipe his mouth, shaking her head. "Just like his father, God rest his soul. Never out of trouble."

She straightened and said to Zach, "Ernie's a natural, lives over by Bramble Creek. He'll set the lad's arm for us."

A natural? She meant a simpleton, Zach realized. Country folk often ascribed healing powers to simpletons, but he wasn't going to let a brave little lad like that be mauled by a well-meaning simpleton. "The boy needs a proper doctor."

The woman shook her head. "No, it'll have to be Ernie. The doctor won't come to us." She smoothed the boy's hair back.

"Why not?"

"Can't pay him," she said. "No money."

"Send for the doctor," Zach told her. "I'll pay."

"*You* will?" For the first time she stopped fussing over the boy and looked at Zach. Her eyes narrowed. She came a few paces closer and squinted nearsightedly up at him.

"It's never—oh, my Gawd, it is!" She staggered back and sat down—*plump!*—on a kitchen chair, staring at Zach as if she'd seen a ghost. "Oh, Lordy, Lordy, Wilks—see who's brought our Robbie home! It's Master Adam, back from the dead!"

J ane left the matter of Lady Dalrymple's letter for a day. She and Abby needed some time to calm down and think things over.

Abby was normally very loving and forgiving and gentle, but in this matter . . .

Jane felt so torn. She didn't want to be disloyal to her sister. Abby had worried and worked and *fought* to keep them fed and safe . . . She was entitled to be angry.

But Jane wanted to hear what the woman had to say and she wanted Abby to come with her—not because Jane felt uncomfortable going by herself, but because she felt, deep down, that Abby needed to be there, to hear for herself.

She decided to try again. She walked around to Abby's house and Abby rang for tea.

"I know she did a terrible thing in leaving us to starve, Abby, but . . . it was a long time ago and we're all right now . . . And . . . she's—it's not as if we have family to spare . . ."

Abby folded her hands across her stomach. "She left us to *die*, Jane. That's not what family does."

"I know. But I want to know why."

"Does it matter? Jane, the letter—letters—I wrote, she

would have had to be made of stone to ignore them." Abby's face crumpled and a tear rolled down her cheek. She pulled out a large masculine handkerchief and wiped it away.

Jane slipped an arm around her sister, feeling guilty. "I owe you everything, Abby darling, and would not for the world distress you . . ."

"But?"

"I want to *know*." She swallowed. "She's Mama's mother. And the other night she looked genuinely distressed, Abby. She fainted."

"Because of the shock. Because she never expected to see us—see you. Because you're the image of Mama. Because we weren't supposed to exist."

There was a long silence. It wasn't like Abby to be hard or bitter. And although Jane could understand her sister's anger, she didn't feel it as strongly. She'd been too young to know what it had really been like for Abby. Her sister had borne the brunt of all their problems. And all before she was even twelve years old.

But Jane yearned for family. And she knew Abby did too, deep down. This was just defensiveness. Abby didn't want old wounds reopened, and unhappy emotions stirred up. Jane could understand that. Abby's life was happily settled now; she had a home, and she had Max, whom she loved to distraction, and who adored her in return.

Abby had everything she'd ever wanted now. Jane didn't.

Jane took her sister's hands in hers. "When we first came here to live with Lady Beatrice, you changed our name from Chantry to Chance—"

Abby frowned. "You know why—it was for our own safety."

"Yes, but you also said it symbolized a fresh new chance for each of us. We each got that chance, didn't we, Abby? Damaris never believed she could wed and yet now she's married to Freddy and I've never seen her happier. Daisy, a maidservant from a brothel, is on her way to becoming the finest dressmaker in London. And you, who were destined to be a governess for the rest of your life, looking after other people's children and never having the chance of a child of your own—"

Abby burst into tears.

Jane was horrified. Abby never wept, and now Jane had made her cry twice in a matter of minutes. "Oh, love, I'm sorry, I'm so sorry. I never meant to upset you like this."

Abby mopped her face with the large handkerchief and gave a rueful laugh between the sobs. "It's not your fault, Jane darling. And I'm not really upset. It's just . . . with all this talk of second chances and family and children . . ." She wiped her eyes, folded the handkerchief and tucked it back into her reticule. "Max says I've become the veriest watering pot since—"

Jane frowned. "Since what?"

For answer, Abby took Jane's hand and laid it on her belly. It took a moment for Jane to understand. "Abby! You mean—"

Abby nodded and gave her a misty smile. "Only Max knows at the moment, but I wanted to tell you first; little sister, you're going to be an aunt."

Chapter Seventeen

It isn't what we say or think that
defines us, but what we do.

—JANE AUSTEN, *SENSE AND SENSIBILITY*

"I'm surprised you recognized me," Zach said as he finished his meal. The doctor—a stranger to Zach—had been, set Robin's arm and left. The boy was tucked up in bed now, fast asleep after having been dosed with laudanum for the pain.

Mrs. Wilks chuckled. "You have your father's eyes—and your grandfer's, at that, my lord."

"Aye," her husband chimed in. "Living spit of old Lord Wainfleet—your grandad, I mean, not your pa."

Mrs. Wilks had cooked and served an enormous dinner, which she'd wanted to serve in the dining room, but Zach had no intention of dining alone in state. Much to her outward horror but secret pleasure, he'd eaten in the kitchen with her and her husband.

"It's not as if I haven't eaten here a hundred times before," he reminded her. He'd forgotten it, but coming here reminded him that this room had been something of a refuge for him as a small boy. It still felt that way.

Now he was here, there were things he needed to know.

"What has happened here since my father's death?" Zach asked. "I remember this place as always busy."

Wilks nodded. "Skeleton staff now," he said. "But we'll be

all right now you've come home, Master Adam. Thought you were dead, we did."

"Thought yon cousin of yours was going to be the new master," Mrs. Wilks said darkly. "Mr. Gerald. He be the reason Wainfleet is in limbo."

"Limbo?" Zach frowned. "How so?"

"Stopped the money," Wilks explained. "Wanted to take control the day your father was buried, but the lawyers said no. Had to wait. Look for you." He sucked on his pipe and contemplated that.

"Got his own lawyers," Mrs. Wilks prompted. "Got the estate—what did they call it, Dad?"

"Frozen," Wilks said. "Assets frozen, they called it. Till the rightful owner be proved." He grinned at Zach and gestured with his pipe. "That's you now, the new Lord Wainfleet."

Mrs. Wilks chuckled. "Mr. Gerald's going to be green as a frog when he finds out you're back. Fancied himself lord of the manor, he did, struttin' around, tellin' us all what to do."

"He still might be if I'm done for murder," Zach said.

They both looked at him in shock. "Bless my soul, Master Adam," Mrs. Wilks said. "You never did kill your pretty young stepmother—not a soul here believes that!"

"Not a soul," echoed her husband.

"Somebody else must have done it," Mrs. Wilks said comfortably.

"Cecily isn't dead," Zach told them. "I got her away from here. I left her with one of her old school friends." They stared at him in surprise, so he added, "She was alive when I left her."

"No, that can't be right, sir," Mrs. Wilks said after a moment. "We saw her body, dead as a doornail she was, poor drownded little thing, just days after you left. But we never thought it was you who did it."

"Never thought it," her husband echoed.

"You *saw* her?" Zach repeated. "And you're sure it was Cecily?"

"Oh, yes," Mrs. Wilks assured him. "It was her all right. All dressed up in that lovely gold dress your pa had bought her, she was. Ruined it was. The weeds and the water had got to it bad."

Zach sat back, stunned by the revelation. It couldn't be

Cecily. He'd left her in Wales. Unless she'd returned . . . But why would she? She'd been in fear of her life.

"When was this exactly?" he asked.

The Wilkses exchanged glances in silent consultation. "Three days after you left Wainfleet," Mrs. Wilks said. "That's right, isn't it, Dad?"

Wilks withdrew his pipe and nodded. "Aye, pulled her out of the lake three days after, we did."

"Then it couldn't possibly be Cecily," Zach said, somewhat relieved. "It took us more than three days to get to her friend's house in Wales, and after that I went to London and back and then I saw her again in Wales—it must have been at least two weeks after I left Wainfleet. And for years after that she wrote me letters; the last one was at Christmas."

There was a short silence. "But we *saw* her," Mrs. Wilks said.

Her husband gave her a nudge and said, "But none of us at Wainfleet ever believed it was you who done her in, Master Adam. I mean, me lord."

"Thank you, I appreciate your loyalty," Zach said. "It's a mystery, but I'm sure we'll get it sorted out." He sounded more confident than he felt.

There had to be an explanation for the dead body—one that had nothing to do with him or Cecily. It must have been some other dead woman. Cecily should be in London by now, safe in Gil's hands.

"Now," he said when they'd finished their dinner, "tell me what's been happening on the estate. And more to the point, what needs to be done. I noticed there hasn't been any plowing or any spring planting."

The Wilkses exchanged glances. "No point, is there?" Wilks said. "Mr. Gerald said he'd get rid of most of the tenant farmers, knock down the cottages and make it all into one big estate. Reckons there's more money to be made that way."

Zach frowned. "What about the tenants?" Some of those families, like the Wilkses, had been part of the estate for generations.

Wilks shrugged. "Find work elsewhere, I suppose."

"In them big-city manufactories," Mrs. Wilks said darkly. "And livin' in a slum, no doubt. I've heard tell they squash whole families into one room."

Zach listened as they confided their worries about the future.

There was logic in changing the way the estate was managed—farming methods did need to be modernized, land drained—the whole estate was crying out for revitalization. But he had no intention of tossing loyal, hardworking tenants off land they and their forefathers had farmed for hundreds of years. Their work, their rents had allowed his family to prosper for generations; it was not for Zach to abandon them now.

He realized now that he loved Wainfleet; he'd just buried that knowledge for the last twelve years.

There was work for him here indeed. A purpose—a good one. A future to build, for himself and for the people of the estate.

Afterward he walked through the house, his footsteps echoing. It was as cold and bleak as he remembered, more so for most of the rooms had been shut since his father's death and the furniture shrouded in holland covers.

But his memories had been colored by his father's coldness and brutality.

Like the estate, it too could change; the house could be made into a home. All it needed was the right woman.

He gave the Wilkses what money he had on him—part payment of arrears owed them—then went to pay a call on the former estate manager and start things moving again. No point in anonymity now—the village grapevine would spread the news of his return soon enough, and in any case, the hearing was only a couple of weeks away.

He was not leaving England again; murder change or not, he'd stay and fight for his future—his future at Wainfleet, and his future with Miss Jane Chance.

"What do you mean she's not here?" Zach stared at Gil. He had arrived in London a bare half hour earlier. "I know North Wales is a long way, but surely by now—"

"The lawyer's man returned the evening of the day you left for Wainfleet," Gil told him. "I spoke to him. He claimed he couldn't find Cecily, or any sign she'd ever been there."

"What?" Zach was stunned. "He did go to Llandudno, didn't he? Not some other village?"

"That's what he said. Claimed he went to the address you gave, but said that not only was Cecily not there, but that the woman who answered the door—a Mrs. Thomas, right?" Zach nodded, and Gil continued, "Said she'd never heard of Cecily."

"Rubbish, she went to school with her."

"She told him she'd lived there all her life, and that no English lady had ever been to the village." He added, "The woman spoke only Welsh. No English at all."

"Nonsense! I met her. I stayed with her, twelve years ago. She speaks perfect English." He ran his fingers through his hair, baffled by the report. "Whoever this fellow talked to, she can't have been Mary Thomas. Or if she was, it must have been a different Mary Thomas. It's a common enough name in Wales."

Gil shrugged. "I'm only saying what he told me. He said he had to use an interpreter to be understood anywhere in the village."

Zach shook his head, unable to fathom it. "I don't understand. Llandudno is small—maybe a thousand people in total. How could anyone not notice Cecily in a village that size?"

"He claimed he also checked every house in the same street, as well as others in the village. The story was the same; no English lady had ever come to Llandudno."

"Rubbish!" Zach thumped the table in frustration. "He's either incompetent or lying. I left Cecily there, dammit—and when I went back two weeks later with the money I got from selling her jewels, she was still there, settling in with Mary Thomas, as happy as a grig. *And* she wrote to me from there—dozens of letters— dammit, you forwarded them on to me."

"I know."

Zach rose and started to pace. "I should never have trusted that blasted lawyer in the first place. I'll go to Wales myself and find her!"

"No need, I've already sent one of my men," Gil said calmly. "He left three days ago, so he should have news for us soon. He's a good man and a native Welsh speaker. I also told him to find witnesses who could swear Cecily was alive after the body was discovered. If Cecily has left Wales—and that seems likely— we'll need to prove that it wasn't her body."

"Thank you." Zach sat down again, somewhat relieved. "Her friend, Mary Thomas—the one who *can* speak English—could testify that I took her there, alive and well. And what about the innkeepers where we stayed at along the way? Even the postilions. Surely someone would recall a nervous young woman with a badly bruised face, escorted by a sixteen-year-old boy, even if it was twelve years ago. And send someone to Wainfleet—we need to find out who that body really was."

Gil nodded and pulled out his notebook and pencil. "Give me the details and I'll send men to make inquiries. It'll cost you, but you won't mind that."

Zach gave him the information, and sipped his cognac as Gil wrote everything down. Perhaps the situation wasn't quite as bad as he'd thought.

Gil tucked his notebook away and regarded Zach thoughtfully. "It might be wise to make contingency plans in case you need to leave the country. Do you want me to make the arrangements?"

Zach snorted. "I'm damned if I'll slink away and let my greedy little tick of a cousin take over my inheritance. Do you know, he's got the estate tangled up in legal tape and nobody can do anything—none of the servants has been paid since my father died. The whole place is stagnating. And he plans to butcher it."

"So you'll stay and risk going to trial for murder?"

"I'll stay." Zach gave him an ironic half smile. "I've risked death for my country a dozen times and more; it's worth it to risk my neck for the sake of my own future, don't you think?"

"And once this is all over—and assuming all goes well and you're a free man again—and you've settled things at Wainfleet, are you planning to return to your old life abroad?"

Zach gave him a cool look. "Don't be disingenuous, Gil, it doesn't suit you. You know perfectly well what I'm planning."

"The girl?"

Zach nodded. "If she will have me."

"Delighted to hear it, though professionally, I shall feign disappointment."

Zach rose and added coal to the fire, stirring the glowing coals thoughtfully with the poker. Gazing into fires always helped him to think.

It was a dammed odd thing, the lawyer's fellow not finding any sign of Cecily. No doubt the man was a fool and went to the wrong village. Welsh village names could look incomprehensible to the uninitiated.

Zach's every instinct was to go to Wales and find Cecily himself, but there was no time. Gil had said he'd sent a good man and Zach trusted Gil. Not long to the hearing.

Long enough to make himself known to Miss Jane Chance, not as a gypsy, but as his true self? A man who could offer her the kind of future she wanted? He might not be as rich as Cambury, but at least he had a house and a title, and he would spend his life ensuring she was never cold or hungry or frightened again.

It wouldn't be a damned cold-blooded arrangement either.

Long enough to get her to be willing to . . . what? Break her betrothal to Cambury? No, much as he wanted it, he couldn't ask her to do that, not while he was still mired in this mess.

Until the murder charge was sorted out, the best he could hope for was to convince her to see him as a possibility. And for that, he needed to talk to her, explain why he'd let her believe he was a gypsy . . . And that he was shortly to be plunged into a murder scandal.

And then to ask her to trust him, and to wait.

Not the easiest of conversations.

He gave the coals one last stir and straightened, finding himself face-to-face with the portrait of Gil's ancestor that was mounted over the mantel. Damned ugly fellow. No resemblance to Gil at all.

The gold frame was stuffed with invitations. Still brooding on his problems, his gaze passed vaguely over them. Noting one was for a party that had been held weeks ago, he pulled it out and tossed it in the fire, then found another old one and burned that too. "Don't you ever go to any of these things?"

"No, and don't change the subject. You could always establish your identity—that'll be quite straightforward, and no need to attend the hearing if we do it properly—and cross to the Continent before you can be arrested."

"What, and skulk in Paris or somewhere until you find the evidence to clear me?" Zach snorted. He wasn't going anywhere. Not while Jane Chance was still free and unmarried.

"I don't believe I mentioned any skulking. I am trying to save you from stretching your neck."

Zach shook his head. "Stop worrying. I know it looks black but I am, after all, innocent. I'll stay and fight the charge." He scanned the invitations and consigned another expired one to the fire. He watched it curl and blacken, then flame up.

In the morning he'd talk to Jane, tell her the truth—all of it, murder charge and all. Throw himself on her mercy. Ask her to trust him. To wait.

Unless Cecily was found in time, all hell would break loose next week, and rather than leave it for the gossips and scandalmongers—for Lord knew how garbled it would be once the tale reached her—he had to tell her the truth himself.

And apologize for the deception.

He went to Berkeley Square the next morning and waited for her in the park. At just after ten o'clock, out she came, radiant in a blue pelisse, laughing and scolding RosePetal, who was straining at the leash as usual, with William clumping along behind her.

Zach's heart leapt at the sight of her. He stepped out onto the path ahead of her, and waited.

She saw him and stopped dead. The laughter died from her face. RosePetal too had seen him and was doing his best to choke himself on his collar in his eagerness to greet Zach. Not Jane.

She said something to William—he couldn't hear what—turned around and marched back the way she'd come, her back straight and stiff, pulling an unhappy dog behind her, as if she were dragging a loaf of bread. A very heavy loaf of bread with four feet that resisted every step.

William shot Zach a smug look and followed.

Woman, dog and footman disappeared back into Lady Beatrice's house. Only the dog appeared regretful, giving longing, martyred looks back at Zach as he was dragged into the house.

It was disappointing, but Zach understood; she thought him a gypsy, after all, and had told him to leave her alone. He went back to Gil's and considered his options.

He had to speak to her. She had to know she had choices other than Lord Cambury. Well, of course she had choices—practically any gentleman of the *ton* would be happy to offer for her, despite her lack of fortune.

But she needed to know *he* was a choice too—a real one—or he would be if—when!—he beat this blasted charge. He couldn't let her throw herself away on a wealthy windbag who saw her as something to add to his collection of beautiful things.

Since she refused to talk to him, he had no option but write to her and explain. He sat down at Gil's desk, selected a fresh sheet of writing paper, sharpened a quill, dipped it in ink and began to write.

Dear Miss Chance,

Forgive this mode of—

No, don't start by groveling. Bad idea. He tossed that aside and started again.

Dear Miss Chance,

Since it is impossible to communicate with you any other way—

Oh, yes, perfect way to start if you want get her back up. Idiot. He screwed it up and selected another sheet of notepaper.

Dear Miss Chance,

I do not blame you for avoiding me—

Not true, he did blame her. It was infuriating. He started again.

Dear Miss Chance,

There are several matters I wish to draw to your attention—

Now he sounded like a clerk, writing to her about drains or something.

Dear Miss Chance,

Please, give me a chance to explain. There are matters—

Oh, good, now he was back to groveling. A groveling drains clerk.

Dear Miss Chance,

I am in trouble, but—

No, it sounded like a begging letter. He wasn't after her pity. In the end he penned her a brief and straightforward message:

Dear Miss Chance,

My situation has changed and I must talk to you. As you may have already guessed, I am not in fact a gypsy, but a well-born Englishman of distinguished lineage. I wish to apologize for the deception, and explain my reasons for it. I ask for nothing but a few minutes of your time. Please meet me in the square opposite your home.

Yours, very sincerely
Zachary Black.

He had the letter delivered by hand and waited in the square. A light, slow drizzle started. Zach adjusted the angle of his hat and pulled up the collar of his coat, and waited. He knew she was home—he'd seen her glance out of the bay window a short time after his note had been delivered.

The drizzle settled in. Zach didn't care about the rain; she knew he was out here, and he was going to make his point, rain or not. Actually he didn't mind the rain at all; it underlined his point.

He'd waited about twenty minutes before William emerged from the house bearing an umbrella. He marched straight up to Zach with a grin from ear to ear. "With Miss Jane's compliments," he said, and tossed Zach a handful of paper torn into tiny bits. They fluttered to the ground like blossoms. "Get the message, gypsy?"

Zach did. He looked down at the sodden remnants of his note. The ink was spreading on the tiny pieces of paper in slow blots, like moldy blight on blossoms. Had she even read it?

He glanced back at the bay window. There was no sign of her now, but he knew she'd be watching.

He swept off his hat and stood, bareheaded in the rain for a moment, then made her an elegant bow. He thought he saw a movement inside. He smiled as a fresh idea occurred to him.

"Don't you get it yet, gypsy?" William said. "No use lookin' over there. It's good-bye and good riddance to you."

Zach laughed. "Do you know, William, I think you might just have tempted fate."

Chapter Eighteen

All the privilege I claim for my own sex ... is that of
loving longest, when existence or when hope is gone.

—JANE AUSTEN, *PERSUASION*

The fool! What was he doing standing in the rain? Jane stood well back from the bay window and glared at the arrogant figure standing so tall and careless in the square opposite, seemingly indifferent to the rain.

He took off his hat—no, swept it off—and the rain soaked into his thick, dark hair. Even from here she could see it curling a little, clinging to his forehead in dark clumps, looking like a victor's olive leaf crown.

He looked straight at her, as if he could see her standing there, and he couldn't, she was sure he couldn't—and then he bowed with such grace and style she wanted to hit him.

He smiled . . . and a warm shiver rippled through her.

She folded her arms crossly and tried to ignore the spreading warmth inside her. He was too good-looking and confident for his own good. Certainly for her good.

She would not see him. Under any circumstances.

How dare he come back! She hadn't seen him for days. Nearly a week. She'd thought herself safe, at last. She hadn't missed him at all. Not a bit. Not in the least. Had hardly even thought of him. Much. In any case, thoughts didn't count. And what she'd been thinking was relief. Yes, relief.

It was the dreams that were the problem. She could control her thoughts—to a point—but in dreams, she had no control at all.

In the past couple of nights, Daisy had had to wake her several times, saying, "Another nightmare, lovie?"

And Jane, hot and sweaty and all twisted up in her nightgown, had agreed.

But they weren't nightmares, so much as . . . enticements. Like the fairy tales of old where some beautiful, magical being enticed away an otherwise sensible girl . . . and she was never seen again.

Her eyes dwelt on the tall figure standing in the rain, bareheaded and imperious, acting as if he owned the place, as if the rain couldn't touch him, as if she had no choice but to see him. He was getting soaked, the fool. Why wouldn't he leave?

He couldn't possibly see her from here.

That faint, entrancing smile . . .

She understood now why Mama had fallen for Papa and run off with him. It was a kind of madness. Irresistible. She shivered again.

Perfectly resistible, she told herself firmly, when you knew the consequences of such imprudence. Had Mama and Papa known how their great love story had ended, they'd never have run off together.

Though they'd never once seemed to regret it—only their circumstances. But the one had led to the other. Had they thought it was worth it? Abby claimed they'd been very happy, almost until the last, when Mama got sick and Papa got desperate. But Abby thought love mattered before everything.

Jane squashed that thought. Love was a choice and Jane had made her choice and a very good, sensible one it was; she would marry Lord Cambury and she would not even think of a tall, impossibly handsome, wholly untrustworthy gypsy.

A well-born Englishman of distinguished lineage.

She snorted. He changed his story as often as he changed his coat. What would he claim next—that he was a long-lost prince in disguise?

Well, she wouldn't stand around all day watching an irritating man getting drenched for no purpose. She smoothed down her pelisse and checked her hair in the looking glass. She was dressed to go out. Abby would be here shortly, to collect her in the carriage. They were going to make a call on Lady Dalrymple. Their first.

Jane hoped it wouldn't be their last. It had taken all Jane's powers of persuasion to get Abby to come with her this time. Now, it all rested with Lady Dalrymple and what she had to say for herself.

Mama's mother. What would she be like? Jane was excited and nervous, eager and anxious, all at the same time.

She glanced out of the window, but the square was deserted; no sign of any tall, dark man standing bareheaded in the rain. He'd gone.

Good. She hoped he'd finally got the message.

Foolish man. He'd probably catch his death of cold. Serve him right.

Lady Dalrymple lived in Green Street. Jane had sent a note ahead, asking whether it would be convenient for her sister and her to call. Lady Dalrymple had sent an instant response, inviting them to take tea with her that very afternoon.

The carriage swished through the damp streets. Abby sat stiffly, clutching her reticule, pale and resolute. Despite her presence, she was far from accepting a reconciliation. "I will accompany you and hear what she has to say," was all she would promise Jane.

Jane was grateful for her presence. She didn't know what to expect, but she was hopeful, at least.

Abby slipped her hand into Jane's. "Don't expect too much of her, love. She's hurt us enough already."

Jane nodded. "It's all right, Abby. I'm prepared."

Abby gave her a rueful smile. "No, you're not. You're too softhearted for your own good."

The carriage pulled up in front of a small, pretty house, and the driver pulled down the steps for them, holding a large umbrella. The front door opened before they could reach the doorbell, and a butler ushered them into a small, elegant parlor.

Lady Dalrymple rose to greet them. Fashionably dressed in lilac silk, she was small and plump, with a soft, pretty face, gently wrinkled about the mouth and eyes, and light tawny-fair hair attractively streaked with silver. Her eyes were blue, the same color as Jane's.

In forty years' time, Jane thought dazedly, I will look a lot like this.

"Oh, my dears, my *dears*," Lady Dalrymple exclaimed breathlessly, hurrying toward them. "I thought this moment would *never* come and I'd go to my grave not knowing—oh! let me look at you!—Jane, the *image* of my darling Sarah—oh! I cannot believe it—my dearest, dearest girl—and Abigail"—she turned to Abby—"Oh, my dear, so very like your papa and with *just* that same look he used to get, the poor boy! But let us not be morbid on this happy, happy occasion!" And apparently oblivious of the tears pouring down her soft, plump, lightly powdered cheeks, she embraced them, first Jane, then Abby, still talking all the while.

Quite stunned and not a little overwhelmed by the effusiveness of the greeting, Jane glanced at Abby, currently standing stiffly in Lady Dalrymple's embrace, to see how she was taking it.

The expression on Abby's face was . . . strange. Jane had no idea how to interpret it.

"Oh, listen to me, babbling on like a perfect *lunatic*—but you must forgive an old lady's emotion—it's not every day one meets one's long-lost granddaughters—oh, and look! I've made you all damp." And unself-consciously she produced a dainty lace-edged handkerchief and proceeded to wipe her tears off Abby's cheeks.

Abby looked half frozen, half panicked. Neither she nor Jane had uttered a word yet; they hadn't had a chance.

Lady Dalrymple continued, "There now, that's better. Oh, what am I thinking? Sit down, my darlings, sit down here with me and let me look at you. And Jarvis will bring in tea and a little something to eat." Clutching them each by the hand, she tugged them down onto a *chaise longue*, one on each side of her. "Oh, my Sarah's daughters, oh!" And the tears came again. "*Tsk, tsk*, look at me, such a sight I must present and I had *such* good intentions for this meeting." She mopped at her face with the soaked handkerchief. "But so happy, my darlings, so happy." She gave Jane a wondering look. "I cannot believe it, here you are, looking just *exactly* like my poor darling Sarah before I lost her, as if more than twenty-five years had not passed. We were very much alike in so many ways. I was once as pretty as Jane here, though you would never know it, to see me now."

Abby's eyes met Jane's. "*Lost* her?" Abby repeated in a flinty voice. Jane could see she was struggling for composure.

Lady Dalrymple looked at Abby and her face crumpled. "Oh, my poor darling child—those letters you wrote—I vow, I never wept half so much in my *life* when I read them. You brave, miraculous, wonderful child, how*ever* did you manage? It quite broke my heart, reading them." She embraced Abby again.

Abby endured it rigidly. Her eyes met Jane's.

At this inopportune point the butler entered, followed by two footmen who brought in a tray containing two teapots, cups, saucers, a milk jug, slices of lemon and sugar and a large three-tiered plate containing a truly staggering variety of cakes, biscuits and cream-filled pastries. The butler also brought a small stack of neatly pressed lace-edged handkerchiefs that he silently placed in front of his mistress.

The girls waited in polite silence as they were served with tea and invited to eat. Jane, having a sweet tooth, selected a delicious-looking cream pastry, and Abby, when pressed, reluctantly accepted an almond cat's tongue. She was looking rather pale, Jane thought.

As soon as the servants had departed, Abby set down her cup and plate, untouched. Jane said quickly, "So you read Abby's letters."

"Yes, I found them in my husband's—your grandfather's—desk after he died. The ones from Sarah herself and your poor, dear papa, as well as Abby's. They *utterly* broke my heart. I never knew where my Sarah was, you see, never even knew she *had* children." She put her cup and plate aside and blew her nose fiercely. She looked at Abby's face. "Oh, my dear, you didn't think—you *did*! I can tell."

She took Abby's hands in hers and said urgently, "I read those letters for the *first* time just a year ago, some weeks—well, probably several months after George—your grandfather—died. If you only *knew* how I regretted not doing it the day he died!" She wadded her handkerchief. "I had *no* idea they were there, you see—he'd *never* told me, and I'd never so much as *touched* his desk—he was always dreadfully fussy and meticulous about that—and so it wasn't until he'd died and I had to clear out all his papers and then . . ." She shook her head. "And by the time I got to that horrid Pillbury place, you'd left it, Jane."

Jane's eyes widened. "You went to the Pillbury Home? Looking for me?"

"Of course I did. For both of you, but Abby was long gone, and you'd already departed for Hertfordshire, only the woman—Bodwin, Bedwyn?"

"Mrs. Bodkin."

"Yes, she said you'd disappeared on the way—some very confusing story, but in the end she said you'd gone to your sister in London." She turned to Abby. "So of course I went there but those frightful people you were working for—"

"The Masons?" Abby said, shocked.

"Yes, *ghastly* parvenues—you poor *darling*, having to work for *such* people—the wife was *frightful*, simply frightful!—and of course, when I discovered they'd dismissed you *without a character*—my granddaughter!—just a few short weeks before!" The bright blue eyes sparkled with indignation for a moment, then she slumped and heaved a gusty sigh. "But you'd gone, and nobody knew where. I even hired a man to look for you, but . . ." She shook her head. "I thought I'd found my Sarah's daughters, but instead I'd lost you again." And more tears rolled down her cheeks.

There was a long silence, then Abby said in a queer, frozen voice, "You didn't even know about us until last year?"

"No, not until your grandfather died. And when I found those letters, I could have *killed* him again! How could he keep it from me, knowing how all these years I've fretted and worried and grieved for my daughter. But George was always a cold, proud, hard man—and stubborn. He never admitted he might have been wrong, when *anyone* could have seen how much those two loved each other."

She saw Abby's expression. "If I'd had the *least* idea where my daughter was, I would have come for her and brought her—brought all of you!—home where you belonged! When I discovered what had happened—your papa—such a handsome, impetuous boy— and that my Sarah died in such a way—" She broke off, emotion choking her.

Jane and Abby exchanged a long, silent look. Abby's eyes were wet with tears, as were Jane's.

It was the explanation they'd craved, the answer to the questions that had haunted them so long.

Lady Dalrymple wiped her eyes and blew her nose again and sat up with fresh resolve. "Now, enough of this weeping—truly, I am not generally such a watering pot—so tell me *all* about yourselves. I want to know *everything*. I want to know why you girls call yourselves Chance and not Chantry, I want to know what your connection is with Lady Davenham—old Lady Davenham, Beatrice, I mean, and of course I am *dying* to know how Abby went from being a governess to those *ghastly* cits one minute and married to the fabulously wealthy—and handsome!—Max Davenham the next—and clever, clever Jane for making the catch of the season—*Cambury*, no less—what a pity he's losing his hair, but never mind, what are hats for?—and I *must* hear all about how that came to be—the betrothal, not the baldness, poor boy—but first Abby, as she is the elder." She looked expectantly at Abby.

Abby stared at her for a long moment, then she gave a shaky laugh. "You sound just like Mama," she choked. "Exactly. If I closed my eyes, and listened to you, I would think she was here with us." And her face crumpled.

"She is, my darling girl, of course she's here with us," Lady Dalrymple said, hugging her. "Where else would she be but with those who loved her best?"

And then they were all three of them in tears.

A short time later, declaring she needed something *much* stronger than tea, Lady Dalrymple dispatched her butler to fetch sherry, and also more handkerchiefs. "Though the way we're going, my dears, we'll need one the size of a tablecloth! Still, there's nothing like a good cry, is there, for making one feel better?"

"I'm still amazed that you went all the way to Cheltenham, to the Pill," Jane said. "And all for nothing."

"Oh, it wasn't for nothing," Lady Dalrymple told her. "I got to hear all about my granddaughters from the woman in charge. Bodkin—was it?—had nothing but praise for you girls."

"Really?" Jane said. Abby, yes, but she doubted that Bodkin would be singing Jane's praises. She'd never had the impression Mrs. Bodkin had any time for her at all.

"Oh, yes, I heard all about what a clever and responsible girl you were, Abby, and how she'd tried to have you kept on as a teacher after you turned eighteen—"

"She tried to keep me on?" Abby said in surprise.

"Yes, for Jane's sake, and because you were such an excellent teacher. Only the governors—foolish men—wouldn't allow it. And you, Jane"—she turned to Jane—"she told me how wonderful you were with the little ones and said it was *such* a shame you couldn't be a governess too, only with your looks it would be *asking* for trouble, and I *quite* see now why she had to send you instead to be the companion to an old lady, depressing as that must have seemed." She wrinkled a nose. "A *vicar's* mother."

"I thought she thought I wasn't clever enough," Jane said.

"No, too pretty and too softhearted, she said. Abby, she said, had more grit to her."

"Grit?" Abby said, half laughing. "She meant I had no looks to speak of."

"Nonsense. She said you had grit and brains." She eyed Abby indignantly. "And it's positively *wicked* to say you have no looks at all—you have the kind of distinguished elegance that will only increase as you age. You get that from your father's side, though there was an expression in your eyes earlier that also reminded me of my late husband. He was also very distinguished-looking." She sighed. "Also proud, stubborn, hardheaded and rigid—quite abominably rigid. When I think of those letters and how, if only I'd found them earlier . . ."

Jane laid her hand over Lady Dalrymple's small plump one. "Let's not dwell on the past too much."

Her grandmother nodded. "You're right, my dear. Regrets are so dismal, and quite useless. You can't change the past. Now tell me, how is your season progressing? That dress you were wearing the night I first saw you—such a divine creation! I *must* know, who is your dressmaker?"

They stayed, talking and laughing, with only the occasional tear, all afternoon. There were still many things they hadn't told her—why Jane hadn't gone to Hereford, for a start, and where they'd met Daisy and Damaris, nor that Abby was going to make her a great-grandmother—but there was time for all that in the future.

Before they left, Lady Dalrymple invited Jane to make her home with her.

Very gently, Jane refused. "Lady Beatrice has done so much for us—we owe her everything. I could not abandon her now."

Lady Dalrymple sighed. "No, I suppose not."

"But I will come and visit you often," Jane promised, seeing the disappointment on the old lady's face. "You don't think you're going to get out of being a grandmother, do you? We have *years* to make up for."

"Oh, you dear, sweet child." Lady Dalrymple groped for another handkerchief.

As the two sisters drove home, Abby said, "Thank you for making me come, little sister. I wouldn't have missed that for the world."

"We have a grandmother." Jane hugged her. "Does she really sound so much like Mama?"

Abby nodded. "It's uncanny—her voice, the melodic pitch of it, the cadence—and the way she rattles on, skipping from one subject to another." She laughed. "Whenever Mama did that, Papa used to tease her about it and say she was *just* like her mother."

Jane smiled and leaned her head on Abby's shoulder. "You've forgiven her?"

Abby nodded. "Impossible not to, really."

"She must have just missed us, you know. By a week or two."

"I know." They were silent a moment, trying to imagine what their lives would have been like if Lady Dalrymple had found Jane at the Pill, and rescued Abby from the Mason household.

"I'm not sorry," Jane said, just as Abby said, "I don't regret it in the least." They both laughed.

"I can't imagine not having Damaris and Daisy and Lady Beatrice in our lives," Jane said.

"No, and I would never have met Max," Abby said softly, placing a hand over the slight swell of her abdomen. "We might have started off in a dreadful place, but it's all worked out perfectly for us, hasn't it, Jane?"

Jane forced her mind away from thoughts of a tall, dark figure with compelling silvery eyes. "Perfectly," she echoed. It sounded a little hollow.

Abby glanced at her. "Are you all right?"

Jane nodded. "Just a little tired after all that emotion. Thank goodness the masquerade ball is tomorrow night. I barely have enough energy to climb into bed tonight."

* * *

"You look delightful!" Jane was going to the masquerade ball as a shepherdess, wearing a gown of pale blue silk, looped up in several places around the hem to reveal a froth of white petticoats beneath. It was an old dress of Lady Beatrice's cut down, much to the old lady's outrage.

"You'd have the gel wear an old dress of mine? To the masquerade of the season? Where everybody who's anybody will be there to see her?"

But Daisy was adamant. "I'm not goin' to cut into new fabric on something that's only going to be thrown away afterwards. And this'll do fine and will save me time as well as money." Lady Beatrice, Damaris and Abby had made their own arrangements for their costumes—Damaris and Abby were keeping them a secret—but Daisy was determined she would make every single outfit Jane would wear for the season. Or bust!

Jane was getting worried it might indeed be bust, but she didn't say so. This was Daisy's dream, after all.

"Save you *money*?" Lady Beatrice was appalled at the notion.

But Jane and Abby had spent their entire lives wearing other people's cut-down clothing, and they understood the need for economy, particularly the economy of time. "I agree with Daisy," Jane said. "I'll only ever wear it once, and besides, it's going to look delightfully old-fashioned, and so pretty."

"And no shepherdess would wear the latest fashion, would they?" Abby added.

The old lady sniffed. "No shepherdess would ever wear hoops either."

"And shepherdesses wear silk, do they?" Daisy said. "Fancy that."

Lady Bea lifted her lorgnette and gave her a beady look. "Wretched gel, would you have Jane dress in *rags*? For the sake of *authenticity*?" She pronounced the word with delicate disdain.

Daisy laughed. "Just sayin'. And there won't be no—yeah, I know—won't be *any* hoops needed when I'm finished with it."

"I suppose she can be one of Marie Antoinette's shepherdesses," Lady Beatrice conceded begrudgingly. "She and her ladies used to play at being shepherdesses and milkmaids and such, poor deluded creatures."

So the dress was altered, and was pronounced to be satisfactory by all concerned, except for one feature. "How will people know she's supposed to be a shepherdess?" Daisy wondered. "She don't look like no shepherdess I ever seen."

"*Doesn't*, *any* and *saw*," Lady Beatrice corrected her absently.

"We could find a sweet little lamb at one of the markets," Jane suggested.

"Nonsense! You'd get attached to the dratted animal, forget its purpose in life is to be dinner, and next thing you know, we'd have a silly great sheep blundering around the house," Lady Bea said severely. "Besides, one does not take livestock to a ball, Jane, not even a masquerade ball. It's simply *not done*."

In the end, the required effect was achieved by Damaris cutting out sweet little lamb shapes from white felt that Jane sewed around the hem of her dress. A shepherd's crook painted white and tied with a blue ribbon, a white velvet mask trimmed with lace and a pretty little straw hat *a la bergère* put the final touch to Jane's outfit, and she left for the masquerade ball feeling very satisfied with her appearance.

Jane, Lady Beatrice, Abby and Max rode together in the carriage, Lady Beatrice magnificent as Good Queen Bess in gold and purple brocade and a splendid ruff and Abby dressed as a mermaid, with a green sequined mask and a green sequined tail peeping from beneath her frothy green skirts and hooked up in a convenient loop over her arm.

Max was nominally dressed as King Neptune, with a trident—nominally because other than the trident, and a black velvet mask, he was otherwise dressed in his usual formal black knee breeches and coat. Over them he wore a midnight green domino, which, he informed them, represented the sea. "I'm not much of a one for costumes," he said as he climbed into the carriage.

"I never would have guessed," his loving aunt told him.

At the entrance to the ballroom, Jane paused a moment, drinking in the sight. Hundreds of candles burned in the chandeliers overhead, their tiny flames reflected and magnified through the myriad of crystals that hung from them, making the scene below shimmer and dance.

Before them was a sea of fantastical and exotic creatures—
Egyptian queens, milkmaids, winged fairies, harlequins, Greek
and Roman gods and goddesses, and more. Of course, not everyone had worn a costume; many had simply worn a domino over
their usual formal dress and donned a mask. The masks ranged
from the simple strips of black velvet worn by a number of
gentlemen to elegant and intricate confections worn by the ladies.

"Oh, I wish Daisy could see this," Jane said.

"She could have come—I did arrange for her to attend—but
she's a stubborn wench," Lady Beatrice commented. "Said she
needed to work. Work!" She sniffed. "Gel works too dratted
much if you ask me."

Jane didn't say anything. Daisy was working flat out, she
knew, but it wasn't the only reason she refused to come. Daisy
was very good at not letting herself want what she knew she
couldn't have. Unlike Jane.

Sometimes, a taste of something was worse than nothing at
all. If you didn't know about something, you couldn't crave it.

Like Zachary Black.

If she'd never met him, never felt the touch of his hand,
never gazed into those gleaming silvery eyes . . . No. She wasn't
thinking about him.

"I can see several milkmaids, but not a single shepherdess,"
Abby said, gazing out over the shifting throng.

"Certainly none with a flock of sheep conveniently attached,"
said Lady Beatrice caustically.

"Oh, look," Jane said. "There's Damaris and Freddy—and
they've gone all Chinese. Don't they look wonderful?" She
waved, and Damaris waved back. She was gorgeously attired
in an exotic-looking Chinese-style dress and Freddy was
dressed as a Mandarin with a long, droopy mustache and a
sumptuously embroidered Chinese robe.

Abby said, "And is that—yes, it's Mr. Flynn dressed as . . ."
She gave Flynn a long, thoughtful glance. "Would you say he's
dressed as a pirate? The gold earring and the black head scarf
with the skull and crossbones seems to indicate it, but I must
say his attire is very . . . colorful. Though I suppose he of all
people would know how pirates really do dress. It's probably
quite authentic."

Lady Beatrice gave her a blistering glance. "Authenticity

again, is it?" She sniffed. "A masquerade ball is about fantasy, not authenticity."

Flynn, seeing them, gave a rakish bow. He was dressed in tight red pants, thigh-high black boots, a violently multicolored waistcoat, a white shirt and a purple and gold brocade coat. He wore a cutlass thrust through his black leather belt.

"A fine figure of a man, Mr. Flynn, though I hope that cutlass is fake," Lady Beatrice commented, watching him make his way toward them through the throng. "Check before you accept a dance with him, gels. If your dresses catch on it, they'll be ribbons in no time. Men never think of such things."

Flynn wasn't the only one who'd noticed their arrival. A number of other young single gentlemen were hastening toward them. "Well, well, Jane's arrival has been noted. Here come your dance partners, gels."

Lord Cambury, who arrived dressed as Julius Caesar, in white robes and an olive wreath, had claimed his dances the day before—the first waltz of the evening and the dance before the supper dance, which was a country dance—and Jane had already written his name on her card. Now a crowd of other gentlemen pressed forward and in minutes every dance had been claimed, mostly by men she didn't recognize, who wrote things like *Henry VIII*, *Lucifer* or *Apollo* on her card.

The next few hours passed for Jane in a happy whirl of laughter and dancing. Lord Cambury had danced his two dances and taken her to supper, then disappeared into the card room to play piquet until the unmasking, leaving Jane to dance to her heart's content. Which she did.

The masks encouraged gentlemen to flirt ridiculously—leering extravagantly at her sewn-on sheep, and saying things like they wished they'd come as the big bad wolf. Most of them were boys not much older than Jane and not to be taken seriously. And because she wasn't Miss Jane Chance tonight, but a simple shepherdess, Jane found herself able to flirt back quite unselfconsciously. It was all the most delightful fun.

Chapter Nineteen

Piracy is our only option.

—JANE AUSTEN, *SENSE AND SENSIBILITY*

It was the last waltz before the unmasking. A shadow fell across her. Jane glanced up and there stood a tall, dark stranger, a pirate by his dress. His eyes glittered through the slits of his mask, not a proper mask, just a ragged strip of black velvet that covered half his face.

She tensed. There was something about him . . . the way he stood there, the shape of him . . . the way he held himself.

His breeches were black and tight and hugged his long, powerful thighs faithfully.

Jane wanted to look away. She couldn't.

His boots were high and black and reached to mid-thigh. A bold red sash cinched his lean waist. Beneath a black leather waistcoat, his shirt was loose, white and flowing, and laced carelessly almost to the throat. Almost. Shockingly, it lay open at the neck.

She could see the faint beat of a pulse in his throat. His naked throat. Tanned and strong-looking and masculine.

She swallowed. It couldn't possibly be him. He would not dare, surely . . .

All she could see of his face—apart from those intense, unreadable eyes—was a clean-shaven jaw, and a square, chiseled, freshly shaven chin. She'd never seen him shaved, but still, she was sure it was him.

His mouth was stern, unsmiling, beautiful—and where did that thought come from, she wondered feverishly.

"My dance, I believe." His voice was low and deep and came straight from her darkest, most turbulent dreams. Zachary Black.

"What are you doing here?" she hissed.

"I came to dance with you, of course—what did you think?" The devil danced in his eyes. White teeth gleamed briefly beneath the mask. "I told you it wasn't good-bye."

"Don't be ridiculous. This is a private ball—a very exclusive private ball! You cannot be here!"

"And yet I am." He gave her that slow, lazy smile.

Zachary Black the gypsy was a handsome, intriguing ruffian, but this man . . . this man was beautiful in his lithe piratical arrogance. She forced herself to concentrate. "You should not be here. You are trespassing. And I am already engaged to dance this waltz."

"Yes, with me."

She checked her dance card. "No, it says 'Radcliffe,' and I know Mr. Radcliffe and you are not he!"

"I'm here in his place." Through the slits in the mask, his eyes gleamed. Did he think it was amusing to be here, an impostor, dressed as a pirate? If anyone realized that a gypsy had somehow managed to gain entrance, there would be a fearful scandal. And Zachary Black would be—she wasn't sure what would happen—a beating, arrest, some kind of trouble anyway.

"This is a private ball. Invitation only. How did you get in?"

He smiled, a flash of white, wolfish beneath the velvet mask. "Purloined one."

"You mean you *stole* an invitation?"

His eyes gleamed through the raffish velvet mask. "Pirate, remember?"

"But why would you do such a mad, risky thing? If you're discovered—"

"Stop worrying."

The orchestra played the opening bars of a waltz and he stepped closer, and reached out lazily. She took a hasty step backward. "No, go away. You must leave. My partner will be here any minute."

He took her hand and swung her out onto the dance floor.

"Stop it! Mr. Radcliffe—"

"Isn't here. I am." His arm was an iron bar encircling her waist, and before she knew it, she was twirling around the dance floor. Being held scandalously close.

She would have to dance with him. She had no choice. She couldn't escape him without making an embarrassing public scene.

He drew her even closer. She could feel the heat of his body, his tall, powerful body, smell the faint tang of his masculine cologne.

"Don't think about the future," he murmured. "Don't think about anything. Just close your eyes and give yourself up to the music."

And to the man. The temptation was irresistible. It was just one dance. A few moments where she could indulge her fantasies. A harmless dance in public. What could it matter? Jane stopped fighting him—and herself—closed her eyes and let him twirl her around the dance floor.

In his arms, she danced in a way she'd never experienced before. She didn't have to think, to remember her steps, just obey the silent, delicious command of this masterful, infuriating, insanely audacious man.

Delicious? She batted the thought away. But oh Lord, he could dance.

So this was what the waltz was all about. It was not at all like her lessons; this was like floating, like a leaf being swept into a swirling wind and whisked off to . . . who knew where.

A dance of pure, magical enticement . . .

The last strains of the waltz faded away.

Jane stood in Zachary Black's embrace, his arm wrapped around her waist much closer than was proper, her hand firmly enclosed in his. She was breathing fast, and not just from the exertion of the dance. Her heart thudded madly in her chest; her mouth was dry.

The dance was over. She wanted to lean against him, to keep her eyes closed and press her cheek against his broad chest and just pretend, for a few more minutes. Her own private fantasy. Cinderella at the ball. She wanted it to go on forever, not caring who he was, who she was. To be just a man and a woman floating in a dream, a blissful dream she didn't want to wake up from.

But in the distance she could hear exclamations and laughter. The unmasking had begun.

Slowly, reluctantly she opened her eyes.

And looked straight into his, gleaming and intense through the slits of the ragged black velvet mask.

"It's time to unmask," she whispered. "People will see you. You have to go." She raised her hands to remove her mask, but he was there before her, his long fingers nimbly untying the strings of her mask and dropping it carelessly, all the time devouring her with his eyes.

She didn't move. She couldn't, couldn't bring herself to move an inch. It was all she could do to breathe.

He remained masked, his eyes glittering in the reflected light from the ballroom. A faint shiver thrilled across her skin as the night air cooled the skin that her mask had kept warm. With a small shock she realized they were outside, on a small balcony, one of several that led from the ballroom, overlooking the terrace a dozen steps below, and beyond that the garden.

A quick glance around revealed that they were alone. The French doors that led back into the ballroom were closed, and the balcony was small and made private by the darkness.

The *darkness*? When she'd arrived at the ball, the whole place—the terrace, the gardens and, of course, the ballroom—had been a blaze of light. The gaily colored lanterns that had been placed along the terrace and strung between the pillars had, in this one small balcony alcove, been extinguished.

Here, where she stood with Zachary Black, there were only shadows, made deeper by the brightness outside. Nobody could see them.

The situation shocked her back to reality. She was no longer an anonymous simple shepherdess, free to flirt and dance and have fun, but Jane Chance, a girl with obligations. And expectations. And a betrothal.

And he was an impostor, here by stealth and dishonesty. There could yet be a scandal if he were found out.

He must have prepared this earlier: extinguished the lanterns, planned every move. It was a scandal waiting to happen.

His presence—his uninvited presence—could compromise her badly. She needed to return at once to the main ballroom.

"You have to leave," she repeated. "It's dangerous to be here. If you're found . . ." There would be unpleasant consequences for both of them.

He made no move. "I came here to talk to you, as well as dance," he told her. "You wouldn't meet me in the park, wouldn't respond to my note—did you read it?"

"Yes." She glanced at the doors back to the ballroom. She was getting anxious. Lord Cambury would be looking for her. "I have to go." She moved toward the door. He stepped in her way, blocking her escape with his big, strong body. "So you know I am a gentleman, but there are other things I need to explain—"

"I said, I have to go!" She tried to push past him but he caught her by the arm and pulled her back.

"I came here tonight to talk to you." And in a low, rapid voice he explained that he was a gentleman with a large estate and a fortune—"not as large as Cambury's but substantial enough." He told her that he'd been away for twelve years, that he'd left England as a boy of sixteen, and had only just returned the day he met her. He explained that while he'd been abroad, he'd been working in various locations, gathering intelligence for His Majesty's government, that he'd become skilled at deception.

As he talked, her temper slowly mounted. To think she'd been having dreams about this man! How could she have let herself fall for this . . . this *charlatan*?

At the end of the recital, he paused. "I suppose you're wondering why I continued to give the impression I was a gypsy."

When she didn't respond, he went on, "I am on the verge of claiming back my inheritance, but there is a . . . an obstacle, a legal impediment—all nonsense really, but I was advised to lie low until the matter was sorted out, and not use my correct name or my title. It's rather delicate and I would ask for your discretion—"

"No need, because I don't want to hear it. And you want to know why?" She tossed her head. " *'Tinker, tailor, soldier, sailor, rich man, poor man, beggar man, thief'*—how many of those are you, Mr. Zachary Black? First you say you're a gypsy, then a pirate, then a spy—and you stole your invitation tonight, so you're definitely a thief! And now you claim to be a *gentleman*? A gentleman with a *title*? A lord in hiding because of some mysterious *impediment* that requires you to dress as a gypsy?

"How gullible do you think I am? This is just another one of your wonderful tales." She snorted. "You're nothing but a big fat liar!" With each word she poked a finger into his broad, hard chest. "You seem to think life is nothing but a game, but my future is not a game to me! It's a very serious matter, and I'm not prepared to listen to any more of your lies, so let me pas—*mmph!*"

She found herself being ruthlessly kissed, pulled hard against him, wrapped in an iron-hard embrace.

She pushed against his shoulders, once, twice, trying to shove him away, but the taste of him, the intense, masculine onslaught of his mouth, ruthless and utterly dominating, slowly sapped her will. His tongue traced the seam of her lips, pressing between them and she gasped. Her mouth opened beneath his and he took possession, his dark, male taste flooding her senses.

Duty warred with desire, and desire won.

The longing for him, so long denied, swelled within her. Intoxicated by the flood of sensation, she gripped his shoulders tighter, pressing herself against him.

He moved, and she found herself sandwiched between a cold stone wall and a hot, hard man. Shivers rippled through her and her grip on him tightened. With a deep moan he settled his big, warm body over hers, pressing her firmly against the cold wall, dominating her effortlessly. Masterfully. Any desire to escape had evaporated long since.

She could taste the hot, hard need driving him. The intensity of it was almost frightening.

Almost. After the first shock of his possession, and as the smoky, dark taste of him entered her blood, she gloried in it, this ravening passion, this seething need for her, for Jane, for the thing inside her that leapt to life at his touch, causing this . . . this firestorm of need to rise within her.

She met him kiss for kiss, a desperate, demanding urgency released within her, driving her to want more, crave more—of him. He made a sound deep in his throat, a growl of hunger, and approval. She pressed herself against him, needing to get closer. His lips were firm and sure, his tongue as darkly velvet as his mask, as he stroked, enticed, aroused . . .

The kisses deepened. She clung on. There was a leashed

power in the way he explored her mouth, feathered kisses across her cheek, her eyelids, her throat, all the while returning to plunder her mouth in an insistent rhythm that called to something wild and primitive inside her.

She could feel the hunger in him, firmly controlled. She was ravenous; without knowing it, she'd craved this all her life. This. Him.

She slid her hand into the open neck of his shirt, the fine linen weave cool against her feverish fingers, and then the warmth, the heat of his skin. Man skin, so different from her own.

Man smell. She breathed in the scent of him, the scent of clean, fresh linen, and underneath the scent of man, a faint musky scent of desire, and some crisp-smelling cologne.

In thrall to his kisses, her hands learned him, the strong column of his throat, the clean, sharp jawline, the faint abrasion of a freshly shaven jaw. Her fingertips, her palms tingled with that delicious abrasion. Her frantic caresses dislodged his velvet mask; it drifted to the floor, unnoticed. She ran her fingers into his thick, dark hair, clean, soft and freshly cut. And all the time, kissing, kissing . . .

Blind with need, she arched and squirmed against him, wanting more. Her tongue tangled with his, she wanted to climb his body like a cat, and dig her way somehow deeper into him.

She didn't know how long she stood there, locked in his arms, given up wholly to the man and the moment, when a sound penetrated her blissful daze. The French doors to her left were rattling. Someone was calling her name.

Chapter Twenty

He shall not be in love with me, if I can prevent it.

—JANE AUSTEN, PRIDE AND PREJUDICE

Zachary Black muttered something rude under his breath and released her.

A faint chill swept over her. She sagged against the wall, her knees strangely spongy.

"Jane, Jane, are you out there?" Lord Cambury stood on the other side of the French doors, his face and hands pressed to the glass, trying to peer into the gloom of the balcony. He rattled the handles in frustration.

"Oh, God," she muttered.

"It's all right, the doors are locked," Zachary told her.

"You have to go."

For answer he gave her a hard, searing kiss. "This isn't over."

"It is. It must be. I'm betrothed." Though perhaps not for much longer. She'd been caught, kissing another man in a dark little balcony.

"To that?" He jerked his head at Lord Cambury rattling fruitlessly at the door.

His scorn stiffened her spine, and she recalled all that had happened before he'd scrambled her senses with his kiss. "Yes, to him. A man of honor. A man I gave my word to."

Cupping her face in his hands, he kissed her again, a hard, possessive branding of a kiss. "You belong to *me*." He leapt lightly over the balustrade onto the terrace below and disappeared into the garden, just as the French doors burst open and a footman staggered through.

Lord Cambury stepped out onto the balcony. "Blasted doors stuck." He waited until the footman had gone, then said, "What are you doing out here in the dark?"

Jane didn't answer. Guilt and embarrassment blasted the remnants of exhilaration. Suddenly her mad, magical adventure seemed a little . . . shameful. She'd made a promise to this man.

But she'd never imagined anything like the power of a kiss . . . those kisses.

She couldn't suppress a shiver. Lord Cambury noticed. "Night air dangerous to your health, don't you know?" He leaned over the stone balustrade and peered at the scene below. "Thought I saw a man with you here before. Couldn't make out his face." He turned and faced her sternly. "There was a man, wasn't there?"

She hung her head. "Yes."

"And you let the blasted fellow steal a kiss?"

She nodded. Though he hadn't stolen anything. She'd kissed him back with all her heart. And was still reeling from the shock of that.

"Who was he?"

"I don't know." She felt guilty not telling him, but what good would it do? Besides, Lord Cambury had threatened to have him beaten up, and she didn't want to be responsible for that. She would handle Zachary Black herself.

If she could. She hadn't exactly done much of a job so far; he'd been firmly in control the entire time. But forewarned was forearmed; she knew the real danger now, the seductive power he could exert over her. If she wasn't careful.

"Don't know?" His eyebrows gnashed together. "You let a man kiss you and you don't know his name? Somebody must have introduced you."

She nodded. "He claimed the dance in the name of Mr. Radcliffe, but I've met Mr. Radcliffe and it wasn't him."

"But you danced with this unknown fellow anyway?"

Again she nodded. It was a masquerade. She hadn't known

half the men she'd danced with. But at a private ball, that shouldn't matter.

He was silent a moment as he surveyed the balcony thoughtfully, noting the darkened lamps. "Did you arrange to meet him here?"

"No, of course not!" she said indignantly. "I know I shouldn't have come out on the balcony, but I didn't realize I was even here until it was too late. He . . . he tricked me."

"But you still let him kiss you."

She blushed but didn't answer. It was too private, too special and magical to . . . admit it, as if it were a crime. Or something sordid. She said, "I have no excuse for being alone with him. All I can say is that I didn't plan to, it just . . . happened."

"*Hmph!*" He regarded her sternly. "Going to have to do something about this. Can't have you going off with strange men at balls and letting them kiss you. Think we should call the banns immediately."

Her head came up in shock. "The banns?"

He nodded. "Bring the wedding forward. Make sure of you before it's too late."

"You mean you still want to marry me?"

He shrugged. "Women are faithless by nature, beautiful ones even worse. Not surprised other men want you. My job is to make sure I get to you first. After you've given me an heir, you can do what you like, as long as you're discreet about it. Until then, missy"—he gave her a hard look—"I protect what's mine."

It was a crossroads moment. Jane had a clear choice between Lord Cambury, who offered her everything she'd ever wanted—except love—and trust—and Zachary Black, about whom she knew nothing, who had a tale for every occasion—and who stirred her emotions like no man she'd ever known, or even dreamed of.

It was the choice her mother must have had.

Jane made the choice her mother did not. "Yes, of course, Lord Cambury, have the banns called, if that's what you think best."

He gave a nod of satisfaction, took Jane firmly by the arm and led her back into the ballroom.

She followed, dismayed by his pronouncement. Not about the banns—the sooner she was married, the safer she was from

Zachary Black. But the casual acceptance that she was a person of no honor, that after her first son he wouldn't care whom she went with, as long as she was discreet—that dismayed her greatly.

She'd imagined—naively, she realized now—that she and Lord Cambury would become closer, that they'd grow to love each other as so many couples did after they'd married almost as strangers.

He, however, seemed to have no such expectations. And the expectation he did have of her . . . that she would be faithless, that he *expected* her to tell lies and deceive him with other men. That she was like some *thing*, that other men would want to snatch—and that she would let them, unless he stopped her.

It made her feel somehow . . . dirty.

And all because she'd been caught kissing Zachary Black.

Which hadn't felt dirty at all. It had felt . . . sublime . . . exhilarating.

But it had been wrong. She had earned Lord Cambury's disapprobation.

The ball was coming to a close. Jane went through the motions of thanking her hostess, saying good-bye to various people, almost in a daze.

She couldn't wait to get to bed, to think about everything that had happened. She was confused, torn, deeply disturbed. And angry with Zachary Black for causing it all.

D aisy was asleep when Jane got home, but just as she was climbing into bed, a sleepy voice said, "How was it?"

Jane had no idea how to answer. Magical? Disastrous? Thrilling? She took the easy way out. "Lovely."

"Any other shepherdesses?"

"No. The costume got a lot of compliments. Some of the boys I danced with were so funny about Damaris's lambs, pretending to be big bad wolves. Really they were more like puppies."

"What about Abby and Damaris—what did they wear?"

Jane briefly described their costumes.

Daisy gave a huge yawn. "Nice. Anything interestin' happen?"

"Not really." Only her first kiss. Kisses. And a magical waltz with a . . . an unabashed scoundrel. Who kissed like a dream . . . Unleashing desires within her that she hadn't known existed.

He'd almost ruined her future with Lord Cambury.

And now the very thought of that same future was . . . disturbing. *My job is to make sure I get to you first—get to you!* As though she were a bitch in heat, put to breed.

But she knew that was the way of things, so why did the idea of it dismay her now? Because the banns were to be called? Because the wedding would be in less than a month?

She didn't know.

She felt a little selfish, not wanting to share the details of her adventure with Daisy, but too much had happened to talk about yet. She needed to be alone with her thoughts, to sort out what had happened, what she thought, what she wanted and what to do. It was all so horribly complicated.

It was at the same time precious and sordid, magical and banal.

As for those kisses . . . she wanted to keep them secret, like her own private treasure. Besides, she was afraid Daisy might crow that she'd been right.

Knowin' you, you'll find the most impossible, unsuitable bloke in the ton *and fall for 'im like a ton o' bricks.*

She wouldn't. She hadn't. It was just one dance. And a kiss, well, several kisses. One . . . incident. Which she would put behind her and never repeat.

Jane blew out the candle, lay down and pulled the covers up to her chin. She lay quietly for a few moments, pondering the events of the evening.

"Daisy," she said after a minute. "Is it wrong to kiss a man if you're betrothed to someone else?"

There was a surge of bedclothes as Daisy sat up. "You kissed a man? Who?" She didn't sound at all sleepy now.

Jane was thankful that the darkness hid her blush. "Oh, no one. I was just thinking. Wondering really. Because after I am married, of course, I won't kiss anyone except Lord Cambury." She couldn't really imagine it.

Daisy lay down again. "If it was me, I'd be gettin' in a bit of kissin' and cuddlin' while I could. I don't reckon Lord Cambury is the kiss and cuddle type."

"Why do you say that?"

"Dunno, really. Just a feelin'. Has he kissed you yet?"

"No. He's been everything that is proper."

"Well then." There was a short silence, then Daisy added, "I reckon if there's a feller you fancy and he wants to kiss you, I wouldn't be saying no, not until you have to. As long as it's just a kiss you're talkin' about, nothing serious."

But it wasn't "just" a kiss at all, Jane thought. There was nothing "just" about it. But she couldn't explain that. It was too precious, too personal, too private—too disturbing—to share. "Night, Daisy."

"Night, Jane." She snuggled down deep into her bed. She couldn't possibly sleep. She wanted to relive—no, *think* about that dance. And those kisses . . .

"And where did you get to last night?" Gil asked Zach over breakfast the next morning. "As if I didn't know by the haircut and shave. Out tomcatting, eh?"

"Far from it," Zach told him virtuously. "I was a complete gentleman." Then reflecting that it wasn't quite the case, he clarified, "I was distressingly celibate. And somewhat of a pirate." He speared another thick rasher of bacon. "English bacon, nothing like it."

Gil directed a skeptical glance at him. "Gentleman or pirate, you can hardly be both."

"You can at a masquerade."

Gil glanced at the mantelpiece, where his invitations and calling cards were jammed into the frame of his gloomy ancestor. "You unprincipled rogue. I might have wanted to attend that."

Zach reached for a piece of toast and buttered it lavishly. "Dear boy, you did attend it."

Gil's eyes narrowed. "I did, did I? And what mischief did I commit?"

"Mischief? Far from it. You waltzed—superbly, I might add—with a beautiful young shepherdess."

"And?" he prompted after a moment.

"And kissed her on the balcony—oh, don't look at me like that. She knew it wasn't you."

Gil poured himself another cup of coffee. "Did anyone see your face?"

Zach didn't dignify that with a response. He ate his toast.

Gil spooned marmalade onto his toast, spread it carefully, then cut the slice into neat fingers. "You're mad, you do know that, don't you?" he said mildly. "How you ever survived these last eight years is beyond me. You're determined to run your neck into a noose, all for a female who don't even—"

"Careful, Gil."

Gil surveyed him over his coffee cup. "Like that, is it?"

Zach took another piece of toast. He was still brooding. He'd spent all night thinking about it.

"She didn't believe me, Gil." Her scornful repudiation of his story had shocked him to the core. He'd told her the truth about himself—the first part anyway—and she thought him nothing but a charlatan. A liar. Playing games.

"I don't blame her." Gil sipped his coffee. "I blame the cat-skin waistcoat. No right-thinking, animal-loving girl would believe a thing you said after seeing you in that."

"Gil, this is serious!"

"I know. I'm enjoying it immensely. I don't think you've taken anything seriously in years. It's quite a promising development." He finished his coffee. "So what will you do now?"

Zach scowled. He'd spent a sleepless night, half the time trying to work out how he could have explained it better, so she would believe him, and half the time—well, most of it, reliving that kiss. He'd woken hard and aching and wanting.

"Think I'll go for a long, hard ride first—"

Gil gave a soft, knowing laugh.

Zach ignored him and continued, "Then I'm going to talk to the lawyer, see if I can question that idiot who said he couldn't find Cecily." And to make some arrangements for the payment and reemployment of the Wainfleet staff who'd been put out of work by his cousin's interference. It was his fault too, he acknowledged ruefully; their situation had been worsened by his tardiness in dealing with his father's estate.

He had a lot of making up to do.

"Cambury's had the banns called," Gil said the following morning at breakfast. "St. George's, Hanover Square. Word is, they'll be married by the end of the month."

"The banns? Damn him for an impatient blasted swine!" Zach clenched his fist. The bastard must have seen them kissing on the balcony after all. And was racing her to the altar before Zach could get her to change her mind.

"At least it's not a special license."

Zach frowned, deep in thought. He had to do something. He couldn't go on with her thinking he was amusing himself at her expense. He had to make her understand he was telling the truth, and that he was . . . that he wanted her. That he could offer her at least as much as Cambury, not quite as much wealth perhaps, and not a castle, but he wasn't a damned bore.

Just a *big fat liar.*

He made up his mind. "Doing anything special this afternoon, Gil?"

Gil's eyes narrowed. "Why?"

"I want you to get me into the old lady's house—don't look at me like that—I mean make a morning call. All nice and polite and aboveboard. It's the only way I can think of to talk to my girl."

"Why do you need me?"

"Because that butler and footman only know me as a gypsy and they won't let me set a foot inside, unless I'm accompanied by that respectable, well-known, gentleman about town, Gil Radcliffe, that's why."

Gil pulled a gloomy face. "All right, but you'll owe me."

Chapter Twenty-one

How hard it is in some cases to be believed!

And how impossible in others!

—JANE AUSTEN, *PRIDE AND PREJUDICE*

At five o'clock, Zach and Gil, elegantly dressed and looking perilously close to what Gil muttered were dashed pinks of the *ton*, called at the big white house in Berkeley Square.

The butler opened the door. Gil, standing in front of Zach, presented his card. "Gilbert Radcliffe and Mr. Zachary Black to see Lady Davenham—Lady Beatrice, that is—and Miss Chance."

The butler glanced at the card. "I'm sorry, gentlemen, but the ladies have gone out."

"Blast!" Zach muttered, causing the butler to frown and try to peer at Zach over Gil's shoulder.

"What dashed bad luck," Gil said, visibly cheering up. "Tell them we called, will you?" And he turned and gave Zach a little push toward the street.

"Of course! They'll be in the park at this hour," Zach said. "Come on, Gil, we'll run them to earth there."

Gil started at him. "Are you mad? Hyde Park? At the fashionable hour? When all the matchmaking mamas and their daughters are on the prowl?" He shuddered eloquently. "Thank you, but no."

"I need you, Gil."

Gil's eyes narrowed to slits. "Why? Anyone can enter Hyde Park—there's no butler there."

"You're acquainted with them, and I need you to introduce me—an introduction in public; she can't wriggle out of that."

There was a short silence.

"Be a good fellow, Gil, I've got to do something. She refuses to see me. She doesn't believe a word I tell her."

"Can you blame her?"

"No, but I have to try. Otherwise she'll marry that oaf."

"You mean that rich and titled, highly cultured gentleman of the *ton*?"

"He's a crashing, pretentious bore—you told me that yourself. He'll marry her for her beauty, not caring who she really is, and squash all the life and the joy out of her."

"It's her choice," Gil pointed out dryly.

"No it's not, not when there's another choice to be made."

"That choice being a man who might, just might end up at the end of a rope?"

"Dammit, you know I'm innocent. And in any case, I have to try. If I don't do something soon, by the time I get free of this mess, she'll be married and it will be too late. You've got to help me, Gil, you've got to."

"You do realize if you appear in public at the fashionable hour, you vastly increase the risk of someone recognizing you?"

"Too late to worry about all that now—besides, it'll all come out next week at the hearing. Though why on earth should they? For all intents and purposes, I've been dead for the last twelve years."

Gil sighed. "I don't see how it will help, but I suppose if I don't agree, you'll come up with some even madder ploy to see her—climb onto her balcony or some such thing."

"Good man!" Zach clapped him on the shoulder. "I don't hold your excessive caution against you, by the way—comes of sitting in an office all day scribbling notes. We men of action are used to taking risks."

"You men of action should just shut your mouth or I'll be off to my club and you'll be without your introduction."

Lady Beatrice and the girls were taking exercise in the park. It was a mild, sunny spring day, and all the *ton* was out promenading at this most fashionable hour of the afternoon, the ladies dressed in their most elegant walking gowns and gentle-men accompanying them dressed in the pink of fashion.

But Lady Beatrice was not happy. Her preferred form of exercise—as she had stated loud and clear on a number of occasions—was to ride graciously through the park in her lan-dau, bowing to other ladies, stopping to exchange greetings and small talk from time to time, perhaps taking up a couple of friends for a short ride while she caught up on the latest gossip. And, she pointed out repeatedly, all the time she was observing her surrounds and *breathing*. Breathing *a great deal*; the air in the park being well known to be *extremely* healthful.

But the girls had said no—they would ride there in the car-riage and then they would *all* walk.

Lady Beatrice's second favorite form of exercise—and the one she had argued strenuously in favor of today—was to be carried in a bath chair by a pair of hefty footmen.

"For seeing them sweat does me a *world* of good, my dears," she argued. "Truly it does."

But on this her nieces were adamant. The doctor had said Lady Beatrice needed to walk for her health, so walk she must.

And being unable to resist the combined forces of all her nieces, she did. With a very bad grace, for the ground was damp and the air was chilly. "And pray, what use is walking when the veriest bores can accost one with the greatest of ease? One has to run, positively run, to avoid them!"

"Do yer good to run," Daisy pointed out, and received a withering glare in response.

Lady Beatrice spotted an old friend, Sir Oswald Merridew, and waved. The sprightly old gentleman hurried over. "Now run along, gels, and leave Sir Oswald and me to chat," she ordered them, and the girls drifted off.

"There she is." Zach indicated Jane, strolling with several other young women and the old lady he'd seen once before: Lady Beatrice. As he and Gil watched, the girls broke into pairs and, arm in arm, strolled away, leaving the old lady talking to a nattily dressed elderly gentleman.

Zach and Gil followed Jane. Gil informed him she was walking with her sister, Lady Davenham.

"Ah, so that's Abby," Zach said. Jane had spoken of her sisters. They didn't look much alike.

As Zach and Gil approached, Jane glanced back and saw them coming. She stiffened, said something to her sister and the two marched quickly away.

Zach and Gil followed.

But every time they drew near, Jane and her sister hurried away.

"Enjoying this a lot more than I thought I would," Gil confided as the girls marched off for the fourth time, almost running this time. "Quite puts me in the mood for hunting season. Why don't you take a flying tackle, bring her down in the mud? Or perhaps I should send for my hunter and some hounds and you can run her to ground that way."

"Delighted to provide you with some amusement," Zach muttered.

It was no use. He couldn't very well chase her all over the park. There had to be another way. He glanced back at the old lady. With that stick, she wouldn't be doing any running away.

"Introduce me to Lady Beatrice," he told Gil.

"Very well, but watch yourself, she's cannier than she looks."

Zach snorted. "I can handle an old lady."

"She's with Sir Oswald Merridew. Knows everyone, Sir Oswald. Knew your father quite well."

Zach nodded. "Better wait until he's moved on, just in case."

It took a few moments, but when Lady Beatrice was approached by a couple of fashionable ladies, Sir Oswald, with an elegant bow, moved off. Zach and Gil reached the old lady just as the ladies were drifting on to their next encounter. It was what the fashionable hour in Hyde Park was all about—seeing, being seen, chatting and moving on.

"Good afternoon, Lady Beatrice," Gil said. "You're looking wonderfully well."

She lifted a lorgnette and scrutinized them one after the other, from head, Zach noticed, to foot—quite a shameless examination for an old lady, practically stripping him bare. He repressed a grin.

"Gilbert Radcliffe," she said. "Long time since you've been seen in civilized company. How is your mother?"

"In excellent health, ma'am, thank you."

The lorgnette was directed at Zach again. "And who is your handsome friend?"

"Allow me to introduce Zachary Black, m'lady," Gil said. "Lady Beatrice, Mr. Black."

"Recently arrived from Italy," Zach added with a bow. He ignored Gil's blink of surprise; an Italian connection would help create a bridge to her nieces.

The lorgnette raked Zach again. "Italy, is it?"

"Yes, m'lady. Delighted to make your acquaintance."

"Are you?" She eyed him narrowly. "Why, may I ask?"

Zach gave her a disarming grin. "Because I wish to meet your nieces, the charming daughters of the *Marchese di Chancelotto*. I suspect we may have friends in common." He glanced across to where Jane and Abby stood glaring at him. "Is that—could that possibly be the young ladies concerned?"

Jane, arms folded militantly, glared across the meager grass at him and pointedly turned her back on him.

Lady Beatrice gave a caustic snort. "It had better be, since you've spent the best part of half an hour chasing them all over the park. Or should I say chasing Jane."

Zach blinked. He darted a quick glance at Gil, who was trying to swallow an I-told-you-so look, though not very hard.

"Doesn't want to talk to you, does she? Can't say I blame her. That's the trouble with this place—anyone can approach anyone—or try to. Now there's a bench—I'm going to sit down. All this dratted walking . . ." She sat down and brought up the lorgnette to scrutinize Zach again, dwelling on his face this time.

Zach felt a prickle of discomfort.

Her eyes narrowed. "Who did you say you were again?"

"Black." He bowed again with a flourish. "Zachary Black, late of Verona. Italy," he added, in case she didn't know either her geography or her Shakespeare.

Her gaze sharpened. "Who was your father?" she demanded abruptly.

Zach said cautiously, "Ah, m'lady, 'tis a wise man who knows his own father."

"His name, sirrah—and don't be bothering with that continental flummery. All that bowing is exhausting me."

"I believe my grandparents named him after a king."

"Hah!" she exclaimed in triumph. "George. I remember him well. Didn't like him much. Nasty temper on him." She gave a brisk nod, as if confirming something. "Zachary Black, my foot. It's Adam Aston-Black, if I'm not mistaken."

It gave him a jolt. There was a muffled sound from Gil, which he turned into quite a praiseworthy cough.

Zach said, "Would you admit to it if you were mistaken?"

"Not usually."

"Neither do I. However, I am not this Adam whoever-you-said," he said gently, as if humoring an old lady. "I am Zachary Black, plain and simple."

"*Pah!* You are neither plain nor simple, my boy, so don't try and flummery me. I might be old but I'm not in my dotage and I know an Aston-Black when I see one. I attended your christening: Adam George Zachary Aston-Black, only son of the late Lord Wainfleet." She grinned. "You howled the church down. No doubt the devil was in you even then."

Zach swore silently. How the hell had she rumbled him?

The old lady continued, "You don't much resemble George, except for the eyes—Aston-Black eyes if ever I saw them! And you have a great look of your grandfather, and him—before you try to deny it—I knew very well. Very well indeed."

"My grandfather was a gypsy, madam."

She gave a crack of ribald laughter. "He was many things, my boy, and a wicked rake to boot—the stories I could tell . . . But"—she fixed him with a severe look—"he was, underneath it all, a gentleman. As are you, I hope, whatever nonsensical game you're playing."

Zach didn't know what to say. He glanced at Gil, who was trying to look as though he wasn't convulsed with silent laughter.

The old lady continued, "So returned from the dead, have you, young Adam or Zachary or whatever you're calling yourself? Thought you might reappear when I heard your cousin was petitioning for the legal ruling. Nothing like a greedy little weasel sneaking your inheritance to bring a missing boy home, eh?"

Zach gave a short, rueful laugh. "You're very well informed, my lady." He hoped she hadn't heard about the murder charge, but he wasn't counting on it.

"I have my sources." She smoothed her skirt complacently. "So you're pursuing my niece, Jane, eh?"

"I am, my lady." No use in pretending now.

"Looks to me like she doesn't want to be pursued."

"We had a misunderstanding."

She arched an elegantly plucked eyebrow at him. "Whose fault was that?"

"Mine," Zach admitted.

The old lady considered that. "What are your intentions toward my Jane?"

"Everything of the most honorable."

"I see." She fell silent a moment, swinging her lorgnette back and forth meditatively. "You know she's betrothed, I assume. Catch of the season—Lord Cambury. A triumph for a gel without a fortune. All the cats ready to scratch her eyes out."

"She's not married yet," Zach said thinly.

There was another long silence, then Lady Beatrice said, "She's a good gel, my Jane—sweet-natured and loving. Not just a pretty face."

"I know."

"Do you? Men don't usually see past a pretty face and a lissome young body."

"A pretty face is the least of her qualities," Zach said.

"How would you know—having just arrived from Italy and all," she pointed out sardonically.

"I've been meeting her in the park—the square opposite your house. We bonded over a dog."

"Good gad!" She lifted the lorgnette again. Zach was getting heartily sick of it. "You're the gypsy!"

He nodded.

"Why?" She stared at him in bewilderment. "Why on earth would Adam George Zachary Aston-Black dress as a gypsy to court a respectable gel?"

"It's a long story."

"Oh, I have plenty of time," she said bitterly. "I have to breathe a certain amount of fresh dratted air before they let me go home. Wretched quacks! So go on, boy, explain. You clearly want—not to say need—my assistance, and I'll hear the whole story before I make up my mind. The full tale with no bark upon it, if you please."

Zach told her everything, held nothing back, not the murder charge, not anything. There was no point in trying to keep it a secret from her. She was apparently some kind of mind-reading witch, and besides, he needed her help. And since she'd clearly had a fondness for his grandfather . . .

When he finished, there was a long pause, then she gave a crack of laughter. "Better than a play indeed." She sobered. "Well, young man, it's a devil of a tangle you're planning to drag my niece into. Why should I assist with that, eh?"

"I'm not planning to drag her into anything," Zach said. "I just want to talk to her, make her understand."

"To understand what?"

Zach just looked at her. What he had to say to Jane was private. For Jane's ears only.

She laughed and patted his cheek. "Such a delicious glower. Your grandfather was just the same."

"The problem is time," Zach said. "It might take weeks to sort out the mess I'm in, and by then . . ."

The old lady nodded. "By then the gel could be married."

"Exactly. His having the banns called has forced my hand. I wouldn't otherwise involve her until I could come to her, free and clear."

She nodded slowly, considering what he'd said. "The gel's not interested in marrying for love, you know. Wants security above all. Had a difficult time of it as a child. Quite happy to make a convenient marriage." She gave him a shrewd look. "You and Cambury both have a title, a fortune and property—or you will have when, as you say, the mess is sorted out. But Cambury is, I fancy, a great deal wealthier than you will ever be."

Zach said nothing. He knew that.

Lady Beatrice continued, "My Jane's not a gel who likes to upset the apple cart—she likes everyone to be happy. If she were to brave the scandal that jilting Cambury would cause—and believe me, it would be the scandal of the decade—she'd need a dashed good reason. So, young Aston-Black, what can you offer her that she hasn't already got?"

Zach looked her in the eye. "Me."

There was a brief pause, then Lady Beatrice went into a peal of laughter. "A chip off your grandfather's block indeed. Not a shred of modesty in that man either." She wiped her eyes. "Well, nobody has ever accused me of being a spoilsport, so as long as you're not playing fast and loose with the affections of my

Jane—and you're not, are you?" She poked him in the chest—quite hard—and gave him a beady look.

"No, my lady, I promise you I'm not." And he meant every word.

She gave him a long look that stripped him bare in quite a different way this time. He wasn't sure what she saw, but whatever it was seemed to satisfy her. "I believe you, dear boy." She glanced at Jane's rigid back, still pointedly turned, and chuckled. "Come to my literary society tomorrow. Two o'clock sharp. And it would be delightful if you could converse in Italian with my nieces—they will simply adore it."

She fished in her reticule, pulled out a card and a pencil and scribbled something on it. "Give this to Featherby, my butler; he'll admit you. And don't fret, I won't give you away. I quite see the need for discretion. You come too, young Radcliffe. We need more young men."

"Delighted, my lady," Gil said glumly.

Zach took the card. A literary society was a more public meeting than he'd planned on, but it was a start. He had to get her alone, had to make her believe him. And to give him time to show her . . .

He glanced across at Jane, bowed to the old lady and smiled. "Thank you, my lady, you won't regret this, I promise you."

The old lady laid a gnarled hand over her heart. "Oh, that wicked, wicked smile—it does take me back." She gave him a wicked smile of her own. "The literary society has been getting devilish dull lately. The arrival of a handsome, Italian-speaking gentleman should liven things up nicely."

As they walked away, Gil commented dryly, "Quite an education, watching you handle a harmless little old lady."

"Smugness does not become you, Gilbert. Besides—harmless? She's a bloody witch! You should recruit her."

"How do you know I haven't already?"

Zach laughed.

Chapter Twenty-two

You want to tell me, and I have no objection to hearing it.

—JANE AUSTEN, *PRIDE AND PREJUDICE*

"M'mother dragged me to Lady Beatrice's literary society once before," Gil told Zach as they approached the big white house in Berkeley Square. "Not the usual kind of literary society. It's packed full of old ladies who can't read small print anymore. The girls read the books aloud, then everyone has tea, then they read a bit more, then they all go home. Sometimes they even read the same book twice!" He shook his head in mild disgust.

"Sounds painless enough."

"The trouble is, every old lady has at least one eligible young female relation that she's trying to palm off on some hapless fellow," Gil said gloomily. "Why else d'you think m'mother dragged me there in the first place? Not for my entertainment, you can be sure of that."

They rang the bell and Lady Beatrice's butler opened the door. His eyes narrowed in recognition.

Before he could say anything, Zach handed him Lady Beatrice's card. "Messrs. Black and Radcliffe for the literary society." The butler glanced at the card, and stood back to let them enter, managing to convey in some mysterious butlerish fashion that while he disapproved of her ladyship's imprudence in inviting such a dubious fellow as Zach, he would naturally honor the card. But he would be watching and Zach had better behave himself.

All conveyed without a word. Marvelous, Zach thought as he stepped inside and found a large liveried footman waiting to collect coats, hats, gloves and umbrellas. "Afternoon, William."

"You!" Having no mysterious butlerish powers, William started forward, clearly ready to throw Zach into the street, but the butler cleared his throat in a discreet and meaningful manner, and with visible difficulty, William restrained himself.

Again, Zach admired the butler's powers. He handed William his hat. "Apologies for my earlier deception, William. Not really a gypsy. Was on government business." He tapped the side of his nose.

Gil shrugged off his coat and handed it to the butler. "Numbers dropped since the start of the season, have they, Featherby?" he said. "Can usually hear the din from here."

"On the contrary, sir," Featherby murmured. "The quiet is because you have arrived a little late. The reading has already begun."

As he passed the still glowering William, Zach slipped a gold guinea into the big man's hand. From the look on the footman's face, it reconciled him slightly to having Zach in the house. Just barely.

Zach followed Gil, who seemed to know his way. They entered a large drawing room, where at least fifty people were seated in semicircular rows, all facing the front.

It wasn't quite full of old ladies, Zach saw. There were at least a dozen younger men, all exquisitely dressed and seated in the front semicircle of chairs.

On a small podium sat three young women. Jane, in the center, was reading aloud. The young men leaned forward, gazing at her raptly.

Puppies, Zach thought. He wanted to bang their heads together and boot them out the door.

Lady Beatrice caught his eye and nodded a regal greeting. Zach nodded back. Most of the chairs were taken, and he and Gil waited just inside the door, so as not to disturb the reading.

Zach stood in the doorway listening, drinking in the sight of Jane, sitting with her back straight, reading aloud, as earnest as a schoolgirl.

*"He came to ask me whether I thought it would be impru-
dent in him to settle so early; whether I thought her too
young—in short, whether I approved his choice alto-
gether; having some apprehension, perhaps of her being
considered (especially since your making so much of her)
as in a line of society above him. I was very much pleased
with all that he said . . ."*

She looked enchanting. Her voice was clear, her reading
ever so slightly . . . wooden.

He found it utterly endearing.

At the turning of a page, she glanced up and saw him. Her jaw
dropped, she lost her place, then fumbled and dropped the book.
She shot a glance at a man seated to her left and flushed. Zach
could only see the back of his head. Sandy hair and a balding pate.

There was an immediate scrimmage as the young dandies
at the front leapt into action, competing gallantly to retrieve
the dropped book and return it to her.

Zach was more interested in the fellow who'd caused that
anxious look. Taking advantage of the disturbance, he moved
fully inside, choosing a position at the back of the room where,
standing, he had a clear view of Jane. Gil followed.

Since that first fraught look, Jane hadn't even glanced at Zach,
but the way she avoided looking in his direction told him she
knew exactly where he was. Beside her, the sister with whom
she'd been walking in the park watched him with an expression
that indicated if she found him hanging from a cliff by his fingers, she'd gladly stamp on them.

She was loyal to her sister. Zach liked that. He smiled and
gave her a friendly nod.

Order restored, Jane resumed her reading, her color considerably heightened.

The sandy-haired fellow turned his head and gave Zach a
long, hard look.

"That's Cambury," Gil murmured.

Zach had thought as much. Across the crowded room the
two men eyed each other. *What can you offer her that she
hasn't already got?* The old lady's question echoed in his head
and he thought of that moment, that split-second instant, when
she'd gone from resisting him to kissing him back.

Did she kiss Cambury like that? His fists clenched at the thought of her golden slenderness in Cambury's pudgy hands. He shoved them in his pocket.

Jane paused a moment, then her voice rose as she read with slight emphasis:

> *"It is always incomprehensible to a man that a woman should ever refuse an offer of marriage. A man always imagines a woman to be ready for any body who asks her."*

Feminine titters rippled through the audience.

Zach's lips twitched as he wondered which one of them she was aiming that at. Him, no doubt. Or perhaps all the men in the audience.

She continued: *"Nonsense! A man does not imagine any such thing. But what is the meaning of this? Harriet Smith refuse Robert Martin! Madness if it is so; but I hope you are mistaken . . ."* and Zach's attention wandered.

He had no interest in this story. He was examining his surrounds, wondering how, in this crowd, he would be able to speak to her in private. The old lady had tricked him. It looked well-nigh impossible.

Jane finished the page and passed the book to the dark-haired young woman sitting on her right, who continued reading. Unlike Jane, she had a real flair for the dramatic.

"Freddy Monkton-Coombes's wife—her sister Damaris," Gil murmured in Zach's ear.

"I thought there were four sisters. The other one not here?"

"Daisy." Gil jerked his chin to indicate her. "The little one sitting in the far corner, sewing. She never reads."

"Why not?"

Gil shrugged.

"For sisters, they don't look much alike, do they?" Zach commented.

"Shush!" A lady turned around with an indignant look. "Damaris is reading!" They subsided into abashed silence. Jane still hadn't looked at him, not since that first shocked glance as she'd realized he was here.

It was, he hoped, a good sign. If she was indifferent to him, she'd look. Surely.

In the break between chapters, while everyone was eating cake and drinking tea, Lady Beatrice caught his eye and waved him imperiously closer. The wrinkled old face was bland, but the eyes brimmed with mischief.

She beckoned her nieces over and, when they'd gathered around her, said, "Gels, I would like you to meet Mr. Black, a gentleman newly arrived from Italy."

Zach bowed gracefully as she made the introductions. She ended, "Zachary is the grandson of an old friend of mine. And do you know what else? He knew your father, gels, the dear departed *Marchese di Chancelotto*." She beamed gently at Zach with a cat-who-ate-the-cream expression, and he recalled that she'd predicted his arrival would liven things up. "And he speaks fluent Italian—what do you think of that, eh, gels?"

Not a lot, judging by the way her nieces stiffened and stepped closer to Jane. Four pairs of eyes fixed him with a hard expression, daring him to do his worst.

He smiled at the mischievous old bat through gritted teeth. So much for her assurance of discretion. "You misunderstood me, my lady," he said smoothly. "What I said was that since I had recently arrived from Italy, your nieces and I might perhaps have acquaintances in common." He glanced at their unresponsive faces and shrugged. "But perhaps not."

He turned to Jane. "Delighted to meet you again, *signorina*," he said in excellent Italian, and went on to apologize—still in Italian—for the misunderstanding, assuring her and her sisters that he'd never met the *marchese*.

Hoping he had reassured them, he was surprised to see four blank—and slightly panicked—expressions on the faces of three of the four nieces. The small one just glared at him with uncomplicated fury.

Jane looked quite frozen. Her sister Abby said hurriedly, "We do not speak Italian, *Signor* Black."

"Only Venetian," Jane added.

Zach inclined his head gracefully. Of course, Venetians were very proud of their distinct culture and history. He said in the Venetian dialect, "My Venetian is a little rusty, but if you would prefer me to use that . . ." And when he received another equally blank and slightly panicked look, he realized the old lady had tricked him. The girls had no idea what he'd said.

"Ah, you don't wish to speak Venetian?" he said quickly in English.

"Not in public," Jane told him. "We were brought up to believe it's impolite to speak a language others in the room do not speak."

"Oh, but Miss Chance," a lady gushed, "I would love to hear a Venetian conversation."

"Me too," said another. "I learned Italian in the schoolroom, of course, but I have never had the pleasure of conversing with a native speaker." She batted her lashes at Zach. "Especially such a dashing one."

Jane's sister Abby stepped forward. "Sorry, but Lady Beatrice has forbidden us to speak Venetian"—she turned to the old lady and said with an edge of steel—"haven't you, Aunt Beatrice, dear?"

The old lady gave Zach the sweetest smile and said, "Indeed I have. I should have warned you, Mr. Black, Italian is bad enough, but the mere *sound* of the Venetian dialect gives me the most frightful palpitations. It was all the fault of the doge. Or was he a *marchese*? I forget—the most divine-looking man, with such eyes—like drowning in chocolate, my dears—and the longest, thickest lashes. And his figure—I vow, his valet must have had to pour him into his breeches. As for peeling him out of them— well . . ." And she sighed with gusty reminiscence.

At that point the butler rang a little bell and there was a general shuffle to resume seats. Jane gave Zach a look that gave him to understand that if she never saw him again, that would be perfect.

Damn and blast. He'd come here to mend the situation between him and Jane, and now—with his Italian/Venetian debacle—it was worse than ever. He glanced at the old lady, cursed her under his breath. It amazed him that she'd lived so long, that nobody had yet strangled her.

She grinned back at him like the veriest urchin brat, filled with such unrepentant glee, he was forced almost to laugh.

Zach inclined his head to her, acknowledging her victory. The devious old hellcat. She'd led him right down the garden path, paying him back, no doubt, for his initial deception of Jane. It had been an impressive performance.

He glanced at Gil to see if he'd witnessed the debacle, and

saw his friend once again battling with silent convulsions. Zach made his way to the back of the room. All was not lost, he told himself. He was still here in the house where Jane lived. There must be a way he could see her, explain. Apologize.

He stepped back to let a lady pass when a sharp little elbow jammed into his ribs, hard. "Oof!"

He turned, rubbing his ribs. The culprit was a small, elegantly dressed young woman, the fourth sister, Daisy. "Sorry," she said. She didn't look the least bit sorry. That elbow had been deliberately aimed. Another one who wanted to punish him for speaking Italian, no doubt. She jerked her head toward the door. "Follow me, gypsy."

Gypsy? Intrigued, he followed. She led him along the hallway and Zach was surprised to see she had a distinct limp. He was also surprised by her accent: pure broad Cockney, nothing like Jane's.

"The old lady told me to say you're to wait in the parlor along 'ere." She opened a door and showed him into a small, elegant parlor. "When the reading's done, she'll send Jane in to talk to you."

"Thank you—" he began.

She cut him off. "Don't thank me, it's the old lady's house so she can 'ave whoever she wants in it. I don't agree, but it ain't up to me. But"—she eyed him grimly—"you hurt or embarrass my sister Jane and I'll gut you like an 'erring, understand, gypsy? Wiv a rusty blade."

Little firebrand. Zach nodded. "Fair enough. For what it's worth, I don't have any such intention. Quite the opposite, in fact."

She sniffed, unimpressed. "Fine words from a fancy gent, but you've already made her cry once." She added fiercely, "Just don't do it again, orright?" and stumped away.

Zach grinned. He liked her, liked the way she was prepared to stand up for her sister and threaten to gut a man twice her size if he hurt her. Jane had good family.

As for the old lady—God only knew what she was playing at. She must have led his grandfather a right merry dance. Or maybe he'd led her the dance and she was paying his grandson back. Whatever her motives, he hoped she really did mean to send Jane to talk to him. Only time would tell.

Zach stretched himself out on a *chaise longue*, and waited.

He wouldn't put it past the old girl to "forget" to inform Jane he was here, leaving him cooling his heels indefinitely.

To his surprise, after the hubbub of the departing guests died down, the parlor door opened and Jane stood there, eyeing him with cool disfavor. "I have been asked to listen to what you have to say," she said coldly. "I don't know what lies you told Lady Beatrice to get her to—"

He rose. "I didn't lie to her."

"Why not? You lied to me."

"No. I misled you, I admit, but I never lied to you."

She gave him a skeptical look. "You can't have it both ways. You're just playing games with me, with Lady Beatrice, with all of us."

"I can understand why you might think that," Zach conceded. "I have a frivolous streak that's gotten me into trouble before, I admit. And in a way, that's how this started off—but it wasn't a game."

She gave an unimpressed sniff and moved toward the door. He caught her by the wrist. "Please, just sit down and hear me out."

She looked pointedly at the hand holding her, and with some reluctance he released her.

"Why should I believe a thing you say? You're a chameleon, a will-o'-the-wisp. A liar."

"Lady Beatrice knows who I am—my true identity. She knew my grandfather, who I'm told I strongly resemble. And she saw me christened as a child."

She arched her brows at that. "Babies change; you could be anyone."

"Gil Radcliffe and I have been friends since our school days. I've been working for him, gathering intelligence for the British government for the last eight years. I'm staying with him at the moment. He will also vouch for me."

She stood with arms folded, tapping her foot, considering his claims, and he added, "It was Gil's invitation I used to get into the masquerade the other night. It was I who wrote his name on your card. Don't blame him, though—he knew nothing about it until afterward."

She thought for a moment, then turned toward the door. "I'm going to check all this with Lady Beatrice."

"Why? You saw how she treated me. She told everyone there she knew me."

"She also said you were a friend of my father, the Venetian *marchese*, and there's no such person. She made him up."

"*She* did?" Zach had assumed the story had come from the girls. And that, he realized suddenly, was why they'd reacted with such hostility to his speaking Italian. Jane, of course, had assumed he was trying to embarrass her.

"I didn't know you didn't speak Italian—or Venetian," he said quickly. "I apologize. Lady Beatrice led me to understand that you did." She still looked mistrustful, and he added, "Truly. I had no idea I would cause you or your sisters any discomfort. I came here today to clear away any misunderstandings between us—do you honestly think I would deliberately sabotage myself, particularly in such a public manner? Truly, I meant no harm."

She considered that, and gave a reluctant nod. "We love Lady Beatrice dearly, but she does have a . . . a mischievous attitude to the truth at times." She opened the door. "But when it's important, she won't lie to me, and I still intend to check." She exited the room, leaving Zach pacing. Would she even come back?

He had to convince her to believe him. And to wait.

After a very long ten minutes, Jane reentered the room and sat down. "Lady Beatrice vouches for you; I am yet to be convinced." She folded her hands in her lap, looking like a demure schoolgirl. "She tells me your name isn't even Zachary Black." Her brows rose sardonically, her voice anything but demure. "And you claim you never lied to me?"

"I was christened Adam George Zachary Aston-Black. When I left my father's home at the age of sixteen, never to return, I was angry. I changed my name to Zachary Black. It's the name I've lived under for the last twelve years." He let that sink in and added, "So, misleading, but not truly a lie."

She pursed her lips. "Very well. What about the gypsy story?"

He explained to her how as a lonely young boy he'd been fascinated by the gypsies who camped on his father's property, and how later he'd been able to use that connection in his work. That he had lived and traveled with them.

Her eyes were opaque, her expression unreadable. "Pirate?"

"Privateer. True, perfectly legal and it was just the once. I really do get seasick."

"What about all those stories you told me, of your travels—the cossacks, that kind of thing."

"True, every last one."

She was silent for a long moment. "Then why didn't you simply tell me who you were? Why did you continue the deception? Why did it have to be all so furtive? And . . . and shabby." Her back was straight, but her eyes were wide, impossibly blue and wounded.

Shabby? Zach swallowed. Yes, in retrospect he had treated her shabbily. "For that I truly apologize." He took a deep breath. "I've been a complete fool," he admitted. "Acting the gypsy, playing games when all the time I should have . . ."

"Told me the truth."

He nodded. "You were right to tell me to grow up. These games and stratagems and disguises have been my life for the past eight years; deception and lies have been my stock-in-trade. When I arrived in England—the day I met you—I had no intention of staying. I thought I'd come to London, deliver the documents my government needed and then"—he spread his hands—"return to my life in the shadows."

"What changed your mind?"

"Two things." And he told her about his inheritance, and that his cousin was planning to have him declared dead, and explained how he'd discovered a murder charge hanging over the head of Adam George Zachary Aston-Black which complicated the claiming of his inheritance. "And that's why I deceived you," he finished. "I need to hide my true identity until I can free myself of this murder charge."

"Whom do they say you killed?"

He explained. Jane sat quietly, listening to the story of how a sixteen-year-old boy had helped a frightened girl to escape her violent husband and took her to live with a widowed school friend in Wales. And about the body discovered in the lake at Wainfleet that had been identified as Cecily's.

She watched him as he recited his story, watched the light change in his eyes, listened to the timbre of the deep voice as he explained.

He finished, "I swear I left Cecily in Wales, alive and well. I've never harmed a woman in my life."

Jane had no doubt he was telling the truth. She knew he was a master spinner of tales, but still, in this she believed him.

She knew he was capable of violence; the way he'd handled those thugs the day they first met had demonstrated that. But she had, after all, met him when he'd come to her rescue, and she'd been a stranger to him.

She'd met dangerous men before in her life, and Zachary Black might be dangerous in one sense—he certainly threatened her peace of mind—and her heart—but she knew he wouldn't harm her in any physical sense.

"Why are you telling me this, Mr. Black? It seems to me you've worked very hard to keep it a secret for a long time."

"Because I want you to know the truth about me. Because you'll hear some garbled version soon enough and I want you to know the truth. The application to have me declared dead comes up next week. I'm hoping to have the murder charge dismissed by then, but if not . . ."

"Because you're having difficulty locating Cecily."

"We'll find her," he assured her. "Gil has men out scouring the country for her."

"If you can't find her, how are you going to prove your innocence?"

He didn't answer, but gave her a curious glance. "Aren't you going to ask me whether I did it?"

"No."

He smiled. "You're assuming I'm innocent."

She gave him a cool look. She hadn't yet forgiven him entirely. "I don't know you well enough to assume anything."

"Yet."

"I beg your pardon?"

"Yet. You don't know me well enough yet." He leaned toward her and added in a dark voice laced with promise, "You're going to get to know me a great deal better."

She raised her brows at that, even though her heart beat a little faster at the intensity in his expression as he said it. "Am I?"

"I'm betting my life on it," he said quietly with a look that burned straight through to her heart.

With as much composure as she could manage she said, "You said two things changed your mind about leaving England. What was the second?"

"You," he said. "I met you and everything changed."

Jane was suddenly breathless. The intensity of his expression, his voice—did she dare believe him in this? He'd deceived her already in so many ways.

"And because I'm a fool, it took me longer than it should have to realize . . ."

"Realize what?" she prompted when he didn't finish the sentence.

"What you have come to mean to me."

There was a long silence. She wondered if he could hear her heart, the way it was thudding in her chest. "And what do I mean to you, Mr. Black?"

The door flew open. Lord Cambury stood there, his face red. "So! It was true!"

Jane rose, frowning. "What was true?"

"That you were entertaining a man in private! Your aunt insinuated as much!"

"I *insinuated* nothing of the sort, Lord Cambury, and well you know it." Lady Beatrice followed him in, leaning heavily on her stick. "I told you perfectly clearly that Jane was talking to another gentleman in the front parlor—as she has a perfect right to do in *my* home with *my* permission. You ain't married the gel yet!"

Her eyes were sparkling with mischief as she added, "Have you met Mr. Black? Lord Cambury, may I present Mr. Zachary Black, whose grandfather was at one time a *very* dear friend of mine."

Zach could have strangled her. What the devil was the old girl playing at now? She'd engineered the entire thing—but to what end, he had no idea. He just wished she'd waited five minutes longer before stirring up her cauldron.

Under her beady gaze, the two men shook hands and muttered polite and insincere greetings.

"Good boys," she told them as though they were schoolboys making up after a fight. "Now, Mr. Black was just leaving, weren't you, dear boy?" She sent Zach a gimlet look, and acknowledging that the moment had been lost and he was not going to get it back today—certainly not with this audience—he turned to Jane.

"Thank you for listening, Miss Chance. Perhaps you will do me the honor of coming for a drive in the park tomorrow. At two?"

She hesitated.

"It's important," Zach said, not caring whether he sounded desperate or not. He was.

"You will do nothing of the sort, Miss Chance!" snapped Lord Cambury. To Zach, he said, "She's not driving anywhere with the likes of you!"

Jane's brows rose. She gave Cambury a considered look, then said calmly, "Thank you, Mr. Black, that would be very nice."

"But—" Cambury began.

"Shall we discuss this in private, my lord?" she said, sweet as honey, cool as ice. His lordship stared at her, baffled, annoyed and, from his expression, also slightly impressed.

Zach took the opportunity to depart. "Nicely handled, Cambury," he murmured as he passed. Cambury's pompous refusal on her behalf was something no girl of spirit would tolerate. He'd practically driven Jane into Zach's arms. It almost reconciled Zach to him. Almost.

Chapter Twenty-three

The very first moment I beheld him,
my heart was irrevocably gone.

—JANE AUSTEN, *LOVE AND FREINDSHIP*

Lady Beatrice expressed the need for a nap after Zachary Black had left, and Jane helped her upstairs. Lord Cambury said he would remain in the parlor and wait for Jane's return. He didn't look at all happy with her.

Too bad, Jane thought; she wasn't very happy with him either.

The interruption couldn't have come at a more inopportune—or frustrating moment. Just when Zachary Black been about to say . . . what?

He'd been so sweet, so serious and remorseful. There had been none of the wicked rogue about him today, and though she'd seen that devilish smile of his too often in her dreams, to see him like this—no games, no mischief, just heartfelt sincerity . . . It was a side of him she'd never seen before and it slipped right past her defenses.

What had he been going to say before Lord Cambury had burst in like that?

Frustration ate at her.

She handed Lady Beatrice over to the ministrations of her maid and returned to the small parlor where Lord Cambury was waiting. Featherby had provided him with a sherry and some biscuits.

Lord Cambury rose, brushing crumbs from his fingers. "Well, missy, what have you got to say for yourself?"

Jane seated herself unhurriedly next to him on the *chaise longue.* "I very much dislike being called missy," she said quietly. "You may call me Jane, Miss Chance, or 'my dear.' But not 'missy.'"

His brows shot up.

"Secondly," she continued, "I don't like the accusation in your voice." She laid her hand over his and her voice warmed a little. "Lord Cambury—Edwin, if I may—you have to learn to trust me. You cannot go on assuming I will betray you at every opportunity."

"Hah!" He shook off her hand. "First you're seen hobnobbing with that shabby fellow in the park, then I catch you kissing some man on a darkened balcony—"

"I told you that was a mist—"

"And now, in your own home, I find you—"

"Talking to a gentleman at my aunt's invitation."

He snorted. "How many more men have you been meeting that I don't know about?"

She tried not to resent the implication, and said wearily, "It was the same man every time."

"What? The same man? This Zachary Black fellow?"

"Yes. It turns out he is a gentleman after all."

"Gentleman?" He snorted again. "I've never heard of him. Who are his people?"

"I don't know, but Lady Beatrice knows his family. His grandfather as well as his father and his late mother. She said she'd even attended his christening."

He frowned.

"But I didn't know he was coming today." She glanced at his expression, and added, "You must have seen for yourself my own surprise when he arrived."

"I saw your *reaction*," Lord Cambury said, his tone implying it was something other than surprise he had noticed. She fought a blush. Had it been that obvious?

"I find your constant lack of faith in me a little insulting."

"I saw you *kissing* the fellow."

She said thinly, "I've already apologized for that and explained that it will not happen again. How often do I need to say it?"

He sniffed. "And yet you've just agreed to go for a drive with this fellow—against my expressed wishes."

"Yes. He came here today to tell me something—something important—and because you burst in when you did, he didn't get a chance to finish."

"What was this important thing?"

"I don't know. But I want to hear what he has to say."

"I don't like it."

"I'm sorry, but I won't be dictated to on this. When I have made my marriage vows I will obey you in all things, but we're not married yet."

His eyes narrowed, then he nodded as if confirming something to himself. "Headstrong beauty. Only to be expected. After we're married I'll tame you."

Jane gave him a cool look and rose. "Now, is that all you wanted to talk to me about? Because if it is, I am expected elsewhere." Which left him with no option as a gentleman but to rise and take his leave of her.

She went upstairs in a thoughtful frame of mind. Less and less was she liking Lord Cambury's attitude toward her. She could understand why he was cross—even suspicious. Zachary Black had been very persistent. And no man would be happy about another man pursuing his betrothed.

But she was getting weary of dealing with Lord Cambury's constant suspicions, and his oft-expressed opinion that because she was pretty and female, she must have no honor.

It was true, she'd kissed Zachary Black on the balcony the other night, and her bones had turned to water . . . and that was wrong of her.

But she hadn't arranged to meet him or encouraged him in any way. And though she had to admit she had returned his kiss—quite shamelessly in the end—she hadn't *invited* it.

The fact that it had taken all of three seconds to go from resisting him to melting in his arms was . . . unfortunate.

But it wasn't a crime.

And today, there had been nothing unseemly between them,

no physical contact—she touched the wrist he'd caught—
almost no contact. She'd simply listened to his story.

And what a story it was. If only Lord Cambury hadn't burst
in when he had . . .

Lord Cambury. She sighed.

She had always assumed she would love her husband—that
she would be the loving one in the marriage, even though it
would be a marriage of convenience. Many couples learned to
love after marriage.

Now it occurred to her for the first time that she might not
be able to love Lord Cambury—or at least that it might be difficult to love him. More difficult than she had expected.

Lord Cambury was acting like a jealous man, but without
love there could be no jealousy, surely? She didn't understand
it, didn't understand him.

She'd always believed that a marriage of convenience would
suit her, that an alliance made in good faith, based on respect
and mutual need, and uncomplicated by extremes of emotion,
would be a sound basis for two people to achieve contentment,
if not actual happiness.

Now she wasn't so sure.

Zachary Black called for Jane promptly at two the next day,
driving a very smart high-perch phaeton pulled by two
gleaming black horses. "Borrowed the whole rig from a friend,"
he told her as he lifted her up into it. "Don't worry, I've given
them a good run already, taken the edge off them." He looked
very dashing in buckskin breeches, gleaming black boots and
a new very smart dark olive coat that brought out the faint green
of his eyes.

Jane settled herself in the seat. It was very high up; she felt
quite dashing and adventurous. She was glad she'd worn her
favorite red pelisse and her new bonnet. She'd been waiting for
this moment all day, hadn't been able to settle to anything much.

What was this important thing he wanted to say to her? She
thought she knew, she hoped she knew. She felt sick, excited,
hollow.

He climbed lithely up, and she felt the warmth of his thigh

as he slid into the seat next to her. It wasn't a very big seat; just barely room for two. Awareness thrummed through her.

Apart from the initial polite exchange of pleasantries, they drove in silence. She assumed he was considering what he was going to tell her; whatever it was must be quite weighty, judging by his expression.

She had her own thoughts on what it might be. They caused the butterflies in her stomach to flutter even more madly.

They drove through the busy streets toward Hyde Park, his hands sure and steady on the reins. She noted his awareness of everything around them, the deft way he negotiated the busy traffic, how he slowed when a child ran onto the road then stopped and ran back, oblivious of the danger. She saw how he stopped to let an old rag and bone man push his cart across the road in front of his smart phaeton.

You could tell a lot about a man from the way he drove.

They drove through the gates of Hyde Park, and continued on to a less fashionable part of the park, where he slowed the horses to a walk.

"Thank you for agreeing to this drive," he said. "I am sorry if it caused you any difficulty with your fiancé."

"It didn't," Jane said tranquilly. Lord Cambury didn't like it, but he had accepted it. "You said yesterday you had something important to say to me."

"Yes." He was silent a moment. The horses walked steadily on, their hooves clopping softly on the road. "It will seem like the most tremendous cheek, but . . ." He swallowed.

Zachary Black was nervous, she realized suddenly. She hadn't ever seen him nervous before. "Is it because of the hearing?"

The horses stopped. He turned his head to look at her. "No, because of the banns being called." His silvery eyes gleamed.

"The banns? My wedding banns?" The thudding of her heart kicked up a notch.

He nodded. "I wanted to ask you to wait." He paused. "Will you wait?"

"I'm not sure what you mean. Wait for what?"

"Will you delay your wedding?"

Delay? What did he mean, delay? Why delay? Why not just say "cancel"? "For how long?"

"Until this mess I'm in is sorted. Until the charges against me are dropped. Until I'm free and clear."

She thought she knew what he was implying, but she wanted him to say it. Needed him to say it. "Free to do what?"

He just looked at her, an intense burning look that seared her to her soul.

She waited.

But he said nothing.

"And if they're not dropped, if you end up going to trial . . . and the worst happens? What do you think I should do then?" she asked softly.

He shrugged. "Forget me, go on with your life as if we'd never met."

The phaeton jerked a little as the horses moved slowly on.

She looked at him, at his grim profile as he stared ahead, contemplating what she could see was a bleak future.

Suddenly she wanted to hit him.

What kind of thickheaded man was he that he would imagine she'd simply wait, keeping two men dangling, hedging her bets while she waited for a verdict? And then if the worst happened— meaning he was *hanged*—she would simply go on with her life? Did he really think she could just shrug it off as if she'd never met him?

But no, she saw. He wasn't thinking very clearly at all. And no wonder, with a murder charge hanging over him. What a frightful thing to come home to.

"I see," she said after a moment. "So you think I should simply tell Lord Cambury that I'd like to delay the wedding until after the trial?"

"Yes."

She was caught between wanting to hug him and itching to box his elegant, oblivious ears. What did he imagine she would tell Lord Cambury? *Let us delay our wedding until after the trial? Then, depending on the outcome, I'll decide who I'll marry?*

"I would need a good reason to delay my wedding," she said. "Can you think of one?" She waited for him to give her the reason.

When he didn't, she continued, "I hardly know you. We've met perhaps a dozen times, we've walked, and talked and now you expect—"

"You left out kissed. We kissed, if you remember. And danced together." And his heated gaze dropped to her mouth, and she felt the tingle of it, the heat, the touch, the possession of it clear through to her bones.

She inclined her head, acknowledging the kiss. And the dance.

"So on the basis of the handful of meetings we had, and a kiss, you expect me to break off my betrothal, which has been formally announced and for which the settlements have been drawn up—"

"No. I'm not asking you to break off the betrothal, merely to delay—"

"Oh, don't be ridiculous," she snapped. "Just give me a reason why I should wait."

The silence stretched. He clenched his fist and looked away. "I can't," he grated.

If she hadn't heard the torment, the anguish in his voice, she might have hit him. For his blind obliviousness. He thought he was being noble, the big idiot.

"You have to give me something, Zachary," she said softly. "I need a reason."

But he said nothing. They completed a full circuit of the park and exited through the gates. In silence they wove through the traffic, a very different silence from before.

Why couldn't he just tell her what was in his heart?

Why couldn't she?

The phaeton turned into Berkeley Square and they pulled up in silence. The groom jumped down to hold the horses' heads and Zachary Black walked around to help Jane down. He placed his hands around her waist and lifted her slowly down, brushing her against his body like a slow-burning flame.

The silver-green eyes glowed green, and she tried to read the words he refused to speak in them. But he put her down and stepped back without giving her any reason to wait, to hope.

"Adam George Zachary Aston-Black, you're under arrest." A thin little man flanked by two burly constables stepped forward. They seized Zachary by the arms. He said not a word, made no attempt to struggle.

Over their heads, his gaze burned into Jane. "Wait," he mouthed silently.

Jane stood in the street, watching, devastated as they bundled Zachary Black into a carriage and drove him away.

He'd warned her this might happen, but to have it happen now, so soon, just when . . .

Oh, how could she just wait? Did he expect her to open up her heart to him—and then wait for him to be declared innocent or guilty?

Clearly he did.

And what if he were found guilty—and hanged? What was she supposed to do then? Switch her feelings off and go back to marry Lord Cambury? As if nothing had happened?

Impossible.

For Jane the worst had already happened. She'd fought against it from the start, tried to deny it for so long, but now, seeing him taken away in custody, bound for prison, possibly to be hanged for a murder she was certain he did not commit, she had to acknowledge it: For better or for worse, she'd gone and fallen in love with Zachary Black.

Gil was at work when he received a message from Zach's lawyer informing him that Zach had been taken to Newgate Prison. He hurried straight over. He had news of his own—bad news.

Zach was being held in a gloomy little cell with several other gentlemen. Gil, being well aware of the conditions in Newgate, had come prepared, and a hefty bribe soon secured Zach a small but clean apartment of his own containing a bed, a table, chair and several small comforts.

Zach was pacing back and forth like a caged tiger when Gil was finally shown to his new accommodations. "They arrested me in front of her, right in front of her!" he said as soon as Gil arrived. "Blast them, why couldn't they have shown a bit of discretion, waited until she was inside! The expression on her sweet face . . . Damn and blast them!" He paced a bit more. "And how the hell did they know to find me there—they were waiting for me, Gil. Right outside her door. Right at the time I was expected back."

Gil made soothing noises and pulled out a bottle of brandy. He'd brought two—the second one had gone to Zach's jailer to ensure his cooperation. He produced two tumblers from his pocket and poured the golden liquid.

"Sit down," he told Zach. "I have news for you."

Zach stopped pacing but didn't sit. He could see from Gil's expression it wasn't good news. "Cecily?"

Gil looked grim. "No sign of her in Llandudno at all. My man returned today."

Zach swore.

Gil went on, "He questioned Mary Thomas, and a number of other people, and they were all adamant they'd never seen Cecily. He questioned them in Welsh and English—and yes, it's the right Mary Thomas—she spoke English and admitted to knowing Cecily from school. But she swore she hadn't seen her since."

Zach sank heavily onto the chair. "I don't understand it. She's clearly lying, but . . ." He glanced at Gil. "At least you can testify you passed on Cecily's letters."

Gil shook his head. "Won't help—they were just letters addressed to you. I can testify they had her name on them, but I can't prove that she sent them."

"Any luck tracing the people who saw us on the journey?"

"Not yet. But we haven't given up."

Zach contemplated his situation. "It's not looking good, is it?"

Gil glanced around and lowered his voice. "Time for you to leave the country. I can get you out of here. The security is quite lax."

"No. I won't flee. That's as good as admitting I'm guilty, and I'm damned well not. I'll stay and fight it."

"It's the girl, isn't it?" Gil said after a moment. "She's the reason you're staying to fight this thing."

The girl. Jane. If Cecily couldn't be found . . . dammit all to hell. Zach examined his situation from every angle. He could see no way out of it. "No, the situation's changed," he said wryly. "I can't embroil her in this mess. She had her life all planned out, and I'm not going to ruin it all for her, not if there's no future. I'm going to have to cut her loose."

"Then if you're going to cut her loose, why the hell won't

you leave the country? It doesn't make sense," Gil said in a low, urgent voice.

Zach shook his head. "I won't run away. When I went down to Wainfleet, I realized that since my father's death everyone there has been left in a kind of limbo—an estate like that needs an owner to run it—an owner who's present. If I'm hiding out in Europe, they're still in limbo. Better that this situation is resolved once and for all—me or my cousin."

"Better for whom? Not you, not if they stretch your neck."

"I'm gambling on my innocence counting for something." Zach lifted the tumbler of brandy in an ironic toast. "To English justice." He drained it, shuddered as it burned its way down his throat, felt the heat of the alcohol lodge in his empty belly and said, "Did you bring any notepaper? I need to write a letter."

J ane had watched until the carriage taking Zachary Black away had turned a corner and disappeared from sight, then she hurried inside and found Lady Beatrice.

"He's been arrested! They've taken him off to jail!" And she'd burst into tears.

After a good weep in the old lady's arms, she'd felt wrung out, but calmer. While Lady Bea wrote notes, canceling their social engagements for the evening and summoning the family for an emergency dinner, Jane had taken herself upstairs to wash her face, and think about what she was going to do.

Her thoughts were in turmoil, but she was clear about one thing. And she had to do it now, before her courage deserted her. She sat down to pen a note of her own.

"Mr. Gilbert Radcliffe to see you, Miss Jane," Featherby said several hours later.

Jane flew downstairs to the drawing room, where Mr. Radcliffe was waiting, looking very solemn, almost grim. "Is he all right?" Jane burst out as soon as she saw him. He blinked, and she collected herself, saying in a more composed manner, "Mr. Radcliffe, so good of you to call on me. What news do you have of Mr. Black?"

He held out a folded paper, looking awkward. "I've brought you a note, Miss Chance."

"From Mr. Black?" She took it, recognizing the bold black writing, and felt suddenly nervous. What reason would Zachary

Black have to write to her? He'd only just been taken. She'd seen him a few short hours ago.

"Well then, I'll be off." Mr. Radcliffe edged toward the door.

"No, please wait," she told him as she broke open the wafer that sealed it. "I might need to answer this."

Mr. Radcliffe looked uncomfortable. "He's not expecting any answer."

"I would be very grateful if you waited." Jane rang the bell and asked Featherby to bring Mr. Radcliffe some refreshment. Zachary's friend provided for, she unfolded the letter and started to read.

Dear Miss Chance,

Firstly I must apologize for the embarrassment caused you by my arrest in your presence. It must have been a shocking experience to a lady of delicate sensibilities, and I apologize, most sincerely.

I also wish to apologize for what I believe might have been a misunderstanding between us. Thinking back over our recent conversations it has occurred to me you might have misunderstood my intentions. As I explained, I expect to be declared innocent of the murder of Cecily Aston-Black, Countess of Wainfleet, but after that, my stated intention is to leave England and return to my former pursuits in the service of my country.

When I asked you to delay your wedding to Lord Cambury, it was simply so that I might attend the wedding, knowing that my current legal position might make that difficult. In our brief acquaintance I believe we have become friends, and it was simply as a friend that I would have liked to witness your marriage.

However, I've realized it was very selfish of me to expect such a delay, only for my convenience. Please take no notice of anything I might have said to cause you to think otherwise. Go ahead and marry your Lord Cambury, with my very best wishes. And be happy.

Yours sincerely,
Zachary Black.

Jane read the letter twice, then put it down, noting absently that her hands were shaking. Mr. Radcliffe was watching her, rather as a mouse might watch a cat, warily, and showing every evidence of a creature heartily wishing himself elsewhere.

"Do you know what he said in this letter?" she asked him.

He looked uncomfortable and made a vaguely negative movement. If he didn't know, he had a fair idea.

"He has given me his blessing to marry Lord Cambury."

"Ah. Very proper of him," Mr. Radcliffe said in a strangled voice.

"Very proper, my foot!" Jane's voice wobbled; she was on the verge of tears again. She took a deep, steadying breath and continued, "He's being noble again. Yesterday in the park he refused to explain why he was asking me to delay my wedding, refused to tell me what he was feeling, and now, today he is telling me that whatever it was I thought he meant, he didn't."

Mr. Radcliffe said nothing.

Jane said, "The situation must be very grim, for him to set me free like this." She hesitated. "I'm right, aren't I? It is looking bad for him?"

Mr. Radcliffe nodded.

"Cecily hasn't been found?"

"No. There's no sign of her in Llandudno, where Zach swears he left her. And Mary Thomas, her old school friend, claims she hasn't seen Cecily since school."

"I see. So Zachary is expecting to be found guilty and hanged." Of course he was, that's why he wrote such a noble, precious, idiotic letter. So she wouldn't feel bound to him. Too late for that.

Again, Mr. Radcliffe nodded.

She rose and started to pace the room. "Isn't there anything I can do? That we can do? My brothers-in-law could help."

Mr. Radcliffe shook his head. "We're doing all we can. I have men all over the kingdom searching for any trace of Cecily, and for any witnesses who saw her with Zach after they left Wainfleet. I've ensured he has a good lawyer for the defense, that his quarters in Newgate are the best that can be obtained and I've arranged for him to be provided with all he needs while in prison. I can't think of anything else anyone can do."

Jane sank onto a chair. Mr. Radcliffe sounded quite . . . pessimistic. "You *will* fight it?"

Mr. Radcliffe nodded. "With all the means we have at our disposal," he vowed. "There will be a pre-trial hearing, but if that goes badly—and without Cecily, how can it go otherwise?—it will be a trial by his peers, in the House of Lords."

"There must be *something* I can do," she said in despair.

"There is," he said grimly. And when she looked expectantly at him, he said, "Pray."

Chapter Twenty-four

*You could not make me happy, and I am convinced that I
am the last woman in the world who would make you so.*

—JANE AUSTEN, *PRIDE AND PREJUDICE*

The note Jane had written earlier was to Lord Cambury
asking him to call on her as soon as was convenient. He
arrived shortly after Mr. Radcliffe had left. Jane was still
downstairs.

She was on tenterhooks, waiting. It was the right thing to
do, she knew it, but still . . .

"That scoundrel won't be bothering you anymore," Lord
Cambury said with satisfaction as he handed his hat to Feather-
erby. "Pity it had to happen when you were present, but it was
for the best. See for yourself the fellow's a blackguard."

Something about the way he said it raised her suspicions.
"You knew about his arrest? And where it took place?" It had
only happened a few short hours before. How could he know
she'd witnessed it? And when he smiled with smug complacency,
she understood. "You arranged it!" Of course. That was how
they knew Zachary Black would be returning her to her home,
and when.

"I protect what's mine."

At his words something inside her settled. "Please come into
the drawing room," she said. "I have something to say to you."

"He's a murderer, you know. He even lied to you about his

name—he's not Zachary Black; his name is Adam Aston-Black."

Jane didn't respond. To Featherby she said, "Lord Cambury and I will be in the drawing room. Please ensure that we are not disturbed." She felt quite hollow, a little sick. But it had to be done.

"I knew from the start he wasn't the sort of man a lady should associate with. I did it to protect you," Lord Cambury said as he followed her into the drawing room.

"Please sit down," Jane told him. Her hands were shaking. She gripped them tightly together.

He sat, looking a little puzzled.

This was it then. She took a deep breath. "I'm very sorry, Lord Cambury, but I cannot marry you."

"What the devil? Not marry me?" Lord Cambury's eyes bulged in shock. "You cannot mean it."

"I'm sorry, but I do." She pulled off the heavy diamond and gave it to him.

"But . . . it's been announced. The minister has commenced the calling of the banns."

She nodded. "I know. I'm sorry, but it cannot be helped. I cannot marry you."

"Why?"

She shook her head. "It does not matter. My mind is made up."

He stared at her for a long moment, then he stood up and stalked over to the mantelpiece. He picked up a china figurine of a shepherdess and examined it carefully. "The years I spent looking for the perfect . . ." He swore, and hurled the little shepherdess into the hearth. It smashed. There was a sudden silence in the room, broken only by the sound of the hollow china head rolling in a circle on the marble hearthstone.

He contemplated the shattered pieces and swung around to face Jane. "Everyone will blame you for this! Everybody knows my high standards and will believe that you're the one who's failed me, that you're flawed and unworthy—and dammit if I don't think you are! You must be, to call it off after all I've offered you! And I won't defend you, you can be sure of that!"

Jane was shaking but strangely calm. With dignity she said, "You must do what you wish."

"Damn right I will." He made a petulant gesture.

"And I must do what I think is right. I'm sorry to hurt you—"

"*Hurt* me? I'm not hurt, I'm relieved, relieved to discover in time that you are flawed and unworthy and quite unsuitable . . ." He continued listing the ways he'd been mistaken in her, the reasons she was so unsatisfactory.

Jane let his rant wash over her, oddly distant from it all. She might have married this man—would have married him. He would've been the father of her children. She shivered, thinking about it, about the impossible standards he would've set them. The demands. The pressure.

And slowly the fears she had held so long, the bonds that had bound her, loosened.

She looked at the pompous little man with his tasteful clothes and his carefully combed hair and felt a swell of compassion.

Underneath all the bluster and pretense he was a sad and lonely man. He'd thought he could buy a beautiful wife, the way he bought his other pieces. And she'd thought his wealth would make her safe from the risk of love. They'd both been so very wrong.

"You can't go on like this," she told him when he stopped for breath. "If you do, you'll never be happy."

"What the devil are you talking about?"

"Expecting perfection, collecting what you think is perfection, surrounding yourself with beautiful things. They'll never make you happy."

"You were ready enough for them to make you happy."

"I know, and I was wrong. I know now they aren't enough. Not for me, not anymore."

His eyes almost popped. "Not enough? I offered you my wealth, my house—houses—jewels—"

"Those are just things," Jane said gently. "And I don't mean to sound ungrateful. I didn't offer you enough either."

He stared at her, perplexed and irritated. "But you're the most beautiful girl I've seen in years. Every season I looked, and after nearly ten years, along you came—absolute perfection."

She shook her head. "Sorry, but that's just nonsense."

"Nonsense?"

"What you're talking about, the thing you call 'perfection,' is such a transient thing. One day I'll be old and wrinkled, and before that, I expect I'll get fat."

"Fat?" He looked appalled.

She almost laughed at his expression. "If I take after my maternal grandmother, Lady Dalrymple—and it seems very likely—I will most certainly grow plump, at the very least. But whatever happens, I intend to age like Lady Beatrice."

He frowned. "But she's old and ugly!"

"That's where we must differ: I think she's beautiful."

"*Beautiful?*" His tone made it clear he thought her statement ridiculous.

Jane nodded. "She's experienced hardship, abuse, grief and illness, and yet not a trace of bitterness shows on her face. She still has a zest for life, and a heart full of love. Wisdom, love, experience—it's all there, in every wrinkle and line—her character and her beauty just get stronger and more refined with age. And that's how I want to be. I want to have children and grandchildren, a body well used and a life well lived. And wrinkles."

He stared at her as if she was insane.

"Everyone ages and gets wrinkled, and that is why your definition of perfection is wrong."

"Wrong? In what way wrong?"

Jane said gently, "It's because you're flawed, because you're worried that deep down inside you, you're not good enough. And so you collect lovely objects, and surround yourself with beauty, and are renowned for the perfection of your taste. And you hope that all this reflected glory and perfection will hide your own flaws."

"How dare you!"

"I don't mean it unkindly. Don't you see, everything that's human and beautiful *is* flawed. It's the flaws that make each of us unique, that make us human and worthy of love."

"Love!" He made a scornful sound. "Vulgar, middle-class claptrap!"

"Worth dying for," Jane said. "And very much worth living for. Do you know, I was ready to sacrifice my own chance of love—and yours—for the sake of having children, for comfort and security . . . No, I thought I could *avoid* love. I *wanted* to avoid it. I thought it was some kind of uncontrollable force that would hurl me into uncertainty and peril. And jeopardize everything I wanted out of life."

"It is. It will. It has."

She smiled. "You might be right. Nothing is certain in life, I know that. But I thought happiness could be bought and could be acquired like"—she glanced at the broken little shepherdess—"acquired like that lovely little statuette. But it can't. Love must be snatched in fleeting moments, treasured, nourished like a fugitive flame in the wind. It's risky and uncertain."

She thought of Zachary Black, locked away in a dank and gloomy prison, facing hanging for a crime he didn't do. His future couldn't be more uncertain, but her own feelings—her love—were strong and sure, burning for him like a flame in the darkness. And because of that, she was prepared to face the risk, had no choice but to love him and face what the future would bring.

The thought brought a strange exhilaration with it.

"I used to think my parents were wrong for eloping together and leaving two very good sensible matches behind. I thought their unhappiness—and my sister's and my childhood difficulties—were the punishment for breaking the rules, for being improvident, for thinking only love mattered. And money does matter, and so does financial security and keeping your family safe, but without love, it's . . . it's as empty as . . ." She gestured at the little broken shepherdess. "As that. Pretty to look at, perfect from the outside, but when tested, ultimately hollow. Empty."

He frowned, and Jane added, almost to herself, "Even in the direst of circumstances, Mama used to call Papa her prince. And she was always his princess, and . . . I want to be somebody's princess too."

"Who? What prince, dammit? English? Foreign? Is it a tiara you want?"

She gave a shaky laugh. "Zachary Black is my prince. I know so little about him—none of the things I used to think were so essential to my happiness. You offered me everything I thought I wanted, but I doubt we could ever have been happy together, could we? And today, as I saw Zachary Black taken away by those horrid constables, I knew that I loved him. And that I was more like Mama than I wanted to be. I've been struggling against loving him for such a long time. He's an impossible man."

"He is! And he doesn't deserve you—he's a murderer!"

"No, he's innocent. As for 'deserving,' while it's true that love must be earned, at the same time, it must be freely given."

"That makes no sense at all."

"It doesn't have to make sense—it just is." She almost laughed at his expression. She was feeling quite giddy with relief. It was crazy—she'd just rejected the most advantageous offer any girl could want, and the love of her life was in jail, facing a capital charge—and yet, somehow, she felt relief. "You're right—I'm afraid it's midsummer madness with me."

"But it's *not* midsummer! It's barely even *spring*!" he said, exasperated.

"I know. And that's another reason why we would not suit—seasonal confusion." He looked baffled and she moved to sit down beside him. "I'm sorry to disappoint you, Lord Cambury, and I hope you'll forgive me eventually." She took his hands in hers. "But even more, I hope you will stop looking for physical perfection in a bride, and stop surrounding yourself with cold, beautiful things. You're a good man, kind and decent, and fond of animals, but . . . you're mistaken about so many things. Stop being afraid of whatever it is about yourself you're trying to hide. You need to *love* someone, not collect *things*."

He blinked at the blasphemy. "But I searched for you for *years*."

"No, you searched for an imaginary ideal, not me. It's not me you wanted, only my face. But to know a person, to love them, you have to look beneath the surface. And love them, perfect or not. Take a risk, Edwin, and learn to love imperfection. Learn to love—let yourself *fall* in love. It's terrifying . . . and wonderful."

"They're going to hang him, you know."

"Not if I can help it. Take care of yourself, Edwin. Good-bye." She kissed him lightly on the cheek—the first time she'd ever kissed him—and hurried from the room, leaving him standing and staring after her, a peculiar expression on his face.

* * *

Dinner was an informal affair: just Jane's sisters, Max and Freddy and Lady Beatrice. Jane barely ate a thing. She started with the news that she'd just severed her engagement to Lord Cambury.

As Lady Beatrice pointed out, it was going to cause a lot of nasty gossip—and none of it would be complimentary to Jane, so they'd better prepare for it.

"But why?" Abby asked, after the initial babble of surprise had died down. "I thought he was what you wanted."

Jane grimaced. "I thought so too, but . . ."

"It's the gypsy, ain't it? Daisy said.

Jane nodded ruefully.

"What gypsy?" Abby demanded, having only known Zachary Black as an annoying man who'd pursued Jane in the park and then turned up at the literary society and embarrassed them all by speaking Italian. And Venetian.

It took a long time for Jane to explain to her sisters' satisfaction, but when she had, once they were convinced . . . There was a long silence.

"So you're finally in love, little sister?" Abby said softly. Her face was full of love, and Jane felt suddenly teary.

"But they're going to hang him." Her face crumpled and the tears came again.

After dinner, the men went off to their club, to seek out Gil Radcliffe and see what they might be able to do to help Zachary Black—or Wainfleet, as they called him. Because, as Max pointed out, Zachary was in fact the Earl of Wainfleet, and had been since his father had passed on, no matter what his cousin or anyone else said. Of course, there was the investiture still to come, but Max also pointed out that it would be harder for them to hang the Earl of Wainfleet than a mere Mr. Zachary Black.

Jane hoped he was right.

Lady Beatrice went to bed, and the girls gathered upstairs. They insisted she tell them everything about Zachary—from the moment she first met him, to what he'd asked her in the phaeton ride. They needed to be convinced he was good enough for Jane. And that he really didn't murder Cecily.

"She's been daft about him for ages," Daisy told them. "She tried to pretend she wasn't, but I could tell. And he's a lot better than that old stuffed shirt, Lord Comb-it-up." She gave them a mischievous look. "I biffed 'im one the other day."

Abby's jaw dropped. "Who, Lord Cambury?"

"No, the gypsy. I give 'im a good 'ard elbow in the ribs, and you know what he did?"

"No."

"Nuffin'. Took it like a man. And then I threatened to gut 'im wiv a rusty knife if he 'urt Jane, and"—she looked at each of them—"he promised me he'd treat her right. Didn't 'old it against me at all. Most blokes wouldn't like bein' talked to like that—'specially not from a little Cockney upstart female—and him bein' a lord, as it turns out—but he knew he'd been actin' the fool, and 'e took it fair on the chin." She gave a brisk nod. "So I like 'im.

Jane gave her a hug.

Damaris said, "There is still the matter of his missing step-mother. I don't understand why, if he really did leave her in Llandudno, nobody there remembers it."

There was a long, depressed silence. It was an unanswerable question.

They hashed everything over a dozen times, and though it was getting late, they made no progress on the question of Cecily or any future for Zachary.

It was clear to Jane that though her sisters tried to put a positive face on things, they simply couldn't celebrate her falling in love with a man whose future involved a noose. They couldn't hide their worry for her.

Jane was only worried for Zachary.

It was in a somber mood that Abby and Damaris kissed Jane good night and wished her sweet dreams. And not to worry.

Easier said than done.

Upstairs, Jane climbed into bed and blew out the candle. "Night, Daisy."

"Night."

She tried to sleep, but though she was exhausted from the

day's events, sleep wouldn't come. She lay there, turning things over and over in her mind. Fruitlessly.

Then out of the darkness, Daisy said, "You said his dad used to bash Cecily."

"Yes, and Zachary."

There was a long silence. She thought Daisy had drifted off to sleep, but then she spoke again. "There was this girl in the brothel once, her sister used to get bashed somethin' shockin' by 'er old man. She could never get away from him—'e always found 'er and fetched her back. And bashed her again. So one day she come and hid wiv us, in the brothel—she'd never even spoken to her sister before that—she was the respectable type. But she was desperate, so she come."

"What happened?"

"He tried all the usual places, and finally come lookin' for 'er in the brothel, askin' questions. And we all of us lied our 'eads off, swore blind we never knew what 'e was talking about." She gave a little huff of laughter. "Some of the girls enjoyed themselves, asking him real awkward questions about why his respectable wife would run off on 'im, and why on earth he'd imagine she'd come to a brothel. Sent 'im off with a right flea in 'is ear, they did."

Jane sat up in bed. "You think Cecily's friend lied to protect her?"

"I dunno, but . . . it's a possibility, ain't it? And if they sent *men* lookin' for her—well, women who been hurt . . . they don't trust men, do they?"

It was indeed a possibility. Jane lay back down in her bed and, staring into the darkness, found a glimmer of hope.

By dawn she had her plan all worked out. The moment Daisy awoke, Jane explained it to her, running it past her for faults. Daisy was full of objections.

"Don't be silly—the old lady won't let you go. Nor will Abby and Max and the rest of them."

"I know. I won't tell them. I'm going to say I've gone to stay with Lady Dalrymple until the scandal of my broken engagement has died down a little."

"But you can't go all that way on your own, so who do you expect to come with you?"

"Don't worry, I'm not going to ask you. You're so busy at the moment, you'd do nothing but worry about all your work piling up." Daisy looked relieved and Jane went on, "And I can't ask Abby, not while she's expecting a baby, and Damaris gets ill in a carriage, and though I know she'd come if I needed her, I'd never ask her. And I know I can't go alone, so don't look at me as if I'm an idiot. I'm taking Polly. And William."

"William?"

"I won't take him with us into the village, but I need him on the journey. For protection. And before you ask, I'll send Polly to hire a traveling chaise. They're the quickest."

"And the most expensive."

"I have enough money, I think. People keep giving me 'pin money' so I can buy what I like for my season."

"Why does it have to be you? Why not send someone else? Hire a woman or summat."

"Because I'm going mad, not being able to do anything to help. And because I can do this. And besides, what woman? How do I know I can trust her with something so important?"

Finally Daisy had run out of objections, but she still didn't like it. Jane expected that; Daisy hated lies and deception. "The old lady's goin' to have a fit when she finds out. So is Abby and Damaris. And if you upset Abby, Max will throttle you."

"They won't worry as long as they think I'm with Lady Dalrymple. They'll be surprised, but not, I hope, suspicious."

"Just don't expect me to lie to any of them; if they ask me, I'm gunna tell them."

"Of course, but just—try not to be asked, please, dearest Daisy."

Daisy sniffed but gave a reluctant nod. Jane rang for Polly and explained what she wanted her to do. Polly didn't like the idea either at first, but Jane promised her she would not lose her position, that Jane would take all the blame. That and the promise of five guineas when they returned from Wales secured Polly's wholehearted cooperation.

Sworn to secrecy, Polly hurried off to pack a bag, and arrange the hire of the carriage. The story was that Jane's grandmother, Lady Dalrymple, was sending the carriage to fetch her, so Polly needed to slip out to do the hiring in secret.

Daisy sat on the bed, watching while Jane packed a valise

for herself. "Don't forget your shinin' armor," she commented sardonically.

Jane looked up, puzzled. "My what?"

"You did say you wanted to be the knight instead of the damsel, dintcha?"

Jane laughed. "Let us hope there are no dragons to slay, then."

Jane was ready to leave by quarter to nine. Lady Beatrice hadn't yet woken. Jane prayed she wouldn't. She left a note for the old lady with Featherby, saying she was going to stay with her grandmother in the country for a week or two, to avoid the worst of the scandal.

Featherby was quite concerned, and not a little suspicious of her sudden need to visit this grandmother that she barely knew—and more to the point that she hadn't yet met and who was sending a *hired* carriage for her. He'd been their friend long before he became Lady Beatrice's butler, but when Jane told him she wanted William and Polly to accompany her, for protection and propriety, he raised no further objection, though he was clearly not happy.

He sent William off to change out of his livery and to pack a bag.

The yellow chaise arrived as ordered, at nine o'clock on the dot—a good omen, Jane thought. She hugged Daisy good-bye, and climbed in with Polly while William packed their things in the trunk. The weather being fine, William was to ride on the outside seat at the rear of the carriage. That suited Jane perfectly, as she planned on keeping William in the dark about their destination until it was too late for him to object.

She sent up a quick prayer that their journey would be speedy, safe—and most important of all, fruitful—and the carriage set off.

"What do you mean her betrothal to Cambury is off? Didn't you give her my letter?"

Gil nodded. "I rather think that was why she broke it off."

Zach stared at him. "But I *told* her to marry him."

Gil shrugged. "Been my experience that women don't much like being told what to do. Especially who to marry."

"But what if I'm found guilty? What will she do then?" And why hadn't he heard from her? He'd expected an answer to his letter, at least. Some kind of message. Not this . . . silence.

It unnerved him. Silence always made him assume the worst.

He resumed his pacing. Was she angry with him? Despite what Gil had said, Zach was sure it was Cambury who'd dumped her, the dishonorable swine. Cambury had had him arrested. So why do that if he was going to abandon Jane? For revenge?

And what was Jane doing? Was she all right? Was she utterly disgraced? A target for scandal and vicious gossip?

The possibilities seethed endlessly in his brain. He paced, not even noticing when Gil quietly left.

He'd trapped a bee in a bottle once when he was a boy. It had buzzed endlessly from side to side, hitting a wall and bouncing in the opposite direction, random, frantic, senseless. Zach felt like that now.

Chapter Twenty-five

The distance is nothing when one has a motive.

—JANE AUSTEN, *PRIDE AND PREJUDICE*

It was the longest journey Jane had ever made. Though the yellow bounders were known for speed and efficiency, and the postilions and the horses were changed regularly, it took more than three days of practically endless traveling to get to Wales. And by the time they reached the small village of Llandudno, it felt like every bone in her body had been shaken loose and every inch of her bottom was black and blue.

Darkness had fallen by the time they arrived, and William, by now well apprised of the intent of the journey, and unable to change Jane's mind, took charge. By dint of questioning and mime, he managed to find them some accommodation; a small local hostelry facing the sea, too small to be called an inn, more a house with a taproom below and two bedchambers to rent above. It was small, but clean and respectable.

Jane and Polly shared the larger bedchamber. They were exhausted, and after a bath and a light supper of hot soup and bread and cheese, both girls fell into bed and slept like the dead until morning.

When Jane awoke and looked out of the small upstairs window, the sun was shining, dancing on the waves below. The sight filled her with optimism.

Over a hearty and delicious breakfast, Jane chatted to the landlady, Mrs. Price, who spoke good English accented with a lovely Welsh lilt.

Determined not to arouse the lady's suspicions by asking questions about Mary Thomas and Cecily Aston-Black, Jane acted the innocent traveler. "Such a pretty place this is," Jane commented. "A school friend of my older sister's was from Llandudno, and she always said it was wonderfully scenic. My middle sister, Damaris, would love to paint this view, I'm sure— she's a talented artist."

Mrs. Price was a plump, motherly-looking woman who clearly enjoyed a chat. They talked about families and sisters and the village for a while and then, as Jane had hoped, Mrs. Price could not resist asking the name of Jane's sister's school friend.

"Mary," Jane told her. "I don't remember what her married name is—Tomlins? Thompson? Something like that. But she's probably not living here anymore—she was widowed, I think, and no doubt moved away."

"Mary Thomas, that will be," Mrs. Price said in triumph. "And she hasn't moved, she lives just down that road there, around the corner and down the hill a short way—a white house with a big blue pot of geraniums by the doorway."

"Oh, I don't think she'd want to see me," Jane said, playing coy. "It was my sister she was at school with, not me. Abby's quite a bit older than me."

The more she demurred, the more Mrs. Price insisted. "She'd love to see you, I'm sure. A sweet, pretty girl like you are, miss— who wouldn't want to have you call on them? Go along with you now."

And Jane went.

She found the house with the big blue pot of red geraniums with no trouble and knocked. A slender, dark-haired woman of about thirty-five answered—Mary Thomas. Jane told her that Mrs. Price had suggested she call, and as she'd hoped, Mary Thomas invited Jane to step into the parlor for a cup of tea. Polly waited outside in the sun.

"I've come about Cecily Aston-Black," Jane said bluntly when she was seated.

Mrs. Thomas stiffened. The friendly expression dropped

away. She stood up. "I don't know any Cecily Aston-Black. You've come into my home on false pretenses. Please leave."

Jane didn't move. "First I want to tell you a story. I know men have been here looking for Cecily, but did any of them explain why they were looking for her?"

Mrs. Thomas shrugged. "They were from England. Like you. Please leave."

"I'm not going to leave until you tell me where Cecily is. I don't know what you think those other men wanted with her, but I'm here because the only person who can save the life of the man I love is Cecily. When he was a boy of just sixteen, he risked everything to save Cecily from the brutality of her husband—his father—so I think it's only fair that Cecily save him now. Because right now he's in prison in London and expected to hang for murder—Cecily's murder!"

Mary Thomas's eyes widened. "*Cecily's* murder?"

Jane nodded.

Mary Thomas sat down again. "I think you'd better explain."

Jane told her everything, and when she'd finished, Mrs. Thomas was silent for a long moment. Then she gave Jane a troubled look. "I would help you if I could, but—"

"Oh, please," Jane burst out, "I've told you what's at stake. If you know where she is, you must tell me!"

"I made a sacred promise that I would tell no one," Mary Thomas told her with a regretful expression. "I understand your problem—and I sympathize—but I cannot break that promise."

Jane said desperately, "You'd let him hang for a crime you *know* he didn't commit?"

Mary Thomas stood up. "I'm sorry, I can't help you."

"He's *not* going to be hanged for her—I won't allow it. I'm going to stay here and *force* you to tell me where she is."

Mary Thomas hesitated. "Perhaps you should try the church."

"The church?" Jane stared at her, trying to fathom the mind of a woman who would let an innocent man hang rather than break a promise. "What would I find at the church? Do they know where Cecily is?"

Mary Thomas shook her head. "I cannot tell what they might know or not know."

"Then why would you send me to the church? What will I

find there?" She added with sudden dread, "Oh, God, you don't mean Cecily is buried in the churchyard, do you?"

"No, she is alive—that much I will say. But go to the church. There you might find peace of mind." And with those words of scant comfort, Mary Thomas ushered Jane out of her cottage, and shut the door firmly behind her.

Polly was waiting outside. "Any luck, miss?"

"No," Jane said bitterly. "She knows, but she promised not to tell, and she won't break her promise, damn her! She told me to go to the church, that I might find some peace of mind there." She snorted. "Peace of mind! How can I have peace of mind when Zachary is rotting in jail? And she could help us save him but she *won't tell*."

They trudged back toward the inn. After all that traveling, to end up with such a . . . a frustrating nonanswer. Jane felt totally deflated.

She is alive—that much I will say. If Mary Thomas testified to that, it might save Zachary's life. And if she refused to go to London to testify, perhaps they could kidnap her and take her to London by force.

William wouldn't like it, though, and without William's cooperation, how could she kidnap anyone?

"Would that be the church she meant, up there, miss?" Polly pointed. On a hill overlooking the town and the sea sat a small gray stone church.

Jane sighed. "I don't suppose it will hurt," she said. "It's not as if we have any other alternative." They climbed the hill to the little church. It was a stiff climb, but when they reached it, puffing and panting, the view was spectacular.

They hadn't come for the view, however. There was no sign of a house; clearly the minister didn't live on the premises. The place seemed deserted.

The churchyard was dotted with gravestones. Jane didn't look at them. The woman had said Cecily was alive. Perhaps some clue might be found inside.

The door was unlocked and Jane peeped inside. It was small, plain and simple, with a spare beauty. A woman was polishing the woodwork. Jane could smell the beeswax.

The woman turned, saw Jane and came forward, speaking Welsh. She was fair and pretty.

Jane shook her head. "Sorry, I don't understand."

The woman smiled. "Sorry, we don't get many English up this way," she said in faintly stilted English with the musical Welsh lilt that Jane found so attractive. "Welcome to our church. Reverend Williams is away at the moment, but I am his wife. Can I help you with something?"

"I don't know," Jane said. "I am looking for an English-woman called Cecily Aston-Black, the Countess of Wainfleet. I believe she lives in this village."

The woman stilled.

"You know her." Jane's heart leapt.

"No," the woman said. "She was here many years ago, but she's gone now. I don't know where she is. And I'm sorry, I have no time to talk. I'm very busy." She turned away and resumed vigorously polishing the wooden fretwork at the front of the church.

"Please, it's very important," Jane said.

"I've told you all I know."

Jane hesitated. She was sure the woman knew more than she was saying, but she could hardly grab a minister's wife and choke the truth out of her, right here in her own church. She glanced at Polly. Polly shrugged, as if to say, "What can you do?" and reluctantly Jane conceded. She left the church on leaden feet. She needed to think. There was some mystery here and she was determined to get to the bottom of it.

She stood in the bright sunshine, gazing out across the sea, trying to work out what to do next. She was feeling rather foolish, having come here in such a melodramatic fashion, behind everyone's back, certain she could make a difference, be the knight instead of the damsel for once.

She'd found out precisely nothing. But—she stiffened her spine—she wasn't finished yet. She would go back to Mary Thomas and demand she tell Jane what she knew. And ask her about the woman at the church.

She headed toward the church gate, and stepped back as a black and white puppy bounded through the gate and cannoned into her, splattering mud all over her skirt. Laughing, she bent to pat him, holding his muddy paws off her skirt, which he took to be a wonderful new game.

A young girl following hard at his heels stopped dead when

she saw what had happened and apologized profusely—at least Jane assumed it was an apology. It was a torrent of Welsh.

"He's a lively little fellow, isn't he? Did he get away from you?" Jane said, hoping the girl might understand from her tone that she wasn't upset. She looked up at the child to reassure her.

And looked straight into a pair of silvery gray-green eyes that were only too familiar.

Something of Jane's shock must have shown in her face for the girl stepped backward, a wary look on her face. She was young, perhaps eleven or twelve, with thick, dark, wavy hair, a pale complexion and a pair of wide, dark-lashed eyes that were like silvered sage leaves.

It was like a punch to the stomach.

Zachary Black's daughter.

And yet he'd sworn there was nothing between him and Cecily. Another of his lies? He could hardly wriggle out of this; the child was his very image, only young and female. Zachary would have looked much like this at the same age, all long legs and endearing, adolescent awkwardness.

"What is your name?" Jane asked gently. "And where is your mother?"

The girl took another step backward. She glanced around, like a gangly young doe about to flee from hunters, but Polly had anticipated the move and had stepped in between the child and the gate, blocking her escape.

"It's all right," Jane assured her, speaking slowly. She had no idea whether the child understood English or not, but she hoped her tone would carry the message. "Nobody will harm you. I just want to meet your mother."

"Maaam!" the girl suddenly yelled at the top of her voice, and a moment later the minister's wife burst from the church and skidded to a halt.

"Leave her alone, she doesn't know anything," she said. She addressed the child in rapid Welsh. The girl gave a quick nod and braced herself to run.

"It's not her I came looking for, Cecily," Jane said. "It's you. And before you try to deny who you are, may I just say your daughter is the living image of her father."

Cecily sagged in acceptance. She gave a defeated nod.

"We need to talk," Jane told her.

"All right, but in private—let my daughter go."

Jane nodded. Cecily said something in Welsh, and the young girl shook her head. "No, Mam, I want to stay," she said in perfect English with only the faintest hint of a lilt. And Jane realized that just now Cecily had spoken with no accent at all.

Cecily shook her head and answered in Welsh, and reluctantly the girl turned to leave.

"May Polly go with her?" Jane asked. She didn't trust Cecily and her daughter not to have hatched an instant plot to run away. "Polly is my maid," she added. "Your daughter will be perfectly safe with her."

Cecily hesitated, then nodded, and Polly and the child left. Cecily indicated a bench outside the church and they sat down.

"Does Zachary know he has a daughter?" Jane asked.

"I don't know any Zachary."

"Zachary Black."

Again, Cecily shook her head, and just as Jane was about to argue, she remembered. "I mean Adam George Zachary Aston-Black, though he calls himself Zachary Black."

Cecily said tightly, "He's not Winnie's father; he's her brother, her half brother."

"Oh. Of course." The tight fist in Jane's chest loosened, though why she should dislike the notion of him having a child, she didn't know. It was long before she met him.

"Does he know he has a little sister?"

"He can't have her."

Jane frowned. "I don't understand."

Cecily didn't bother to explain. "I'm not going anywhere. I don't care how many men—or ladies—the earl sends, I'm not going back, and neither is my daughter."

Daisy was right: Cecily had been hiding from her husband. "It's all right, Zachary—I mean Adam—is the earl now. His father died last year, as I underst—" She broke off, frowning. "But you must have known that—you said you were the minister's wife."

Cecily paled. She looked down at the ground and said nothing, her face tense and set.

And Jane understood. No wonder Cecily wanted to keep hidden, and why it was all such a secret.

"How long have you been married?" she asked quietly.

Cecily swallowed. "You mustn't tell. He—my husband doesn't know." The husband that was away at the moment.

Jane tried not to let her shock show. Cecily had not just married bigamously—she'd bigamously married a *minister!*

"I had no idea when I first came here that I was with child," Cecily explained in a low voice. "I must have conceived just before I left Wainfleet. And I didn't want anyone here to know who I was, in case my husband came after me, so Mary and I agreed I should live under my maiden name. She introduced me as a spinster friend of hers from school."

"It must have been awkward when you learned you were increasing."

Cecily nodded. "It wasn't until I started getting fat that I realized. I had no morning sickness, nothing—and my courses had always been irregular, so by the time I realized it, I was well along."

She gave Jane an embarrassed glance. "In fact, I didn't even realize it then—I was shamefully ignorant, I'm afraid. It was Michael who broke it to me."

"Michael?"

"Reverend Williams, my . . . my husband. He's a good, kind, compassionate man, and he realized before I did what the problem was. He assumed I was an innocent girl, you see, taken advantage of by some English rake." She gazed out over the sea. "He told me I was going to have a baby, asked me about the father—of course I couldn't tell him, in case he wrote to the earl—Michael is such a good man, he has no idea how . . . evil . . . other men can be." A shudder racked her slender body.

"He told me then I must marry him, and give the child a name." She glanced at Jane. "Of course I refused him, but he kept on."

She bit her lip. "I know it was wrong, but by then, all the villagers knew—I was really showing, and the looks I was getting . . . It was horrid."

"Why didn't you explain?"

"I couldn't. What if someone wrote to the earl?"

Jane could sympathize, but the thought crossed her mind that Cecily could have simply explained she was widowed. But she was the gentle, helpless type and no doubt the thought of raising a child on her own—among villagers who would probably suspect the child was a bastard anyway—would have been quite daunting.

Cecily continued, "And then talk started in the village that I was carrying Michael's babe. Which was so dreadfully unfair—Michael is so kind and gentle and caring . . ."

And then Jane understood. "You were in love with him."

Cecily nodded. "I knew it was wrong and a mortal sin—and a crime—but I did it. And for nearly twelve years we've been so happy. He's a wonderful father to Winnie—he loves her and she adores him." She gave Jane a piteous look. "He doesn't know and I would rather die than tell him."

"It's Zachary—Adam—who will die if you stay in hiding."

"*What?*" Cecily turned to her in shock. "What do you mean?"

"Don't you know? He's in prison, and likely to be hanged for murder—your murder!"

"*My* murder?"

Jane nodded. "He needs you to come to London and prove his innocence." She frowned. "Why do you think those men came looking for you before?"

Cecily looked shamefaced. "I don't really know. Mary warned me that a man had come on the Earl of Wainfleet's business, and I panicked." She bit her lip. "We told everyone he was a tax collector from England come after me, so everybody pretended they spoke no English, and he went away. When the second man came, we knew—or we thought we knew—what he wanted, so we did the same. He was cleverer than the first one, but he went away in the end, and I thought I was safe again."

"Both those men were sent by Zachary, because he needed to prove he hadn't murdered you and stolen your jewels."

"And you have come because . . ."

"Because I love him. And because I know what it is to have to flee from evil men."

"Not Zachary!" Cecily said, horrified.

Jane laughed. "No, not Zachary," she said softly. "He's a rescuer of women, not a bully." She looked at Cecily. "So, Cecily, will you come with me to London and prove his innocence?"

Cecily hesitated, looking troubled, but just as Jane was about to threaten to drag her there—by force if necessary!—she nodded. "Yes, of course I'll come. Michael is away at the moment. With any luck I can go to London and be back before his return."

Jane wasn't particularly impressed by Cecily's priorities, but as long as she saved Zach from the hangman, she could keep her secrets.

They walked down to the village together in silence. Jane was preoccupied by the problem of how to transport herself, Cecily, Polly and William back to London. In her rush to get here, she hadn't considered that. The post chaise could carry two, three at a squeeze, and besides, it had departed the morning after they'd arrived. One didn't keep a post chaise waiting, not if one had limited means.

She would have to send William to the nearest large town to hire a vehicle.

They reached the main street of the village just in time to see a smart traveling chaise and four pull up outside the little village hostelry. A groom ran to take the horses. The driver, a tall gentleman in a dusty, elegantly cut, many-caped driving coat, buckskin breeches and dusty black boots, swung down and stalked toward them.

He was unshaven, weary and furious.

Cecily clutched Jane's arm nervously. "Who is that?"

"My brother-in-law," Jane said, delighted that her transport problems had been so neatly solved. "Max, what a surprise. And what excellent time you made. Have you come for me?" She braced herself for a tongue-lashing.

"I ought to throttle you!" Max growled, drawing her into a hard, relieved hug. "Frightening Abby like that. And Lady Beatrice is beside herself."

Jane stood on tiptoe to kiss his cheek. "But I was perfectly all right. I had Polly and William with me all the time. And see—it was worth it." She drew Cecily forward. "This is Cecily, former Countess of Wainfleet. Cecily, my brother-in-law Max, Lord Davenham."

Max blinked. "You found her!"

"Yes. And she's agreed to come to London with us and testify that she's not dead after all." Jane couldn't help grinning; she wanted to dance and sing and cheer. Zachary Black was safe.

"Why the devil didn't you simply ask me to drive you?" Max said over luncheon. He'd decided to give the horses a two-hour spell and set off for London that same day.

Jane agreed. The sooner she could get Cecily to London, the sooner Zachary would be out of jail.

"I didn't think you'd agree," Jane told him. "Would you have?"

"Probably not," he conceded.

"Are Abby and Lady Bea really upset?"

"Very." He gave her a baleful look. "It helped that you took William."

"How did you find me so quickly?"

He said dryly, "Next time you go to stay with your grandmother in the country, you might remember to tell that grandmother it would be better if she didn't then come to make a morning call in Berkeley Square."

"Oh."

His lips twitched. "It wasn't hard to guess where you were heading for."

"I thought Daisy would have told you—she tried so hard to talk me out of it."

He grinned. "It was Daisy's uncharacteristic silence that got Lady Beatrice so worried in the first place. The poor girl almost burst from trying to avoid speaking at all." He quirked an eyebrow. "Made you a promise not to talk, did she?"

Jane nodded.

After a quick lunch they set off in Max's chaise. It was a bit of a squash—Cecily had brought her daughter, Winnie, with her. It seemed Winnie had known all along that Michael Williams wasn't her real father—though Cecily conveyed with a warning look at Jane that she didn't know anything else—and now that she'd discovered she had a big half brother, she was eager to meet him.

Cecily had left a letter for Michael, saying she'd had to go to London on a family matter, and she and Winnie would be back in about ten days.

On the journey Jane got to know Zachary's little sister better. She was a shy child, but sweet-natured and very eager to learn all she could about her newfound brother. Cecily was one of those people who, like Polly, could sleep a journey away. Since Jane was not, she was delighted to talk to Winnie about her brother, relating some of the stories she'd heard from him.

By the end of the journey she and Winnie were firm friends.

Max's chaise was better sprung than the post chaise—they weren't called "yellow bounders" for nothing—but it was still an exhausting and relentless journey. Max changed horses every twenty miles, and they made good time, arriving in Berkeley Square midmorning of the third day.

Featherby must have been watching out for their arrival, because he ran down the front steps and spoke to Max before the carriage steps were let down to let the ladies alight.

Max opened the carriage door himself. "You have ten minutes to relieve yourselves and tidy up." He looked at Jane. "Freddy and Gil Radcliffe have managed to get a preliminary hearing set up for Wainfleet—a magistrate will hear the evidence against him and decide whether there is a case to answer in the House of Lords. It's already started, so hurry!"

They raced inside, used the necessary, and in less than ten minutes were weaving through the traffic to the place where the hearing was being conducted.

Chapter Twenty-six

Know your own happiness. Want for
nothing but patience—or give it a more
fascinating name: Call it hope.

—JANE AUSTEN, SENSE AND SENSIBILITY

"We were damned lucky to get a preliminary hearing," Gil said. Zach knew it. Gil and Freddy Monkton-Coombes—a fellow whom Zach didn't even know!—had moved heaven and earth to make it happen. Cousin Gerald had fought just as strenuously to prevent it.

But Freddy Monkton-Coombes knew people and had pulled strings on Zach's behalf, and Gil and his lawyer had managed to cause enough doubt to get a magistrate to agree to hear the evidence and decide whether or not there was a case to answer.

The hearing was being conducted in a large meeting room, not a formal courtroom. Zachary was seated at a small table to one side, flanked by Gil on one side, and his lawyer on the other. At another table sat Cousin Gerald and his lawyer. He'd claimed to be representing Cecily, the murder victim, as the heir to her husband, the late Lord Wainfleet.

At the front sat the magistrate, a hawk-faced elderly man, sharp, fiercely intelligent and something of a radical; he'd made it clear that he didn't have much time for aristocrats who thought they could get away with murder. Or pull strings on their friend's behalf.

Just Zach's luck to get one of the few scrupulously honest magistrates in London.

The doors were opened and a crowd of people surged in. Zach was taken aback. He'd imagined it would be a small affair.

"That's the Wainfleet contingent," Gil murmured in Zach's ear as a dozen or more people took seats down the front. Zach nodded dazedly as he glimpsed faces he hadn't seen in years, as well as some he'd met on his recent visit to Wainfleet.

"My man had instructions to bring up only those witnesses who could give actual evidence—there was almost a riot when he limited it to eight people."

"Eight? There looks to me more than that."

Gil nodded. "We had to hire an extra carriage. Everyone wants to testify that it couldn't possibly have been you who killed Cecily." He glanced at Zach. "Do you have any idea how they feel about you down there? It's positively feudal."

Zach nodded, a lump in his throat as he watched the Wainfleet people file in—his people. Some faces, like the Wilkses, were familiar, and a man he thought might be Briggs, the gamekeeper. There was Sykes, his father's old coachman, and a number of others Zach couldn't place—maids, footmen, gardeners—it looked like Gil had imported the entire Wainfleet staff.

"We argued their testimonies were vital; was a way to delay the hearing," Gil murmured. "I don't have much hope that their evidence will help, but they were all determined to argue on your behalf."

Zach swallowed, touched by their loyalty. "No sign of Cecily?"

Gil shook his head.

Others filed in. To Zach's surprise, Lady Beatrice arrived, and took a seat at the front of the room. She was accompanied by three of her nieces—none of them Jane—and a lanky, elegant fellow that Gil said was Freddy Monkton-Coombes. Who'd pulled strings to help get this preliminary hearing. Zach nodded to them all. Why had they come?

And more to the point, where was Jane?

Why had her family come, but not Jane? She couldn't be ill—if she were, her aunt and sisters wouldn't be here. So . . . was she angry? Upset?

He examined their expressions and decided they looked more dutiful than anything. No smiles or hopeful nods such as the

Wainfleet servants were giving him. Was her family here to bear witness to his downfall? Because he'd ruined her life?

A small knot of smartly dressed young men caught his attention as they entered and took seats near the back. Each one of them nodded to Zach, and with amazement, he recognized boys he'd gone to school with, friends not seen for twelve years, now grown up. He nodded to them, his throat full.

Everybody from Zach's world was here; everybody—apart from Cousin Gerald—had come to show support. Except Jane.

He felt gutted by her absence. But he couldn't blame her. He'd sent her away, fool that he was. And she'd believed him when he said he felt for her only what a friend would feel. Though why had she called off her betrothal? The same old questions, endlessly circling in his brain . . .

The hearing started. First the original coroner's report was discussed. Then one by one the witnesses from Wainfleet were questioned by the magistrate.

The gamekeeper, Briggs, began by stating his firm belief that young Master Adam had had naught to do with it, that Master Adam was a good lad and never did no harm to man nor beast— nor woman. Then he'd gone on to describe how he'd seen the countess's body caught in the reeds.

The magistrate fired questions at him. Briggs answered them in a firm voice.

"Yes, it was definitely the countess's body. She had been missing for three days before they found her body."

"Yes, young Master Adam *had* disappeared at the same time, but he couldn't have—"

"Yes, sir, her skull was cracked and she'd been thrown in the water. But Master Adam had naught to do with it. He couldn't have . . ."

For all Briggs's good intentions, the testimony was damning. Zach gave him a friendly nod as he sat down, to show he had no hard feelings, but Briggs couldn't look at him.

Next, one of the former Wainfleet maids came forward. She also testified to it being definitely the countess's body. Yes, she was certain. She knew her ladyship well; she'd attended her in the bath. But she too was certain it couldn't have been Zach, even though it was true that he'd disappeared the same night as the countess. "He was always a nice, quiet boy."

As she returned to her seat, the magistrate turned his head and gave the "nice, quiet boy" a hard, you're-wasting-my-time glance.

Several of the servants testified that Zach and his father had argued often and that the arguments frequently ended in violence. They'd insisted the violence was all on the late earl's side, but as the magistrate pointed out, the late earl wasn't there to defend himself.

As one by one the Wainfleet people stepped up, defending Zach with nothing but faith and loyalty—and love—the lump grew in his throat. He felt guilty for his long neglect of them—*his* people, they'd made that clear—and of Wainfleet. He loved it, he realized—and only understood that now, when he was about to lose it all. And disgrace it.

He was sunk. He was going to hang. He just wished . . . No, better that he didn't see Jane again, not while he was in prison. Nor on trial. Better that she forget him and marry . . . someone else.

There was a slight stir at the back of the room, where it was standing room only. Late arrivals, come just in time to see him indicted for murder.

Dammit, why had she severed her betrothal to Cambury? He might be a bore, but he would at least have taken good care of her.

The laundry maid was called next, but instead, a tall, elegantly dressed man in buckskins and high boots arrogantly pushed his way to the front of the room. The hawk-faced magistrate frowned in irritation. "Yes? Yes? What is it? If you have evidence to give, you can wait your turn." He waved the tall man aside.

He took no notice. "I am Lord Davenham, and I believe producing the so-called murder victim, alive and well, supersedes all other evidence." There was an audible gasp, then the entire room held its collective breath as he said, "Cecily Aston-Black, Countess of Wainfleet, is not dead."

The calm, authoritative statement caused a sensation.

Zach sat up, his heart beating frantically. He scanned the crowded room, but half the audience was on its feet and everyone was weaving back and forth and craning their necks in an effort to see what was going on and he couldn't see.

Hawk-face was the only one in the room who remained unimpressed. He called for quiet, then said, "I presume you have evidence to support this outrageous statement?"

The tall man inclined his head. "The best evidence of all—the so-called victim herself, Cecily Aston-Black, Countess of Wainfleet, in person."

Zach's fingernails bit into his palm. He waited, his throat dry, his heart pounding. Pray God this wasn't another trick of Gil's. If he had found someone to imitate Cecily . . .

He glanced at Gil, but he looked as surprised as anyone.

There was a stir at the back of the room as a woman started slowly forward, a pale, pretty young woman with fair, curly hair and frightened blue eyes. *Cecily!*

Shaking like a leaf, she threaded her way to the front of the room. Nobody moved; nobody spoke.

It really was her! Zach started to breathe again. Hope, dammed up for so long, broke free, first in a trickle, then in a flood. Cecily was here. He was saved.

The magistrate gestured, and one of his men brought a chair forward for her to sit. Hawk-face might not like aristocrats, Zach thought, but he wasn't immune to a pretty face.

Whispers rippled through the audience as she faced them and sat.

She'd changed a little in the twelve years since he'd last seen her—she'd put on some weight, and was looking more matronly, but it really was Cecily. How had they found her? Where? Relief swamped him.

It didn't matter how or where—she'd been found. She was here. Zach owed Davenham his life.

The room fell silent as Cecily folded her hands in her lap and waited.

"Your name?"

"Cecily Aston-Black, former Countess of Wainfleet." She spoke almost in a whisper. A hushed ripple echoed through the audience.

"Can anyone here vouch for your identity?"

Cecily looked around helplessly. She stood and looked at a group of women in the third row. "Is that Joan? And Mary? And . . . I think . . . is it Mabel?"

"And who are Joan and Mary and Mabel?" Hawk-face asked.

The three women stood. "Please your honor," said one. "We were maids when her ladyship was at Wainfleet."

"And do you recognize this woman?"

All three nodded vigorously. "'Tis the countess, for sure," one said. "Bless you, my lady, we all thought you dead." Tears streamed down the woman's face.

Zach knew how she felt.

Hawk-face stabbed a long, bony finger at one of the maids. "You told us all, not ten minutes ago, that you saw 'her poor drownded body' pulled from the lake. That it was definitely the countess."

The woman looked ready to burst into tears. "I was certain too, me lord, but"—she looked at Cecily—"that's definitely the countess. I don't understand it, but that's her, all right."

Mrs. Wilks stood. "I'll vouch for her too. That's her lady-ship, sure as I'm standing here. God be praised, m'lady."

And one by one, all the Wainfleet servants rose to their feet and agreed that it was a mystery, but yes, that was Cecily, Countess of Wainfleet. No doubt of it.

Hawk-face gestured in disgust for them to sit down again. He surveyed them sourly. "Then if this is the Countess of Wainfleet, who was the woman you fished from the lake?" He looked at Briggs, the gamekeeper, who looked bewildered and shook his head.

"Why did you think it was the countess?"

"She was small and slender and fair, just like 'er ladyship," Briggs said. "And 'er ladyship had gone missing."

"Surely you looked at her face," Hawk-face snapped.

Briggs gave an apologetic shrug. "After three days in the lake, there ain't much face left, yer honor."

One of the maids put her hand up.

"Yes?"

"It was her clothes, yer honor—the countess's clothes. She was wearing her new dress." She turned to Cecily. "You remember, my lady, the lovely gold dress with the satin ribbons that the earl bought for you special?"

Cecily shuddered. "I didn't care for it." Zach's father often gave her expensive gifts after a particularly bad night. "I gave the dress to Jeannie, for her wedding—my personal maid, Jeannie Carr. She was going to be married the next day. She loved the dress, and we were the same si—" She faltered and her hands flew up to her mouth as she realized the implications. She finished in a horrified whisper, "We were the same size. I gave her the gold dress to wear at her wedding."

There was a ripple of conjecture, then a maid said, "We thought Jeannie had jilted Bobby Looker, left him standing at the altar . . . but all the time . . ." She burst into noisy sobs.

"If the body was that of Jeannie Carr," Hawk-face said, "there is still a murder to be investigated."

Sykes, Zach's father's old coachman, got heavily to his feet. "I reckon I know what happened to her," he said. "I've thought about it off and on for years, but . . ." He scratched his head worriedly. "I weren't sure enough to stir it all up again."

"Get on with it, man," Hawk-face snapped.

"When his lordship learned young Master Adam had run off with the mistress, he were that furious—he were a man of temper, but I never saw him so enraged. He'd been drinkin' a fair bit," he said in an apologetic aside to Zach. "He insisted on setting out after you in his curricle, even though it were well dark by then. And he were determined on driving himself—well, you know what he were like, Master Adam."

Zach nodded. When his father was drunk and in a rage, the devil himself couldn't reason with him.

The old man's face crinkled with emotion. "We hit something on the way out, just before the bridge. I thought it were a sheep, honest I did—I heard a little bleat. I went back when we got home the next morning to check—I don't like to let animals suffer, but I never found nothing, so I never thought much about it. But thinking back . . . I reckon he might have hit young Jeannie, going to meet her Bobby, all dressed in her finest . . ."

There was a hushed silence as people in the audience pictured a joyful young bride, crossing the grounds of the estate in the dark, dressed in her beautiful new gold dress, going to meet her groom, only to be struck by a curricle driven by a drunken maniac . . . and drowned.

They pictured the groom waiting at the altar the next morning, the slow devastation as the minutes passed and it dawned on him that he'd been jilted. And the question of "why" never answered . . . until now. So very tragic.

Hawk-face made a note and said briskly, "In that case, I find there is no case to answer. Cecily Aston-Black is alive and well, and the death of the maidservant, Jeannie Carr, I rule as accidental death, and since the driver has gone to his eternal rest, that is the end of the matter. Lord Wainfleet, you are free to leave."

There was a moment of utter silence, then cheers burst out. Zach rose to his feet, half in disbelief at his good fortune, half exultant. He was free, free to build a new life. Now he just needed to find the girl he wanted to build it with . . .

And at the back of the room, a beautiful young woman rose to her feet, her smile a dazzling sunburst in a sea of happy smiles. Zach thought his heart would burst.

She was here, after all. Waiting for him. Jane had come.

Jane stood at the back of the room, jostled by the throngs of people all wanting to personally congratulate Zachary, unable to get to him.

Across the room her eyes met his. His glowed, shining silver-green. She smiled back, close to tears—happy tears. They'd made it in time, after all. She'd found Cecily and brought her to London, and Zachary Black—Lord Wainfleet, as he was, though she would always think of him as Zachary—was free.

A little hand slipped into hers. It was Winnie. "It'll be all right now, won't it, Jane? My brother is free? Mam spoke up and set him free?"

Jane hugged her. "Yes, my love, he's free. Your mam set him free."

Cecily was still down the front near Zach. She was looking quite terrified by all the attention, but it looked like Max was looking after her. She would have some explaining to do, but not here, not now—this was all for celebration.

Jane watched Zach, surrounded by well-wishers, shaking hands, smiling. Winnie leaned against her trustingly and Jane glanced down. The child's resemblance to Zach had initially endeared Jane to her, but those long days in the carriage had taught her to love Winnie for herself.

"See that tall, beautiful man over there?" she said to Winnie.

"My brother, you mean?"

"That's the one. He doesn't know it yet, but I'm going to marry him."

Winnie's thin little face lit up. "Really?"

"Yes, really. But don't tell a soul yet—it's a secret."

"I promise." Winnie's eyes were shining. "Will that make you my sister?"

"Yes." Jane hugged her. "I've always wanted a little sister."

"I've always wanted a sister too," Winnie confided.

"Well, now you'll have four, because you can share mine: Abby, Damaris and Daisy." She pointed them out. "And I suspect you might get an aunt as well—see that old lady? That's Lady Beatrice."

Winnie looked at Lady Beatrice, leaning heavily on her stick, glaring at the milling throng blocking her exit. She caught Gil Radcliffe by the coat and said something to him. He nodded and cleared a path for her.

"She looks a bit scary," Winnie whispered as the old lady stumped toward them.

"She does, but she has the kindest heart in the world," Jane told her. "I promise."

"Come on, we're going home," Lady Beatrice declared. "Can't tolerate this racket any longer. Freddy's taking Damaris and Daisy home and Max will bring Abby."

"But—" Jane began. She wanted to speak to Zachary.

"Told young Radcliffe to bring him along later. They're both coming to dinner." She frowned at Jane. "Well, you didn't imagine you could have any kind of private talk here, with all this rabble looking on, did you? Do it better in the parlor at home. Don't fret, gel—he has obligations to his tenants, but he'll come. I doubt wild beasts could keep him away from you now his name's been cleared."

Jane looked across at Zach and sent a silent signal, pointing to Lady Beatrice and indicating she had to go. He nodded and mouthed the word *soon*. She blew him a kiss, and across the room he sent her a blazing look, a silent promise that dried her mouth and sent her heart racing.

Lady Beatrice observed the exchange, gave a snort of laughter, then looked at Winnie, clinging to Jane's arm. "Well now, who's this?"

"This is Winnie Williams, Lady Beatrice. She's Lady Wainfleet's daughter, and Zachary's half sister. And," Jane added, drawing Winnie closer, "I've just been telling her she might be getting a new aunt."

Lady Beatrice's eyes gleamed. "Ho! A new niece, is it? Excellent. Now, come along, Winnie child, Max—that's my nephew—is bringing your mother, so no need to worry. After all this excitement, I need a drink, and I expect you could do with a cake and some lemonade, eh?"

Winnie nodded shyly and, still clinging to Jane's arm, followed the old lady out to the waiting carriage.

There was no way Zach could get away quickly from his well-wishers, and to be honest, he couldn't bring himself to brush them off, even though there was nothing he wanted more in life than to go to Jane.

But these good folk had made what was, for most of them, the longest journey of their lives, just to show him support, and he was grateful. More than grateful, he was deeply touched.

So he invited them all—his Wainfleet people and the men he'd been to school with and anyone else—even Cousin Gerald— to join him at the tavern over the way, where he bought drinks for the next two hours.

At the commencement of the first round, once everybody in the taproom had a drink in their hands, he made a speech, thanking them for their support, for their faith in him. To his school friends he promised a dinner at Gil's club—soon to be his own as well—and to the folk from Wainfleet he promised a proper celebration on the estate—a May Day fete, celebrating his return to England—

"Your return from the dead, me lord!" some wag in the audience called, and they all laughed.

"And the beginning, I hope, of a new, prosperous era for all at Wainfleet," Zach finished. "To the future." And they all drank.

Zach glanced at the door. He'd need to stay at least another hour before he could leave. He toasted and joked and laughed and talked, a drink in his hand the whole time, but he hardly drank a thing.

There was only one thing he wanted now: Jane.

Chapter Twenty-seven

*I cannot fix on the hour, or the spot, or the look or the
words, which laid the foundation. It is too long ago. I was
in the middle before I knew that I had begun.*

—JANE AUSTEN, *PRIDE AND PREJUDICE*

B ack at the house on Berkeley Square, Jane was on tenterhooks. She participated in the conversations, and she hoped
she made sense, but the whole time she was listening for one
thing: the front doorbell, signaling the arrival of Zachary
Black.

Finally the bell jangled in the hallway, and without waiting
for Featherby to announce Zachary's arrival, Jane jumped up
and rushed out. And skidded to a halt.

"I believe my wife is here, the former Countess of Wainfleet." A soberly dressed man of medium height stood in the
hallway, hat in hand.

"Mr. Williams?" Jane said, coming forward. "I am Jane
Chance—delighted to meet you. Yes, Cecily is here, and Winnie too. They are in the drawing room taking tea. If you would
care to come this way—"

"Thank you, but no," he said, his face rather grim. "If you
don't mind, I would rather speak to my wife alone first. If there
is somewhere . . ." He glanced around.

"Of course," Jane said, her heart sinking. This did not look
good for Cecily. "Featherby, will you show Mr. Williams into
the front parlor, please? I will fetch Cecily."

She hurried back to the drawing room. "Cecily, your husband is here."

Cecily started, looking instantly apprehensive. Winnie, on the other hand, exclaimed "Papa!" and flew from the room.

She was still hugging him when Jane and Cecily arrived. He clearly loved the child and she him, which made Jane warm to him a little. Taking Winnie with her, she left a pale and clearly nervous Cecily alone with her husband, presumably to break the news to him of her bigamy.

Cecily looked at Michael, twisting her handkerchief between nervous fingers.

"Well, girl, do you not have a kiss for me?" he said quietly.

His voice was so gentle she wanted to burst into tears, but she was too filled with guilt. She hurried over and kissed him nervously. "How did you find me?"

"I followed you back here after that hearing."

"You were there?" She stared at him. "But how?"

"I've been to Wainfleet, where I heard all about the countess—drowned in the lake, some said; run off with the son, others said. And I heard all about the old earl who died last year, who had a way with his fists when in drink, and not choosy about where those fists landed. He's not much mourned by anyone."

She thrust a shaking hand against her mouth. "Oh, my God—you *know*?"

He nodded.

"About the . . . the bigamy?"

Again, he nodded.

"But how? What made you go to Wainfleet in the first place?"

"That lawyer's man. There he was, asking about the Countess of Wainfleet, and you and Mary Thomas all in a tizzy about him and convincing the whole village to speak only Welsh to the poor man. And what do we have to do with the Countess of Wainfleet, I wondered, so I had a quiet word with the fellow."

"Oh, Michael." Cecily's eyes filled with tears.

"He told me she'd gone missing twelve years ago, and that the earl needed her in London now. And that her name was Cecily."

At that, a sob burst from Cecily. "Oh, Michael, I'm so sorry, so sorry."

He pulled out a handkerchief and wiped her cheeks. "Hush now, girl, don't take on. What's done is done."

"Why didn't you say anything?"

"Well, see, I remember how you were when you first came to stay with Mary Thomas. Jumpy and nervous, you were, *cariad*, like a dog that's been ill-treated and has learned to fear the hand of man." He stroked her cheek with the back of his fingers. "I knew you were running from something bad—from someone bad. I knew you were in hiding, knew you were full of fear and secrets." He smiled. "But, God forgive me, I wanted you."

"Oh, Michael . . . I should never have agreed to marry you, I know. Bigamy—it's a serious crime. And you've always been so upright, so pure—"

He laughed. "Not so upright or pure that I didn't want you the instant I set eyes on you. And still do." And he drew her into his arms and kissed her.

"What are you going to do?" Cecily said after a while.

He tucked a stray curl behind her ear. "I suppose you'd better make an honest man out of me."

She blinked. "I don't understand."

"I think a quiet London wedding will do the trick. Then we go back to Llandudno and go on with our lives."

"You mean you're not going to tell?"

"What good would that do? You're my wife; I made promises in the presence of God, promises I still consider sacred—bigamy or not. God knew the truth, even if I didn't. Perhaps that's why He never blessed us with another child."

She bit her lip.

"But our Winnie is blessing enough for me," he continued. "And we'll face Divine Judgment when the time comes. My mind is easy."

His goodness, his acceptance, brought on more tears. "Michael Williams, you're such a good and decent man, I don't deserve you. But I love you so much."

"Hush now, *cariad*. Just tell me you'll marry me in London and give us a *cwtch*." He opened his arms to her and she threw herself into them.

* * *

The doorbell rang just as Cecily had brought her husband into the drawing room and was in the middle of introducing him to everyone. Before Jane could excuse herself, Featherby ushered Zachary into the drawing room.

There was a chorus of greetings and congratulations.

"Thank you, everyone," he said. "I would love to discuss it all with you, and I will later—I believe I've been invited for dinner?" Lady Beatrice inclined her head graciously. He thanked her, and turned to Cecily. "And, Cecily, there are things we need to discuss, but first—" He turned back to Lady Beatrice. "May I speak to your niece in private?"

"Certainly, dear boy, but which niece? I have five for you to choose from."

He grinned, began to turn away, then glanced back with an odd look. "Five? I thought there were only four."

Lady Beatrice smiled. "I have a new niece, one you have not yet met. Lady Winifred Aston-Black, better known as Winnie Williams—your sister."

"My sist—" He broke off and Jane saw how he looked, really looked, for the first time at Winnie. The child sat like a little mouse on the edge of her chair, gazing up at him—her magnificent big brother—with her heart in her eyes. Jane held her breath. Don't let him rush this, she prayed.

"I have a sister?" Zach said in a wondering voice. He looked at Winnie and gave her one of his slow, heart-curling smiles. "I have a beautiful little sister. You cannot know how happy this makes me, Winnie," he told her in his deep voice. "I have always wanted a little sister."

If Jane hadn't already fallen in love with him, she would have fallen at that moment.

And then he took his little sister's hands in his big ones and lifted them one after another to be kissed. It was just right. Winnie blossomed under his gentle care and smile.

"I have always wanted a brother too," Winnie said shyly.

Zachary laughed and caressed her cheek with one long finger. "I shall try to be a good one," he told her. "But I will need lots of practice. I'm looking forward to showing you Wainfleet, little sister. The people there will be thrilled to meet you—a new daughter for Wainfleet."

Cecily made a little sound in her throat and Zachary turned to her, saying, "First you give me my life back, and now, a sister, a precious gift for which I have no words." He kissed Cecily's hand. "Thank you from the bottom of my heart."

Cecily snatched her hand back. "You can't have her! I won't give her up!"

Zachary took in the situation at a glance. "Of course I won't take her from you, Cecily. I have no intention of separating you from your daughter—good God, what sort of a man would I be to even think of such a thing? She is your daughter and always will be."

She eyed him doubtfully and he gave her a little nod of reassurance. "But you will let her come to Wainfleet sometimes for a holiday, won't you? Bring her with you, I mean." His gaze included Cecily's husband, to whom he hadn't yet been introduced. "All of you."

Cecily stammered, "You forgive me then? For hiding?"

Zach smiled. "There is nothing to forgive. I gather the lawyer's agent was an idiot who used my title and made demands—it must have frightened you half to death."

Cecily sighed, and nodded. "It did. But I'm sorry I was such a ninny—I should have trusted you."

Zach looked at Max. "I haven't thanked you properly yet for finding her. I don't know how you did it, but—"

"I didn't do anything," Max said. "Jane found her."

Zachary looked at Jane in shock. "*Jane* did?"

Max said, "She hired a post chaise and went to North Wales, found Cecily and convinced her to come to London. I just drove everyone back to London."

Zach glanced at Cecily, who nodded.

"But—" He closed his eyes briefly. "First things first. Lady Beatrice, may I speak to your niece in private?" He took Jane's hand. "This one."

And without waiting for permission, he hurried Jane outside into the hallway. He looked around. "Where can we—"

"In here." Jane opened the door of the small parlor and drew him inside.

Kicking the door shut behind him, he pulled her into his arms and kissed her.

He kissed her like a man dying of thirst in the desert, desperately, hungrily, needing to taste her, feel her against him, needing to wrap himself around her.

To claim her.

"I thought I'd lost you," he muttered.

"I thought I'd lost you." She hugged him tight.

"I've been such a fool."

"That letter you sent me . . . so noble, so precious—so idiotic. *You care for me like a friend*." She laughed softly and pushed his hair back from his forehead. He kissed her hungrily.

"When I heard Cambury had dumped you—"

She pulled back. "Excuse me? I broke with *him*."

He frowned. "But why?"

She rolled her eyes. "Why do you think?"

"But I was in jail. On a charge of murder."

She shrugged. "You were innocent."

"You didn't know that."

"Of course I did."

"And you went to Wales—all that way—oh, God, how did I ever deserve you? I'm going to spend a lifetime trying to deserve you."

"A lifetime?" She quirked an eyebrow at him.

He looked at her, arrested. "Oh, Lord, I've forgotten to say it." He moved off the *chaise longue*, where they'd ended up, knelt down on one knee, took her hand in his and said, "My dearest Jane Chance—Chantry—Chancelotto, whoever—you are the love of my life. I don't deserve you, but I do adore you, and I will spend my life trying to make you happy, if only you will marry me. Will you marry me?"

She looked at him thoughtfully. "I'm not sure. Do you expect me to live in a gypsy wagon?"

"Only in the summer," he said promptly. "In the winter we can sleep in haystacks. Very warm things, haystacks. Cozy, if a bit prickly at times."

She gave a mournful sigh. "Don't you have a proper home?"

"No, just a big old house," he said in a downcast voice. He added hopefully, "But it could be turned into a home, with a bit of work, I mean. And the right person."

"Do you think I might be the right person?"

"I know you are. Now will you please say you'll marry me, because kneeling like this is dashed uncomfortable, not to say silly-looking, and I want to have my wicked way with you on that *chaise longue*."

"Oh, well, in that case, I would love to marry you, my darling Zachary Black—or whatever your name is." And she slipped off the *chaise longue* and into his arms.

D inner commenced with Zach and Jane announcing their betrothal. There was a slight delay as Lady Beatrice pointed out caustically that Zach had failed to provide his betrothed with a ring.

She could, however, solve his problem. She snapped her fingers and the ever-prepared Featherby produced from his pocket a small leather box. "I have so far provided all my nieces with a betrothal ring," the old lady said, "so we might as well keep up the tradition. Unless you have any objection, Wainfleet?"

Under her beady gaze, Zach wouldn't dare. He accepted the box graciously, and opened it. It was magnificent, a glowing red ruby, surrounded by tiny diamonds. He showed it to Jane.

"Oh, it's beeyoutiful," she exclaimed happily. "Put it on me, Zach, put it on!" He slipped it on, and sealed the deal with a kiss.

Jane, cradling the ring on her hand, kissed Lady Beatrice, then showed it to all her sisters, and they exclaimed and admired and hugged her all over again.

She paused, and looked at Lady Beatrice. "You never mentioned this ring when I was betrothed to Lord Cambury."

"No," the old lady said. "The rings I've given each of you gels are for love, not show. An emerald for Abby, a sapphire for Damaris and now a ruby for Jane, the girl who tried to deny her warm and loving heart"—she winked at Zach—"and was foiled by a handsome gypsy."

And then the champagne flowed. It was a large, happy gathering, with Lady Beatrice, all Jane's sisters, Max and Freddy, Gil, and Cecily and Michael and Winnie, who was reluctantly allowed by her father to have her first ever sip of champagne. The only missing member of their loose extended family was

Flynn, who was spending a few weeks at the country home of a certain Lady Elizabeth, daughter of an impoverished earl. An interesting announcement was expected.

Over a dozen courses they rehashed the events of the day, Zach thanked everyone again, Jane described her trip to Wales, and then Cecily and Michael quietly announced they were going to marry again, and more champagne was brought out.

"You must have a honeymoon," Jane said.

"Oh, no," Cecily demurred, but she looked at Michael with a hopeful expression.

"No," he said, "simple country ministers don't go on honeymoons."

He meant they couldn't afford it, but Jane could see Cecily loved the idea. She looked at Zach, who picked up her silent message beautifully. "It would be my pleasure to have you holiday at Brighton for a couple of weeks, if you would permit it, Michael," he said. "A small thanks for saving my neck from the noose. And a tiny part of what the Wainfleet estate owes Cecily. That's what I meant to talk to you about, Cecily—as my father's widow, you are owed money."

"Oh, but—" Michael began.

"All drawn up in the settlements before her marriage to my father," Zach told him firmly. "Legal and binding—no choice in the matter at all. But the Brighton trip would be a wedding gift from me, if you will accept it."

Michael and Cecily looked at each other. Cecily's eyes were shining.

"And if you will permit," Jane added, "Winnie can stay here with us, and Zachary and I can show her around London. Lady Beatrice?"

"Can't think of anything more delightful," the old lady said promptly. "Charming gel. Fond of her already."

Cecily turned to her daughter. "Would you mind staying here while your da and I go away for a little holiday?"

"*Mind?*" Winnie exclaimed. "Stay in a house with *three* cats, a *dog*, *two* sisters and an *aunt*—and be shown around *London* by my *brother*?"

They all laughed. "Then it's settled," Zach said.

* * *

While Cecily and Michael were away on their honeymoon, the household at Berkeley Square swung into preparation for Jane and Zachary's wedding. It was to be held at St. George's Church in Hanover Square, the parish church for Mayfair and the setting for all the fashionable weddings, but no banns were called there for Jane and Zachary's wedding.

"It would be too embarrassing to have the banns called for my wedding to Lord Cambury one week, and then the banns for my wedding to you the next," Jane told Zachary and he laughed.

"Suits me. The sooner we're wed, the happier I'll be." And he obtained a special license. The date was set for two weeks—just in time for Cecily and Michael to attend and, more to the point, Winnie.

In the short time they'd known her, they'd both become so fond of their little sister. She was sweet and shy, and expected so little.

The day after her parents had left for Brighton, Winnie had been sitting upstairs with Daisy and Jane, watching a fitting of Jane's wedding dress. Luckily Daisy had been working on it for weeks, and the change of groom and date didn't bother her in the least.

"Jane," Winnie said diffidently, "I don't suppose . . . I mean . . . I know children aren't usually invited to weddings, but I was wondering . . ."

"Oh, dear," Jane said, keeping a perfectly straight face. "I didn't plan on inviting you as a guest, Winnie."

"Oh." Her little face fell. She mustered a brave smile. "That's all right, I didn't think—"

"I hoped you would be a bridesmaid."

There was a moment of silence. Winnie's jaw dropped. "*Me?*" she squeaked. "You want *me* to be a *bridesmaid*?"

Jane hugged her. "Of course I do. We've already started on your dress. Daisy and you will be bridesmaids, and Abby and Damaris will be my matrons of honor. I want *all* my sisters with me on my wedding day."

Chapter Twenty-eight

You have bewitched me body and soul,
and I love, I love, I love you.

—*PRIDE AND PREJUDICE* (FILM SCRIPT)

Zach stood with his best man, Gil, waiting at the altar. The church was filled with spring flowers and their scent, brass cleaner, incense and beeswax formed a heady mix.

"Have you got the ring?" he asked Gil.

"For the fifth time, yes."

"She's late."

"She's not."

Behind him stood his brothers-in-law to be, Davenham and Freddy Monkton-Coombes, looking perfectly relaxed and a little smug—damned married men. They had no idea how blasted jumpy he was feeling. Flynn now, he seemed almost as nervous as Zach. With four bridal attendants, he'd had to have four groomsmen, and Jane had suggested Flynn. Zach didn't care who was in the wedding party, as long as Jane was.

Where was she? What if she'd changed her mind?

The church was packed, almost all there for Jane and her sisters, half of them from the literary society, but some of Zach's relatives had turned up, relatives he barely remembered, but seeming glad to see him, much to his surprise. Even Cousin Gerald had graced the event with his presence, though he wasn't exactly exuding sweetness and light. Fences to mend there, Zach thought.

But where the devil was Jane?

The organist, who'd been playing some blasted creepy tune for the last ten minutes, fell silent, and then—Mendelssohn's "Wedding March."

He turned, and saw his little sister, slender and earnest, marching with slow, careful steps down the aisle toward him, holding a bunch of freesias and some kind of white blossom in a death grip. His throat swelled. She was followed by Daisy, and behind her . . . the love of his life.

Jane, walking toward him in a dress of some white stuff, silk maybe or satin, with a foam of lace that cupped and caressed her breasts and shoulders . . . Aphrodite rising from the waves. He swallowed. Was there ever such a beautiful sight?

For a moment he couldn't breathe.

And then she smiled, and he thought his heart would burst.

His Jane. His wife. His life.

She was accompanied by Lady Beatrice and her cane on one side, and by her grandmother, Lady Dalrymple, on the other.

She handed her flowers to Winnie, while Daisy and the other two sisters arranged her train. Jane took no notice; she had eyes only for Zach.

Outside it was a gray spring day, but in the dimness of the church, her eyes shone blue as the sky over the Aegean, shining and full of love. And he was happily drowning . . .

"Dearly beloved . . ."

Zach held Jane's hand and tried to breathe.

"Who gives this woman . . ."

"We do." Lady Beatrice and Lady Dalrymple stepped back.

"Will you, Adam George Zachary Aston-Black, Earl of Wainfleet, take this woman . . ."

"I will."

"And will you, Jane Sarah Elizabeth Chantry, take this man . . ."

"I will."

He fumbled with the ring, his hands were shaking absurdly—why, when he wanted this so much—but it slipped smoothly onto her finger. She smiled up at him, and Zach gazed down at her and heard nothing more until, "You may kiss the bride."

At last.

He cupped her face between his hands, and made her

another, silent promise with his eyes, and then he lowered his mouth to hers.

At last, after twelve years of wandering, homeless and alone, Zach was home.

For his wedding night, Zach had booked a suite at the Pulteney Hotel.

Jane had never stayed in a large hotel before, and the Pulteney was the grandest and most fashionable hotel in London. The Czar of Russia himself had stayed there only a few years before.

Zach slipped the porter a guinea, and leaned against the door watching his bride as she explored the suite in delight. A bottle of champagne had been opened for them on arrival and she lifted a gently fizzing glass, drank it down all in one gulp, then shivered deliciously.

"Lovely," she exclaimed. Then turned to look at him. "Well?"

"Well what?"

"You told me *weeks* ago you'd have your wicked way with me and I'm still waiting. Isn't it time?"

"It certainly is," Zach said and, striding forward, swept her up into his arms.

Jane laughed as he caught her up and fell with her onto the enormous bed. She was eager to make love with Zach, but also a little nervous. Her sisters had told her not to worry, that it might not be comfortable at first, but with a little practice, it was utter bliss.

She remembered the look on Abby's face as they were riding to the masquerade. The love, the connection between Abby and her husband, had almost been tangible that evening. Damaris and Freddy had it too, and Jane wanted to know their secret.

She wanted to know it with Zachary so very much.

As he scooped her up and fell with her to the bed, she expected him to pounce, and to be ravenous, the way he'd been the day he proposed. Instead, he was heartbreakingly tender.

In an echo of her wedding kiss in the church, he cupped her face between his hands, as if cradling something precious and fragile. His fingers were cool against her suddenly heated skin. Gently he tilted her face toward him.

"I love you so much," he murmured, and with achingly slow deliberation, he lowered his mouth to hers.

He brushed his lips across hers, so lightly that she could barely feel it, a warm, spicy drift of gossamer. She wriggled and pushed closer, and he smiled at her impatience.

"*'Come live with me and be my love, And we shall all the pleasures prove,'*" he quoted softly. "The pleasures, love, all the pleasures."

She smiled. "That sounds nice."

"Better than nice . . ." Again, his mouth drifted over hers, caressing her lips so lightly; it was a tease, a slow, tantalizing temptation. The delicate friction of his mouth over hers, his warm breath, the hint of his enticing masculine taste shivered through her. And in between, his deep, murmured words of love.

She sighed, closed her eyes and gave herself up to him.

The delicate tease of his mouth soon turned into slow, hot, deep, drugging kisses . . . and she slowly turned into a hot puddle of desire. It was utter bliss. His hands roamed over her and she plucked impatiently at his waistcoat, his shirt.

"Yes, I think it's time to get rid of these." He rose from the bed, and without taking his eyes from her, he pulled his coat off, his waistcoat, his shirt. And he was bare from the waist up.

He turned and sat and pulled off his boots, then he stood and pushed his breeches down his legs and kicked them away. He turned and stood before her, clad only in a pair of white drawers. She lay on the bed, boneless, feasting on the sight of him. Lord, but the man was beautiful. He smiled, that slow, irresistible smile that never failed to make her insides curl with pleasure.

"Now you." He held out his hand, and she allowed him to pull her upright.

He kissed her again, but her knees sagged and she sank helplessly back to the bed.

With a soft, deep laugh, he reached around her for the buttons down the back of her dress. "There must be a hundred of these things," he murmured as he fought with the buttons. "Daisy likes to make things difficult, doesn't she?"

"It's a beautiful dress."

"I'm more interested in the beautiful woman inside it."

Jane was too busy exploring his beautiful naked chest to

care. So this was how a man was built, all hard, elegant planes, lean and powerful. Sculptured. Beautiful. She leaned forward and licked one tiny, hard male nipple and he gasped.

"If you care about this dress, I wouldn't do that," he warned her with a look of dark promise.

"I care about it. But would you please hurry?"

For answer, he drew her to her feet, pulled the dress over her head and tossed it aside. And frowned at her corset and petticoat and chemise. "Wish I had my knife," he muttered, and got to work on her corset strings.

Jane was more interested in what was happening inside his drawers. Something was . . . different. She longed to pull them down and look, but she was too shy. Yet. She wished she'd drunk a little more champagne.

And then her corset fell away. He tossed it aside, and in one swift movement he lifted off her petticoat and chemise. She was naked. She ought to be embarrassed, ought to have moved to cover herself modestly from his hot, masculine gaze, but somehow she couldn't move.

He devoured her with his eyes. And then he dropped his drawers and she forgot all about her own nakedness in the fascination of his.

He was magnificent. She stared at that part of him standing proud and unashamed and longed to touch it, but she wasn't sure whether he would mind or not.

He brushed the back of his fingers lightly over her breasts and her breath hitched in a series of escalating gasps as his knuckles moved back and forth and she ached where he touched her, and her insides clenched with wanting.

Pushing her back on the bed, he lay down beside her, skin to skin, kissing, his hands roaming over her, her skin so tender and sensitive, each touch seemed to shiver through her.

She squirmed to get closer to him, exploring his big, beautiful, masculine body, her hands feverishly stroking, squeezing, learning him. And all the while they were kissing, kissing, and she could barely think, only touch, only taste, only feel.

His mouth moved to her breasts and she gasped and shuddered beneath his tender onslaught, barely remembering how he'd reacted when she'd licked him there. But she did remember, and pushed his head away so she could taste him there, to nibble and suck on his small male nipples, and it was his turn to groan and shudder.

"Not me, not yet," he muttered, and lifting her face, he kissed her deeply, possessively, and then kissed his way down her throat and back to her breasts. His mouth closed over a hot nipple and sucked; she arched against him, pulsating with need, with pleasure, with . . . something.

His fingers slipped between her legs, stroking and teasing and she heard the sound of wetness and made a little sound of embarrassment.

"No," he reassured her, his voice a dark rumble of love, "this is perfect, you're perfect, love." He moved his fingers and deep ripples shuddered through her. "You're beautiful. All beautiful."

And he stroked, and his clever, insistent fingers drew such response from her that all awareness, any self-consciousness, simply evaporated under the demand, the rising tide of . . . the insistent drive to . . . to . . .

"Please, please . . ." she pleaded, not knowing for what. Her legs thrashed; shudders ran through her body.

And he claimed her with his mouth, and his fingers moved and she thought she could not bear any more and then . . . she shattered, in a million sunbursts.

And before she could recover, he moved over her, and he was there, between her legs, thick and hard and hot. "Easy, love, easy," he murmured, and he stroked her and again she felt the pressure inside her building.

Now she wanted to feel that thickness, that hard, blunt masculinity, inside her, and she thrust up against him, and as he entered her in one long, smooth movement, she felt a sharp sting, but then he was moving, and it felt right. She wrapped her arms and legs around him, gripping tight, and suddenly they were moving together in a rhythm some deep primeval part of her recognized.

The shudders deepened and the pressure rose, and she hung on tight and felt him moving deep within her, and it built and built even more than before until she was swept away in a maelstrom of sensation. The world splintered into a thousand glittering shards, and he gave a harsh groan and shattered within her. And for a moment she knew nothing more.

When she opened her eyes, the worried expression in his eyes faded, and he smiled and kissed her gently. "The French call it *la petite mort*, the little death. Are you all right?"

She went to stretch and found herself still wrapped around him. He'd turned so he was on his back and she was lying on top of him. It was a position that she decided she liked very much. "Perfect," she murmured, and planted sleepy kisses on his chest. "Just perfect. Bliss . . ." And she lay her head over his heart and slept.

Zach pulled the bedclothes over them, careful not to wake his precious burden.

He lay there, trying to come to terms with how his life had changed. He'd come to London with nothing, no name, no future, no family, and now . . .

This loving, sweet-faced girl had given him . . . everything. He was the luckiest man in the world.

He went to shift out from under her.

"No," she murmured sleepily. Her legs and arms tightened around him. "I don't want you to move . . . ever."

In the morning he awoke to find her standing by the window, wrapped in nothing but a shawl, looking out at the gray drizzle of a London spring. He slid out of bed and, naked, padded silently toward her. He wrapped his arms around her and planted a slow, heated kiss on the nape of her neck.

She shivered deliciously and turned in his arms, smiling at him with sleepy, loving eyes. She kissed him. "Good morning, my darling." She stretched. "I feel wonnnderful. So that's what you meant by *'all the pleasures prove'*?"

"No." He gave her a slow smile. "That was just the beginning. It gets better." And he drew her back to the big, wide, rumpled bed.

Epilogue

"'Tis too much!" she added, "by far too much. I do not
deserve it. Oh! why is not everybody as happy?"

—JANE AUSTEN, *PRIDE AND PREJUDICE*

The May Day fete at Wainfleet was a huge success. People
had come from miles around—villagers, tenants and all
kinds of people not connected with Wainfleet. All of Jane's family was there, including her newfound grandmother, a group of
Zach's friends from school, even some members of the literary
society.

To Winnie's delight, she'd been crowned Queen of the May
and had led the dancing. There was maypole dancing, and folk
dancing, and competitions of all sorts, from baking competitions
to shooting and tug-o'-war, and wrestling. Zach had provided a
feast with a whole ox and several sheep roasted on a spit, barrels
of ale and cider, platters of roasted vegetables and mounds of
bread, followed by cakes and sweet pies of every sort.

A bonfire was built that lasted through the night, and as
evening fell, a gypsy band had appeared and there was music
and dancing and fortunes told and trinkets bought and sold.
Zach had introduced his wife to his gypsy friends; they would
always be welcome at Wainfleet, he told them.

The following night, there was just Zach and Jane and their
immediate family seated around the big oaken table in the
dining hall at Wainfleet, and Lady Beatrice was educating the

newer members of the family in the history of the Chance sisters—according to her.

"The Chantry gels, you see, being orphaned, were taken in by my dear half sister Grizelda—"

"Imaginary half sister," Max murmured *sotto voce* to Zach. "All this is quite imaginary."

Zach grinned. He liked the old lady, and it was good to know he wasn't the only focus of her mischievous tongue.

"Grizelda, of course, was married to a *marchese*, Alfonzo di Chancelotto—"

"Angelo," Max corrected her dryly.

"Of course, dear boy, I always get those Italian names confused."

"Venetian."

"Precisely." She gave him a beady glare and continued, "So when Abby and Jane's widowed mother passed away in the sanitorium in Italy—"

"Not Venice?" Max asked innocently.

"No, dear, in the mountains of Switzerland—the Italian-speaking part," she added before Max could interject again. "So dear Grizelda and her husband decided to take in the girls and raise them as their own dear daughters."

"Along with dear Damaris, I presume," Freddy said.

"And Daisy," Damaris added, giggling.

"Oh, she was only discovered later, sadly." Lady Beatrice had to account for Daisy's Cockney accent somehow.

"I never went to Italy," Daisy said firmly. She didn't approve of these flights of the old lady's fancy. "And I never been to Venice either."

"But we'll take you there one day, Daisy darling," Abby told her. "You should see it, so beautiful with the houses rising out of the water."

"I been in houses like that," Daisy said, unimpressed. "It's called rising damp."

Abby laughed. "No, they're beautiful, and not at all damp, you'll see."

"And there are pigs," Freddy added. "The famous experimental Chinese swimming pigs of Venice—oof!" as Damaris elbowed him in the stomach. He gave her an injured look. "What? My father *loves* those pigs."

"Nonsense," his loving wife told him. "He's never even seen them, and he won't because they don't exist."

"Ah, but he *dreams* of them," Freddy said soulfully, and they all laughed.

The newly proclaimed Earl of Wainfleet slipped his arm around the waist of his countess, and said, "Well, delightful as this gathering is, my wife and I need to . . ."

"Inspect the grounds," Jane said.

"At night?" Lady Beatrice said.

Zach smiled. "There's a full moon out there and it needs attending to."

"Ahh." The old lady nodded.

At the mention of a full moon, Abby and Max, Freddy and Damaris and Cecily and Michael all decided they needed to inspect the grounds too, different parts of the grounds, attending to the moon.

Lady Beatrice and Lady Dalrymple looked at those who remained, Daisy and Flynn. "Well," Lady Beatrice said, "are you two going or staying?"

"Staying," Daisy said. "The country gives me the creeps at night. Anyone for cards?"

Patrick Flynn gave her a dry look and rose to his feet. "I might as well walk the dog, then. Come on Caesar or RosePetal or whatever your name is, we can bay at the moon together."

Jane and Zach strolled slowly through the gardens, stopping to kiss every few steps. The scent of roses, freesias, lilac and a hundred spring blossoms filled the air. Overhead a full, fat golden moon hung in the sky, blessing all beneath it. They were home, both of them.

"Happy?" Zach murmured.

Jane gave a blissful sigh. "More than I ever believed possible."

"Me too." He tightened his hold on the woman nestled against his heart, the woman who'd made dreams he'd never dared to dream come true. Bathed in moonlight, they kissed.

Read on for a special excerpt from
the first Chance Sisters Romance

The Autumn Bride

Available now from Berkley!

Chapter One

"Give a girl an education and introduce her properly into the world, and ten to one but she has the means of settling well, without further expense to anybody."

—JANE AUSTEN, *MANSFIELD PARK*

London, August 1816

She was running late. Abigail Chantry quickened her pace. Her half day off, and though it was damp and squally and cold outside, she'd taken herself off as usual to continue her explorations of London.

Truth to tell, if her employers had lived in the bleakest, most remote part of the Yorkshire moors, Abby would still have removed herself from their vicinity on her fortnightly half day off. Mrs. Mason believed a governess should be useful as well as educational, and saw no reason why, on Miss Chantry's half day, she should not do a little mending for her employer or, better still, take the children with her on her outings.

What need did a governess, especially one who was orphaned, after all, have for free time?

Miss Chantry did not agree. So, rain, hail or snow, she absented herself from the Mason house the moment after the clock in the hall chimed noon, returning a few minutes before six to resume her duties.

Having spent most of her life in the country, Abby was loving her forays into this enormous city, discovering all kinds of wonderful places. Last week she'd found a bookshop where the owner let her read to her heart's content without pressuring her to buy—only the secondhand books, of course, not the new ones whose pages had not yet been cut. She'd returned there today, and had become so lost in a story—*The Monk*, deliciously bloodcurdling—that now she was running late.

If she returned even one minute after six, Mr. Mason would dock her wages by a full day. It had happened before, and no amount of argument would budge him.

She turned the corner into the Masons' street and glanced up at the nearby clock tower. Oh, Lord, three minutes to go. Abby picked up speed.

"Abby Chantry?" A young woman, a maidservant by her garments, limped toward her with an uneven gait. She'd been waiting opposite the Masons' house.

Abby eyed her warily. "Yes?" Apart from her employers, Abby knew no one in London. And nobody here called her Abby.

"I got a message from your sister." She spoke with a rough London accent.

Her mouth was swollen and a large bruise darkened her cheek.

"My *sister*?" It wasn't possible. Jane was hundreds of miles away. She'd just left the Pillbury Home for the Daughters of Distressed Gentlewomen, near Cheltenham, to take up a position as companion to a vicar's mother in Hereford.

"She told me where to find you. I'm Daisy." The girl took Abby's arm and tugged. "You gotta come with me. Jane's in trouble—bad trouble—and you gotta come now."

Abby hesitated. The girl's bruised and battered face didn't inspire confidence. The newspapers were full of the terrible crimes that took place in London: murders, white slavery, pickpockets and burglars. She'd even read about people hit over the head in a dark alley, stripped and left for dead, just for their clothing.

But Abby wore a dull gray homemade dress that practically shouted "governess." She couldn't imagine anyone wanting to steal it. And she was thin, plain and clever, rather than pretty, which ruled out white slavers. She had no money or valuables and only knew the Mason family, so could hardly inspire murder.

And this girl knew her name, *and* Jane's. And Abby's address. Abby glanced at the clock. A minute to six. But what did the loss of a day's wages matter when her little sister was in London and in trouble? Jane was not yet eighteen.

"All right, I'll come." She gave in to Daisy's tugging and they hurried down the street. "Where is my sister?"

"In a bad place," Daisy said cryptically, stumping rapidly along with an ungainly gait. Crippled, or the result of the beating she'd received? Abby wondered. Whichever, it didn't seem to slow her down.

"What kind of bad place?"

Daisy didn't respond. She led Abby through a maze of streets, cutting down back alleys and leading her into an area Abby had never felt tempted to explore.

"What kind of bad place?" Abby repeated.

Daisy glanced at her sideways. "A broffel, miss!"

"A broff—" Abby broke off, horrified. "You mean a *brothel*?"

"That's what I said, miss, a broffel."

Abby stopped dead. "Then it can't be my sister; Jane would never enter a brothel." But even as she said it, she knew the truth. *Her baby sister was in a brothel.*

"Yeah, well, she didn't have no choice in the matter. She come 'ere straight from some orphanage in the country. Drugged, she was. She give me your address and arst me to get a message to you. And we ain't got much time, so hurry."

Numb with shock, and sick at the thought, Abby allowed herself to be led down side streets and alleyways. Jane was supposed to be in a vicarage in Hereford. How could she possibly have ended up in a London brothel? *Drugged, she was.* How?

They turned into a narrow street lined with shabby houses, and slowed.

"That's it." Daisy gestured to a tall house, a good deal smarter than the others, with a freshly painted black door and windows curtained in crimson fabric. The ground-story windows were unbarred, but the higher ones were all barred. To keep people in, rather than out. *She didn't have no choice.*

As she stared up, she saw a movement at one of the highest windows. A glimpse of golden hair, two palms pressed against the glass framing a young woman the image of Abby's mother.

Abby hadn't seen her sister for six years, but there was no doubt in her heart. *Jane!*

Someone pulled Jane back out of sight and closed the curtains.

Her sister was a prisoner in that house. Abby hurried across the street and started up the front stairs. Daisy grabbed her by the skirt and pulled her backward.

"No, miss!" Her voice held so much urgency it stopped Abby dead. "If you go in there arstin' questions now, it'll only make things worse. You might never see your sister again!"

"Then I'll fetch a constable or a magistrate to sort out this matter."

"Do that and for certain sure you'll never see your sister again. He—Mort—him who owns this place and all the girls in it now"—she jerked her chin toward the upstairs—"he pays blokes to warn him. Before any constable can get here your sister will be long gone."

Abby felt sick. "But what can I do? I must get her out of there."

"I told you, miss—we got a plan." The sound of carriage wheels rattling down the street made Daisy look around. She paled. "Oh, my Gawd, that's Mort comin'! Go quick! If he catches me talkin' to anyone outside he'll give me another frashing! I'll meet you in the alley behind the house. Sixth house along. Big spiked gate. Go!" She gave Abby a shove and fled down the side steps to the basement area.

Abby, still in shock—Jane, in a brothel!—hurried away down the street, forcing herself not to look back, even when she heard the carriage draw to a halt outside the house with the black door.

She turned the corner and found the alley Daisy had described running behind the houses. It was narrow, gloomy and strewn with filth of all kinds, the cobbles slimy, the damp stench vile. Abby covered her nose and grimly picked her way along the lane. From time to time something squelched underfoot but she didn't look down. Whatever she'd stepped in, she didn't want to know. All that mattered was getting Jane out of that place.

She counted along the houses and came to the sixth, set behind a tall brick wall, the top of which was studded with shards of broken glass. A solid wooden gate was set into it, topped by a line of iron spikes.

The sinister row of spikes gleamed dully in the faint light. Ice slid slowly through her veins. With her dying breath Mama had made Abby promise to keep Jane safe, to keep them both safe. It hadn't been easy—Jane's beauty had always attracted attention, even when she was a little girl—but Abby had kept that promise.

Until now. Jane was imprisoned *in a brothel*. Abby raised a hand to her mouth and found it was shaking.

Her whole body was trembling.

How long had Jane been there? Abby tried to work it out, to recall what Jane had said in her last letter, but she couldn't. Over and over, the question pounded through her mind: How had Jane come to be in a brothel?

Abby shoved the fruitless question aside. She had to think, to plan what to do to get Jane free. What if Daisy didn't come? Abby would have no option but to fetch a constable.

Do that and for certain sure you'll never see your sister again. Abby shivered. She was entirely dependent on the goodwill—and ability—of a girl she'd never seen till a few minutes ago.

If constables and magistrates couldn't help, how could one small, crippled maidservant make a difference? And where was she?

The minutes crawled by.

Abby was almost ready to give up when she heard something on the other side of the gate. Her heart gave a leap of relief, then it occurred to her it could be anyone. She pressed back into the shadows and waited.

The gate cracked open an inch. "You still here, miss?" came a whisper.

"I'm here."

The girl poked her head out. "I got no time to explain, miss, but come back here in an hour with a warm cloak and some shoes."

"Shoes, but—"

"I was going to try and get your sister out now, but I can't while Mort's here. But he's goin' out again shortly."

She turned to leave, but Abby grabbed her arm. "Why? Why would you do this for us? For Jane and me?" It was obviously dangerous. Why would this girl—a stranger—take such a risk?

Was she expecting payment? Abby would gladly give all she had to save her sister, but she didn't have much.

The girl shook her head. "'Cause it's wrong, what Mort's doing. It never used to be like this, stealing girls, keeping them locked up—" She broke off. "Look, I ain't got time to explain, miss, not so's you'd understand. You'll just have to trust me. Just be back here in an hour with a warm cloak and some shoes."

"Why?" Some kind of payment for services rendered?

"'Cause she hain't got nothin' to wear outside, of course." She jerked her chin at the filth in the alley. "You want her to walk through that in her bare feet? Now I gotta go." And with that the girl was gone, the gate shut behind her. Abby heard a bolt slide into place.

Numbly, Abby found her way back to the Masons' house.

An hour.

A lot could happen in an hour.

"What time do you call this?"

Abby, her foot on the first stair, turned back. Mr. Mason stood in the hall entry, fob watch in hand, glowering. "You're late!"

"I know, and I'm sorry, Mr. Mason, but I only just learned that—"

"I shall have to deduct the full day from your wages, of course." He puffed his chest up like a particularly pleased toad.

"It was a family emergency—"

He snorted. "You have no family."

"I do, I have a sister, and she has come to London unexpectedly and—"

"No excuses, you know the rules."

"It's not an excuse. It's true, and I'm hoping . . . I was wondering . . ." She swallowed, belatedly realizing she should not have argued with him.

"What were you wondering, Miss Chantry?" Mrs. Mason swept down the staircase, dressed in a sumptuous puce silk dress, a feathered headdress and a cloak edged with fur. "Have you forgotten, Mr. Mason, we are to attend the opera this evening? I do not wish to be late."

"It's fashionable to be late," her husband responded.

"I realize that, my dear." Mrs. Mason's voice grated with sugarcoated irritation. "But we are going to be more than fashionably late—you don't even have your coat on."

The butler arrived in the hallway, heard the remark and went to fetch Mr. Mason's coat.

Mrs. Mason pulled on one long kid evening glove and glanced at Abby. "Well, what is it, Miss Chantry?"

Abby took a deep breath. The Masons were very strict about visitors of any kind. Abby was allowed none. "My younger sister is in London, ma'am, and I was wondering if she could stay with me, just for the night—"

The woman's well-plucked eyebrows rose. "Here? Don't be ridiculous. Of course not. Now come along, Mr. Mason—"

"But I haven't seen her for years. She's just left the orphanage and she's not quite eighteen. I can't let her stay in London on her own."

"That's not our concern." Mrs. Mason frowned into the looking glass and adjusted her headdress. "A stranger, sleeping in the same house as my precious babies?" She snorted.

"She's not a stranger; she's *my sister*."

"It's out of the question." Mr. Mason allowed the butler to help him into his coat. "Blake, is the carriage here?"

The butler opened the door and peered outside. "It's just turning out of the mews, sir."

"And this is your last word?" Abby asked.

Mrs. Mason turned on her. "Why are you still loitering about? You heard my husband; the answer is no! Now get upstairs and attend to the children."

There was no point in arguing, so Abby went upstairs. She had no intention of obeying anyway.

She checked on the children, as she did every night. They were all fast asleep, looking like little angels, which they absolutely were not. The two older ones were full of mischief. Abby didn't care. She loved them anyway.

Susan, the toddler, was sleeping on her front with her bottom poking up as usual. Such a little darling. Abby gently turned her on her side and the little girl snuggled down, smiling to herself, still fast asleep. Abby tucked the covers around her.

These children were the joy and also the agony of her job. Abby loved them as if they were her own. She couldn't help herself—she knew it was foolish, and that one day they'd break her heart. She knew they'd be taken away from her, or she'd be sent away from them as if they'd outgrown her like a pair of old shoes.

It was heartbreak waiting to happen, loving other people's children.

She'd learned that hard lesson from the Taylors, her first position. Two years she'd been with them, loving the little ones with all her hungry heart. Not thinking ahead. Never even considering that one day she'd be dismissed and never see the children again.

They lived in Jamaica now.

She would lose the Mason children now too, but she would not—could not—leave her sister alone in a London hotel—not after what she'd been through. Even if she hadn't, if Jane had arrived in London unexpectedly, as she'd told the Masons, they had six years to catch up on; Jane had been a child of twelve when Abby saw her last.

Jane.

She bent and kissed each sleeping child and hurried out to collect the cloak and shoes for her sister, adding a shawl to the bundle, just in case.

G aslight had not yet reached the more sordid parts of the city. In the evening gloom the alleyway seemed more noisome and full of sinister shadows. Abby trod warily, counting the houses until she reached the high brick wall with the spiked wooden gate.

She stationed herself opposite the gate and waited, watching the windows like a hawk, noting every passing flicker of light, every shadow of movement. Was that Jane? Was that?

The time passed slowly. A distant clock chimed the hour. It was taking much longer than she'd expected. Had something gone wrong?

Something ran over her foot, a flicker of tiny damp claws and a slithery tail. She jumped, stifling a scream. She loathed rats.

She was concentrating so hard on the windows above that the scrape of the bolt on the gate opposite took her unawares and she jumped in fright.

The gate creaked open. A head peered out. "Abby?" A low whisper.

"Jane?"

A pale wraithlike shape slipped through the gap and then her sister was in her arms, clinging tightly, trembling, weeping and laughing. "Abby, oh, Abby!"

"Janey!" Tears blurred Abby's vision as she hugged her little sister. Not so little anymore, she realized. Jane was as tall as Abby now. She hugged her tighter. "Jane, dearest! Are you all right? How did you come to be in London? I thought Hereford—"

A hard little finger poked her in the ribs. "Oy! We're not out of danger yet, y'know. Escape now, happy reunion later!" It was Daisy. "Now quick, where's them shoes?"

"Of course." Abby released Jane and as she stepped back her jaw dropped. Her sister was naked but for a thin chemise. "Good God, Jane, where are your clothes?" She pulled the cloak out and threw it around her shivering sister.

"It's to stop us leaving," Jane said between chattering teeth. "We can't go into the streets dressed like this."

Abby crouched to slip the shoes on Jane's cold feet, which were filthy from the alley. She wiped them clean as best she could with a handkerchief, her hands shaking with rage and distress. For her sister to be kept in such an indecent state, without even clothes to keep her covered! And in such cold weather!

"Put this on as well." She passed the shawl to Jane.

"No, Damaris can use it."

"Damaris?" Abby glanced up and saw another girl hovering uncertainly outside the gate, shivering, her arms wrapped around herself. She too was scantily clothed, but unlike Jane, this girl looked exactly like a woman out of a brothel.

She wore a thin red-and-gold gauzy wrapper that barely reached past her thighs. Her dark hair was piled high, spiked into place with two sticks. Her face—clearly painted—was a dead white oval. Her lips and cheeks were garishly rouged, her eyelids had been darkened and the line of her eyes was elongated at the corners.

"Damaris is my friend." Jane took Abby's shawl and tucked it around the shivering girl. "She's coming with us."

Abby frowned. Take this painted brothel creature with them?

Jane saw Abby's hesitation and put a protective arm around

the other girl's shoulders. "She has to come with us, Abby. She saved me. I owe her everything."

"Come with us? But . . ." It was going to be difficult enough to smuggle Jane into the Mason residence, let alone this . . . this person.

"Damaris is the only reason I wasn't raped," Jane said urgently. "She has to come with us, Abby!"

Shocked, Abby stared at the garishly painted girl. *The only reason Jane wasn't raped?* Suddenly she didn't care what Damaris looked like, how much paint she wore, how scandalous her clothing was, what her past was. Whatever she'd done before this moment, she'd saved Jane from rape.

Daisy shifted restlessly. "Goin' to stand around all night talkin'?"

It jolted Abby to her senses. "No, of course not. Here, Damaris." She unfastened her own cloak and wrapped the shivering girl in it. She tugged the hood up to conceal her face and hair.

Abby glanced down at Damaris's narrow feet, pale against the dark mud of the alley. "I don't have another pair of shoes, but here." She passed Damaris her mittens. "Put them on your feet. It's the best I can do."

"Thank you," Damaris said in a soft voice. "I don't mean to be a burden."

The girl's gratitude made Abby ashamed of her earlier hesitation. "You're not a burden," she lied. "You helped my sister and for that I owe you. Besides, I wouldn't want anyone to return to that horrid place." They would manage. Somehow.

She turned to Daisy. "I cannot thank you enough for what you've done. I have a little money. It's not much, but . . ." She proffered a small purse.

"I don't want your money!" Daisy stepped back, offended.

"But you risked so much—"

"I didn't do it for money. Anyway, I got me own money. Now, are you lot goin' or not?"

Abby stepped forward and hugged her. "Thank you, Daisy." Jane and Damaris hugged and thanked Daisy too; then, with whispered good-byes, they hurried down the alley.

Almost immediately Abby heard footsteps behind them. Had they been discovered? She whirled around. It was Daisy, carrying a small bundle.

"Are they Jane's belongings?"

Daisy clutched the bundle tightly against her chest. "No, it's me own bits. I'm getting out too."

"You?" Abby exclaimed. "But why?"

"Mort'll flay me alive when he finds out what I did." She must have noticed Abby's hastily concealed dismay, because she added proudly, "Don't worry about me, miss; I can look after meself. Now hurry! They'll be out lookin' for them girls any minute now. Valuable property, they are."

Slip-sliding as fast as they could down the alley, the girls broke into a run as soon as they reached the street. They turned down the first corner, ran several blocks, turned another corner and kept running. When they had no more breath, they collapsed, panting, against some railings bordering a quiet garden.

A minute passed . . . two . . . The only sound was their labored breathing. They watched the way they'd come, ready to flee at the first sign of any movement.

But no one came. Nobody was following them. They'd escaped.

"Right, I'll be off then," Daisy said gruffly when they'd caught their breath. "Good luck to you."

But Abby couldn't let her go like that. "Where will you go? Do you have family in London?"

"Nah, I'm a foundling." She shrugged. "But don't worry; I'll find somewhere." She went to push past them but Abby caught her by the sleeve.

"It's my fault you're in this situation—"

"Nah, I was going to leave anyway." Daisy pulled her arm out of Abby's grip.

"Abby!" Jane turned pleading eyes on her sister, but Abby didn't need any prompting. If she could take a painted prostitute under her wing, she certainly wasn't going to let this small heroine stump gallantly off into the night, alone and friendless. And bruised.

She took Daisy's hand in a firm grip. "You're coming with us, Daisy, for tonight, at least. No, don't argue. After all you've done for us there's no way in the world I'm going to let you wander off in the dark with nowhere to go. Now come along; let's get Jane and Damaris into the warmth."

FROM AWARD-WINNING AUTHOR

ANNE GRACIE

THE
Winter Bride

 A Chance Sisters Romance

Damaris Chance's unhappy past has turned her off the idea of marriage forever. But her guardian, Lady Beatrice Davenham, convinces her to make her coming out anyway—and have a season of carefree, uncomplicated fun.

When Damaris finds herself trapped in a compromising situation with the handsome rake Freddy Monkton-Coombes, she has no choice but to agree to wed him—as long as it's in name only. Her new husband seems to accept her terms, but Freddy has a plan of his own: to seduce his reluctant winter bride.

PRAISE FOR *THE WINTER BRIDE*

"Exquisitely written, perfectly plotted."
—*Library Journal* (starred review)

"A romantic winner, with Gracie's typical witty charm and sweeping emotion."
—*Kirkus Reviews*

www.annegracie.com
penguin.com

 BERKLEY SENSATION | Penguin Random House

M1621T0115

FROM AWARD-WINNING AUTHOR

ANNE GRACIE

THE

Autumn Bride

⚘ A Chance Sisters Romance ⚘

Governess Abigail Chantry will do anything to save her sister and two dearest friends from destitution, even if it means breaking into an empty mansion. Which is how she encounters the neglected Lady Beatrice Davenham, who agrees that the four young ladies should become her "nieces," eliminating the threat of disaster for all. It's the perfect situation, until Lady Beatrice's dashing and arrogant nephew, Lord Davenham, returns from the Orient—and discovers an impostor running his household...

"I never miss an Anne Gracie book."
—Julia Quinn, *New York Times* bestselling author

"Treat yourself to some super reads from a most talented writer."
—*Romance Reviews Today*

annegracie.com
facebook.com/AnneGracieAuthor
facebook.com/LoveAlwaysBooks